Rich Man's Coffin

14601-GARD

Rich Man's Coffin

THE LEGEND OF BLACK JACK WHITE, AN AMERICAN SLAVE IN NEW ZEALAND

Kenneth Gardner

To order additional copies of this book, contact:
Xlibris Corporation
1-888-795-4274
www.Xlibris.com
Orders@Xlibris.com

Contents

FOR THOMAS JAY

The existence of this book owes an endless amount of gratitude to the following people of New Zealand and especially Blenheim. I would like to thank Steve Folster, first and foremost, for his unwavering patience during my use of his facilities for the transcription and editing of this manuscript. Also helping significantly in these endeavors were Suzie and Brian Stevenson, along with their good friend, Rick Manson. For those who do not write their first-draft longhand, you cannot fully appreciate just how generous a person with a computer can be when you are penniless out in the middle of the wop-wops. Thanks to Ron McEwan and the rest of the crew at Montana Wineries for the camaraderie and moral support during the long nights of vintage. My gratitude to Don Sykes and Keith Watson of zzinc.com.

For factual information and story background, my thanks go strongly to Mr. and Mrs. Joe Mills, still living on the Para farm; and to Jock Penny and the good people of the Brayshaw Park museum. Also, a big thank you to the people of DOC, for meticulously maintaining White's Bay and the placard which inspired the entire work of this book. To Mike Taylor at the Picton museum, I owe much appreciation for his guidance and generosity with original documents. That brings me to perhaps the largest suppliers of valuable documentation, Mr. and Mrs. John Guard still living at remote Guard's Bay. My thanks to them for their hospitality and openness about their past.

Most importantly, I would like to thank the man himself, Arthur Alesworth, for living such a courageous life.

Foreword

Sitting here at White's Bay on a beautiful summer day, I am reminded of exactly why Black Jack White was so fortunate to have chosen this spot to wash ashore so many years ago. He claimed not only his freedom, but his indelible spot in history as one of its most remarkable yet lesser-known figures. I first found out about Black Jack White by reading the Department of Conservation's sign here at White's Bay, New Zealand; and since that time have not been able to stop thinking about him. After months of research, it became clear that his life and times would provide an incredible biography; however, I began to see him and the events of history in which he was involved, as legendary. At that point, I decided that I not only wanted to gather the detailed facts about the man to the best of my ability, but also to write a believable and enthralling story about him.

The first forty years of Black Jack's life were the most interesting, not only for the particular events occurring in his life, but also for the world history that paralleled this time of his life. It was also a time of little record keeping in

New Zealand; and I believe that Black Jack, being a former slave, did not possess the means to inscribe his account. This void of information did not represent a total loss for me, however, as I saw the elements for a great tale and even an honorable and impressive biography already in place.

Therefore, I set out armed with the facts that I had gathered about the man to write his story. I focused on three factual subjects of Black Jack's life which I considered to be most significant; and which all occurred within the same brief time: Namely, his self-won freedom and the exciting new life which it brought him; next, the Maori wars that were raging right at the spot where he washed up on shore; and finally, the whaling industry which had also just begun at the time and the place that he arrived in Kiwi land. All of these things are of tremendous historical importance not only to New Zealand, but for the world; and for them to have been experienced, shaped, and influenced by any one man makes for an incredible saga.

Yet, I was faced with the added and unifying dimension of Black Jack's former slave status: The fact that he was doing all of these incredible deeds under his own powerful will while hundreds of thousands of his fellow Afro-Americans toiled under the height of slavery, makes him heroic to me; and moreover, legendary.

As a work of fiction, this story would stand on its own merits; and without championing my own story-telling ability, let me emphasize that I have worked hard to integrate the facts about this man's life and to pay respect to him in areas where I needed to embellish the truth. I have not, however, found it necessary to inflate his stature, nor to unduly create fantastic aspects of his life in order to make his life readable. Black Jack stands on his own as one of the unique men of history; and his life serves to inspire all of us.

Clichés aside, this man should pique the interest of European and Afro-Americans alike, as well as native New Zealanders; and it should help to form a common bond between these two nations who seem to share so little history despite the parallels of period and purpose in their pioneer eras.

Discovering and writing about Black Jack White has been a journey: From tracking down the exact location of his unmarked grave, to finding the intact remains of his hut at Para (one of the earliest European structures on the South Island of New Zealand still standing), to camping out on the same remote beach where he first washed ashore in 1828; tracing Black Jack's odyssey has created one for me. Neil Armstrong's famous words, " . . . one giant leap for Mankind . . ." might just as well have been uttered by this new world explorer, Arthur Harper Alesworth, as he unknowingly made a huge step for his fellow Afro-Americans, and for Mankind as a whole.

Here was a man, who before the automobile, electricity, the Civil War, and the Gold Rush, was living free and making a very lucrative career in what was then one of the richest trades in the world: Whaling. This happened for Black Jack long before Melville's *Moby Dick* took place; even before Richard Henry Dana, Jr.'s, *Two Years Before the Mast*—long considered to be the first of the genre of the great American novel; and all during the worst period of American slavery. Yet, Black Jack remains a remarkable historical figure in and of himself, regardless of having been a former slave and civil rights pioneer.

Hopefully the reader will appreciate this account of the man's life. I believe that the man himself would have approved of it.

Prologue

"You never know when you are gonna have to know how to swim. You know that, Arthur?" She was a large woman. She threw him up once again and his slippery small belly slapped back into her raised palms, as though she were catching a large fish falling from the sky.

"Yes, mama, I know." he said with a disrespectful sigh.

She ignored his attitude for the moment, stealthily baiting her catch. "You *never* know when you gonna need to swim, Arthur. You know that?" she asked more emphatically.

"Yes, mama . . ." he had begun to yell; however, he was stopped by the sudden sensation of water flooding his throat.

"You mind your back talk!" she snapped as she added a dash of simulated anger; and promptly plunged the boy just under water before he knew what was happening. She was a big woman, but not obese. She had always maintained that 'the White man's food' had done something to her: Changed her natural African physique somehow. Now, she had a layer of thick skin, over a light pad of fat; all covering an ample rack of muscle which she freely admitted was rather abundant for a woman. But she was strong; and she didn't mind the additional framework as long as it was useful. Besides, she attributed it to too much potato and pig.

He came back up coughing and sputtering, and gasped, "Mama! All right Mama, I'll swim, I'll swim!"

She let the little Black boy go; and although he was nearly eight years old and well developed, she had no trouble lofting him over her head. "Go on, swim then." she said in an antagonistically loving voice; and then shoved him away in the water.

These sunny summer days in the estate's duck pond were a welcomed treat for her, as they only occurred when the Master was away visiting or on errands; and the manager would be kind to her and let her and a few other mothers frolic with their children in the pond for the afternoon. It was well known to all, though, that it was a strictly prohibited activity, and that the consequences of being caught red-handed would land squarely on the backs of those apprehended.

Therefore, mothers always kept a keen eye poised on the end of the row for the first sign of the Master's carriage in preparation for slipping out behind the hedge to the slave quarters. On this particular day, that readiness paid its way, as Arthur's mother spied the earliest glimpse of the dust cloud behind the trees at the road.

"Swim, Arthur, swim!" she yelled; but she had already begun to overtake him in his first attempt to reach the bank. She scooped him under one arm as her feet began to meet mud; and she galloped up onto the grassy shore, dripping as she ran beneath the weeping willow, dashing behind the hedge ahead of the other women.

Chapter 1

THE MAORI COURT

"Call me 'Arpur'. I came from Sydney to New Zealand, to Kapiti, on the Shibboleth. The ship went down in Rio de Janeiro where she was a whaler."

"Who is she?" interrupted the court judge with a perplexed tone.

"Pardon?" the Black man shot back.

"*She*. You said, 'where *she* was a whaler.' Who is *she*?"

The Black man looked surprised, as if he thought the man were joking; and then in a careful tone replied, "The ship, Sir. The ship's name was 'Shibboleth.' We whalers referred to our ships as *she*."

"I know that, Alesworth! You made it sound as if some *woman* was a whaler, Harper; and we all know that women don't whale!" The Judge seemed proud to doubly humiliate the Black man. He used the familiar 'Harper', a name which few people used for Arpur, and to which he gave even fewer the blessing to utter. The name was a nick-name, given to him by someone deep in a painful and almost forgotten past; and such spiteful reinstatements of its functionality only served to dredge up anger and ha-tred. The courtroom burst into laughter; and Arpur laughed with them, his laugh heard above the rest.

"Now, Arpur," The Judge had conceded a bit of re-spect upon the witness owing to his surprise at the Black man's humility. "Please continue."

Arpur looked around, grin fading as eyes swam the courtroom. "The chief man at the station was Tom Evans, the owner was Johnny Jones. I was six or seven seasons whaling at the Island." He referred to the Island of Kapiti, in the Cook Strait of New Zealand.

The judge broke in again, "What Island? Norfolk Is-land? Stewart Island?" The courtroom erupted into laugh-ter again, and Arpur followed along nervously, "Oh, you mean the little island just above the southern half of this great nation of ours!"

Arpur spoke up, "Yes. There were four boats on the Island."

"Is that it then? Of your whaling days? And what about now?" asked the Judge.

"I live at Picton Road. Major Baillie was my employer going on ten years. I arrived in this country just after the Battle of Kuititanga." said Arpur.

"And for the record, my Maori brothers who may not remember, that battle took place 16 November 1839." the Judge said in a paternal yet pedantic voice. "Now con-tinue, Jack."

"I don't know the year she came here, it was not 1840. I made up one of the boat's crew and was the after oars-man. We commenced whaling a month after I arrived."

The Black man looked as though he were going to say more; and then he closed his mouth and folded his hands.

"And?" prodded the Judge.

"And that is all." said Arpur calmly. He knew these Maori courts could be rough; but he also knew that he was not on trial and that all the information he supplied was strictly voluntary. He was merely giving an account of his life, as he had been invited to do at the request of the elder men here who knew that he had played a role in the Maori wars.

"Now Arpur, what year is it?" coyly inquired the Judge.

"It is 1890." stated Arpur.

"And how old are you?" the judge asked.

Arpur knew it was a leading question; however he replied with a smile, "Seventy-eight years old."

"And in those seventy-eight years, you are asking this counsel to believe that all you have done is a little bit of whaling and a little bit of gardening?" The court chamber roared with laughter while Arpur sat silently staring back at the Judge.

He did not know what to say. Certainly, Arpur had had a rich and full life, with experiences that some men did not even dream of. How would he explain some of the things that he had done? There were situations and actions that he had never imagined taking part in; and now it was all rushing back to him. The thought of reliving his life, of giving account of things that he had buried in his mind, began to overwhelm him; and it showed visibly on his sweaty face.

"Court adjourned!" yelled the Judge with a wave of his hand. The elder men grumbled and chortled as they milled out of the courthouse. The Judge approached Arpur, now alone with him in the room; and put his arm around

Arpur's broad shoulders. "Now, my friend. You will have dinner at my house with my family; and we will hear the whole story, won't we?" he said in a tone bordering between friendly and commanding.

Arpur walked softly with short, uncertain steps beside his friend, as a child being led to bed; and he searched through his mind for a way to begin. He rehearsed the line as if it were a speech: "Most people know me as Black Jack White . . ."

Chapter 2

THE DECISION

January, 1828, Mississippi:

"Y ou want to be a what?" his mother asked in excited disbelief.

"A whaler, Mama." said Arthur earnestly.

"That's what I thought you said." his mother spoke distantly, and paused before saying, "Not a sailor, a *wh*aler." She emphasized the 'wh' sound on the last word, allowing the word to register before she could grapple with its full weight. "And how does a Black man from the South go about finding any whales?" she asked with a biting tone which convinced him that she was not joking.

"The ships: They leave from up North all the time. Jeff was tellin' me." He had begun to talk fast, preparing to go into details when she cut him off.

"And what the hell does Jeff know about ships up North? Hell, he hasn't been anywhere but knee-deep in cotton

14601-GARD

his whole life. You tellin' me that he knows didley 'bout sea adventurin'?" she asked, beginning to sound disparaging to her only son.

Arthur stood up from the kitchen table and respectfully put his hands in the air as he calmly tried to explain. "Mama, Jeff's been places. Ain't nobody knows that 'ceptin me, and now you; but Jeff gets around."

"Bullcockey!" His mother slapped at his hands as she turned from the wood-burning stove. "The only place that Jeff's been is out cattin' at night 'round the old-timers' whiskey shed. He ain't got nothin' but gossip and second-hand stories from other big talkers. You willin' to hang for that, Arthur?"

"No, ma'am; but . . ." Arthur looked up from the floor and tried to tell her more.

"But nothin', boy! You got responsibility here. You got a wife already. That's more than most of these dogs around here got. And Lord knows I don't need you to look after *me*, but *she* might! What do you think of that?" she demanded as she stared at him sharply.

"Mama, I know all that. That's why I've got to do this. I want to be free; I want *us* to be free. I hear one year out there, and a man can support his family, his *free* family, up North for a whole 'nother year." Arthur told her with the eagerness of a small boy.

"You'll hang, son! You'll get all of us lynched, you know that?" his mother yelled.

He knew she was partly right. Attempting a run from this far south could be suicidal, he knew. Slave owners this far inland were not at liberty to get new chattel as cheaply and easily as coastal plantationers; and therefore, they were fanatical about holding onto, or hunting down as the case might be, the slaves they did own. He offered a solace. "Mama, I can make it. I've got it all planned out. I've been talkin' with Jeff and he says there's a trail up the mountains that White folk know nothin' about. Goes clear through to New York."

"New York City! Hell, why don't you jes' go down to Shreveport or Nawlins and hop on a boat down there? There's got to be some men doin' some whalin' down there." she said with enough interest to have him believe that she was beginning to give in.

"There is, Mama: But Louisiana is just another slave state. I'll be caught if I go down there." he informed her.

She looked down, shaking her head in concerned contemplation of his plan. "Lord, Lord, child. You's as crazy as your daddy." she said forlornly. She was speaking of the man who had plotted his escape many years ago, with similar expectations to Arthur's; and he had not been heard from since. It had been a devastation to Arthur's mother; and the thought of losing her son strained her visibly.

They both stood there at arm's length, looking down at the same patch of floor for a moment. "Mama, it will be all right." he said finally.

"That's what your father said. Remember, Arthur?" she asked sadly.

"Yes, Mama. I know. But I just got a feelin' about this. Every man's got a destiny." he said gravely.

"Destiny, pshaw! Listen to you. Soundin' all like Moses, or someone." she said, suddenly sounding amused. "What's wrong with what you got right here?" she asked, beginning to sound indignant again. "Heh, Arthur? Why do you want more than you got here? You got your friends, plenty to eat, and a roof over your head. What more do you want?" she asked, her temper starting to flare.

He seized her clutching hands, and said into her eyes, "I want to be free, Mama. I want freedom."

"You don't even know what that is Arthur! You don't even know!" she shrieked. "How can you have something you don't understand? You were born a slave, Arthur. That's what God made you." she said, driving her words into him.

He looked away, visibly hurt as he said, "Well that don't mean I'm gonna die a slave." He spoke these words with a prophetic ring in his voice, and he walked out the door and off the porch to go work his last day in the fields.

His mother hesitated in her grief before running to the edge of the porch and shouting after him in a mocking voice, "All right Arthur, you do what you got to do. But don't go changing your family name to Whalesworth!"

He continued walking away from her, his proud grin concealed from her view.

Chapter 3

THE ESCAPE

The dogs tracked him relentlessly. Leaving in January had not been his choice; but he had heard that the ships were departing in Winter to meet the whaling season in the South Seas at the beginning of that winter. Jeff had told him all about it. Now, as he trekked across frozen fields of fallow Mississippi mud, the thought of going winter to winter did nothing to alleviate his anxiety.

He had found the trail all right, after traveling a few days by foot upstate. He had never ventured so far, and by now, the endless fields and hills before him blended into a mesmerizing tunnel which carried him in only one direction with two names: Forward, and North.

"Follow the hills." Jeff had told him as they carried their wood in for the evening. "Keep the hills in front and the morning sun to your right. When the sun gets overhead, find a creek with some trees and rest up. When the sun gets over to your left shoulder, start after them hills again. Find another creek at night and stay there. That way, if you're sniffed out at night, you always got the creek to cover your tracks. If'n you find a creek flowin' down out of the hills back at you, follow it up. The trail's about three days out. When you start seein' big rocks stickin' out of the sides of the hills, you's real close. Find a field with some Black folk workin', and blend in long enough to find out 'xactly where the trail starts. Then you's be in Gawgia."

Very good Jeff, he thought: If he could just get away from these damn bloodhounds his first day out. He hadn't even had time to sip any stream water, or nibble at the salt bread his mama had baked. Who had told? he wondered. From the sound of it, the plantation hounds and the recovery party must have started out after him straight away. He had planned it all out though: Get into the fields at day break with everyone else so as not to be missed. Work a full morning until lunch, for the head count and for the last meal before heading out. Work toward the back of the field and slip over the stream while the field foreman was counting the morning bales. That would have given him an hour, maybe two, at least before they realized he was gone.

Someone must have told. He had explained it to everyone he trusted. Although, his missus did have that look in her eye. He had wondered about her. She really wouldn't know any better if she had truly wanted him to stay. She was young; she had not yet had to witness a Black man being strung up and mutilated to hinder his further escapes. She might have told, she was young. But how many times had he reassured her? "Sugar, I'm comin' back real soon for you and the youngin', I promise. I'm comin back rich, and we's gonna live free like decent folks, you'll see."

He had almost pleaded with her as he explained. But she seemed to only pretend to understand the complex details. Her eyes had told another story, almost betraying her pregnant silence.

His mind raced over more pressing issues than holding court for an informant at the moment. Right then, his lungs stung with the icy air as he trotted non-stop along the tree-lined edge of countless fields, ever vigilant to connect the ones which lay dormant and vacant so as not to be seen by workers. And in that way, the cold became a blessing as it not only limited the number of his footprints which were actually made, but it also broadened his path through the number of fields which lay empty at this time of year. It was actually an easier time of year for him and his kind, he admitted to himself, as the rhythm of his run came over him. With virtually no crops to harvest except for the late cotton, slave activities turned to the likes of chopping wood and tending livestock. It made life a little more interesting for his people, but no more enjoyable; as most were not particularly fond of the cold weather. It also brought out the hunting mentality of the plantation staff; and now he had unwittingly given them an opportunity to hone their sport.

The dogs were a couple of miles back; as he gauged from the echo of their barking. Their wailing came in waves, fading in and out. He knew that continuing on a direct forward course would only bring them straight to his flank by sunset. He knew that he had to maneuver somehow, without losing time: Possibly a switchback. He thought as he ran. In the clarity of his stride, a plan emerged. Along with the hard bread, his mother had given him a glass flask of 'medicine': A pint of 190 proof liquor to help him along the way. "Now don't drink this, Arthur!" she had sternly warned. "Just a sip at night to keep you warm. And God forbid, if you get hurt, be sure to wash your wound with it!" Arthur pulled the bottle from his breast pocket and watched as the clear contents shook with his swift steps. He looked ahead and saw one of the many irrigation streams which cut across the fields of these low, flat farms. As he approached it, a scheme quickly developed in his mind; and he began to put it into action immediately.

Without stopping, he swooped down to scoop up a hand-sized stone from the furrowed field. As he looked from the vessel of spirits in one hand to the rock in his right hand, he brought the two together smartly at the lip of the bottle. Just as he had hoped, a small triangular sliver broke free from the neck of the flask, leaving a jagged crotch extending from its rim to its shoulder. The contents remained inside, as the cork not only held them in place, but reinforced the now compromised neck as well. Arthur hurriedly dropped the rock; kept running; removed the cork; and swiped his right hand across the jagged edge of the bottle. He succeeded in producing a deep gash in the meat of his palm; and his pain was offset by the sting of the splashing liquor and the trance of his exertion. He shook his hand and promptly corked the flask, returning it to his coat pocket. He let his injured hand trail to his side, the blood dripping in a substantial stream behind him. When he was within one-hundred yards of the creek, he removed his handkerchief from his pocket, being careful not to use his bloody hand. At fifty yards, he had the bottle out and grasped with his handkerchief-clad left hand, looking like a magician readying for a trick. With his left hand, he flicked the cork free and allowed the fluid to begin spilling from the upright flask onto the handkerchief. As he reached the stony edge of the water, he squatted and began pouring the alcohol into his wound. He allowed the liquor and the blood to collude with the flowing water as he cleansed his cut. When it was clear of blood, he quickly wrapped his gash with the spirit-soaked rag and tied it tightly. Standing, he swigged the remaining alcohol and smashed the glass on the rocks where the blood droplets met the water. Satisfied with his work, he wolfed down a slab of bread and washed it down with a handful of water. He turned upstream and continued to run, skirting the creek along the edge of its sandy bed. He would run until sunset, he thought, and cross the stream in the morning near its head. He was entirely confident that his quick actions had foiled the hounds. However, someday they would pay for his shed blood with their own, he promised himself. "Free men don't get hunted with dogs." he said out loud. The sound of his own voice in this vast expanse of empty fields made him feel important.

Chapter 4

AN HONORABLE CHARGE

Arthur stood nervously at the quay end of the gangway. It would be the first time that he had walked out over the sea, he thought; and the first time on a ship, for that matter. This was the harbor, though: The man had said. All the whalers came here. He had even told Arthur which letters to look out for: "H. M. S." ; "else you end up right back down South", he had said. Being as the kindly Black gentleman had driven the wagon the last leg of the way to New York, Arthur was inclined to heed his advice.

New York was beautiful, even in winter. The harbor was bustling with busy tradesmen and shops; and tall, new ships came and went constantly. Everyone seemed happy; and life was vibrant. Arthur smelled snow and opportunity in the air. In his dark, dusty, worn clothes, he was hard-pressed to seem the beggar in a city where sown about were sooty chaps, the ever-prosperous, self-support-ing chimneysweeps. Besides, he was bolstered by his success of having made it to Fortune's front door. It was of no consequence, as he walked the planks leading to the brig, that he could not read the sign which read, 'Whalers wanted. Men of fortitude: Inquire within.'

The First Mate met Arthur walking across midship, asking if he could be of help. "And what might your name be, Guv'nor?" he asked in an artificial, bubbly voice.

Arthur blinked at the man in curiosity. He replied, "Arthur Alesworth, sah." He waited for the man to yell at him; or worse, to grab him and shackle him to the mast, awaiting the authorities.

The First Mate replied in an even more manufactured zeal, "Arthur Alesworth! 'A', 'A'! As in, aye, aye, Guv'nor!"

Arthur was confused by this man's enthusiasm, but he went along; and said, "Yes, sah, I suppose so."

The First Mate, standing a couple of inches taller than Arthur, said, "And you are by far worth your ale. Do follow me inside for a refresher!"

Arthur hesitated as the man gingerly turned and walked toward the aft cabin door. The First Mate reached the door, set in the bulkhead formed by the rise of the deck at the stern of the ship; and he motioned with a turn of the head and a grin for Arthur to accompany him.

Arthur warily followed him into the compartment at the rear of the ship. The space opened up to reveal large tables extending from the bulkheads out into the center in orderly rows; and a makeshift bar in a rear corner with kegs anchored to the deck. The First Mate was already at one keg with a stein, dispensing a beer for Arthur.

The First Mate, one hand on the mug and the other on the tap, turned his head, still smiling, and asked, "So you want to be a whaler, then, Guv'nor?" He finished pouring and presented the mug auspiciously to Arthur. He said, "Best ale under the Crown. It's a bit cold, sorry. Should do, though."

Arthur, staring blankly, accepted the cup and replied, "I think I'd make a good one, sah." He took a sip of the foamy brew, peering around the dim cabin as his eyes adjusted.

The First Mate paused without breathing, as if summarizing an equation in his mind, and exhaled the words, "Well, yes, I think we might have something for you." He looked down and around at the tables as if he hadn't realized that they were there before; and he put out his arm and palm. He said, "Please, sit here and enjoy your beverage while I see about matters. I shall return." He briskly exited, leaving Arthur to look at dark timbers and brass fixtures.

Arthur sipped his ale; and after a few moments in the cool chamber, bobbing gently on the harbor swells, he began to feel extremely relaxed. He started to envision himself, sailor suit and all, out on the high seas. What would it be like, he wondered, to see nothing but water? Would there be islands? Would there be storms? How well would he sleep on the waves? he wondered. A seagull screeched past the small aft porthole.

The First Mate returned, approaching Arthur as would an actor. He said, "I have some good tidings. The Captain would like to have a talk with you!" His excitement seemed to imply that Arthur should reciprocate in kind.

Arthur looked up at him from his bench and naïvely asked, "You mean you're not the Captain?"

The First Mate held his gaze on Arthur as his eyes passed through a range of focal distances and conflicting emotions. He finally sputtered and chuckled, saying, "Good heavens, no. I wish!" His tone changed dramatically to the less obsequious, and he added, "You're a funny fellow. The Captain will be pleased to have you on board, to be sure!" He bolted ahead of Arthur, out of the aft door and down a ladder. Arthur struggled to keep up.

As Arthur followed the fleeting dark form of the First Mate down ladders and through low passageways, he became mindful not to strike his head or knees. A light appeared from behind a partially opened door at the end of a long passageway. Arthur heard the familiar voice of the First Mate speaking in low tones behind the door. He slowed as he approached, allowing his bumps and future bruises to escort him. As he drew near the door, the First Mate's talking turned to whispers, and Arthur heard bits and pieces of his phrases: Things such as, " . . . he's the one, I swear . . .", followed by " . . . you should have seen . . .", and " . . . then he said . . ." , all followed by an uproar of laughter between the First Mate and an unseen man.

The First Mate spoke up from behind the door, "You there, Arthur, is that you? Do come in."

Arthur pushed the door open slowly and stood in the doorway. The First Mate took his hands off the man's desk and stood back. The man sat, hands folded, looking back at Arthur with an amused smirk. The small cabin, no more than six feet deep and the width of the ship, was situated directly below the aft topside deck. It had windows across the entire aft bulkhead, which also constituted the stern of the ship. The bulkheads and overhead were completely whitewashed, and the deck was covered with a luxurious mat of some unknown material. Arthur was impressed with the stately cabin; although he showed no emotion.

"You must be Arthur!" said the Captain, standing and extending a hand across his large desk. The Captain wore a red jacket with brass buttons, and white trousers. He looked as though he were always at the desk, and always in a clean uniform.

"Yes, Captain." Arthur said, almost asking, as he shook the Captain's hand timidly.

The Captain vigorously shook Arthur's hand and motioned for him to sit down with the other. "Do sit down. Let's discuss some things." he said, sitting himself, and continuing to smile.

Arthur sat erect in the chair in front of the desk. The First Mate stood just to the right of the Captain; and they both beamed at Arthur. Arthur felt slightly self-conscious.

"First Mate, this calls for a brandy!" boomed the Captain, as he reached for a decanter behind him on the shelf. The First Mate produced two small glasses. The Captain poured a generous amount for Arthur, and a jigger for himself. Lifting his glass, he nodded to Arthur as he extended his arm. "Cheers!" he said gleefully, as he anticipated Arthur's response. Arthur's face developed an expression of realization, as he belatedly leaned forward and lifted his glass. The Captain quickly clinked his glass against Arthur's and proceeded to drink his cognac in one swallow. As he slapped his glass down on the desk, he said, "Welcome aboard the Elizabeth, Arthur!"

Arthur lifted himself to his glass, and after taking a cautious sip, replied with a slight slur, "Thank you, sah."

The Captain continued after reclining. "Now, Arthur. The First Mate tells me that you want to be a whaler. Is that true?" he asked with a second question lurking behind his voice.

"Yes, sah. I hear it's good." said Arthur, as his head began to take in the harbor air and the bright whitewash in a more sensitive, sensory capacity.

"That's excellent." replied the Captain quickly, as if opening for a speech. "Because we may have an offer that you cannot refuse." The Captain's words echoed in Arthur's ears. "Right now, we have several openings which we are hoping to close. We have made some changes within our staff, and we are looking for some very quality personnel to fill the gaps around here. There are some general seaman jobs available; however, there are also a handful of other, more select positions which are being offered." Arthur's head began to swim as the thought of being offered a job washed over him. Where was the foreman dragging him by the cuff? Where was the whip? he wondered. The Captain continued, "Now, you are a Negro, are you not?"

Arthur was shocked by the frankness of the question. He stuttered, "Y-yes . . . I believe so. My folks came from Africa, if that's what you mean." He paused, as if for approval.

The Captain pursed his lips, and said, "That is fine. You have never sailed in a ship yourself, though, correct?" He looked back at Arthur, as a doctor examining a patient.

"No." said Arthur. He anticipated trouble.

"Very well. That is fine. Now, I understand that your people have had some difficulty in this country." the Captain said.

"What do you mean?" asked Arthur.

"Well, with this issue of slavery and gross mistreatment and such. You see, our laws don't allow all of that in my country. I don't own slaves, for sure, nor would I want to. With all of this talk about liberty, freedom, and justice that this country brags about—no offense—we just think that your people are not sharing in those so-called ideals. We want to help you." the Captain expounded.

Arthur thought that he was dreaming. He tried to cover his embarrassment; and said, "Well, you know, I'm all right, sah. We get along all right." He did not know what else to say.

The Captain paused, turned to his First Mate who gave a nod, and then said, "Well, Arthur, my point is: We're prepared to charge you with a commission on this fine vessel which will elevate your privilege beyond what the average sailor will experience during the next few months at sea. Here it is: I want you to be my personal assistant; to be by my side in all of my most sensitive operations; and to take care of some very important jobs for me. How does that sound?"

Arthur grappled with all of the new information and choices, and replied, "I don't know, sah. If you'll have me, then I guess I'll try. Jes' don't give me something too important to handle; I don't want to mess somethin' up."

The Captain slapped his palm down on the desk, and exclaimed, "Arthur! I think you'll do just fine! I think that you'll find that this opportunity is just what you've been looking for. From what we've seen all ready, we really want you! Do you think you can handle it?"

Arthur considered his options. It was either brave the cold in New York harbor for an indeterminable amount of time in search of work, or who knew what, he thought. This sounded like the answer to his prayers and hard work, Arthur thought. He perked up and said, "Well, yes sah! I'll do the job."

The Captain smiled and nodded in assumptive approval. He said, "That's the spirit, Arthur. You'll see that you've made the right choice. Now, there's a small matter of a contract that we need to square away; and then the First Mate can see you to your quarters and get you your uniforms." The Captain's smile began to slip away and his movements became less excited as he rifled through his drawers. "Ah, here it is. Now, this just states that you agree to provide service to the ship for one full year in return for room and board; and the rest is just quite simple, really. You can read it later. Just sign here." said The Captain, as he slid the contract toward Arthur with a pointed finger, and handed him a quill.

Arthur hesitated. He had signed his name only once before in his life. He carefully scrawled a large 'A', followed by some wavy lines. It sufficed. The Captain snatched the contract back and held it to his knitted face. He motioned for the First Mate, who stepped forward and signed as witness. Then, The Captain lit his wax stick and placed his official seal on the document. He then tossed the paper with a spin to the side of his desk and folded his hands behind his head.

The Captain nonchalantly said, "Very well. That is all. The First Mate will explain everything to you." He said to the First Mate, "Mate, see the Cabin Boy to his chamber, if you would be so kind."

The First Mate stepped up to Arthur and flatly said, "Let's go." as he pointed out the door. Arthur stood, confused, and shuffled out the door. Arthur stopped down the passageway a bit, realizing that the First Mate had not immediately followed him. Arthur heard low voices again. He thought that he heard the Captain say, " . . . and get that nigger a bath. Jesus Christ, he smells worse than a dead whale. When he's done with that, my chamber pot needs emptying. Then get him started on the bilge." The Captain and the First Mate laughed, as the First Mate came bounding out into the passageway to find Arthur.

"Aye, aye, Captain." said the First Mate, still chuckling.

Chapter 5

AROUND THE HORN

"Station the piloting party!" yelled the First Mate at regular intervals as he roved the ship from deck to deck. It was a cry which could strike dread or ecstasy alike in the hearts of sailors, depending on the time of day, condition of weather, or purpose of port call.

Today it came at dawn on an April morning. It was only the second time that Arthur had heard the order issued: The last being upon departing New York. Now, over two months later, the command came as a welcomed announcement that heralded the impending mooring of the ship to actual terra firma. Arthur would walk on land once again, he thought, at a place which his shipmates had raved about in anticipation for months: Rio de Janeiro.

The ship had had to sail a course well outside the influence of the Gulf Stream, and in so doing, had avoided all of the Caribbean sea and its legendary liberty hot spots.

Arthur had experienced nothing but open ocean for seventy-five consecutive days. He looked forward not only to escaping the confines of the ship, but also to eating something other than hard bread and water.

The ship had been well supplied at the beginning of the voyage, with extra stock of various bulk items being stacked in passageways and other out-of-the-ordinary places; however, one by one, certain things had begun to run out at different times throughout the trip, until all that remained was the barest essentials of survival. The coffee had been one of the last things to go, and its absence compounded the depletion of the tobacco. The crew was a miserable lot. Having been forced to forego their vices at unexpected times, they fell prey to the monotony of the austere life at sea. Sometimes the wind was the only sound which challenged the silence; and it was said that a man's suffering its singular song for hours on end could either soothe him or send him senseless. It never bothered Arthur much. He would either play his mouth harp or hum a simple tune to himself.

Seasickness was another scourge by which Arthur had been passed over. Other sailors had warned him about it, and had even watched 'the Negro' to see how he responded to the sea; however, it was not to be, and Arthur often watched in modest amusement as several of his more experienced shipmates would sour a freshly swabbed deck. To their surprise, and his, Arthur took readily to the sea. He sensed his colleagues' perceptions about his potential culturally influenced disadvantage to adapting to everything nautical; however, he brushed aside all doubts as he soon swung freely as a buccaneer through the rigging. In fact, his cavalier performance on deck and his matching knack for learning knots endeared him to some of the saltier scalawags onboard.

So much so, that one day the following scenario unfolded: The Captain had assigned Arthur several tasks, many of them more menial in nature than usual. Arthur had been extremely compliant to the Captain's wishes for the first forty days, carrying out his duties to the last dirty detail in an effort to please his new boss. However, it seemed to Arthur that the harder and more meticulously that he worked, the more that the Captain expected him to do. Arthur didn't mind at first, because being used to working tirelessly without appreciation, he still saw the Captain's actions as mild at best. Then, as Arthur's duties began to spread into the realm of other ship's activities such as rigging aide, lookout watch, galley wash, and the like, the Captain continued to increase his demands on Arthur in his role as Cabin Boy. It were as though the Captain had turned a blind eye to the significant and additional amount of work that Arthur had been required to perform; and also as if he totally disregarded the importance of the operational duties in light of the less desirable and seemingly optional jobs which he had begun to heap on Arthur as of late. Arthur tried to work faithfully without interjecting any personal opinion or attitude about the matter; however, after a time he began to grow weary, and he could not help but feel strained under the burden. It seemed to Arthur that the Captain was trying to work him to death, out of spite in some secretive unspoken way. It confused Arthur. It was not the amount of work that bothered him, just the way that the tasks began to conflict in timing and priority. Arthur felt silly in wondering why the Captain would try to undermine himself in being so contradictory. Arthur really began to think about it; and it made no sense. There was no humanly possible way to complete the tasks in the order and the time that the Captain had assigned them to him. On this particular evening, the First Mate came to Arthur as he was helping to set a jib, and told him that the Captain required to see

Arthur. Arthur, not wanting to release the boom and send the ship careening, stated that he would be there as soon as possible. No sooner than the words had left his mouth, it seemed to Arthur, then the Captain was standing by his side, having returned with the First Mate.

"What's this I hear about you disobeying my orders?" asked the Captain with a calmly horrifying tone.

Arthur, ropes in straining hands, turned his head and said, surprised, "Sah, no sah, I didn't disobey. I jes' can't do two things at once." He finished with a bit of shine on his words, hoping the Captain would understand his dilemma.

"Harper! Step down from your post and come with me!" the Captain suddenly shouted.

Arthur felt a twinge of anger, but he remained restrained. He said calmly, "Sah, I can't let go . . ."

The Captain cut him short and screamed, "First Mate, confine this man to his quarters. Have him flogged and then report to me."

The First Mate jumped in Arthur's face as the Captain wheeled and departed. The First Mate breathed down Arthur's neck as he motioned for a nearby seaman to take the ropes from Arthur. He escorted Arthur to his rack with a firm hand around the back of his neck.

Some time later, the First Mate appeared at the Captain's desk. "Sir, I cannot find anyone who will flog the Cabin Boy." he said urgently.

The Captain slammed his ruler down and looked up at the First Mate, infuriated. He commanded, "Then do it yourself; or I will."

The First Mate squelched a look of distaste, and replied hastily, "Sir, the crew is acting very unsettled. There's much grumbling about mutiny."

The Captain immediately exploded, "Mutiny! Mu-

tiny! I'll pull into port right now and have every one of
them hung!" His face turned red and the veins in his neck
bulged. As he took a breath, his eyes fluttered with a wild
stare; and then he put his head in his hands on his desk.
"Oh, God, just forget it. Just forget it. Dismissed." he
said, as if in emotional agony.

II

Arthur stationed himself in the crow's nest. He liked
being the lookout during maneuvering. He would be the
first to see port and the first to be seen by the Harbor
Master. He was like a highly visible ambassador, being
carried along aloft three-quarters the way up the mainsail
mast, standing just forward of the last crosshatch. From
the sights of anyone's looking glass, he provided an ominous vision which transfixed even the more experienced
horizon watchers; especially if volatile precipitation pre-
vailed which pushed patches of vapor or parts of sail past
the person's viewing-pipe perspective.

Arthur would relieve the off-going lookout, the man
who had had the honor of crying out, "Land ho!" after a
long hard night suspended above the ship. The oncoming
piloting party and subsequent maneuvering watch sported
not only the advantage of being fresh from a full night of
sleep, but also the jubilation of being the on-duty crew to
deliver the ship unto a new day of liberty.

That is, if the Captain allowed liberty call. The likeli-
hood of liberty not being granted was extremely slim, however, given the level of tension that had recently developed
onboard, and the relative prudence of the generally prag-
matic skipper. Liberty would go down, the Captain surmised, and he figured it best to allow it before requiring

that the new stores be loaded. Besides, he had a pressing matter to attend to on shore himself.

The Captain gave the order for the Brazilian colors to be flown, as a friendly gesture; and also out of partial loyalty to his interests here. For the Captain had a Brazilian wife. It was common knowledge among most of his longer-standing crewmembers; however, it was not openly discussed. That was due to the fact that the Captain also had a Mrs. Stewart in the United Kingdom who would probably not take kindly to the rumors that she was married to a professional polygamist. The crew did joke about the matter, however, periodically during the rare hours; but it was widely held that no matter how saucy the affair or how unpopular the Captain, indiscriminate gratuitous indiscretion would provide no positive returns for any loud-mouthed member of the crew who mistakenly thought that he could boast of his knowledge in the presence of the Captain, no matter how boisterous the surroundings. Stupidity being adept at compounding itself, every good sailor knew to merely smile and toast the Captain when he appeared with his dubious bride. Besides, she was extremely attractive. Being an Indio-Spanish mix, and embodying all the best traits of each influence, she was always a welcome sight among the revelry and drunkenness that, to her at least, seemed to herald her coming.

Arthur tied his end of the chord to the mast, and the many gaily-colored pennants flapped in the breeze. The ship was emblazoned with regalia, as if for a homecoming. The smells of land-trees and grasses, cooking food, and farm animals-began to arrive in waves and waft across the deck. The odors brought with them memories of all the finer pleasures of life to all the crewmembers; and each man began to privately anticipate his own experiences to be had during the brief but intense time on shore. Arthur was overwhelmed with the possibilities that freedom might

hold for him on land. He did not know where to begin
planning his holiday activities. For the time being, he
needed all of his faculties to help steer the ship to the pier.

Rio in the morning was breathtaking. As Arthur called
out landmark bearings to the Helmsman, he took in the
spectacular scenery. He had heard of the Spaniards and
the great land to the south which they had conquered.
Now, he could see it firsthand and how vastly it differed
from the austere New England coastline. Wildly undulating peaks and irregularly shaped valleys, all covered in lush
emerald-green and banana-yellow canopy, draped onto
white, sandy beaches. The water in the bay was the color
of turquoise stones that Arthur had seen back home. It
was certainly prettier than the murky lakes and ponds that
served up those well-suited catfish, he thought. The Spanish houses and buildings were quite different as well; however, like the catfish, they seemed to suit their surroundings. They were white like the sand, and their windows
required no glass because the wind was always warm. From
a distance there seemed to be much color adorning everything: Bright reds, yellows, greens, blues, and oranges in
varying hues were abundant on building edges and along
street walls.

In addition to the sights, Arthur began to hear a rhythmic sound as the ship drew closer to the pier. It sounded
like music, yet it seemed so chaotic and flamboyant compared to the marching music of the militia band back
home. It was also a far cry from the orchestral music which
was sometimes performed on the verandah of the plantation mansion. The music that Arthur heard now was slightly
arousing, and he felt it stirring different remote and unidentifiable sentiments within him. He liked it. Yet, it was
so early in the morning; and it seemed that the parade he
saw now had been going on for some time. Arthur wondered if it were some dawn ritual, or perhaps some wel-

coming party for the ship. He could not work out how that could occur, however, unless the city always had a large welcoming committee ready to go at a moment's notice. Arthur had never heard of such a thing, so he reckoned that Rio must be a rather rowdy town.

The ship reached the quay and the lines went out. The boat was secured, along with the maneuvering watch; and the Captain called all hands to General Quarters at midship. He addressed the crew:

"Now gentleman, I realize that we have had our share of run-ins on this first leg of the journey. I'm willing to let by-gones be by-gones, and I urge you to do the same. Remember, what happens underway, stays underway." The crew stood at relatively respectful attention, maintaining ranks with only the odd snigger and glance or two. The Captain continued, "Now, we have the business of stores loading and general repairs to attend to; however, I have postponed that until tomorrow morning at oh-eight-hundred hours." Cheers began to break out as the men became visibly excited; and the Captain calmly raised a hand to restore order. He carried on, "Now, we have approximately forty-eight hours liberty here, starting shortly; and I am not requiring midnight musters. So you are free to bunk on the ship or about town. Please be on your best behavior, as you are an ambassador of the Queen during your stay, and a guest of the Brazilian government. We do not want to do anything to affect our welcome status here, as it would be very difficult for Britain to shoot over the horn without this stop! Do I make myself clear? Good! Muster for all hands at oh-eight-hundred hours. First Mate, make sure the ship is squared away, and then call liberty. That is all." The Captain walked toward his cabin. The men broke ranks with a hurrah and scrambled for their racks.

The First Mate inspected every man and every bunk

and gave the all clear. He instructed the men to queue at the gangway for their liberty pay. Standing behind the strongbox, he dispensed each man with a sum and a salute, and they were away. Arthur had queued last, it being his first time, and he wanted personal instruction from the First Mate on how to go about liberty and the business of spending money. When the last man had barreled down the gangway, Arthur stepped up and looked eagerly at the First Mate.

"Yes?" asked the First Mate, indignantly.

"I'se like ta get my money, now, Sah." said Arthur.

"You what?" asked the First Mate in disbelief.

"I need ta get my money, so's I can go to liberty." said Arthur respectfully.

The First Mate began to laugh and then abruptly forced a stern look. He said, "Harper, you'll be lucky to see topside for the next two days. Now go see what the Captain needs. He's preparing to visit his family here."

Arthur looked perplexed, and he said, "But Sah . . ."

The First Mate yelled, "But nothing, Harper. Do your job! Didn't you read your contract? By the way, you're duty cook as well, so get moving!"

III

Colored paper flowers and confetti streamed past on a rippling black surface highlighted by a myriad of broadening white rays of light which trailed back to a converging source: The lanterns of the procession dancing past the pier. The festival had continued all day; and now as night thickened, all Arthur could do was watch from his post at the ship end of the gangway. A dubious honor, the topside watch was nothing more than a glorified doorman's job, filled with some poor soul who had been chosen to remain tied to the ship, either spiritually or physically-it mattered not-and feign a sense of duty to his floating ball and chain as the other prisoners rioted in the street.

Arthur watched the carnival from the deserted, dark, deck of the ship, as a child who experiences one of his parents' parties from a distant door down a dim hallway. People whooped and yelled; laughed and gibbered; drank and sang; all to a raunchy, raucous, rhythm which flowed smoothly down the street. Arthur enjoyed the unrehearsed production, yet he was unsure if he could have joined the procession.

Occasionally members of his crew would stumble out of the crowd, either alone or in noisy gangs, and stomp across the gangway. Depending on their level of drunkenness, the reactions to Arthur's face ranged from sympathy to outright mockery of his position.

One sailor said, "It's a good one, Arthur. Don't worry, though, you're not missing much. Just got to get some things from my rack. See you in the morning! Cheers!"

The leader of another group of sailors who had stampeded all the way across the gangway before recognizing the Cabin Boy, said, "Arthur! You sorry son-of-a-bitch, you're missing all the fun. By the way, you're unsatisfactory!" They all exploded in a chorus of guffaws and set out again into the throbbing mass.

Several more came and went, until at midnight, a lone sailor came strolling up, sober and straight as an arrow, and said, "I'm here to relieve you. I have word from the First Mate that you are to have breakfast ready for the crew at oh six hundred; and you need to prepare the Captain's quarters for departure. Anything I need to know?"

Arthur had not expected a relief. He was happy that the man had not come at one of the times that Arthur had sneaked away from his post and fetched a cup of coffee from the galley. He was overjoyed to have been given the opportunity to confidently reply, "No Sah, all conditions normal. Aft draft is high and dry and the tide is drawing nigh. I stand relieved."

IV

Warm, soft lamplight flowed over the Captain's desk and flickered across the large map in Arthur's outstretched arms. Although he could not read, Arthur had become familiar with world geography; and he could readily identify all the continents and oceans on the globe. He found nautical symbols easy to learn as well, along with some of the simple math that sailing required. Everything about seamanship seemed to come naturally to Arthur; and as he sat surreptitiously in the seat of his ship's superior officer, he fantasized about one day becoming a great sea captain himself. Perhaps when he returned from whaling, he thought, he and Lalani could purchase a boat in New York.

Arthur's musing was interrupted by the clamor of a commotion occurring on the pier. He stepped to the portside porthole above the Captain's bunk and peered out. Coming across the gangway in a hail of hysteria and a flamboyant, frilly, red dress, was a tall, raven-haired woman with brown skin. She was unaccompanied, even though she looked like one of the carnival dancers. Her clothes looked Spanish, and so did she. As she stormed across the gangway to the surprise and obvious dismay of the watch, one of her shoe's heels became trapped in the grating of the bridge, causing it to come off of her foot. Visibly infuriated further, she wheeled around to retrieve her slipper. However, she was foiled by the fault of her fashion, the berth of her skirt being too big to let her see her own shoe. She whipped around in frenzied circles screaming and

cursing in Spanish, finally abandoning her frustrating efforts and blowing past the sentry. The topside guard, recognizing her as the Captain's Brazilian wife, let her pass.

As she crossed onto the deck, she disappeared from
Arthur's view. He quickly resumed his readying of the
Captain's chamber, in case the visitor was an acquaintance
of his sent ahead to spring an impromptu inspection.
Arthur heard her irate, irregular clumping, as the mysterious woman violently lumbered unishod across the upper
deck. He heard the sound shift, as she stumbled down the
midship ladder. Her hurried faltering gait gave the impression of a renegade with a wooden peg leg running
down the passageway. She burst through the Captain's
cabin door, and standing over Arthur at the desk, breathless, stammered, "High yam Senora Stewhart. Who are
hugh?"

Arthur sat, sextant in hand, and said, "I am Arthur."

"Lieutenant Arthur. I have not heard of you. But that
is typical. My husband did not mention that he had a
Moroccan officer under his command. Pleasure to meet
you." She lurched forward slightly, and extended a dainty
and unsteady hand.

Arthur stood, happy to improvise in the role of junior
officer, and shook her shaky hand. He said, "A pleasure."

She immediately broke and slumped onto the Captain's
bunk, sitting and staring at nothing in particular with
glassy eyes. With a heavy Spanish accent, she began to
speak, "Well I am here because the good Captain would
rather spend the evening drinking rum with his crew than
be with me. His last night in port; and he is acting like a
little boy! Can you believe it? You men are all the same."

Arthur sat fiddling with stacks of maps and nautical
instruments at the Captain's desk. He took advantage of
her pause, and said, "Yes ma'am."

She studied him with swimming eyes, surprised by his sincerity, and said, "You are nice. Why are you not out enjoying yourself?"

Arthur put on a slight air of importance and said, "The ship gets underway tomorrow. I am preparing the Captain's navigation aids, Mrs. Stewart."

Senora Stewart said, "Please, call me Monica." She paused again, a curious smile floating on her face.

Arthur, keeping his eye on his work, replied, "All right."

Monica, jumping up suddenly, sprang across the cabin and began rifling through shelves. She exclaimed, "I know . . . Let's have a brandy. You have worked enough. You stop now, all right? Let us drink and talk!"

Arthur, not wanting to disobey the wishes of the Captain's wife, removed the decanter from its secluded spot on the top shelf. He produced two glasses; and she hurriedly poured ample amounts of the Captain's liqueur. She quickly drank the better portion of hers, as if very thirsty, and sat back down on the Captain's bed.

She said abruptly, "He treats me like chit! Just like chit. Does he treat his crew like that? I hope not for his sake. I don't know why I put up with it." Arthur sat across the cabin from her, paying respectful and slightly sympathetic attention to her. She continued, "He doesn't give a damn about me! Eight months! Eight months I wait; and does he write to me? No! Does he send me any word or gifts by way of one of his captain friends? No! Like chit, I say." She began to sob, lightly at first, and then she burst into tears. Arthur did not know how to respond, except with kind looks and open ears. She went on through her sobs, "I am sorry. Forgive me. I think it is because I am Spanish. He does not think of me as a real wife. I am just a plaything that he visits for pleasure. Besides, he makes fun of me, I know. I hear his crew mock me and the way I talk. I cannot help it!" She cried harder.

Arthur felt compelled to offer solace. He said quietly, "I think you sound jes' fine, Monica. I would be proud to have you as a wife. Captain Stewart is very lucky."

Monica abruptly stopped crying, and her head snapped upright, "Oh you kind man. You are so nice. Please, come sit here. I want to talk to you." She motioned with a patting hand beside her.

Arthur looked at her one bare foot, her wet face, and her puffy eyes. He felt sympathy for her as he carefully sat down next to Monica.

She looked him in the eyes and asked, "Tell me. Does he treat anyone else this bad? I want to know."

Arthur averted his eyes, swayed his shoulders, and said, "I don't know."

Monica ducked her head to catch his eyes and asked again, "You do know. Tell me, is there anyone whom he treats like he does me?"

Arthur hemmed and hawed another moment, and then said quietly, "Yes."

Monica triumphantly said, "Yes. I knew it. The bastard. Tell me what he does to other people."

Arthur looked at her sheepishly; and like a child confessing to his mother, said, "I think he called me a nigger. I just didn't 'spect that from Mister Stewart. And now he picks on me. I can't do nothing right. I don't think he likes Black folks."

Monica seemed to regain her senses as she stared sternly at Arthur. She said, "Are you serious? That is terrible." She spoke in a rational, concerned tone; however, inside she was becoming even more enraged than before. Her mind began to clear considerably and thwart the effects of the evening's libations. For now, what had started as a general coquettish quest for stray surplus sympathy, became her keen and resolute conviction to take emotional revenge on the man who had claimed to love her. To cherish her for who and what she was; and part of her was African, from her father's side. Her husband was fully aware of that; and the thought that he would harbor any racist opinions only added further doubt in light of his recent boorish behavior. She defused her threatening bomb of anger with a simple, sudden realization: She had married the wrong man. As her newfound calm settled over her, she sauntered over to the Captain's desk and extinguished the oil lamp. Slipping back to Arthur through the dark, she came to sit in a single stark ray of light which shone through the porthole above the skipper's bunk. She placed a hand softly on Arthur's shoulder, and said, "Please, teach me how to speak better."

Arthur said, "I don't know."

Monica said, "Yes, I want you to teach me, sometime. Please stand up."

Unsure of her intentions, Arthur obediently rose as she wished. He stood rigidly and nervously as she slowly began to grapple with the intricate lacings of his jumper pants. She fumbled with the many buttons that formed a long gauntlet around the front of his trousers. Finally, she reached her goal and began the oral lesson that she had requested.

Arthur hesitantly spoke up, "But I thought you wanted me to teach you, Mrs. Stewart."

Monica quickly pulled back and said, "You are, more than you know. Please be quiet. I need to concentrate." And as she continued with her studies, forming several consummate vowel sounds with her skilled lips and demonstrating a firm grasp of dangling participles in her native tongue, Arthur's enthusiasm grew as his student learned faster and faster. After much intense instruction, the two agreed that she had absorbed enough for one night; and that Arthur simply could not pound any more into her head. As the session came to a climax, however, the unthinkable occurred.

Unbeknownst to them, the Captain had returned to the ship, and could now be heard rambling loudly down the passageway. As he burst through the door of his dim cabin, he seemed to pay no mind to his wife seated primly on his bed. Nor did he notice the dark figure hovering just beside his wardrobe. No, the Captain did not seem to notice much of anything as he continued to sing a slurred sailor song at the top of his lungs. As he rambled on, he lifted an object to his face and struggled to focus upon its stiff, black form. It was a high-heeled shoe. Before the Captain realized the identity of his possession, however, he proceeded to pass out from drunkenness, landing squarely on his face.

V

Heading for Cape Horn could be one of the better or worse parts of the voyage. At best, it was roughly the half-way mark of the trip, and rounding it successfully meant beginning the downhill leg of the long journey. It also meant the last sight of land for an additional two months; and so, even in the best of conditions, it provided only a reserved amount of adulation. At its worst, it could sink a ship within minutes. Set deceptively off the actual mainland of the tip of South America, 'The Horn' as it was known was really a vestigial island emerging from the end of a sunken spit. Similar to the Florida Keys, the area consisted of shallow reefs and narrow straits, which when combined with the awesome storms that arose from the waters meeting between two major oceans and a polar ice cap, could create a calamitous climatic cauldron that was capable of boiling and stirring a ship down to its pulp. Circumnavigating the tip of the horn was an artistic symbol in itself: Sail between land and the horn and the ship would be speared; or, drop in too far below the horn and miss the turn North, therein cruising into the icy waters of the Antarctic; or cruelest of all, mark the turn spot-on only to slam straight into a lurking squall. It was the actual 'rounding' of the horn that was such a semantic challenge: Get 'around' the Horn was the word; ironically the 'Horn' that was not so round.

The Captain obviously felt confident in his preparation for the long arc. One day out, and he still hadn't given the order for battening and load securing. He seemed unconcerned, and moreover, unusually happy following his time in Rio. As the ship began to turn into the setting sun, he flitted about the deck cheerfully, even stopping to make idle conversation with random members of the working crew.

Arthur arrived topside fresh from supper on the mess deck, ready to assume his evening watch. The Captain approached him in the twilight, and smiled. He said, "My good man Harper, I have a new friend whom I would like you to meet."

Arthur became curious and confused, first at the Captain's friendliness, and then at his enigmatic declaration. He asked, "And whom is that Captain?"

The Captain said, "You'll see. Now, if you would kindly go to my cabin and open my wardrobe, you will find a bird cage. Inside the cage, you will see the newest addition to our crew. Bring her to me, please."

Arthur obediently walked away quickly, and disappeared down a ladder well. He searched his mind, trying to figure out what the Captain was referring to. He knew that he had been on the ship the whole time in port. He reached the Captain's dressing closet, and opened the doors. There, suspended from the crossbar, was a beautiful brass cage. Inside the cage, calm and regal, sat a large green parrot. Arthur scratched his head. Had he been that busy during stores loading that he had missed a bird arriving onboard? he wondered.

Arthur carried the cage back to the Captain. The Captain thanked him and asked, "Have you ever seen a parrot before, Harper?"

Arthur said, "No, Sah."

The Captain said, "I didn't think so. It is a beautiful creature, don't you agree?"

Arthur said, "Yes, Sah."

The Captain said, "The parrot is traditionally a sailor's best friend. Unlike the seagull which can be seen at sea sometimes far from land, the parrot will appear only when land is close. Furthermore, once a parrot is onboard and out of sight of land, it will remain around the ship. Also, the parrot is quite affectionate; and it can be taught to speak. Did you know that, Harper?"

Arthur said, "No Sah."

The Captain said, "Well then, let this be a pleasurable lesson for you. This parrot is going to be my companion for the second leg of the trip. The man I bought it from said that she is already domesticated, but she doesn't know any words yet. I want you to help me take good care of our friend here, Harper; however, I want to be the only one who teaches her to speak. Is that clear?"

Arthur replied, "Yes Sah."

The Captain said, "Very well, then." He proceeded to open the cage. He carefully placed a finger up to the bird's perch; and it cautiously clasped onto his finger. He brought the bird out slowly, murmuring reassuringly, and coaxed it onto his left shoulder. He looked at the bird for a time, and confident that it would remain, turned to Arthur with a beaming smile. The Captain said, "You see, Harper, a mate in the making."

Arthur said, "Yes, Sah."

The Captain said, "That is all. Carry on. I will give you feeding instructions in the morning."

Arthur said, "Yes, Sir." and turned to walk away.

As he was approaching his post, he heard a strange, high voice say, "Please Mister Arthur!" He turned on his heels in time to see the Captain, parrot on his shoulder, frozen with one foot on the first step of the ladder.

Arthur said, "I beg your pardon, Sir?"

The Captain said, annoyed, "I did not say a word."

The parrot squawked, "Please Mister Arthur!"

The Captain flew into a rage, wildly waving his arms and circling the deck, the parrot emulated and reflected his agitation, launching into a flurry of "Please Mister Arthur's, one right after the other. The pair created a comical spectacle that sent the topside crew into similar hysterical antics. The Captain, seeing the deteriorating condition of his command, lashed out with a final act of anger and flung the poor bird from his shoulder. Dazed and confused, the parrot took flight into the early eaves of the dropping night.

VI

Countless threats of flogging Arthur were thwarted by counter threats of mutiny; and the Captain and crew settled into an uneasy standoff in preparation for the coming test. The ship's entire operating system was overhauled: Sails and masts were inspected; rigging was secured; hatches were battened; and portholes were bolted. Heavy-weather clothing was issued and lashed to the deck at each watch station. Stores and hardware were tied down. Dishes were racked and strapped. Leash lines were placed at the helm and bow. The cage was fitted on the crow's nest. Flags and pennants were hauled in. Loose gear was stowed. Hull fittings were sealed. The bilge was pumped. The deck was tarred. The Captain's small windows were stopped with soft gum and boarded. The rum and java were distributed just as the sun gave its final flash; and the Captain, putting on his lucky red hat, pointed out many playful penguins flanking the stripped and streamlined ship. "We are close to making the turn." the Captain broadcast, as he browsed and chatted with several of the men who stood ready on the lines. The Captain then gave the order that the nets be run along the sides of the ship. These formed a web, which being tightly integrated with the peripheral of the ship, served as a platform of stop gates to try and save any person who had not been successful in competing with the stifling ocean and its crashing waves.

Arthur was sent up to the crow's nest to monitor the horizon. He bolted himself within the cage securely. Then came the task of counting down to the turn. In the twilight, he was provided with the visual navigational clues of both day and night. In the darkening sky, he could see a bright, familiar northern star; and low where the rim glowed golden still, he was able to make out a speck of land.

"Bearing ought-three-ought." Arthur bellowed down to the Helmsman.

The Captain, standing next to the man at the wheel, gave him instructions to continue, "Steady as she goes." The night remained peaceful; and as the crystal clear sky turned indigo, Arthur mentally marked where the island last appeared under the star.

"Bearing ought-four-ought." Arthur yelled after one-half hour of silence. The Captain once again ordered steady on course; for even though the ship was steering straight, he knew that prevailing currents around the horn would actually sweep the ship in an arc, thereby aiding his navigational efforts. A bearing of forty degrees meant that the island around which he wanted to turn was out to the right at a modest angle. When the call came that the horn was directly off the ship's starboard, then he would take the helm himself and turn the ship hard.

"Eleven O'clock and all is well!" came the cry from the roving watch on the forecastle.

Another fifteen minutes passed before Arthur was heard to exclaim, "Bearing ought-five-ought!" He thought he saw land approaching on the dark horizon; however, he knew that the plan was to turn far south of the mark. He yelled out in a concerned voice, "Captain, the Horn is getting bigger!"

The Captain looked up, and then exchanged a confused stare with the Helmsman. They both smiled and shrugged, as if to discount the opinion of their junior seaman. The Captain chuckled and mumbled something about seeing a flash of white in the sky whenever Arthur spoke.

At roughly eleven-thirty, Arthur called out, "Bearing ought-seven-ought!" Having been ignored earlier, he remained silent about the immense dark mass looming dead ahead. He heard the Captain and Helmsman laughing and making small talk. He heard the low voices of the relaxed crew. He heard the gentle wind rustling in sails. He heard the bow sluicing through the calm water. And as he ever so gently began to doze in the warm breeze, he thought that perhaps he had heard the firing of a distant cannon. Something struck his face. It was a single drop of rain.

Eleven-forty-five arrived and Arthur shouted, "Bearing ought-eight-ought!" He saw the Helmsman preparing to step aside as the Captain put on his gloves. The two shrugged again, this time looking around skyward. The rain began sporadically. A few sailors kicked at their weather gear, unable to generate interest in the oppressive clothing. They focused their efforts on readying the sails for the turn.

The Captain cried out across the deck to the First Mate, "Prepare to mark the turn!"

The First Mate yelled back, "Prepare to mark the turn, aye."

At the call of midnight, Arthur jubilantly exclaimed, "Bearing ought-nine-ought!" The boat at that moment was close to the bottom of the earth; and a fitting place it was for the hellish events that were about to unfold.

The Captain stepped in to take the helm. He cried out, "Mark!"

The First Mate yelled out, "Mark!"

The starboard crew laid hard into the lines and the sails roared in protest as the masts groaned. The Captain arrested the wheel and wrested it to leeward. He leaned into the helm, calves straining, as the ship lurched and crackled loudly. The ropes sang and the hull hummed, while the keel drummed on the choppy swells. The rain accompanied the wind as they played the sails and peppered the deck.

Suddenly, the wind shifted violently. It seemed to blow straight down out of the sky, cascading heavily like a waterfall; and appropriately so, because along with it came a torrent of water-the term rain not being applicable due to the absence of any intervals of air between the nonexistent droplets. What fell that night onto the deck of The Elizabeth could only be described as solid streams, like gutter spill, of cold stinging water. Before the sailors could set the lines, the precipitation followed its dramatic entrance onto their stage with a devastating duet with the wind, which had now decided to dance sideways. The ropes were ripped from the raw hands of the riggers, the sail sheets were rented, and the boom slammed into the stay, upsetting the Captain from his precarious stance. The wheel spun from his hands, allowing the ship to pitch back and tilt over in the opposite direction, all in one heaving hurdle. Many of the crew were thrown to the deck and the rest were blown and scattered. The sails flailed and flapped unrestrained, tearing to tatters, as the lines waved and whipped in the wind. The lightning started next, giving the sporadically illuminated ship the look of an eerie and angry Medusa. The Captain had just righted the ship as the sailors scrambled to secure the sails; and he struggled to steer without the sheets. Then the swells started. With the ship having already turned away from the current, the large waves came across the path of the bow at an odd angle and even less forgiving intervals. The mountains of water were big and swift enough to lift the ship high; and they came faster than the boat could properly settle. Therefore, the crewmembers could feel the awesome sensation of rising high into the air, only to experience the sickening delay preceding the drop through space, and the jarring impact with the surface of the void left by the vacating wave. One after the other, the ship and the crew rode the rolling humps of the rampaging sea serpent. Walls of water walked across the deck, marching to the thunder as troops to war. The phantom forces thoughtlessly tipped the ship steeply to one side as they climbed aboard; and they exited with an equally rude disposition as they plunged from the opposite rail.

This battle raged on for what seemed like hours to the drenched and defeated crew; however, its last assault actually came shortly before one. As the wind and rain slowly ceased, the seas stilled and the ship once again sailed smoothly. The Captain assessed the damage; the crew secured the sheets; and the situation returned to normal. The ship had successfully made the turn and survived its worst. The crew began to let out spasmodic cheers as they slapped one another on the back. A head count was ordered by the Captain, even though no one was visible in the nets; and the word of all accounted for being returned, the Captain looked skyward. There was Arthur, dismantling the crow's nest cage against the backdrop of a clearing night sky. As he lay the cage to one side and stretched his arms, he heard a fluttering sound in the rigging above him. He looked around in the darkness for a shred of tattered sail, but saw nothing. Exhausted from the ordeal, he decided that all inspection work could wait for the morrow and daylight. He was just happy to have lived through such a turbulent and terrifying display of nature, he thought. He prepared to exit the crow's nest and descend. Suddenly, he was startled by a rustling sound near his right shoulder. He turned his head just as the bird lighted, and his brow brushed its feathers.

The parrot said, "Por Favor Señor Arthur."

VII

Two months is a long time to go without seeing land or women. One time, Arthur thought he saw a man in the distance, walking on the water; but he couldn't be sure.

He named the bird Mary.

Chapter 6

THE LANDING

I f the view which lay before the advancing dinghy that morning was to be foretelling of that night's events and the fate of those souls rowing toward the shore, then it was surely to be as dark and foreboding as the scene unfolding before them. It was as some had described while documenting this forsaken inlet, the 'Golgotha of the Whale': The ungodly resting place for the strewn remains of countless hapless and unfortunate leviathan. However, for one lucky soul, the landscape's features could not be more at odds with the good fortune which was destined to prevail for him during the course of the ensuing evening.

Arthur Harper Alesworth, one Negro slave crewman of The Elizabeth, cut the water hard with anticipation from his seat third back from the bow, as he cast his eye eagerly toward shore. Arthur had embarked with The Elizabeth, one of the very few British whalers to set out from

New York, to the reportedly bountiful coasts of New Zealand; and the four month journey during 1828 had taken its toll on this strong young man.

He yearned for land, and the fresh scent of a strange new world was just what he needed to revive. What struck him first, though, was the sharp stench of the rotting sea giants that littered the beach, and his heart plummeted into his churning stomach. He looked around wildly, searching the beach for an open space which might be free of the carrion-clad bones of the offending beasts; but his panic only increased as he saw no relief from the hellish smell of boiling flesh and putrid oil. His acute suffering was punctuated by the stinging crop of the First Mate, seated astern, as he cried sharply, "Row harder boy, or swim with the sharks!"

Arthur flinched on the gunwale whilst on the shore they flenched the whale.

Chapter 7

THE DEBUTANTE

May 22nd, 1828. Te Awaiti:

Alesworth did not have time to get his land legs back before he was called to attention for the work detail assignment. Standing in a line across the beach, arms stiffly held to his side and chin out, Arthur felt the resurgence of the nausea which he had fought with and conquered at journey's start. Could there be such a thing as land sickness? he wondered. The wild smell of charring whale flesh helped his condition little; and his inspection uniform certainly did not seem appropriate for the lurid tasks he saw being performed on the gargantuan fish lying about the beach before him.

One large burly black-bearded man walked away from a group of men he had been supervising whale-side; and he carefully inspected the company of new arrivals. He turned on his heels at the end of the line, gingerly stepped back to front-and-center; and began to shout, "Right! This is my beach! There will be no mucking around!" He looked each man squarely in the eyes one by one as he spoke. "This is the first successful whaling station on the South Island of New Zealand. I intend to keep it that way! Understood?"

The sailors broke stance and began to hiss and snigger as they cajoled one another with snide remarks.

"Right!" began the man again. "At attention, eyes front, or you can row right back out to your ship and tell your Captain it's open-ocean whaling for the lot of you!" This statement achieved its goal, and the men straightened up once again. "Right! Now each of you will find plenty to do here on shore between actual whale hunts. Every one here helps everyone else, regardless of who killed which whale, or which ship that whale's bones and oil are leaving on. Whales brought in by a ship's crew will be marked; and that whale will be tracked through processing from flenching to boiling. Everything is above board here, and no one is to be cheated. We're counting on your honesty!" he said honestly. The men again began to turn their heads in mocking chatter.

"Right! While on shore, work hours are normally from six a.m. until six p.m., unless we get a late whale; at which point, all hands will assist in securing the whale to the sheers for the following day's processing. Whales will be hunted in rotation, unless more than one whale breeches in the bay, at which point, each ship's hunting party will be dispatched in order according to the roster. Should the case arise that all hands are at sea in the chase, the station will continue processing with a skeleton crew of local natives and whomever else remains available. The order of returning boats will determine the order of the next roster, irrespective of the original dispatch queue. It's a case of the rich getting richer, gentlemen. That should give you some incentive with the chase!" the man said, watching his words sink in and take effect on the men. He continued, "Right! For now, I don't know what you know about shore-whaling, but I am going to assume that it is next to nothing!" The men had begun to respect this man; and they did not move a muscle. He went on, "Each of you spread out and find your own working party in progress. Do not get in the way! Do not ask questions unless absolutely necessary! When you feel comfortable with the task being performed at your station, then lend a hand. Remember, everyone's success depends on you. Any questions?" the man asked as he looked up and down the line. He finished by saying, "Good! Dismissed!"

The men looked around hesitantly; and then began to walk up the beach slowly in all directions.

"Move!" the big man bellowed.

The men ran. They each assimilated into a different group: One or two stopped at different steaming try-pots; more gathered around several large carcasses being stripped of blubber; and the rest crowded around the odd collection of bones being dried and cleaned.

Arthur started with the try-pots. He remained silent as he had been instructed. He soon realized that these large cauldrons were arranged in groups of three, connected closely in a triangle; hence the name. He soon learned by listening to the more experienced workers that the process involved with the pots was also itself called 'trying', which referred to the boiling and breaking down of the large chunks of blubber into useable oil. He watched as long strips of blubber, two-feet wide and about twenty-feet long, were carried over from the flenching station where they were being peeled off the side of the leviathan. He witnessed the cutting of the strips, cross-ways, into one-foot sections, so that one-foot by two-foot blocks were laid out

ready to be cast into the cauldrons. Loose chunks and remnants were thrown under the pots into a makeshift 'furnace'; the whale supplying the bulk of its own fuel for
burning. The smell of incinerated whale fat did not wholly
sicken Arthur, as he had grown accustomed to roasting
whatever wild game he had killed back on the plantation.

This seemed to be the easiest job on the shore from
what he could see; however, Arthur hedged his enthusiasm and kept his head down, so as to hide any nubile
frailties which may render him vulnerable to the as yet
unsolicited jibes of his unfamiliar coworkers. Everything
went well, though; and Arthur soon began to pick up
chunks and place them into the pots. His colleagues were
either completely disinterested in their new team member, or they had become indifferent to everything in the
face of long, hypnotic hours of monotonous labor. Arthur
had happily resigned himself to believing the latter, when
suddenly one of the men spoke up.

"Where are you from, mate?" he asked in a British
accent. The front of his uniform had become dingy with
oil and dirt, yet his spirits seemed high.

"America." Arthur responded nonchalantly.

"Ah, a Yank!" the man quickly said, gaining a distinct
gleam in his eye. "John, we got a Yank in our midst!" the
man blurted to his fellow crew member.

"I heard, I heard." the other Brit said disinterestedly,
as he stirred the blubber.

"Go on, mate. Which ship is that you came in on?" he
asked, looking over his shoulder toward the bay; and then
turning back with a broad grin on his face. "That's not
American, is it?" he asked sincerely, knowing that no
American whaling vessels had as yet made the journey this
far south.

"The sh . . . sh . . . Shibboleth." Arthur sounded the
word out; and then waited nervously for a reply.

"The what?" asked the first Brit with an air of disbe-lief. He had heard the name of the ship among conversa-tion as it was mooring; and he knew what Arthur had said was not correct. His brows lifted as he remembered; and he said, "Oh! The Elizabeth! That's right. But what are you doing on an English ship, mate?" he asked, not bela-boring the point of Arthur's less-than-spot-on pronuncia-tion of the name.

Arthur appreciated the man's semantic oversight, as well as his liberal use of the word 'mate'; and he said, "Yeah, that's it. She was in New York, takin' on supplies and men. The First Mate said somethin' about 'no whales off Nantucket, goin' to New Zealand.' So's I said take me! Hell, I didn't know it was this far. Neither did they, if you ask me." Arthur finished with a grin. Both men chuckled.

The Brit said, "Mate, you're all right. I don't think I've seen any Black men down here. In fact, last I heard, they don't let your kind out of the country where you come from, right?"

Arthur shrank at the question. He said, unsure, "No. They don't. I's one of the lucky ones."

"Well, mate, I think that's just great! The first Yank down here, and a Black Yank at that!" the first Brit ex-claimed. Then he asked, "What's your name, mate?"

Arthur spoke up proudly, "Arthur, sir."

The first Brit was taken aback by Arthur's servile re-sponse. He said, "Sir? What the hell you calling me 'sir' for? I work for a living, just like you." He rebounded from his amused repugnance, however, and said, "Never mind mate, it's just as well. We call everyone new around here 'Jack.' Isn't that right, John?"

His friend responded with a belch and said, "Yeah, sure, Jack."

The first Brit turned back to Arthur and said, "Your

name's gonna be 'Black Jack'. What d'ya think about that, mate?"

Arthur didn't see that he had much choice but to cheerfully accept his new moniker. He replied flatly, "Yeah, sure mate, that's great." Then he asked, "What's your name?"

The first Brit perked up at Arthur's interest in him; and he replied, "Groggy Jack, mate!" He laughed; looked around; and then said in a cheekily clandestine voice, "And tonight you'll find out why!" He laughed heartily as he rolled his head back, stirring the brimming cauldron.

II

"Work's almost finished, Black Jack!" exclaimed Groggy Jack. He turned to his other, less gregarious partner, and said, "Get the wash water ready, Happy Jack!" The other man snorted and grunted some sort of agreement. "You can start getting ready for your bath, Black Jack."

Arthur was unsure of what he meant; and he stood there for a moment looking around the beach. It was just past six, as the roving foreman had informed each party; and by now Arthur could see several men from each group putting down their tools and standing fast. No whales had come in that day: It was early in the season; and it was not unusual for the migratory animals to arrive sporadically. Arthur had been fortunate to experience some of the waning warm weather of the South Pacific, and as the sun stood high in the sky at this evening hour, he became grateful that he would at least see a bit of fall before the cold, wet winter set in.

Without any new work being dragged in from the sea and no ships arriving, the men were free for the night. Although riotous celebration usually only followed a large catch; Arthur could see that the men of the beach were in a festive mood at the prospect of a completely uncommitted evening.

"What are you doing, Black Jack?" Groggy asked. "Get those clothes off, and get ready."

Arthur paused for another moment; however, as he scanned the beach further, he saw men engaged in happy chatter who were unceremoniously undressing. Also, many women, both white and brown-skinned, had begun to move among the groups and collect the discarded garments, seemingly indifferent to the natural state of the nude whalers. Arthur began to undress.

"Mate, what the hell is wrong with that uniform?" demanded Groggy in a joking manner. "Did they issue the cabin boy's spare to you?" he asked.

"I am the Cabin Boy." said Black Jack blankly. He didn't fully understand the deprecation behind Groggy's comment. "I think I grew a little bit on the trip." said Black Jack sincerely.

"A little bit!" exclaimed Groggy in sarcastic disbelief. "Mate, your hem is three inches above your ankle! Your shirt is above your navel. You look like one of those Arabian dancers!" he almost squealed.

Black Jack blushed. "I suppose." he said. He had gone through a tremendous growth spurt during the four month journey. Just under six-feet tall when he signed on in New York harbor, he had not immediately noticed an outward physical change due to his rigorous adjustment to sea life. However, once underway, he had noticed that his bunk seemed to be getting rather cramped; and he began to regularly bump his head on passageway doors. The ship's physician at first dismissed the Cabin Boy's awkwardness to inexperience and a case of 'getting his sea legs on'; however, Arthur's lengthening process progressed so rapidly that it even became apparent to the naked eye of the doctor. As Arthur stood towering over him one day midway through the voyage, the doctor had exclaimed, "Good God, boy, you're becoming a giant!" The doctor became so fascinated with Arthur as a special case that he dedicated additional time and care to studying the Captain's personal attendant. He eventually concluded that the added foods in a former slave's diet (the sailors did eat well!); the rigorous physical demands of operating a ship on open seas at full sail; and the sun and salty air had all contributed to Arthur's accelerated development.

The extra attention paid by the doctor began to influence the rest of the crew; and before long, Arthur had attained a veritable celebrity status. In the galley during mess hours, crewmen would openly inquire as to what he was eating, and how much of it; and lively discussion would ensue around Arthur concerning his activities of the day. On fine weather days, seamen would cluster around him topside to engage in carefree question-and-answer sessions; good-heartedly needling him on various subjects ranging from abolition in America to zealots in Zaire. Now standing well over six-feet tall and black as the whales they hunted, Arthur Alesworth seemed authoritative to the sailors; and they respected the young man and his opinions on everything.

On balmy nights, Arthur would break out his mouth harp on the forecastle and play tremendous melodies to the delight of the midnight-to-six a.m. watch crew. His popularity grew to match his proportions; and life on the ship seemed to begin to revolve around him. In turn, he was pleased to be accepted for who and what he was; not being judged as solely a person with black skin.

His growth in stature and prominence in such a short period had not gone unnoticed by the First Mate; and it had certainly not escaped the attention of the Captain. One night as the Captain sat pouring over his cabin chart table, he heard the melodious playing of Arthur's harp

streaming over the deck and down through his open stern
windows. He stood to listen; and to watch the porpoises
frolic in the moonlit wake of the ship. He saw the water
glowing and the eerie shine of the schools of fish gliding
just beneath the surface. He took out his sextant and
pointed it at the cloudless, starry, indigo sky. Diamond-
encrusted sapphire, he thought, as the singing of the night
crew played harmony to Arthur's pied piping.

The crew sang:

> "Come all you whalemen who are cruising for Sperm,
> Come all of you seamen who have rounded Cape Horn,
> For our Captain has told us, and he says out of hand,
> There's a thousand whales off the coast of New Zealand!"

Suddenly, the Captain noticed an unfamiliar star staring back at him through the sextant. Hold on, he thought:
We're off course! The Captain cried out for the First Mate,
but no response came from the adjoining cabin. The Captain rang the First Mate's bell. Still no response. He yelled
out again. All he heard was the continuous caroling of the
crew, and the confounded conducting of Arthur's harp!

Blast! he thought, as he raced from his cabin, down
the passageway to the first ladder. Bouncing off bulkheads,
he climbed topside and stood fuming at midship. He stood
there amid the music, unnoticed for perhaps an entire
minute, until he could stand no more. "Harper!" he yelled
at the top of his lungs. Again, "You there, Harper! Cease
and desist!"

All at once, the music and singing stopped as the First
Mate wheeled around, almost falling from his perch on
the forecastle. He immediately recovered and shouted the
customary, "Attention on deck!" All hands stood rigidly
where they had been caught.

"Mate! Are you aware that we are thirty degrees off

course?" the Captain shouted across the deck to the First
Mate. He then shot a scathing glance at the Helmsman.
"And where is the damned Lookout?" he loudly demanded
as he looked up at the empty crow's nest. "Helmsman,
bring her right hard thirty degrees, then steady as she
goes." he said sternly, his rank and bearing now regaining
their place over his emotions. "Lookout, back up the mast,
now!" he said smartly. "First Mate, belowdecks." he said
nonchalantly as he turned back toward the midship's ladder. Approaching the rails, he suddenly turned and shouted
a final command, "And no more music! If I hear anything
tonight, there will be no liberty in Rio. That is all!" The
Captain spun on his heels and stormed belowdecks, the
First Mate close behind. The only sounds after that were
the methodical clicks of the Captain's asternship cabin
windows being carefully closed, followed by a muffled one-
man storm which raged with gale force for over an hour;
and then silence.

All Arthur remembered of that night was that the First
Mate had come back topside, seemingly angry with him;
and curtly told Arthur that he couldn't play his mouth
organ on watch any more. From then on, his treatment at
the hands of the First Mate had gotten worse; and this ill
will had seemed to spread to the Captain, who eyed Arthur
with disdain and became increasingly disparaging in his
treatment of him. The crew had remained loyal, however;
and from that night on he had acquired a new handle in
order to revere and honor the timeless event. From then
on, Arthur was addressed as 'Harper' by his mates. However, the new name was a double-edged sword, being used
also by the First Mate and the Captain; though in a much
less flattering and impersonal way. They called him, 'The
Harper'; and it was meant to serve as a reminder to him
and everyone else that his actions had been unprofessional,
and had endangered the operation of the ship that fateful

night. So adamant had the Captain been about securing the black mark, that he had altered the ship's records to reflect it. The ship's log came to read, 'Cabin Boy-Arthur Harper Alesworth.'

"Get undressed, Black Jack!" Groggy snapped. Arthur reeled back to the present. "T'isn't anything that these ladies haven't seen before, mate!" Groggy said. He proceeded to place a small pot of sea water on an open corner of the furnace, and strip. He continued, "I'll show you how we make our soap." He scooped out a handful of partially melted blubber near the top of the try-pot; and held it in the his cupped palm. As it cooled, he sprinkled a pinch of sand on it with his free hand. Then, as it was almost solidified, he dropped it into the hot salt water. Black Jack watched as it sank to the bottom, streaming trails of oil behind it, but remaining mostly intact. After a few moments, it began to bubble; and then it slowly floated to the surface, effervescing. Groggy quickly grabbed it and began to lather his body with it. "Better than what the Queen herself has in the Royal Toilet!" he exclaimed. He then rinsed himself by pouring a jar of cold, fresh water over his head. Arthur repeated his example. By the time they had finished with the ritual, a woman had been by and left a neatly folded stack of clean clothes, sorted by size, for each man in the group. "Reminds me of what they gave us in prison." remarked Groggy jokingly. "Eh, Happy?" he asked. The other Brit grunted. The men put on their accouterments, pants first. Arthur noticed the material was much like the spun-cotton fabric back home; but it was a little stiffer and not as soft. It was a dingy off-white; however, it had a very pleasant, crisp, clean smell. In addition, all the articles were ample and loose-fitting; and Arthur began to feel very relaxed and comfortable. "Don't bother putting your boots back on, mate!" said Groggy. And then he asked, "What do you like to eat?"

III

The table of food laid out on the deck of the grog shop was a feast for Black Jack's eyes. He looked over the steaming dishes as more were carried out by the women of the village. Beginning at the closest end was a large serving pan full of boiled giant crayfish. Black Jack had seen the small crayfish around the creeks in Mississippi; and he had had a chance to see big lobsters up North before setting sail. However, these were crustaceans which were much larger than American lobsters with all the characteristic anomalies of the more exotic South Pacific crayfish. They were colored like Indian corn, with bright oranges, yellows, shades of brown, and occasional specks of purple and blue. Each of them must have contained a pound of meat, he thought. Next were the many kinds of shellfish: The mussels (which the sailors called 'sea ears'), both green-lipped and other varieties, which were the size of a man's hand; the scallops, the oysters, and the giant clams. Then, the Abalone, which the natives called Paua, with its glassy rainbow shell. There were fish of all types and sizes: None smaller than three pounds, he thought. Further along, there were birds: The most notable to Black Jack being the Takahe, which he thought looked and tasted like chicken. Down the table further was the mutton, coming from the few sheep that the White men had carried along the year before. Also there was wild pig, which roamed freely around the hills, and had an equally wild flavor. At that point, Black Jack saw where the fruits and vegetables began. It seemed that the natives shared with him their favorites: Boiled potatoes and cabbage. For dessert, Black Jack tried a fruit which resembled a cucumber, but which had a very rich, creamy, ripe melon flavor. The natives called it a Fejoha.

Of course, Black Jack could not eat everything on one

plate; and so, much to the delight of his female hosts, and in response to the good-natured prodding of his newfound mates, he made several visits back to the table. The men ate and drank for approximately two hours; each enjoying at least four platefuls; and none diminishing in voracity throughout the meal. After a time, many began to smoke peacefully while the women cleaned up the remains; and most of the group had wandered off to their respective huts as the sun set. The non-resident ship dwellers not afforded or not desiring libations or accommodation for the evening began to push off and row back to their ships.

Groggy Jack, seated on a whale backbone, rolled heavily on his buttocks toward Black Jack. He groaned with a smile; held his distended belly with one hand and a makeshift toothpick with the other; and said, "So, you think you'll stay for a little grog, mate?"

Black Jack, equally content in his bloated state, stiffened a little on a whale tailbone; and said, "Better get on back to the ship, mate. The Captain will be 'spectin me."

"Bah!" said Groggy disdainfully. "The cook will have his nightcap ready just the same. After ten, he'll be dreaming about the Queen. Won't even know you've gone missin'." Groggy assured Black Jack, as he leaned on one elbow and sucked his sliver of wood.

"I don't know." said Black Jack, with the same wavering voice as a child late for curfew.

"Stay! You'll have a great time meeting all the blokes. Won't he, Happy!" he said as he nudged his shipmate.

"Mmm, yeah, sure." said Happy Jack.

"See! Happy thinks it's a good idea. And you wouldn't want to make him 'un-happy', would you?" Groggy asked, as his eyes grew wide at Black Jack, and he began to laugh.

"All right, but I'm not a big drinker of spirits." said Black Jack seriously.

"This isn't spirits, mate, its grog!" said Groggy. He turned to Happy Jack to nudge him again, asking, "Right, copper, right?" He burst into laughter again, continuing to jab his mate and laugh, alternately.

IV

After night had fallen completely, the three men walked inside the grog shop. It had the same air as a British pub, with a bar at the back, high benches along the sides, and high round tables and chairs down the middle. There was a door to the kitchen behind the bar. At the bar was a single tap; because here they only served one beverage: Grog.

"The first shout is on me!" shouted Groggy Jack, and he bounded for the bar. As the grogshop keeper reached for the brass handle of the tap valve, Groggy stood quietly and let his eyes slowly walk from the foamy brown liquid streaming into the metal mug, up the cloth hose snaking its way from the back of the tap, to the rafters above where a large oak barrel lay on its side. A wonderful invention, he thought; and he silently congratulated and envied the man who had invented it. He paid the shopkeeper, and carried three mugs back to the bench along the wall to his waiting mates. "Ah, I love this place!" exclaimed Groggy, as he proceeded to put lips to head.

Black Jack, unsure if Groggy referred to the pub or the whaling station, cautiously followed suit and sampled his first sip of grog. It tasted to him like distilled molasses. He had tasted something like it around the old-timers' shack; but only when they were low on good solid corn sour mash, or even the extra special secret vodka they were so proud of. Molasses mash was the lowest form of alcohol, if his memory served him right, that a man could relegate himself to. Made from livestock feed-grade cane, it was distilled only after the winter stores of corn and potatoes were run through; and then only if all the men folk agreed that they would lower themselves to it. Some of the slaves from the Caribbean had sworn that they could take molasses to rum in only a few days in the still; however, they had all individually given up the fight and learned the hard way that the feed-grade molasses of Mississippi was a far cry from the quality of the sugar cane of their sunny island homes. Everyone knew that you could never thin it with water enough to rid it of that sickening burnt-butter flavor without losing the sugar content needed to start the liquor coming. This made for a product which, before being put through the still, was thick, brown, bubbly, slightly bitter, and disgustingly sweet all at the same time. It could gag a maggot; and still not get a man drunk. A few days in the still made no difference. As the alcohol increased, so did the sludge; so that the amount of effort required to produce even a cup of spirits was not worth it. What alcohol did come out always reeked with vile fumes; and no man nor beast could be found who could stomach the brew.

"Pretty damn good, eh?" goaded Groggy, as he elbowed his two mates from his seat between them. "You oughta hear how they make this stuff. Simply amazing for mere sailors, I'll tell you what!" Groggy said, as he went on in his slap-happy fascination for the drink.

"I can't imagine." Black Jack said smugly.

The three of them engaged in idle chatter about different things; mostly the work day, as the evening progressed. Groggy did most of the talking, introducing Black Jack to his other mates from his ship and around the village; while Happy Jack just sat there for the most part, offering the occasional grunt of agreement. The three of them began to migrate around the shop; mingling with different groups, individually and together, eventually drifting back to reclaim their seats on the bench along the wall. Black Jack was surprised to notice that his ghastly brew was nearing its bottom, along with those of his mates.

"My shout." Happy Jack said nonchalantly and abruptly, as he gathered the group's glasses and headed off to the bar. Black Jack was relieved, as he had no money. As a servant on the boat, he wasn't entitled to any.

"What do you think of Happy?" Groggy asked Black Jack as soon as their mutual mate was out of earshot. Black Jack was surprised at the question: Not by its nature, but by the fact that he had been asked his personal opinion regarding a White man by another White man. Even though he had grown confident in the newfound camaraderie of his shipmates, he was not prepared for this kind of advice seeking. He tried to hide his apprehension.

"He's all right, I reckon. A bit quiet, but I like him all right." Black Jack said authoritatively, but unpretentiously.

"He's a poofter, you know." Groggy said surreptitiously in a low voice, as he looked into Black Jack's eyes.

"You don't say." said Black Jack quietly, returning the gaze of false concern. He knew from his time on the ship that it was a British word; and that it meant their mate had an intense like for his own gender.

"Yeah, Nick from the ship caught him trying to crawl into his bunk with him one night after liberty in Rome." Groggy explained. A quick look over his shoulder revealed that his unsuspecting mate was returning with a fresh round. "Shh, shh. Here he comes!" Groggy hoarsely whispered.

"I heard that." said Happy in a resigned voice. "I wish you'd stop it, Groggy." he said in protest as he sat.

"Now, Happy." Groggy said, pushing his shoulder into Happy's; and causing Happy's drink to slosh and drip. "You know we weren't talking about you!" he said to Happy

in a sing-song, patronizing voice; like a big brother cajol-
ing a temperamental baby sister. He immediately turned
to Black Jack, and winked.

"Yeah, sure." said Happy with a pout in his voice.

"Now drink up. Both of you!" Groggy yelled into the
air, looking up at his now hoisted stein.

Black Jack noticed that he did feel rather cheerful.
The room had grown busier and rowdier; and the noise,
which consisted mostly of loud, boastful conversations and
mugs being rammed together for countless unknown agreements on manly matters, began to uplift his mood. Even
Happy seemed happier. And then the women and the
Maori began streaming in.

Black Jack had caught distant glimpses of the brown-
skinned people along the beach while he was working;
but he hadn't really had time to get a good look at them.
Nor had he wanted to stare; as any rudeness might be
considered threatening or intolerable, especially at the in-
stigation of such an odd newcomer as himself. However,
he saw them clearly and close now, through the enhanc-
ing looking glass of his mild inebriation. What had appeared at a distance as dirt, and possibly stains on their
faces, now became resolved as intricate and elaborately designed tattoos in symmetrical curves and lines. The males
had their entire faces covered; whereas the females had
only involved their chins from the point in their jaw to
just beneath the lower lip. The tattoo stain was a dark
green, and it attractively complemented their smooth,
brown skin. Anything like that on him wouldn't even show
up, thought Black Jack. The Maori people's hair was con-
sistently thick, long, and crow-black. They had high cheek
bones, hazel eyes, and magnificent teeth. They were, to
Black Jack, a striking and beautiful people. They reminded
him of the Indians back home, although these people pos-

sessed a certain fierceness and presence of spirit which Black Jack could not quite equivocate to the natives of North America. Also, their language had a more rhythmic, pleasing cadence to it, with a consistent and frequent use of 'T', 'K', and 'R' sounds.

"Those buggers eat their own people, ya know." Groggy said quietly to Black Jack, leaning into his ear and disrupting Black Jack's erudite study of the crowd.

"Huh?" Black Jack said, shaking off his stuporous stare. "What did you say?" he asked with lips as moist as his squinting eyes.

"They're cannibals. Savages. They make meals out of mothers and brothers." said Groggy flippantly. Then he said directly, without seeming affected by his own comments, "Give me your mug, I'll get the third one." He asked Happy, looking at his mate's mug, "Happy?"

"Yeah, sure." came Happy's flat reply.

Black Jack and Happy Jack were left standing together. Black Jack made conversation in light of his mate's unfounded reputation. He asked, "So, Happy, is that true what Groggy says?" Happy looked at him in disbelief. Black Jack quickly ascertained the reason for his company's shock, and asked again, "I mean about the cannibals?"

Happy sank in relief, paused, and said, "Groggy says a lot of things. You have to learn to listen to him with a grain of salt." This was the first complete sentence Happy had spoken; and he sounded very intelligent to Black Jack. Black Jack began to eye him warily. Happy continued, "I haven't seen anyone be killed or eaten around here. Except for the occasional brawl, it's a pretty quiet place." Groggy returned with the third round of brew.

The three men began to drink more swiftly as they delved into more serious topics. Groggy asked Black Jack, "So, what's the deal with slavery, mate?"

Black Jack bristled and asked, "What do you mean?"

Groggy replied, "Well, are you gonna be one forever, or what? I mean we don't have slaves. Where we come from, a Black is a Black, sure, but that don't stop him from earning his own money and doing what he pleases. How do you feel about that?"

Black Jack loosened again, and said, "Right now, I am in service to the ship, and specifically the Captain. As far as I gather, he owns me the same as the Master owned me back on the plantation. I thought that I was free as soon as I got to New York; but now it don't seem like it. I guess when the Captain says I can go, I can go. Maybe next year, maybe the year after that. I'll see."

Groggy looked at Black Jack with a stiff pose, as a salesman would eye a reluctant prospect, and he rebutted, "Now mate, who sold you that crock of shit?" He looked at Happy, and then back at Black Jack; and said, "Mate, just from the little bit that you've told me, I think that I've got news for you." Black Jack seemed unaffected by Groggy's growing enthusiasm. Groggy continued, "Mate, in case you haven't realized it, you're now in one of the remotest parts of the world getting in on the ground level of one of the most lucrative enterprises to come along since digging for gold!" Groggy waited for a reaction, but Black Jack remained unfazed. More big talk from a dreamer, thought Black Jack. Groggy went on, "Mate, in this business, no one owns you. You own yourself. Isn't that right, Happy?" Black Jack anticipated Happy's expectedly lackluster response as much as he believed in Groggy's zealous ramblings.

Suddenly Happy spoke: "That's correct, Groggy." He turned and looked squarely into Black Jack's surprised eyes and said, "Shore-whaling is the opportunity of the future. At present, there are close to a thousand vessels from various nations roaming the world's seas in a vain search for the dwindling number of Sperm Whales. Shore-whaling is a little-known, and hence underdeveloped profession which has limitless potential. It involves the hunting of an entirely different whale, which migrates closely along the coasts of areas of the world which are largely unsettled and free of competitors, both natural and Man. Therefore, once a station is established, we won't have to go to the whales; they come to us, and in great numbers. With the establishment of a successful shore-whaling station, comes the associated territory, which can be hunted and harvested in cooperation with as many or as few select ships as fit the criteria for partnership within a season or several seasons; depending on their productivity and ongoing relations with the station owner." Black Jack's jaw began to drop as he stared at his mate's now overflowing mouth. He continued to sip his drink. Groggy remained silent, nodding in agreement with everything that Happy said. Happy went on: "This station is the first of its kind on the South Island of this burgeoning nation. Australian companies pull the strings for most of these places in the South Pacific; however, Jackie, the station owner, has been let go to operate rather freely: Partly due to his proven experience with seals, which are now mostly gone, and partly due to the trust which he has established in the minds of his benefacting corporation. In its one year of operation, this station has produced a total monetary profit of approximately 20,000 British pounds. That figure is expected to double next year. Each of those whales you see out there produces about ten tuns of oil. At 28 British pounds per tun, that spells profits. And the bones? On average about 3500 dry-weight pounds at 125 monetary pounds per. That is good money, no bones about it. In addition, each Right Whale is naturally much larger than the Sperm Whale: Approximately 300 feet long as opposed to just 90 feet long, making the per-catch efficiency higher as well. By next year, there will be so many new ships down here in need of established stations, anyone with any experience here will be a prime candidate for capitalizing on the business and opening a station down the coast. Does it sound like something you'd be interested in, Black Jack?" Happy asked, as he concluded.

Black Jack stared at him saucer-eyed, mesmerized, and said, "Yeah, sure."

Happy cocked his chin arrogantly, and said, "Good," as he gathered the empty steins and headed off to collect round four.

"Enough about business, Black Jack." Groggy said after his long but attentive silence. "Look at the females in this place!" he uttered.

V

The noise of the crowd was a roar now, with tight clusters of close friends being milled around by aimless souls and the luckless lonely. Black Jack's eyes wandered over the crowd as Groggy and Happy's chatter droned in the back of his ear. The room had become a warm, uninhibited stage that people played across in a plotless drama. There were countless crusty and hardened men, now mellowed by imbibing, recounting numerous similar yet all-important sea stories to one another in loud voices. There was the odd wistful loner, standing precariously between circles of conversation, pretending to be invisible. There were groups of women, along the walls and with tables all to themselves, gabbing and cackling, bobbing their heads in sniggering laughter about various men and things. And then there was her.

Black Jack had noticed her only since beginning his fourth grog; and now it seemed to him that she was everywhere at once. He noticed her when she had squeezed behind him and his mates; her ample hips brushing his buttocks. She had had to turn her silver serving tray on its side and hold it above her as she pushed through. It had barely grazed the back of his head. Black Jack noticed her when she cruised down the wall, in and out of people like a nimble mink, collecting forgotten glasses. Black Jack would catch a glimpse of her again now and then walking quickly to and fro behind the bar, busying herself with different tasks and waving and smiling to the occasional mate. But most importantly, Black Jack noticed her when, late in the evening, she stopped short of walking through the kitchen door; turned her head fully; and looked him dead in the eye from across the crowded pub. She made a point, it seemed to him, of holding her chilling stare for at least two ticks of the clock; and then she whipped her long black hair around and proceeded through the door, slamming it behind her.

"Did you see that?" Black Jack interrupted his mates to ask.

"Groggy snapped his head around in mid-sentence to Happy, and asked Black Jack, "Excuse me, see what, mate?" He then turned back around to Happy with a disapproving shake of his head and resumed his conversation.

It seemed that Black Jack had been the sole target and witness of her display. He knew that look that she had given him. He began to realize that it had stirred something inside him. He began to pull away, he felt: To rise above the din of the crowd and glide across the room. His senses became clearer, now smelling and seeing more sharply. No one had been shaken by her slamming of the door; in fact, no one had even twitched. However, for Black Jack, it had jarred loose some deep feeling which he raced to identify in his currently altered ego. He knew what he knew: It was desire. Emboldened with his self-awareness, he made his way through the crowd with the stealth of a wolf. At the door, he looked around and feigned the moronic actions of a drunkard in search of a loo; and he slipped unnoticed through the kitchen door.

In the dim light of a single oil lamp, he could see that the empty kitchen had been tidied and secured for the night. Everything was immaculate and packed up, forming a neat museum of silhouettes. None of the shadows was hers: She was not there. Toward the back of the kitchen was another doorway, and drifting past its opening he spied a lazy puff of smoke. He attempted to walk straight to the door; and stumbling out onto the rear deck of the shop, he walked straight into her.

She was stunning, Black Jack thought. She eyed him amusingly; and then offered him her cigarette. He obligingly took a drag of the hand-rolled fag, tasting tobacco and a hint of something else, as he looked her in the eyes. He could not get over her beauty. She had long, shiny, raven-black hair which accentuated the supple young skin of her face, neck, and shoulders. She had a strong, yet delicate face; with high cheek bones, a sleek feminine jaw line, and a pointed, albeit flared, nose. On her chin, she wore the faintest beginnings of what Black Jack would later come to learn was her 'moko': a tattooed symbol of her beauty and power as a Maori princess. Black Jack had never seen anyone like her; and he tried to convey his admiration with a broad smile, as he returned her cigarette. Her hazel eyes twinkled. She liked him, he thought.

The night, save for the distant din of the party within, was quiet. A warm breeze was gently blowing in from the bay; and the small waves rhythmically lapped the shore. The full moon shone brightly in the cloudless night sky, illuminating the water, the sand, and the trees around them. They stood face to face in awkward silence for an immeasurable moment; until finally, she giggled. Somehow, each of them knew that it would be a fruitless endeavor to attempt spoken communication; however, they succeeded in relating their feelings to one another quite well. Black Jack ran the back of his hand down one side of her hair and over her blouse, both of which were fluttering slightly in the wind. She responded with a curious hand to his shoulder. His height seemed to impress her. He followed by leaning in to kiss her. As his lips were just about to touch her receptive and willing mouth, a gust blew across the deck and a large wave crashed. She jumped forward and clutched at his arms. His heart quickened only because of her sudden closeness: The actions of the sea could no longer unnerve him. The tide was coming in, he thought. As he was noting the swelling of the ocean to himself, she pulled back, took him by the hand, and hurriedly led him off the deck. They disappeared down a bushy footpath, a set of unfamiliar stars guiding Black Jack's way.

Chapter 8

THE DREAM

A dark figure sits bow-legged, back bent over his legs with arms stretched down to shackles binding wrists and ankles, to a wooden floor in an early-American cottage. The swing and sting of the cat-o'-nine-tails punctuates each utterance of the white-wigged gentleman wielding the whip.

"It's your attitude, boy!" *Whap* goes the whip. "That's the problem!" *Whap*. "You know that though, right?" *Whap*. "Right?" The prim and proper Pontius pauses. Then, *whap!* "Right?"

The sweaty, lean, half-clad figure inhales with a rush, shudders, and musters a seemingly sincere, "Yes, Sir."

"That's right!" *Whap*. "And we've been through this . . ." *Whap*. "Time and time . . ." *Whap*. "Again!" *Whap*. "You are the problem." *Whap*. "You have always been the problem." *Whap*. "I have tried with you, Arthur." *Whap*.

"I have never . . ." *Whap.* "Ever . . ." *Whap.* "Had this much trouble . . ." *Whap.* "With anyone!" *Whap.*

"But, but, Sir . . ." stammers the big, dark man imploringly.

"Don't argue!" *Whap.* "I am sick . . ." *Whap.* "And tired . . ." *Whap.* "Of your petty arguments, boy!" *Whap.* "I have my limit." *Whap.* "I will only tolerate so much back talk!" *Whap.* "We have been very good to you, Jack." *Whap.* "We take very good care of you." *Whap.* "If you were anywhere else . . ." *Whap.* "You know what that would be like!" *Whap.* "You've heard about other masters, right Jack?" Another pause. Then, *whap!* "Right, Alesworth?" *Whap!*

"Yes Sir!" the slave utters, this time feigning a bit more enthusiasm.

"Some of your people don't even get last names around here!" *Whap.* "Hell, they don't even get to stay with their families." *Whap.* "Or have wives!" *Whap.* "What if I take your wife away for awhile, Arthur? Will that improve your attitude?" *Whap.* The frilly-clothed man hesitates, beckons the bound man's woman for a cup of water, wipes his brow with a lace handkerchief, and reassures his grip upon the leather crop of the hydra. The Black man lifts his head slightly, ears perking.

"Ah, yes!" *Whap.* "I see that I am finally reaching you, man." *Whap.* "Will that do it, then, my opinionated planter and picker?" *Whap.* "That is it then, I shall remove her from your cabin for a month!" *Whap.* "She will take up residence with the Pastor . . ." *Whap!* "Who is a decent man without a wife." *Whap.*

The Negro begins to strain against his shackles, chains clinking.

"And he shall instruct her in the ways of respect and decency." *Whap.*

His chains begin to rattle as the collars of the binding irons begin to vibrate.

"Will that improve your attitude toward working for this honorable estate?"

The leggings and arm irons shake violently and all at once fall from the ebony man's body as he stands to face his punisher. He pauses to take his wife by her hand and then continues walking toward the Master. As he passes him, he emphatically says, "No Sir!" and bumps his shoulder against the man's chest.

"What is going on? Where are you going?" the Owner shouts. He tries one last crack of the whip, only in vain, as the back of Arthur fades into a cloud of vapor going out the cottage door.

"Anywhere but here, sir, anywhere but here." a husky African male voice replies.

Black Jack awoke suddenly on a flax floor mat under a wool blanket in a large room with strange, red, wooden carvings next to a Maori woman.

Chapter 9

GOOD MORNING NEW ZEALAND

Anxiety flooded his heart as his eyes darted around the great room and over the hilly outline of the feminine form lying beside him. He struggled to recall the strange events of the previous night, and how he had come to be there. The still figure lay with her back to him, her line rising and falling beneath the blanket like the mountains he could see distantly through the window. Her thick, dark hair and smooth, brown skin reminded him of his betrothed back home, and the many mornings that they had shared in their quarters on the estate in Mississippi. His mind raced to discern the difference in the present scenario, however, and it suddenly occurred to him: The light! Good God, he thought, it was mid-morning; and no one stirred, from what he could tell, anywhere in the house or outside.

Only the throng of bird song bristled the morning air, as the chilly dawn clouds evaporated from the brilliant azure sky. He attempted to remain still there on his back as he scanned the magnificent and strange curved carvings that lined the ceiling beams and columns that ran down the walls. He tried to calm himself and put aside the urge to beat the imaginary Master coming through the door to rouse him and his sleeping beauty; to spring into action and complete the round of chores in the darkness before breakfast.

But it was light! And all the beauty and calm began to work their spell on Arthur as he realized that for this brief moment of serenity he was free. Free to think his own thoughts, free to ponder the unknown events of the day ahead, free to choose what to do next. Well, sort of; as he was still faced with the task of making his way back into the milieu of shorewhalers and workers; to blend in undetected and eventually join up with a party returning to his ship before the day's muster. It was a kind of semi-freedom, a working furlough of sorts, for those going ashore to work the whales. Granted even to the slaves on the ship, it had come as an unexpected and pleasant surprise to Arthur when they had told him he could exchange the dirty and smelly confines of the ship's bilge for the back-breaking duties of the beach. He had likened it to a glimpse of freedom, with close supervision; but he had not imagined the loose comings and goings that he had been allowed once joining the myriad of grimy men upon the shore.

He was almost let go to do what he pleased! Moving from group to group, lending a hand to a boiling pot here, giving a back-wrenching heave-ho there to secure an incoming whale, or running an errand to the shop. He had tried to contain his jubilation; but he had beamed the entire day, with his fellow workers not being able to avoid noticing the enthusiasm of this dark-skinned pearl-toothed fellow, until at the end of the day's work he had become so popular that several of the more boisterous and rambunctious men had shouted out to him, "We are going to the grog shop tonight, man!"

Lying there with his prior night's catch, he was now bursting with a newfound excitement and a feeling that was unfamiliar to him. He had never felt as if his actions were his own, or that they could make him feel good about himself. He tried to think about a word he had heard others use occasionally. He thought about a thing he had heard mentioned and discussed, and now he thought he must be experiencing it: He thought it must be Pride.

Yes, Arthur was proud of himself, whether he had felt it before unknowingly, or whether it had just flown through the paneless window of this South Pacific hut; it felt wondrously new to him. He swelled inside, and if the feeling had a sound, it would have been heard throughout the house. The emotion was accompanied by something else, however.

Black Jack suddenly felt a strain and a stretching like never before, and the pain that it brought caused him to writhe and turn on his side toward his sleeping beauty; and he realized the origin of his discomfort as a certain extension of himself suddenly jabbed the more tender outer fleshes of her motionless body.

She started and turned; her sleepy eyes coyly and knowingly gazing into his; and during this silent stare, he realized that her eyes were golden-brown. She lay perfectly still, glancing at him, and then shyly down under the blanket through the gap between them; and then cautiously flittering her eyelashes before returning her eyes fully into his.

Black Jack felt the heat of his unwieldy weapon inten-
sify, along with his remorse that perhaps he had stabbed
his unsuspecting and trusting mate with an unwelcome
dagger. Suddenly though, she broke gaze as her eyes fluttered and rolled back into her head at the same time that
she turned leeward, slowly and heavily, onto her back; her
arms relaxing to her side; her head continuing to roll to
her far side; and her legs gently parting. She let out a long
ingenuous sigh, flicked her tongue furtively a few times
through the furrow of her lips, and slowly closed her eyes.

Black Jack rose up vigorously on one elbow, confidently
bolstered by her display of welcoming signals; nimbly
hopped onto the other elbow, and directly sheathed his
sword.

Chapter 10

THE FIRST WHALE

Black Jack watched the big, burly man walk from workstation to workstation along the busy beach. From his vantage on the high bluff, he could see the village (or 'pa', as the Maori call it), the entire beach, and the handful of ships moored in the bay. He felt as though he were a sentinel, like one of the Indian scouts back home, secretly spying on the activities of an enemy tribe.

Things seemed normal with the camp; and in fact, he thought, it seemed as though they would remain so regardless of his presence or contribution. Never having had attended school, Arthur had no knowledge of the feeling of playing 'hooky'; however, in this suspended moment of observation, he could not help but feel a certain mischievous satisfaction in his—as yet to be determined as unnoticed—absence from work. He had never missed a scheduled day of labor on the plantation; and so, beyond his

day of escape which lay well outside the scope of context
of his present situation, this was a completely new experience for him.

'Laying out' was what his mama had called it; and
beside the imposed conscience of the work ethic brought
about by the thought of physical punishment and pain,
she believed that a person should work every day (except
Sunday, which was another matter entirely and a sensitive
subject with her as she tried to overlook the Master's fla-
grant disregard for the Sabbath and any spirituality or
expression thereof in his slaves). Not to do so was lazy and
demonstrated an ill character, she would assert quite often, regardless of any real illness which may present itself;
which, in her opinion, was a matter between the man supposedly afflicted and his god.

So Black Jack was laying out; and here it was an hour,
maybe two, before lunch, he thought. Maybe he'd stay
up on his grassy perch behind that rock, and breathe the
ocean air all day, he told himself. Then he considered the
consequences, and thought better of it. But how to slip
into the mix without being detected and suffering the full
recoil of the authorities, both on ship and shore? he wondered. He began to carefully place his feet, one over the
other, down the steep rocky bluff. It was completely different terrain than to what he was accustomed; however,
its beauty fully compensated for its treachery. The dark
foot path had made for an unconscious passage through
the brush the night before; however now, there was no
trail. Large, angled rocks protruded from the grassy hill
face in the places not occupied by the more predominant
vegetation: Large hedge-like bushes with small but wiry
trunks that gnarled and twisted in dense clumps. Their
randomness of clustering in combination with their individual entanglement made for an intertwining juggernaut

culminating at head height. It were as though Tantalus
had stumbled into a rogue bonsai garden.

Birds flew everywhere: White Seagulls, gray Terns, green
Kakapos and blue Kakas, and black and red Takahes.
Tramping under the bushes, Black Jack stumbled upon
what at first looked like scurrying vermin. They were little
brown Kiwi birds. He stopped in sudden fascination to
watch them. They had long thin beaks like quills without
the feather. They had an odd shape much like an oriental
vase; and they had no wings. A bird without wings! Black
Jack chuckled to himself. Then he plopped down in the
moss and the grass; and he began to laugh uncontrollably.
He laughed until tears came to his eyes; and he began to
roll in the grass. A flightless bird, he thought loudly to
himself. He burst forth again with thunderous guffaws,
until he could not breathe. There he lay for a fair number
of minutes, rolling and laughing; runny bird dung dripping onto him from the leaves above. A true motley fool.

He said out loud after a mild recovery, "A bird that
cannot fly. How odd!" Even though he thought to himself
that this bird and he had a lot in common.

Slowly Black Jack made his way down to the rocky
cliffs. He was close to the sand by now, as the cliffs stood
only a few yards high. They were like Japanese curtains on
the sides of a large stage, only suggesting the structures of
walls while they served to frame the space between bays.
The cliff walls themselves were mottled with hand-sized
holes, jagged yet weathered, which provided perches and
nesting ledges for many different sea birds. They all took
flight as Black Jack carefully scaled the cliff, facing inward.
Placing his feet into the oval-shaped holes, it was difficult
for him to see the nests from above; and he regretfully
smashed several eggs on his way down. He found the rock
edifice rather easy to climb down; and he soon reached
the point where the sand cleanly met the cliff. On his last

step, he swung out, turned, jumped, and casually strode toward the shore-whaling station. He had come down a remote corner of the bay so as not to be detected; and as he came around a rock, he tried to slip unnoticed into a group of flenchers at the side of a whale.

"G'day, Black Jack!" hailed a man in an Australian accent. Arthur was surprised to hear his name from a complete stranger. "Glad you could make it." the flencher added, without pausing in his slicing of the skin.

"How, how . . ." Black Jack had begun to stammer.

"How did I know?" the man cut him short. "Mate, you've been the talk of the town since you missed the six o'clock muster." he said with gloating glee.

Black Jack seared with embarrassment. He began to breathe and taste the putrid fumes of last night's grog. He envisioned retching; but his gut held, and he retained his composure in spite of losing his cover. "So everyone knows?" he asked, trying to sound unconcerned.

"Sure, mate, you've been missing all the fun." the Aussie said sarcastically. He then let his new acquaintance off the hook by saying, "Don't sweat it, mate. Jackie expects all the new guys to have a slip up or two anyway. Just keep your head down for the rest of the day; and don't let it happen again. She'll be right!"

Just then, the big burly man came around where the head of the whale used to be. He yelled out, "Oy! Black Jack. There you are!" He spoke with a broad, toothy grin; and his jovial demeanor caught Black Jack off guard.

The Australian spoke up, "It's all right, Jackie, we've got him now. I'll make a flash flencher of him for sure."

"Right!" said Jackie. "Anyway, word has it that a group of whales is coming down the coast. Should breech sometime today if they wander into the channel. Go over the basics with him, will you Sam? Thanks." He finished his address to the men as he walked behind them, scanning the slits Sam had made in the side of the whale. "Beautiful, just beautiful." he said happily, disappearing around the fluke.

Sam handed Black Jack a flenching pole with a fresh blade, and said, "Just watch the bones mate. Don't get stuck in. The rest is common sense. When she's ready to drop, just let it hit the sand. Don't let a stack of blubber be the last thing you see."

"Right." said Black Jack, feigning confidence as he made his first incision with the giant scalpel.

"So, your first whale, eh? You ready?" asked Sam.

"Yes." Black Jack replied with the only word that he could imagine would reveal as little as possible.

Sam eyed Black Jack as he stripped and stabbed, looking for any signs to the contrary of Black Jack's affirmative response. "You didn't do any out at sea?" asked Sam.

"No." said Black Jack.

"Oh, that's right, only the Yanks have the whole kit packed up onboard with 'em. Well, that's all right." Sam said. He was referring to the American open-ocean whaling setup. These ships were equipped with virtually everything needed for putting down boats, giving chase to, and fully processing a large whale: Right down to the try-pots and furnaces. The Australians being somewhat local in the South Pacific, and the British laying claim to the country, were not obliged to be self-contained whaling operations on the open seas; as they were afforded the dubious luxury of being supported by shore-whaling stations. "Bah! Bugger that, being on one of those floating rubbish heaps!" he said, alluding to the insidious and unavoidable accumulation of carrion and its associated stench which had become the trade-mark of many open-ocean whaling ships.

"Yeah, really." said Black Jack, taking credit for his

good fortune and the irony of his placement aboard an English vessel.

"Going after the Right Whale: Where to start?" Sam asked himself out loud for Black Jack's benefit. "Well, you know why they call it the Right Whale?" Sam asked Black Jack.

"No." said Black Jack after a thoughtful pause.

"Because, unlike the Sperm Whale, after the Right Whale dies, it turns over in the water, nice and easy; and it floats there, waiting to be towed in. Therefore, it's the right whale to hunt!" Sam said, chuckling.

"Oh." said Black Jack, not expecting the joke.

"Also, the thing is huge. It's close to two ships in length, maybe more. It's also got two spouts. That's how you can tell you got a Right Whale when she breeches: The Sperm Whale only blows once.

"All right." said Black Jack, attentively absorbing the information.

"The mouth, mate! You never want to see that coming back at you; but if you do, you'll see the gates of Hell!"

"What do you mean?" Black Jack asked curiously.

"I've seen it once, mate, and once was enough. A big wrinkled head, and she looks like she's smiling. She's not smiling, mate! And what looks like a big black iron curtain where the teeth should be; and sharp as razors! I've heard tell of the Headsman going right through them on a charging whale. Found nothing but shreds and blood, mate, shreds and blood." Sam repeated himself, as if fascinated with his own words.

Black Jack stopped himself from gawking at the storyteller. "Really." he said, hiding his amazement.

"So, you want to be a Headsman? That's where they put the new men, you know." said Sam coolly.

"Sure." Black Jack said confidently, rising to his mate's false challenge.

"No, Black Jack, I'm only joking with you. They'll probably put you on after-oarsman. You'll be good ballast there!" Sam said, slightly condescendingly, but in all seriousness.

"That'll be fine as well." said Black Jack, still showing his poker face.

"Right, so here's how it goes." Sam began. "My crew is first on the roster, so we'll be going out first. I happen to be the Headsman, so you'll see me drop my pole where I stand and start running for that skiff you see down there on the beach." Sam said proudly as he pointed to a boat just beyond the tail of the whale. The boat was approximately thirty-feet long. He continued, "You'll see about eight other men scrambling from all over and helping me to right the boat and throw the gear in: That'll be our water jug, our biscuit bin, and our line. But we're not going out there for a picnic mate. It'll probably be the rest of the day, if we stick the fish or not. When we do shove off from the beach, you're gonna see eight men row faster than you've ever seen your ship sail, no lie. That fish will be one, maybe two miles out there, and they don't wait around. I'm gonna be standing on the bow, though, with an oar longer than this pole, steering us right up to the whale. I'll be saying silly things like, 'Send us alongside, laddies, now give way!' and 'Hurrah, my bonnies, hearty and strong!' Sounds stupid now; but believe me, it really gets the boys going. Especially when they know I'm the Headsman!" he boasted again. He went on, "Now, when the boat touches the back of that whale, I've got to be quicker than the ferryman in Hades. I'll notch that oar, so hopefully it will still be there when the fun is all over; 'cause this is where it gets good. You payin' attention there, Black Jack?"

Black Jack swallowed hard and said, "Uh-huh."

"Good." said Sam. "I pick up the harpoon, which is

heavier than a Hickory log in a cabin; but it's got balance, see: If you lift it just right, it swings itself out over the target and waits for you, nice as a feather. One hand on the fulcrum, one at the back to drive it home. Then I scream at the top of my livin', lovin' lungs—I scream Jack, like my Celtic forefathers back on the highland battle-grounds—'All clear! Give it to her!' For that timeless second, the salt air and the acid in my bile make for a wickedly galling cocktail; and my body becomes God's cannon. The harpoon comes out of me like Thor's hammer and parts the black mass that is the almighty whale. And if ever a man could dread more the coming together, back to back, of any two events in time, it is when he must stand witness to the release of the harpoon and the reaction of the whale. For whether he has fallen from a great height and lived to tell about the experience; or can show the scar from a shot fired directly at him during a duel; or perhaps even boast of being treed by a tiger: No man can honestly claim that he has suffered all of the effects and feelings that come just before death, save for the actual departing of the last breath from his body; as those which beset the whaler when his skiff takes flight after the tethered leviathan." he said, as he turned from his flenching to look at Black Jack. "You catch my drift, Black Jack?" he asked.

"Rightio!" Black Jack fired back immediately, demonstrating mature enthrallment.

"The beast dives for Hell;" Sam carried on, "Trying to quench the fire in its back, but to no avail. It begins to drown on its own blood, being cursed with lungs in its would-be watery grave. Can you believe that, Jack? A fish with lungs! What was God thinking on that day, Jack?" Sam asked cynically.

"I dunno." said Black Jack, knowingly. "The Bible says Job was swallowed by a whale; so maybe God needed a way for Job to get air so he wouldn't drown." he concluded.

Sam was surprised by Black Jack's frankness; more so than at the fact that Black Jack had seriously considered the question.

"All right." said Sam modestly. He continued more quietly, having suffered a mild setback to his bravado. "But lungs, Jack. It just seems like a cruel trick for God to play on the largest creation in the world: 'Here's the biggest creature in my kingdom. Now I'm going to set him in water and watch him try not to drown for the rest of eternity.' That's a bad joke, don't you think, Jack?" Sam asked his student.

"Maybe." said Black Jack. "But it all depends on how you look at it, I reckon." he said, preparing to assume the role of teacher. "Mama always told me, God makes examples that are plain to see, so all his children can learn from them, if they open their eyes. If it's the biggest living thing in the world, then I suppose God is sayin', 'Look here, fool, and witness this soul's trials in getting his daily breath of life.' Or a bird without wings: that would surely cause a thoughtless man to stop and think about that poor soul's plight. I think God shows us things, so we will come to know him better if we make up our minds to." Black Jack finished, free of pretense and arrogance.

Sam stood there stunned for a moment; and then not to be outdone in this bout of amateur philosophy, said, "Well, what about the deaf and blind beggar, Jack. Will he come to know God? Will he come to know God if he 'chooses to open his eyes'? Tell me, Jack." Sam asked Black Jack earnestly. Yet, he seemed to be mocking Arthur's words.

Black Jack remained patient, and replied, "Every man has a mind; and every mind has an eye with which to see what it chooses. That's what Mama always told me."

Sam accepted Black Jack's wisdom; and not wanting

to trespass within the subject of his pupil's mother or religion, he returned to whaling. "Right! Well, then, the whale
is pretty much done then; if I've done my job. If not, look
out!" Sam said wryly.

"How so?" asked Black Jack curiously.

"Well, I've never had it happen to me, but I've seen it
happen to less experienced crews. If the harpoon does not
find its mark, then you get a flying fish!" Sam said smiling, trying to pay homage to Black Jack's lesson. "The
giant turns, and gives chase to its hunters. It bears down
like a train on the water, staring straight at the skiff; and
just short of the sloop, shoots into the air leaving its prey
to pray to that monumental black monolith for a momentous moment. Following this second of silence, the whale
falls to the water, like a slick, wet Sequoia being felled; and
the subsequent explosion of wind and sound blasts far
harder than any cannon that man could fire. It is then
that the men must prove that their intent was to bring the
fight to the fish; and not the other way around, as the
dying black island furiously flourishes her tail and fins, as
unfurling a flag to claim her final resting plot: The very
spot directly beneath their bloody boat." Sam concluded
with the pitch and force of an orator.

Black Jack stood in awe of Sam's speech. He said, "That
is fantastic. And you are quite the poet. Did you know
that?"

"I get on a roll, now and then. The chappies like it.
They set the words to song sometimes. Keeps 'em happy
when we're towing that bloody bitch back in from five
miles out!" Sam said, hiding his pride with a rationale. He
quickly changed the subject to avoid embarrassment; and
said, "You know, they also call the Right Whale a Black
Whale." He was trying to maintain a masculine sense of
authority.

Black Jack stood up straight and said, "Well, maybe

that is why it is the right whale to hunt!"

Sam laughed hard, and said, "Sharp, Jack, very sharp."
He continued to laugh, admiring his friend's sense of humor.

II

The beach was remarkably quiet for a place so full of
people. The bright sun shone down out of a clear sky; and
the warm breeze blew relatively dry air out of the bay and
over the sand and washed-up kelp. An occasional gull
screeched overhead; but other than that, no metal from
men's tools clanged, and they did not speak as they worked.
It was as though the whalers had achieved a hypnotic
medium between the excitement of welcoming new arrivals and getting to know them. Everyone moved about as if
in their own world, while still working efficiently hand-
in-hand with all whom surrounded them. There had become no need to talk, and so nature's song played beautifully in the background.

The ships moored side-by-side in the bay bobbed in
successive order as waves cut obliquely across the channel
and sprawled out on the shore. The salty, meaty smell of
seaweed mingled with the greasy odor of simmering whale
oil; and both fragrances took turns sparring with the aroma
of rancid flesh which held rank above each on the beach.

"Are you scared?" Sam asked Black Jack out of the blue.

Arthur thought pensively for a moment, and responded, "I don't know what to be scared of."

"You've never killed a whale, then." Sam stated as a
question.

"I've never hunted something that large, no." Black
Jack said, qualifying his answer.

"Well, mate, if you're scared, say you're scared. There's

no shame in it. That's part of the game." Sam replied with his ready answer.

Black Jack responded defensively, "Like I say, I won't know if I'm frightened of the whale or killing the whale, until the time comes."

Sam relented a bit, and said, "Well mate, how about this: When the time comes, go out with me and my crew, and see how it's done properly. One of my blokes will be happy to trade places with you."

Black Jack eyed him, and asked, "I don't know if that is right. What will my crew think of me then?"

Sam smiled and told him, "Jack, it's like this: Right now, your men are all nubs. They don't know what they're doing; and chances are they won't come anywhere near getting a whale their first time out. Now along comes you, with some experience under your belt, and they won't think twice about it. They'll make you Headsman, and you'll be king of your boat!"

Black Jack thought about Sam's proposition. It did seem to make sense, he thought. "All right." he said. "I'll give it a go."

Sam grinned and said, "Great, now listen closely . . ."

Suddenly, from up on the hill, the cry came: "Thar she blows! And close . . . two miles! Two spouts! Thar she blows!"

Sam's face had frozen as he heard the Lookout, listening for the vital subtleties hidden among the report such as type, number, and distance of the whales. Sam yelled to Black Jack, "C'mon, then! Follow me and do everything I tell you." as he scrambled for the gear, throwing items into Jack's arms and running for the water. As they reached the water, he shouted, "Now, Jack, grab the aft. Let's turn her right. That's it, now into the waves. Chuck the gear in. Here come the boys!"

Men came sprinting from all points on the beach, sand flying behind them as they pumped their arms and legs. They bounded into the waves and stampeded into the skiff, splashing Sam and Black Jack as they stood waist deep in the waves steadying the boat. The oars came out as the two men on the end hoisted themselves in; and the sloop was away.

"Dig in, boys! I've got the sights on her!" Sam shouted as he slapped the steering oar into the salty spray.

Black Jack scarcely had time to consider the fantastic speed of the boat, as he was soon racked with searing pain and gasping for breath. The other men rowed mechanically and swiftly, tight-lipped and silent with stone faces. Their steely-eyed glint reflected determination as they pounded incessantly and efficiently on the blurred surface of the sea, all in perfect unison. The fury of their stroke combined with the barking of the Headsman to create a hypnotic marine opera which held the aching aft-oarsman spellbound. Before the entire effect of the mesmerizing scene could settle completely on him, they reached the whale. The oarsmen stopped and the boat fell silent, save for its gurgling wake.

"Alongside, boys!" Sam yelled. The whale floated calmly in the water. It seemed to be resting, almost waiting for its hunters; not at all like the frenzied quarry that Arthur had anticipated. Sam peaked his oar and picked up the harpoon. He looked around to see the other boat still struggling to approach its catch, about one-half mile away.

To Black Jack, the great animal seemed docile: Much like the cows back home. The whale did not seem to be the great unwieldy beast that had been described to him.

"She's got a calf!" exclaimed Sam, standing; as a much smaller whale surfaced and spouted along the far side of their prey. "Stand by!" shouted Sam, as he considered his options. It was well known to the experienced hunter that a mother whale could be that much more unpredictable and unruly, given her protective nature. The men in the boat relaxed slightly, still knowing that the time was close at hand, but taking the opportunity to rest their arms and lungs. Black Jack was very grateful for the chance to recover; and he wondered how long the reprieve would last. He thought about the cows with calves back home, and how easy it was to lead the mother once the calf was in tow. That did not seem to be the case here. Still, he thought, there had to be an easier way than attacking the whale head on: Even a gentle cow would turn demonic if run through with a sharp stick.

Suddenly the headsman tensed up. Sam said, "All right, it's on! Ready!" He leveraged his harpoon into position, the line trailing behind to its coil sitting just in front of Black Jack. The oarsmen simultaneously brought in their oars with the precision and timing of riflemen in a firing squad. They clenched their hands on the rail just inside the gunwale, and braced their feet inside the notches on the floor. Black Jack perceived their urgency and followed suit. Sam braced his back foot, and said, "All right, Jack." He asked Black Jack, "Do you see where the line comes over the loggerhead and into the boat at your feet?"

Black Jack gave an affirmative nod and said, "Yes."

Sam said, "Good. That is where you will see smoke. You are to pour water on the line, and keep pouring no matter what, or the line will part and we will lose the whale, understood?"

Again, Black Jack nodded.

Sam said, "Excellent . . ." like a happy snake, and without hesitating, he turned his head and launched his harpoon into the back of the whale, just aft and below the blowhole.

To Black Jack, it all occurred in slow-motion: The blade glinted as it met the shiny, wet, black skin. A slicing sound followed, and then the razored hook disappeared. Within a split second, thick, purple blood began to weep from the wound, forming a large dome-shaped droplet around the shaft of the harpoon. Black Jack watched as if the cut were his own. He envisioned the pain of past childhood scars: How the sensation hesitated before rushing in. It must have been the same for the whale.

When Black Jack's head returned to its upright position from having bounced off his back, the smell of smoke and the burning in his neck gave him an immediate bearing on reality which helped to quell his urge to vomit his heart out through his nose. He could vaguely make out the line and the loggerhead, but nothing else within the tunnel of water would consent to focus as it rushed by. Black Jack could scarcely hold on to the rails, let alone pick up a pale and dowse a hot rope. However, he was relieved from his duty of bucket brigadier by the wave which crashed in from behind him as the whale stopped and the inertia of the boat halted its forward acceleration and associated thrust. The skiff, half-full of water, coasted into the back of the whale with great force, and the impact sent everyone who had lost their grip on the rail reeling forward to the aft of the boat. Black Jack found himself sitting among a pile of his comrades, drenched in blood and salt water; all looking and feeling as though they had dropped from a great height.

Sam stood up and shouted, "Ready, ready, Lads! Hold fast!" as he sprung from his seat at the bow and surveyed the whale, waiting for its next move. The blood from the wound was oozing out, not spurting; and no spray emanated from its spout. It floated motionless in the water as its ends began to sag visibly lower in the waves. Sam yelled out, "Yes, boys! This was an easy one. Hurrah!" The boat exploded into cheers from men who had hardly had the strength to breathe not seconds before; and much waving of arms and slapping of backs took place. As they all looked around, the men saw the second whale, about three miles in the offing, slap its fluke menacingly at an approaching skiff. Sam looked back into the boat, and said, "They'll be right, mates. She's just about to meet this one in whale hell!" The men laughed and cheered wildly again, in a fervor over the prospect of two whales being brought back to the beach. Black Jack stared, wild-eyed at the entire scene, taking it all in. His head buzzed and his blood coursed; and he felt as if his very soul was on fire.

"Black Jack, you all right?" Sam shouted to him over the cheering mob.

"Oh yes, oh yes!" he shouted back to Sam, his face flush and tingling as he smiled.

"Good!" Sam said. "Everyone ready for the tow home?" he shouted. The men yelled affirmatively. "Right then! We'll wait 'til she rolls and off we go. Everyone have a biscuit!" he said in the festive spirit of the moment; and he sat down once again to join the crew in their revelry.

Five minutes passed, and the fever pitch of the hunt began to evaporate from the boat as the men and their muscles began to settle. "Bloody hell." a few exclaimed, as they stretched their arms and rubbed their legs. "Goddamn." some were heard to grumble, as they vomited over the side. Black Jack began to shiver as he shared in their agony. His legs began to cramp, and a torn sensation spread across his damp chest. A cool southerly wind began to blow, and dark clouds moved in over the sun. The whale had yet to turn over.

"All right, boys. Me thinks someone is telling us something here. This one's not going to roll, so let's get her moving." Sam said doggedly. "Black Jack, let me show you something." Sam said to Arthur, beckoning him to the spot where the boat met the behemoth. Black Jack crossed the wavering sloop slowly, carefully patting men's shoulders for support as he stepped. "Step up here with me." Sam said calmly as he leaned out over a foot placed on the broad sloping arc of the leviathan's back. "C'mon then!" he said, turning back to look at Black Jack in the skiff he had left rocking. Black Jack put a foot on the gunwale, paused, and then all at once sprung onto the back of the whale; and trotted up to meet Sam at the spine. "Good on 'ya, mate. Now look at this." Sam said enthusiastically to Black Jack. "This is your classic dead whale. No worries. See how easy it is when you make a clean kill? No mucking around with flying fish!" Sam said proudly as he put an arm around his young ebony prodigy. He continued, "Now! This is unusual: I've seen a whale that doesn't roll; mind you, not that often. We've just got to be careful on the tow: Fins flippin' out, undertow if she finally does pitch, you get the drift!" Black Jack nodded, too exhausted to speak. Sam went on, "Right! Now, before we go, I want you to examine the classic signs of a post-mortem whale. Note the limp, dangling posterior, with associated oblique lateral wrinkles. That tail has had it. Note how blood has ceased to issue from the wound." Sam pointed to the place where the harpoon sat mired in a mound of thick, clotted, brown fluid. He finished his lecture by saying, "And notice how you can already feel the little fishies and sharks tapping away at the sides of her belly!" Sam looked around confidently and pointed alongside, as Black Jack perused with him.

"I don't see no fish or sharks, Sam." Black Jack said sincerely after a moment.

Sam froze; and his eyes snapped to the harpoon. He

scrutinized it for a stretched second, watching it rise in synchrony with the waves that the beast encountered; and he strained to detect any aberrant movement. The pole suddenly twitched. "Hang on!" Sam cried out as he ran to the weapon. He immediately dropped to his knees at the harpoon and thrust his hands into the crusty wound. He peeled back the sides of the slit; and a solid stream of bright red blood gushed onto his face, bathing his entire head. He opened his mouth to scream, and almost immediately, another hot, bloody geyser shot onto his face and into his throat. He choked and gurgled as he pulled away, struggling to yell, "Set to, boys!" Instantly he sprang backward into the boat, sputtering and coughing. "Jack! Get in, Jack! She's not done yet!" Sam warned frantically.

The men watched as Black Jack took one step forward on the rising back of the beast; before the vortex of the blue, gray, and black torrent swept him violently and swiftly from their vision.

Chapter 11

MEET THE FERN POUNDER

F oam swirled around Arthur's head as he bobbed in the ocean. Gray swells churned the waves and carried him up and down through areas of smooth and rough undulating sea. Cold rain pelted his face, as froth and fog played havoc with his eyes; and wind howled in his ears. Brine filled his mouth and washed his nose like a strong saline elixir. His only defense against the onslaught was to further tread the water.

He could see the bluish-gray outline of the hilly coast. Cutting across the waves at a sharp angle was the tidal current which he credited with moving him along his shifting littoral vantage to land. He was rushing past, as if carried on a large, swift river offshore; and as the earth was passing north, he thought, then he must be progressing south. Further and further, faster and faster he sped within the torrent, its velocity ironically providing him with a conciliatory buoyancy, roughly one-half mile from tide's

113

edge. He began to make out features as they appeared through the mist: Jetties giving way to bays, then bluffs conceding to beaches; all in alternation. Fairly hospitable terrain, he thought in his attempts to comfort himself, if he could just break free of the stream and swim.

As he rounded a sharp outcropping of rocky cliff, he was granted a brief reprieve from the undertow. Its pressure reduced as it slowed; and its remnants splayed out and dissipated over a large kelp bed breaching the surface with its thick tatters. The water calmed and rippled slightly in a mildly turbulent circle; and it regained its aqua-blue tincture as it bathed the brownish-green garden. Black Jack waded among the plants and felt relief amid the tranquil grotto. He had entered a small, peaceful bay.

He began to swim, sea vegetation tickling his body as he stroked through the forgiving tendrils. He had lost his clothes. As he strived for shore, seaweed gave way to sand as the surf became shallow; and soon he was able to stand. As he did so, the clouds slowly separated and the sun shone. The parting vapors refracted the emerging sunlight, so that as Black Jack walked from the waves, several sharply defined rays lighted upon his head and shoulders. He felt their touch and he immediately became warm. The dry sand before him was bright and hot: It was as though the rain had not come to this bay. Birds sang loudly and flew about, and copious colorful fruit dangled from emerald trees.

There he stood in all his glory, naked and freshly baptized, saved from death and delivered to this place seemingly devoid of people. The bay shore was smooth and crescent, and Arthur stood at mid arc, like an actor alone on a large amphitheater stage. The beach extended from a low reef on the right, across the sand, to a cathedral rock cave protruding into the water on the left. All in all, he thought as he looked around, roughly five-hundred yards wide. But how far from Te Awaiti? he wondered. His time adrift was a blur now, and he could not accurately measure his travel down the coast. He figured that it must be close to normal quitting time; and that soon the men would be bringing the whales back to the station and lashing them to the sheers. There would be jubilation throughout the village, he knew; but would they look for him? he wondered. The question hit him hard. Black Jack asked himself: How likely was it that an exhausted man, bent on celebrating his bounty, would want to venture once again into dark foreboding waters to chance rescuing a possibly drowned man (cabin boy, servant, ex-slave, Black, fellow whaler)? Arthur ran through the combinations of choices in his mind before giving himself a fair go at the question. How important would any of those people, he wondered, consider risking a search for him? Black Jack began to think of the issue in terms of his value; as if he were a slave again. He thought it ironic that as a slave, his loss seemed an incontrovertible necessity to warrant his capture and return; whereas now that he were free, it seemed that the urgency of his 'missing in action' status might not run as high among even his more socially liberated compatriots. So, if correct in his assumptions, he realized bitterly, his actual value as Slave might have more to do with the amount of control his Master was permitted over his person and spirit; rather than his monetary worth as a unit of chattel. Consequently, he continued thinking, his value now to the station or his ship would come down to, regardless of how much work he was capable of producing on his own, his value in the eyes of White men as a free Black man. A dead, drowned, Black man, he thought, heaping additional coals on his own head.

As he stood there stewing in his own spite, he saw something strange among the trees at the back of the beach. Perhaps it was his exhaustion, coupled with intense hun-

ger; or perhaps it was the residual salt in Arthur's eyes:
Whichever the case, he would have sworn to his mother
on a Bible that he saw a chicken that was the size of a
horse! It ran past an opening in the brush, paused momentarily, and then vanished. A bird that size wouldn't
have eaten worms, Arthur thought: It would have devoured
snakes! But come to think of it, he hadn't seen any of those
in this paradise.

II

Being quite warm and dry from the sun now, Black
Jack began to explore the bay in the remaining daylight.
He realized that he was extremely thirsty, and so he welcomed his discovery of a small, fresh-water stream running out of the brush and right over the middle of the
beach into the sea. It must come out of the high hills
rimming the beach, he thought. The rear of the beach
remained fairly flat for a few hundred yards, until it met
the base of the hills where it began to rise steeply yet
smoothly. Next to the stream in the middle of the beach
just beyond the high-tide line were two large rock forma-
tions, side-by-side, about the size of huts. Black Jack squatted and drank from the cool stream with a cupped hand as
he eyed the structures. He noticed that they rested on
grassy knolls just above the level of the stream so that they
were afforded not only protection from the rising tide in
front, but also from an unexpected flooding of this small
tributary. In addition to the high grass around their bases,
the rocks were surrounded by large plants which consisted
of a radiata of long, blade-shaped leaves growing from a
center at the ground and spreading out and up to Black
Jack's height. In the very center was a single straight, slender, brown stalk which sported several pods of stringy,

silky, white clumps. It seemed to Black Jack to be the tropical version of a cotton plant.

Circling the two rocks, Black Jack found an opening in one at ground level. It was a small cave, obscured by the exotic plants; and perfectly suited for a man. The floor consisted of warm, dry, soft sand; and the walls and ceiling were composed of solid, smooth stone. The entrance was about three-feet high and the same wide; and that height and width persisted to a depth of about twelve feet. The axis of the cave ran parallel to the beach, and thus perpendicular to the wind and the waves. Black Jack crawled in and found that he had more than ample room to sit, lie down, or even sprawl out. He thought that unless better housing revealed itself in the fading remains of the evening, that this cave would most certainly be his accommodation for the night. Besides, he thought, he would be up early to look for his crew's approaching boats; and so, this humble domicile need only serve him for one night.

Moving about the rock edifices, he began to gather the smooth, long, broad leaves of the exotic cotton plants. He was drawn to them for a reason other than their billowy, white bounty: The leaves reminded him of a plant his mama used in weaving baskets. They were tough and sinewy, and yet soft and smooth at the same time. They were ideal for making a mat on the floor of his abode. Within several minutes he had covered the ground of his hole lengthwise; and a few moments later he had completed adding a crosswise layer on top. He didn't see much that could be done to improve upon his basic design; and so with fresh water and suitable shelter close at hand, his efforts turned to food.

Wandering further upstream, perhaps them little freshwater crayfish would be hidin' out somewhere after all, he thought. After a time, Black Jack's failure to find the familiar delicacy was overshadowed by his sighting of another object; as he once again discovered a completely new creature in this incredible land. Stopping and looking into the water, he believed that he saw a dark object dart from one side of the stream to the other and disappear. After several seconds of unsuccessful staring, he started searching again. Suddenly he saw something. It seemed similar to a snake; strangely somehow, it was swimming. A submarine serpent! Now he had seen everything, he surmised. He surreptitiously secured a stalk and stealthily sneaked to the stream, slipping the stick silently under the surface and soundly striking the black eel as it slithered from side to side.

The eel went limp and floated to the top; and Black Jack fetched it with his stick. It dangled and curved as it wrapped around, with smooth, flat, black sides and fish eyes. Upon close inspection it looked more like a fish than a snake, Black Jack thought; and he wondered if the same held true for its flavor. With no means of starting a fire, Black Jack was faced with enjoying his catch as a cold, raw entree; however, he did not view it as an allegory of his situation, and his spirits were lifted by his good fortune rather than dampened. Black Jack laid the eel upon a rock in the sun; and before long it was warm. His search for a sharp implement in the meanwhile had proved fruitful; and he commenced to slicing open the skin and gutting his find. He managed to produce two large boneless filets; and all in all he ended up with about a pound of meat in hand. He gorged himself. In fact, he made so little time of consuming his booty, that it took another few minutes after finishing to realize that he was full. And shortly after that, he began to feel sleepy. He took a few gulps of the refreshing stream water; meandered back down to the beach; and crawled lazily into his cave. As warm hues of yellow, orange, violet, and blue filed past his dwelling door in their respective salutes, he recounted the blessings which had been bestowed upon him since being washed from the back of the beast. He said his prayers, respectfully requesting God to forgive his nudity and guide his rescuers; and he drifted blissfully off to sleep.

III

Blue strawberries. Arthur was back home in a field on the plantation in Mississippi, naked, picking blue strawberries. Strangely though, it was Winter; for the cold mist of the hoary frost battled with the early morning sun. And weirder still, Arthur was lying down in the frozen black earth between the rows of low plants. The foreman approached on his horse and shouted down to Arthur, "The Master's found a way to cross the Blueberry with the Strawberry. And grow 'em in winter. Now that's progress, Alesworth!" The overseer laughed maniacally as he cracked his whip, stinging Arthur in his exposed fleshy flank.

Black Jack swatted a biting mosquito on his shivering leg as he awoke. He had reflexively curled into a fetal position in his sleep; and now his clenched fingers and drawn-up legs ached and cramped as he attempted to unfurl in all directions. This stretched-out position provided only momentary relief; for as the blood flowed back to his extremities, it took with it what little warmth was left in his torso and abdomen. The ambient temperature of the night air was not anywhere near freezing; however, it was a deep, solid, steady chill which left him with the impression that he might never get warm. As he curled up again, he peered over his shoulder and out at the moonlit night sky. The cold had sharpened his senses and cleared his mind; how-

ever, he was still tired. As he closed his eyes and attempted
to drift back to sleep, he thought that it must be somewhere between one a.m. and four a.m.: No-man's land for
the sleepless.

He awoke again sometime later, chilled to the bone,
and cramping. At some point, he figured, his body had
given up shaking to try and warm itself. Now, he was like
a living dead man, he felt; accepting an inner absence of
heat which was intolerable, but to which he must become
accustom. He could imagine only one solution for his situation: He must move. Crawling from the cave he realized
that his stomach was burning with hunger as well. The
sensation was like drinking cool acid; and its combination
with his overall condition intensified his agony. He felt as
though he wanted to fling himself from the rocky cliffs to
relieve his pain; or even run through the scratchy brush in
order to generate heat upon his skin. He was miserable.
He had not anticipated such an extreme climate swing
between day and night.

He began running back and forth across the beach;
however, he realized after a time that he could not exert
himself enough to offset the chilling effect of his own wind.
Besides, he was only succeeding in intensifying his hunger, he realized. As he passed the rocks on the far end of
the bay, a glimmer at water's edge caught his eye; and he
stopped to investigate.

Gleaming in the moonlight with shells open, as if captive audience to the stars, were hundreds of mussels
perched just above the water. Black Jack had lucked upon
low tide. He reached down to pluck his first snack; and as
he touched the first mollusk, its shell snapped shut as
tightly as the lid on a rich man's coffin. Black Jack studied
the intriguing object in his hand, turning it side to side in
front of his face. Funny, he thought, how even his close

inspection might not reveal that a living creature dwelled inside; save for the fact that he already knew. Now with the casing irreversibly sealed, the effort required to remove its delicious innards would negate the benefit from the actual amount of food gained. It wouldn't be worth it, thought Black Jack. But eat he must; and so he hatched a plan: He would simply place his finger inside the open mussels as he picked them from the rocks, thereby pulling each of their contents out with the stroke of his opposing thumb.

His scheme worked well. The shellfish were tepid and slimy; yet they had a certain tenacity which gave them enough of a rich, meaty quality so as to satisfy Black Jack. He ate continuously for close to an hour, consuming almost fifty mussels. Toward the end, he had forgotten the cold; and he even began to feel relaxed and energetic. It was a more pleasurable awareness than his previously increased alertness. As his suffering and anxiety melted away, he once again began to feel sleepy. Sitting on the sand, he looked at his pile of discarded shells, and then up at the stars. For the first time, he really took the time to look at them. He had stargazed occasionally in Mississippi, but nothing compared to what lay before his eyes here. Running across the sky, the Milky Way was brighter and crisper even in the three-quarter moon light than he had ever seen. Not only did the thicker bands of light show themselves; but he saw well-defined dark holes in the middle of the presently enhanced white area. It seemed that in addition to its dimensions lengthwise, the formation had developed depth and structure. Black Jack suddenly felt as though he were witnessing thousands of silvery fish swimming across the night sky.

Growing weary of his amateur astrology, he helped himself up and began to pad back to his cave. He felt reassured by the impending dawn and the bonanza of sus-

tenance available to him; and he began to plan the coming day. Sleep would come first he thought, as the still
calm of the bay began to blanket him and make him feel
at home. As he was parting from the tide line, however, he
heard a distant lapping sound, like oars in the water. His
feet were being licked by the small waves of some mysterious wake; and he turned a hopeful glance toward the sea.
He strained to see what he thought were shadowy figures
rowing toward the shore; alas the silhouettes dissolved in
the cold mist, sending him no consolation save for the
remnants of their ripples to die upon the sand.

IV

A figure adorned in feathers stands upon a great hill
looking east out over the Pacific Ocean. He sees a large
sailing ship in the offing.

"Ha!" his companion says. "They are good people who
are sailing on the sea; and if you conquer this land and
hold talks with them, you will obtain guns and powder
and become very great!"

V

Black Jack awoke to heavy rain and gray light. The
shifting wind buffeted his home's portal and brought water with it. Fortunately, the downpour was lukewarm and
he was able to shelter himself toward the rear of his cave.
Having missed the dawn, his sense of time was skewed, as
the sun was completely obscured by thick clouds. Huddled
there, he realized that he was sore all over, hungry; and he
needed to relieve himself in both capacities. The full weight
of his predicament was beginning to bear down on him,
he thought. From his bitter brooding sprang an idea. He

would simply begin to weave the sturdy leaves that he had already gathered, into a rain shed of sorts. It seemed entirely feasible to him, looking at the number and size of the long flat blades. He began to weave: A simple over-and-under pattern until he had a working template that began to grow. He became excited as he worked, the activity and pleasure of creating something vitally necessary serving to warm not only his body but also his soul.

The leaves came together tightly and bound one another. For an extra measure of strength, he split the ends and used the sinewy strings within the slats to secure all the sides and corners. Within an hour, he had formed a sizable mat, probably four-feet long by three-feet wide, which promised to shed water. Perhaps he would sail back to Te Awaiti on it, he joked himself.

With a quick glance around, he prioritized his 'to-do' list for the day, and set out into the world. He had seen a log previously lying just upstream and back a ways in a little clearing in the brush. It became his first friend in the bay as he sat upon it and extolled its virtues. The mat performed its duty impeccably as well, fending both wind and rain from Black Jack's head and back. Sitting there dry, warm, and relieved, he began to feel a queer sense of relaxation that seemed to run deeper than the gratification of the immediate moment. The feeling was akin, he thought, to the comfort that comes from a pleasant familiarity with one's surroundings. Like being at home. That was it, he realized, as a single cool drop of rain leapt off the back of his shield and tip-toed down his naked spine: This bay felt like home. He grabbed for a soft fern to complete his job, and was surprised as the plant broke loose from the soil, roots and all. Black Jack noticed a large bulb at the base of the plant, and he thought that it resembled a small potato. With caution, he nibbled at the tuber, and found it to be quite starchy. More food, he delightfully thought to himself. His skin stippled; his scalp tingled; and his groin itched as he stood to mark his territory and the momentous occasion.

Moving back down the stream, he could not see any sign of the previous day's prey, as the rain pelted and rippled the little river's surface. He would gather fern roots, he thought; and then swing by the beach and grab a few mussels. It began to occur to him that a good deal of his time was going to be spent in the act of simply gathering food. He began to pull up fern plants, holding his mat over his head with one hand and pulling the wild potatoes with the other. He went on in this way for about twenty minutes; gathering plants and forming little stacks spread out along the bank; until he had several substantial piles strung out down the side of the stream. As he reached for his next plant, he suddenly heard a sound that startled him; and a murky object scuttled away into the water, too quickly to be identified. Black Jack stared at the spot where it had submerged, his heart racing. Given the variety of new creatures to which he had already been exposed, he feared to imagine this latest revelation of creation. As its dark outline slowly formed beneath the ripples; Black Jack stepped back. When it broke the surface and sprang upward, Black Jack jumped. It had eyes like a fish; and its little head was precariously perched on a long, odd-shaped neck above a round, limbless body which floated on the water. Its nose and mouth had seemingly grown together into one large set of scales protruding from its face, and one large tooth sat at front-and-center of the big proboscis. The duck quacked; and Black Jack laughed. It was the first audible welcome that he had received since arriving at this bay.

From somewhere in the weeds, another duck emerged and joined its mate, treading water and staring back at Black Jack. Slowly they turned, before drifting downstream and eventually hopping back up into the grass. Black Jack wondered how many there were; and how cold duck would taste. Fowl and fern root: It sounded like a decent meal to him, even uncooked. And so, it was not a great stretch of his imagination to gather up his stick from yesterday and hide behind his mat along the edge of the creek. In this virtually uninhabited environment, the birds were actually more curious than fearful; and they began to return upstream as if investigating Black Jack's disappearance.

He stunned one with his first throw; and plunging into the knee-deep creek, he wrung its neck in midstream. Its partner took flight; flapping, flailing, with a furious squawk, a forgotten flurry of floating feathers falling in a fluffy squall. A female, thought Arthur, as he proceeded to pluck the more painted patriarch of the poignantly parted pair. After disposing of the entrails, he decided to eat the bulk of the bird while it was still warm. Black Jack licked the fat from his fingers, gobbled a few fern bulbs, and drank a copious amount of water. At this point, he concluded, his meal must have served as a late brunch. The rain had abated, but he still could not see the sun or determine its position. He wandered back down to the beach to look for boats. As he walked, he realized that he might like some clothes should he meet any would-be rescuers. His awkward situation busied his mind, and he was able to stave off the impending urge to sleep. However, he thought, searching for items to hide his nakedness would only draw him away from his lookout on the beach. In this compromising situation, he opted for the fastest solution and simply tied his mat around his waist. It afforded him little flexibility; however, it served its purpose, and he was free to stand unashamedly in the middle of the beach and scan for boats.

What if they didn't come? he began to wonder. His mind considered every scenario it could generate. He

couldn't stand there indefinitely, he thought. He had to
eat and sleep. And if they cruised by during one of those
times, what then? he pondered. Surely, they would stop
to thoroughly investigate each shore; if they were going to
take the time to travel this far along the coast, he assured
himself. But he wasn't sure. Maybe they wouldn't come
down this far; he worried. Perhaps he should begin walking the rough terrain back to the base, he wondered. What
if he came to an impasse, or worse, became lost, he argued
with himself. Then he began to question whether he
wanted to return at all. After all, he wasn't entirely desti-
tute, just marooned. Standing there with an eye on the
ocean, he began to weigh his incentives: What was waiting for him at Te Awaiti? Surely greater monetary wealth,
but was that what he wanted? he asked himself. His first
encounter with the whale had abated some of his enthusiasm. But what of his family back home? he thought. He
couldn't just suddenly abandon his plan of returning rich,
he told himself. What was happening to him? he quizzed
himself. His entire motivation was shifting like the wet
sand beneath his feet. He was wavering between he knew
not what. Perhaps possible pots of gold or godly paradise.
All he knew was that at that moment, he was full, happy,
and totally free. The realization overwhelmed him, and he
thought that it must have been the same feeling which
had prompted the first man to ever the utter the word,
'Hallelujah!'

He began to grow more and more excited, and hop
from one foot to the other while standing in place. He
threw his arms in the air and spun as he hopped. He began to run back and forth across the beach; and he shouted,
"This is my bay, Lord. This is my bay!" Steadfast in his
newfound resolve, he abandoned his watch on the beach
and dedicated the remainder of the day to the task of home-
steading.

To build a fire, or not to build a fire: He pondered the issue. It seemed natural to him to want a fire. However, without the means to make one for the first time that he could remember, it seemed a wholly unnatural goal. Where the hell did fire come from? he asked himself. The Master had always provided hot coals in a bucket for all the slave quarters. The potbelly stove was always kept going, at least for coals, all year long. If Mama wanted to cook, she lit the wood stove off of the potbelly. If they needed to roast a hog on the spit outside, they carried coals from the potbelly. Come to think of it now, Arthur had never seen a flame spring from nothing. He had always figured that there must be some eternal fire somewhere from whence all flames were seeded. Certainly, he had heard the old-timers talk about rubbing two sticks together; or striking two flint rocks together. However, Black Jack had never seen either method put into practice.

Now that he thought about it, he didn't really need a fire. It was just something that he had always had; and so he had grown accustomed to it so much so that he no longer even appreciated it as a comfort. However, its absence tended to create a vacillating craving within him: Periodically he would obsess about fire in general; eventually he would forget about it for a time. Then, with or without encountering a need for it, the idea of fire would reenter his consciousness. It was a continuous struggle with his desire for fire.

Then there was the practicality of the fire: It really would serve many purposes, he convinced himself. First of all, it would let him be in two places at once, doubling his manpower with one application. His thinking went: He could leave the fire to signal his presence, day or night, while he was free to pursue the other pressing needs of basic living. He really liked that idea. Secondly, he could use the warmth until he made suitable clothing. He really didn't think that he could stand another frigid night. But could he spend the time on starting a fire? he wondered. Where would he begin, and with what materials? And if he were not successful before nightfall, then he would have no fire and no supper. He allowed the thought of being cold and hungry to sharpen his wits.

He knew that friction made heat from handling ropes on the ship. He knew that dry rope, cloth, paper, and wood burned. How did heat become fire? he wondered. He was truly perplexed. Black Jack went to his cave, sat down on his mat, and began to think methodically. He could tell it was the middle of the afternoon, even though the sky was still overcast. It had long since ceased raining; however, everything was covered with moisture. Everything outside his cave, he realized. Looking around, Black Jack saw several pieces of small driftwood within his reach, all bone-dry. He also spotted many desiccated, brown strands of the same leaves as composed his mat. These papery pieces were brittle and flaky; and Black Jack thought that they would make excellent tinder. Along the bottom of the cave wall lay the fragments of many various shells in the sand. He thought that these might be hard enough to mimic flint. A few mussel shells still had their halves connected at the hinge; and he practiced clapping these together like castanets. The idea occurred to him to load the shell with the kindling of dry leaf and wood strands. He closed the shell, allowing a certain amount of tinder to protrude from the tight, thin lips. He then located a broad, flat area on the rocky cave wall; and he began to stroke. Slowly at first, he developed a rhythm as he rubbed the shell continuously back and forth in long swathes across the rock face. As he attained a sustainable pace, he began to increase the speed, pressure, and intensity with which he moved the makeshift mollusk match head. He knew that he must pit his diligence against his curiosity: For frequent stops to look and see would only reward him with what he already knew was not there; but persistence would proudly and graciously display its victory torch for him without his prompting. He rubbed incessantly, just as he had run that day in the fields. Then he was running away; now he was running toward. He pursued the flame. He wanted the fire. He began to sweat. He controlled his breathing. He kept stroking. His arm ached. He exhaled. He ground on. He inhaled. He smelled smoke. He saw no smoke. He rubbed. He exhaled. He sweat. His muscles burned, but the tinder did not. He prayed. He stroked. Nothing.

Finally, he could wait no longer: He turned the shell toward him and looked. The thin edge of tinder had been rubbed black from the heat and had receded back into the lips of the shell. He popped the shell open and saw that the blackening stopped just inside the rim. His analysis: Not enough heat to start a fire. He knew from common sense that he had worked long enough to achieve maximum temperature. Any more rubbing would be a waste of time and effort, and would take away from the need to gather food. He resigned himself to the fact that he would be cold for another night; but he would not allow himself to be hungry.

Black Jack made a quick sweep of the stream. He gathered up his stacks of previously picked potatoes and carried them back to the cave. As he set them down just inside the entrance, a small cloud of smoke met him and stung his eyes and nose. As he winced and wiped his tears, he looked down and noticed the open shell on the floor of the cave. Where once there had been slightly singed tinder, there was a small pile of ash. Arthur's soul soared. He immediately refilled the shell with kindling and set to stroking. He worked a little harder and faster this time; stopping when he smelled smoke. Instead of flipping open

the case like an anxious child, however, he carefully eased
open the shell slightly and began to blow into it gently.
There, suddenly, he saw them: A faint constellation of
dim sparks striving for life, glittering orange against black
as the few sparse flecks of gold in the bottom of a hopeful
prospector's pan. His mouth close to the lips of the shell,
he pensively breathed life into the precarious tinderbox
cupped in his hands; until suddenly a tongue of flame
leapt out at him as a genie from its lamp.

Black Jack set the flaming green-lipped mussel down
and immediately began to place small sticks on top of it.
The twigs were happy to burn, and they welcomed more
wood in turn. Black Jack added bigger pieces as the fire
accelerated. Before long, coals began to form; and Arthur
set out to find larger logs for his flames to lick.

Piles of driftwood lined the shore. Although the top
layers were thoroughly soaked, Black Jack quickly found
dry wood as he searched through sticks which steadily
became less and less damp the deeper he went. Starting
with small stuff, he began to carry the wood back and
stack it just inside the cave as he kept the fire stoked. Soon,
the fire settled into a steady blaze; one which could be
maintained without constant attention. It was a beautiful
fire, thought Black Jack. With an ample bed of coals rimmed
with embers and ash, it lay just inside the cave entrance,
flames dancing a foot high and smoke drawing up the
outer rock face. He left it, confident that it would be strong
enough to roast the duck with which he would return.

Black Jack opted for an eel, actually. He knew what
roast duck was like, and so he wanted to sample the cooked
version of his serpentine friend. Besides, the process was
much less involved, from hunting to cleaning, for the eel;
and Black Jack was in a hurry to return to his plaything,
the fire.

There it was, just as he had left it, minus a few flames. He promptly prodded it, and it leapt back to life. He left the eel outside and decided to investigate the temperature of his cave. It was Heaven, he thought. The air was as warm as sail sheets on a sunny day, and the rock sides reflected the fire's ambient glow. Tonight, he thought, he would be glad that he did not have clothes. He crawled out, rammed a stick into the eel's mouth and down its gullet, and rolled it in the flames until its skin sizzled and bubbled. Then he peeled the hot eel and ate it. All before sundown, he thought boastfully, all before sundown. He felt a sense of progress and accomplishment. He was becoming tired of seeing his own nakedness, however; and now with the presence of fire, he felt that it would most likely be in the best interest of safety, as well as decency, if he procured some type of covering.

The problem of finding something which was actually comfortable enough for him to wear began to loom greater than had the challenge of starting a fire. He had general ideas about solutions, as he had had with the fire; but again there were no quick and easy ways to go about it. Feathers would be good, he thought; however, it would take days to gather enough for just a small loincloth. Then there was the issue of fastening them. Which led Black Jack to think about skins. But he hadn't seen any animals, save for the monstrous apparition that first appeared briefly upon his arrival. He only hoped that the creature had been a figment of his tired imagination. Sitting there feeding wood to his fire, an idea lit upon Black Jack as a divine inspiration: Bird wings. The duck being the largest and easiest to catch, it would be the first thing on Black Jack's busy agenda, he thought. Tomorrow. Darkness knocked nightly near nine he knew; and so now nine drawing nigh, he knocked off for the night. He gave his fire a final feed and retired amidst its mellow orange and yellow glow.

VI

"Who the hell do you think you are, boy?" his foreman snarled as he stared down at Black Jack and kicked
sand on the fire. The man stood tall against the bright
blue midday sky; while Black Jack cowered in the cool
shadows of his cave. "No one asked you; gave you permission to; wanted you to build this fire." the White man
stated as his hostility gave way slightly to sincerity. His
long, brown riding leathers and his matching cowboy hat
were unfamiliar to Arthur; and they made the man's figure all the more intimidating. "Do you want to get us all
killed?" he asked, as he kicked the last blast of sand into
Black Jack's eyes.

Black Jack awoke with sand in his eyes. Rubbing them
made them worse, with the subsequent tearing granting
him at least a blurry compromise. The first thing that he
noticed was the darkness. Then the cold. Had his fire already gone out? he wondered. He fumbled in the dark
until he located an edge of moonlight and crawled toward
it. He came upon the remnants of his fire and reached out
to touch it. As his hand sank into a pile of warm sand, his
heart froze. He instantaneously tried to race through all
the possibilities that did not include someone actually having come along and put out his fire. Wind, protective animals (he had heard of that!), his own thrashing about:
Anything which eased his fear sounded good to him; and
he reported the most convincing choices to himself as he
attempted to utilize sleep as a savior of his sanity. As he
shut his eyes tightly, he thought he saw the first dim beginnings of the dawn. He felt his sovereign resolve to call
this place home begin to dissolve; and he prayed that his
beloved cave did not become his tomb.

VII

Arthur's ear stung from slapping at a phantom mosquito in his sleep. As he came to consciousness, the low whining buzz created the auditory illusion that it was right outside his ear, and then far away simultaneously. It bothered him immensely, and he wrestled with the urge to slap his ear again. As he began to focus on the sound with both ears, it seemed to him to become more like the twanging of a single guitar string. But who and what would pluck incessantly at a single-stringed instrument in the pre-dawn light? he wondered. He sat and looked at his deliberately extinguished fire from inside his cave and listened to the strange music come in and out in waves. After a time, he thought that he heard other bizarre sounds around the instrument at various distances, but all in relatively the same area upstream from him. They sounded like moans. The moaning persisted for awhile and then fell away, along with the string, and all was silent again. The dawn got lighter.

Black Jack sat staring at his dead fire, contemplating what he would have for breakfast. His hunger took precedence over his fear of the unknown noises; because, he reckoned, whatever he had to face it would transpire in the light of day. Granted, he admitted to himself, he would not go in pursuit of his mysterious company; however, he was ready for its confrontation should the occasion arise. Obtaining food was job one at the moment. Thinking it too much trouble to start the fire anew, he decided on cold fern root and mussels for his morning meal. With plenty of bulbs already on hand, Black Jack shot off to the rocks to grab some shellfish. However, when he arrived, he found himself staring down through the pulsating seawater to the elusive beds of mollusks. It was high tide. Bugger, he thought. He would have to wade into cold water, or forego the richer part of his breakfast. As he stood staring out over the bay at the rising sun, he was stunned by a blast of sound from behind. It was like a blow from the Master's hunting horn, only twofold deeper and more terrorizing; and as Black Jack's neck reflexively snapped around to face the threat, his eyes were met with a sight ten times more frightening than the sound itself. There across the beach that he had traversed only moments before were at least a hundred huge men; and in the center stood the massive conch shell blower. As Black Jack's eyes sprung wide with horror, he was more correct in his light-speed surmisal that these men were natives, than in his subsequent thought that their eyes bulged in mimicry of his. For as he suddenly forgot about his nakedness and the proper control of the remainder of his natural entities, the men launched into a militaristic march toward Black Jack which anchored him to his spot like cold iron.

The men sported the same facial tattoos which Black Jack had seen on the Maori in Te Awaiti; however, these men had their long hair tied back; and they wore a loin cloth in lieu of the White man's clothes. They seemed extremely angry with Black Jack. He watched, frozen, as they advanced in unison. They would throw out a foot and lunge down on their bent leg, slap their knee, lunge on the other leg, slap their chest with both hands, snap their head to the side, stick out there tongues as far as possible, and protract their eyes again: All in a heavy, staccato verbal rhythm dominated by what sounded to Black Jack like loud, mad cursing. After a few seconds, Black Jack realized that their movements had the timing and coordination of a precise ritual, rather than an act of aggression; and his fear abated at least as much as he was sure that they were not going to charge upon him and kill him for another few seconds. They did seem intent on scaring the hell out of him, though, he thought. Aside from the fear of being killed and eaten for breakfast, Arthur began to view the onslaught as a loud, scary show. The men wielded spears, which they twirled like batons; and made threatening gestures in the air. They were obviously warriors; however, they occasionally pranced as if dancing. The rhythm they created came mostly from their voices with low, loud, deep—and most of all sharp—blasts of 'ooh' and 'ah' sounds, with their chests and legs serving as drums. It was a far cry from the prim and proper parade detail of the militia back home, Arthur thought, but different still from the snatches of primitive dance that the old-timers had often demonstrated to him late at night. If the African beat he knew could be referred to as rich, heavy and musky in character; then the rhythm being displayed before him was slightly lighter and sweeter, with an inflection of intermittent harmony that unified the body of the music into an eclectic dirge, despite its heavy overtones.

As for the words, Black Jack swore to himself that they were profane insults. Some of them sounded English, and his mind began to piece together recognizable syllables. The staccato chant went, in English phonetics:

TALK-ee, TALK-ee, TALK-in-TAH-mee;
NOT, MAN-you, O THE WRONG-ee
FALK AT YOU, AH REE KEE;
FALK AT YOU, AH REE KEE;
WHERE you, KEE tay, RAY cow, FALK AH RAH;
WHERE you, KEE tay, RAY cow, TAP POO;
WHERE you, KEE tay, RAY cow, FALK ah WAH
    HA;
RAY ah, TAY ee hee
RAY ah, TAY MAH HA
RAY ah, TAY TAP POO

All with strong emphasis on the capitalized syllables.

Ironically, and of course unbeknownst to Black Jack,
the chant actually contained a beautifully spiritual meaning:

Arise and come forth
Illustrious offspring of the gods;
Come forth illustrious ones;
Come forth illustrious ones;
Here the token of alertness;
Here the token of sacredness;
Here the token of acceptance;
Reveal your excellence,
Reveal your power,
Reveal your sacredness.

As this ballad was being extolled vigorously; one warrior broke from the ranks, pranced in front of Black Jack
with high kicks, and retreated. Black Jack at first felt threatened by this sudden advance; however, he held his ground.
Soon, another warrior advanced and retreated with similar
gesturing. Finally, a third warrior moved forward and placed
something on the ground. At the moment he rejoined the
line, all of the men stopped instantaneously, staring bug-
eyed at Black Jack from their frozen positions. The entire
experience had been overwhelming; and he was unsure
what to do next. What he did know, however, was that the
whole ordeal had been directed at him; and that no matter what, he would wager that the object on the ground
was either a welcome or a warning. Seeing as the men
seemed to be waiting at great lengths for Black Jack to
make the next move, he deduced that the object was most
likely an offer of some sort. He knew what his mama had
always told him about offers-'you don't ever want to refuse
'em lest you really want to insult your host'. Black Jack

took his mother's advice to heart at this moment; and he uprooted himself from his spot and picked up the small token.

At the moment he picked up the token, the instantaneous shift in mood within the confined bay was so great, it was as if a large stone had been rolled away from the entrance of some awesome and sacred cave; and as if he had been granted sanctuary among all the people of the world. In the recesses of his mind he heard a large tower bell tolling the strokes of twelve noon in some distant imaginary square. In reality, a hundred women in full Maori dress began to sing and dance in a lovely harmony even more refined than that of their men. Black Jack was led up the hill by the huge entourage into the forest. He was amazed to see a full Maori village just a few hundred yards from where he had spent the last couple of days. Hidden among the trees and brush were many huts, canoes, and one structure which actually resembled an English house. Its frontal facade consisted of large red beams joined in a sloping gable, covered with elaborate carvings. It reminded him of his recent tryst.

Being brought into the great house, Black Jack was offered a robe of soft skins and feathers by several women. Upon being clothed, he was led to a great table at which sat three large men in similar robes and feather caps.

"Kia Ora." said the biggest man. He meant, "Greetings."

Black Jack felt very welcome now; and he began to feel more so when the women started bringing in the food. They brought in various dishes, one after the other, until the table was full of steaming delicacies much like those at Black Jack's first feast. Of course, two new additions to which he had been recently introduced were present: The duck and the eel. Also, a new item caught Black Jack's eye; one that seemed familiar: A basket of big, orange, egg-

shaped vegetables piqued his curiosity. As the men ges-
tured for him to eat, Arthur went straight for these strange
objects and discovered that they were, indeed, sweet potatoes. If ever a gustatory sensation could evoke emotional
memories and connect one to so many experiences of the
past, it was Black Jack's tasting of the familiar yams. He
instantly felt closer to his present company, regardless of
their cultural differences; and he even began to feel a bond
forming for the place above and beyond his original personal predilection for what he had perceived as a private
paradise.

The large man spread out his arms over the table, then
up at the ceiling. He looked around with a distant gaze
that seemed to penetrate the walls and encompass infin-
ity; and he said, "Pukatea!"

The other feathered men grimaced and smiled; and
said, "Pukatea!" as they stuffed their faces with both hands.

Black Jack kept pace with the men and did not slow
down on his eating. He and the men had been left alone
in the large hall, with women scurrying in occasionally to
replenish certain dishes or attend to one thing or another.
The men did not talk for the first hour; and so didn't
Black Jack, as he definitely wanted to please his company.
Besides, the food was excellent; and oddly, he felt very
relaxed. He realized that the men were very important
within this villa; and that he was being treated, at least for
now, as an equal. It was for him a very honoring yet hum-
bling experience. As the meal proceeded into the second
hour, Black Jack saw that the rest of the pa seemed to be
getting on with its daily activities, leaving him with the
impression that perhaps he and the men would be attended to hand-and-foot for some time to come. His theory
proved correct. When the men were through eating, they
made no movements that suggested that they intended to
rush off to work. Black Jack was game for that plan. He

leaned back with them, and waited for them to initiate conversation. The first thing they did was break out their pipes and light up a smoke. Then they commenced to engage in animated chitchat and manly laughter. Black Jack remained the pleasant observer, sitting there attentive and smiling. He wondered how he would ever communicate with them.

In the middle of one of their exchanges, the largest man turned from his compatriots in mid-sentence and began to address Black Jack in Maori, as if he were saying, "Yes, yes, dear fellows; and what do you think of the matter, chap?" His friendly inquisitor looked at Black Jack and smiled; however, the embarrassed tension began to spread across his face, as the inevitable, and perhaps heretofore known, issue of the verbal barrier raised its ugly head. And after such a lovely breakfast, thought Black Jack. All four men seemed to silently voice the mature opinion that it would be naïve of them to pretend that the purpose of their gathering, if not originally planned to be so, could at least now begin to serve as a learning experience for each of them. Their male sensibilities fell into place and they logically began with the simplest of social niceties. The Maori men began by individually putting their hands to their chests and stating their names. The largest of the Maori pointed to his chest and said, "Ruaoneone." Black Jack reciprocated with his whaling moniker, as he wanted to maintain an authoritative image, at least in the minds of his obviously power-oriented hosts.

"Black Jack!" they all repeated in unison, impressed with his name. These men had all encountered the White man's language before; and aside from being accustomed to hearing and even speaking bits of it, actually found many of the sounds and syntax to be strikingly similar to their own. The group proceeded with the basic etiquette of introductory subjects; and progressed to more complex topics as the day went on. These Maori men, it seemed to Black Jack, had all the time in the world to do whatever pleased them. All of their needs were attended to throughout the day, and Black Jack was content to remain with them and learn the Maori language and customs. The men actually knew enough English to fill in the gaps when an impasse arose; however, Black Jack soon picked up enough Maori words to communicate a good deal of his story. What could not be immediately understood verbally was frequently facilitated with body language. Between hand gesturing, Maori, and pieces of English, the following represents the gist of what transpired over the course of the day:

"You speak the White man's tongue, and yet you are as black as night. What of that?" the Chief asked Black Jack.

"I come here from the land of the White man. They captured my people as slaves from the land of the Black man." said Black Jack.

"I did not know that such a land existed. That is good to know. But to me, you are a black White man. I shall call you, 'Black Jack White'; and it shall be known among my people forever that on this day, Black Jack White came to Pukatea." The Chief leaned forward and took one of Black Jack's hands and clasped his fingers. With his other hand, he pulled Black Jack's head forward and touched his nose to Black Jack's. He stared into Black Jack's eyes for a moment, and then released him. The other two men repeated the gesture, or 'hongi', with Black Jack, and then all four men laughed happily. They continued to eat, drink, smoke, laugh, and talk.

"When you first came out of the water, we thought you were the Taniwha." continued the Chief.

"What is the Taniwha?" asked Black Jack.

"He is a great beast of the land, sky, and sea. He takes many forms, and one never knows where he will appear next. We must always keep a lookout for the Taniwha, or he will destroy us." said the Chief.

"I am not the Taniwha." said Black Jack smiling.

"We knew that when you did not kill the Moa. The Taniwha would have seized upon the Moa." said the Chief, slightly disappointed. Black Jack knew that he spoke of the giant bird. He was relieved that it had not been a hallucination. "Then we thought you were the angry ghost of one of our ancestors." continued the Chief. "You see, when one of our people dies, we leave their bodies in a cave until they turn completely to bone. Then we return for the bones and bury them. When you went into the cave, we thought that perhaps we had overlooked someone, and they had come back to punish us!" The Chief began to laugh at his own story, and the other three followed suit. The Chief went on, "Then you ate, drank, defecated, and slept! No ghost that we know of would desecrate his own tomb, so you had to be human! From then on, we just watched you to see if you were the kind of person we wanted to meet." Black Jack chuckled nervously. He supposed that he had passed the test. The Chief began again, "You show great skill and power in using your surroundings, Black Jack. That impresses us. We have never seen a White man do the things you have demonstrated. Especially the fire!" The Chief sat back as he finished, truly admiring Black Jack.

Black Jack basked in the glow of approval for a moment, and then feeling emboldened by the acceptance of these wonderful people, asked, "If you liked it so much, then why did you put it out?"

The Chief looked at his advisors, who returned his concern; and they all turned to Black Jack, hesitating to respond. The Chief spoke up, "Black Jack, my people are under serious threat these days. We have word that a great warring chief is moving south along the coast in hopes of conquering all alien tribes. Therefore, we cannot risk being detected at this point; and that includes building fires. You yourself can attest to how difficult it was to detect us." The Chief said with a pensive smile. He continued, "You will also recall that you saw no canoes, and no people. We have been fishing and hunting at night."

Black Jack allowed the Chief's words to sink in. He was surprised at the concept of Maori fighting Maori. In his limited knowledge, he thought that it was all one large tribe. He said, "Well without fire, then how was this food cooked?"

The Chief perked up as if to compliment Black Jack's astute question, and he replied, "The Earth is our oven. No flames dance about and say, 'Here we are', so that our enemies may come and cook and eat us with our own fires!" The Chief seemed angry; however, Black Jack knew that the anger was not directed toward him.

In an effort to appease his host, Black Jack quickly changed the subject and asked, "Who is this chief that you speak of?"

The others looked at one another with knowledgeable concern; and then Ruaoneone replied, "It is Te Rauparaha." A heavy shadow seemed to fall over the room as the name was spoken. A moment of morose silence followed. Then Ruaoneone said, "He is a bad chief. He makes war for no good reason. We don't like him." Ruaoneone looked at his men as he said this; and they laughed nervously at the frank admission of their chief, mimicking his gestures of dislike. Then Ruaoneone seemed to grow indignant again as he drew up his chest and grimaced. He motioned for one of the nearby women to come to him. He spoke with her in hushed tones of fluent Maori; and Black Jack could not understand him fully. The Chief seemed to be asking her to bring him something.

She returned with a large, smooth, round stone. It was elongated and thinner on one end, and broader along the bottom. The Chief removed one of the uneaten fern roots from the table, placed it on the floor in front of him; and slowly brought the large stone down on top of it. The bulb was pulverized. He then turned his eyes up at Black Jack as if to determine the effect of his lesson on his guest. Black Jack was not completely certain as to the purpose of the display in context with the current topic; however, he humored the Chief with an obligatory series of nods and smiles.

Ruaoneone then motioned to the woman again; and this time she produced a human skull and presented it solemnly to the Chief. Ruaoneone placed the skull on the floor facing Black Jack and brought the round rock above his head with both hands. Shooting a glance at Black Jack to ensure his attention, he slammed the stone down squarely onto the skull; smashing it to smithereens while simultaneously shouting, "Te Rauparaha!"

Chapter 12

THE DAYS

They gave me a house and a wife. Fed me like a king, and told me to enjoy myself. They must like me. Said I was the first White man to come without a canoe or the evil spirits.

It seems that they believe the White man travels with some sort of invisible demons that kill their people without weapons. They have told me that every time a new White man's canoe arrives, the bad spirits march slowly down the coast from village to village. The spirits are cowardly warriors, the people here say, for they attack without showing their faces; and they kill the children and the very old. The people here say that the evil spirits have killed more Maori in the last few years than all the marauding chiefs put together. The only good thing about the spirits: The people here say that the evil White man's spirits kill all Maori equally, without favoring one tribe over the other. In that way, they say, the killing has been fair without destroying the balance of power. Although, they say, with all the tribes being smaller now, it is the more peaceful tribes which suffer at the hands of aggressive chiefs like Te Rauparaha.

Their language is not very hard to pick up. I have been here a week now, and I can talk more freely now with everyone without as much hand waving and finger pointing and jumping around like some fool. The young ones love that. They point and laugh and carry on something fierce when I try to ask the simplest things like where the toilet is or when the next meal is or even what I am supposed to do to help around the place. The Chief told me to relax, but I can't sit around and do nothing. Even he goes hunting with his mates; and my wife busies herself with womanly things with her women friends. They start early in the morning getting the fire in the ground all hotted up again. It seems they do the same thing like we did back home with the potbelly stove. They just keep the coals going, forever and ever. And there's always meat of some sort stewin' away down in them pits, turnin' nice and soft. It gets wrapped in the big leaves that grow around here. Then they cover it up with rocks and it's just like a proper oven.

The ladies also sit around and make things all day long. They make the feather robes and caps, the woven mats and baskets, and even some whale-bone tools. However, they are absolutely not allowed (and I have seen this enforced quite strongly) to engage in or go anywhere near the wood when it is being carved. The men believe that the carving is sacred only to them; and that even the scent of a woman around the wood while the shavings are present will destroy its magic. The same holds true for something else that I have come to know here. There is a very precious looking green stone here which everyone holds in the highest regard. They use it for weapons, jewelry, and tools. Some of it is harder to see light through and has swirls in it, while other pieces can almost be seen through with nothing but the most brilliant green present. I myself am impressed with this stone, as I have never seen anything like it. It is unique unto itself even in this remarkable place. I have seen no other precious stones here, nor even a hint of gold or silver. Aside from an obvious material value, however, it seems that the green stone is held in the highest mystical regard by everyone here.

Everything that requires an implement can be served with something fashioned in whale bone; however, the higher members of the tribe, or 'iwi' as they call it here, have all the identical items made in greenstone. That includes fishhooks, knives, necklaces, and battle-axes.

For the Chief, his greenstone accessories seems to be indispensable, as though they are part of his spirit and strength. He went to great lengths to show me his prize possession: His 'mere'. It is a big, long, flat blade, about sixteen-inches long and six-inches wide at the broadest point. It is hard to describe, but it is shaped like a flounder fish or a beaver tail, with a handle at one end. The rounded edge is sharpened somehow, and I reckon they use it like some kind of weapon in battle. To see the Chief wave it back and forth in the air makes me think that he must go after people with it; but I can't imagine it being much use for nothing more than slappin' people up side the head with. I mean, it don't have a point like a sword; and I can't see it gettin' stuck into someone or anything like that. Maybe that's why this tribe is so peaceful. All this big loud talk about war and killing and eating people: I just can't see it. All these people want to do is eat and be happy. I think they just like to keep their enemies scared away.

II

Ten days here and I have learned a lot. I went out with the Chief and his men; and we speared a pig. I made the spear myself from a really hard wood here they call 'Rimu'. They say I have the magic and that I will make a good warrior, perhaps even a chief.

I have been training with the men and boys of the pa, learning all the moves and chants. I have my own mere, which is only whalebone now for practice, and an assortment of fishing gear and jewelry. They say when I make my first kill that I will no longer be a White man, but they also say that I will be the first White man to become a true Maori. They really like me, I can tell.

III

After a fortnight with my new wife, I think she loves me. I believe that I am falling in love with her as well. I think of my beloved back home and our unborn child, and I feel rather guilty. However, I could not refuse the gracious offer of my hosts. Besides, what man can turn away a beautiful woman when she is offered as a willing bride? I tried to remain above my feelings for her, as a visitor in a temporary situation which he cannot control; however, her constant attention and affectionate admiration for me have softened my spirit to the point that I cannot resist feeling kindred toward her. She is exquisite. I could not have chosen a more beautiful woman if the Chief had lined up all the females in the village and let me take all day to pick. She seemed to be ready for marriage. She was brought in by the Chief's attendants; and she made no attempt to be coy or avert her eyes or appear unreceptive in any way.

She is remarkable. Unlike any woman I have seen in the pa, except for the Chief's wife, she has green eyes. Green like the stone. It is shocking, really. And although I must remain mature and hide my embarrassment at the fact, the young women of the pa dress themselves so that their bosom is fully uncovered and visible at all times. For someone who is not used to it, the sight can be quite distracting; however, I must confess that my Kumari has the finest pair in the village, and my eyes have no problem whatsoever remaining faithful to her in that regard, either face or figure. She spares no effort in pleasuring me, yet I do not feel as though she is my loyal servant. We truly seem to be developing a spiritual bond, deeper somehow than what I shared with Lalani back home. Getting betrothed to her was like a ritual to formalize a fact between childhood sweethearts. It seems now that she had just always been a good friend, and the only girl around who was even remotely attractive. We were always close, but there were always those gaps which we couldn't reach across (like absolute trust and understanding); and because of the lack of choice, we overlooked those differences in light of holding on to what we did have.

Now, strangely, I have many new choices and no choice at present concerning her. For now I will let Lalani, and her memory, rest somewhere in my soul until I can pay her some attention. I have Kumari, and she is becoming my world. I awake at dawn and her hands are already upon me, exploring my body like a new land. We make love like sharks make blood in the water; and we are always late for breakfast. At night, she has begun to break away early from her work mates; and she is waiting for me when I get in from training. She attends to every particular detail of my grooming; and she asks me what I think about everything that she makes and wears. The women have begun her moko. She wants to know if I am going to start my face. I tell her I don't know and laugh; and she respects me when I change the subject.

IV

Kumari, the Chief, his wife, and I took the pa's war canoe out on the bay for a little tour today to mark the passing of my first moon here. Well, we and a couple-hundred men in full war dress. It was an exercise of sorts; that's what the Chief told me; but I think he had told his wife it was a pleasure cruise, judging from the quarrel they were having. It was a beautiful day: Clear, sunny, and warm with very little breeze. It's one of the reasons we went out, being that the visibility showed no sign of advancing war vessels of any kind. Our boat is about one-hundred-feet long, carved from a single tree. The Chief says that he can go pretty far; he just doesn't want to. Besides, he says, he would never want to go as far as the White man goes. The Maori boats can't take that much water. The Whites are here, he says, because they have killed all of the whales that they were originally given. The Maori only kill one occasionally for what they need, he says. He also says that he likes how the White man has put a top over the boats to keep the water out, but he doesn't want to do that. He thinks that is how the evil spirits hide to get over here.

His is a small war canoe, the Chief says: The one which Te Rauparaha comes in will be much larger and will carry several-hundred men. Ruaoneone says he doesn't know how Te Rauparaha finds such large trees. He seems a little jealous to me on that point. He says that he does not know for sure when Te Rauparaha will come, but that he is ready. I hope the old bastard never comes. I just want to live here in peace with Kumari forever.

Chapter 13

ROBULLA COMETH

June 24th, 1828. Tory Channel:

*A*h, *The Elizabeth, my darling. Good to see you again. You float so gracefully, so properly, when you come to dance in my waters. But you and I both know that you are my whore, and that you have come to do my bidding once again: For a price! Right my precious? And what will your price be this time? Eh, my little bobbing British brothel bitch? Never mind, you will give me what I want in the end, just like last time.*

It will start just the same. You will see me coming in this big boat which is so odd to you. Your captain will throw out some fake greeting and ready your men on deck as he shits his pants. This time he will know my name, though. At a distance, he will recognize me, and order his men to stand down. Fool. I could have you all for lunch without breaking a sweat. But you don't know that I can't afford that. Can't afford hav-

ing your flax-white asses telling everyone back home how savage we are. No, because then you would stop coming. And stop bringing your guns. My guns.

Here they come. Roll out the barrel! Yes, that's it. Try to appease me with your tobacco and your junk. Very nice. Is that how you conquer all your lands? Very impressive. Oh yes, lots of whale meat and bones. Haven't seen that before! Idiots. Yes, I'll play your game, but not for much longer. Your captain can see that I am growing impatient. He wants to protect his interests here. His business venture. Yes, captain. I can help. I will keep those other bad, mean, nasty Maori at bay, so to speak. With what, you say? No, no, I couldn't, I shouldn't, see this year's model of muskets? Oh, Captain, you make me blush. They're so big. You can't see me mocking your dumb white ass behind my battle-hewn stone face, can you? All right, name your price, captain. Make it good though; I really don't feel like getting bloody today.

A man you say? Have I seen a White man in the water or on shore? Well, yes, captain: There's more of you all the time. Your point? I like the way you kowtow to me when I am standing impudently upon your deck.

He's White, but he's not. Now, you've been hitting that grog again, right captain? He's black. A black White man. Goes by the name of Arthur. Your cabin boy. Gotcha. You want him back. Five muskets now as a deposit, and twenty more with ammunition when I return with your manservant. He's somewhere close. Like where, at the bottom? South or North? You don't know. Big help you are. You don't really want your boy back, do you! These are old muskets, aren't they, I just feel it. Without powder, they are useless. You're slogging us off, aren't you captain? All right, I'll play your silly little game. I'll find your black White man, and I'll be back. And stop calling me 'Robulla'. I don't know where you got that shit. My name is Te Rauparaha.

II

There he goes: Robulla the scoundrel. Like a rogue possum rummaging through alleyways at night, that one. But I've got his number, oh yes; no one pulls the wool over this captain's eyes.

It seems that our illustrious friend imagines himself to be some great chief; from up North at Kapiti, all the way down to Kaikoura. It seems that he has four or five tribes under his thumb. To me, he just sails around with the same group of rejects bullying his own people. All the Maori I've encountered don't want anything to do with him. They're all quite settled now in their respective tribes and lands, with peace and plenty to go around. They say Robulla—sorry, Te Rauparaha—just wants to cause trouble. Worse than that, they say that he is just an opportunist who is seeking glory. He fights his own people with the White man's weapons. Now there's a hero! Poor dumb bastard.

Yes, we chuck him a few of our muskets that have rusted in the hold. Somehow, he gets them working; and, oh, the sound! Like a child with a new toy, he is. I think he believes himself to be the new God of Thunder when the hammer finally chances upon a spot of dry powder. And then off he goes, to terrorize innocent people. Oh well, at least it can be said that it sends him on his way as quickly as he came.

What an odd bird, though. He's a bit old to be running up and down the countryside like a young warrior. I reckon he's got to be getting on sixty or so, which would put him being born right around the time Captain Cook was first here. A shame the good Captain didn't fire a well-placed shot then.

Then again, I've got to give some credit of intelligence to my dubious mate. He did ferret us out for what we were worth. Weren't here a fortnight last year when he comes sailing up in his fortress with his hundreds of men. I must admit, it did put me on the ready. They disarmed us straight away though when their intentions became clear. What a riot! They offered up some poor bugger who had jumped ship years before and been pushed around from tribe to tribe until he had learned to dress and feed himself, but not much else. He wasn't much good to us with his wits being gone and all, but we took him anyway just to show good will toward our local shore patrol.

We just wanted them to shove off and leave us alone to bring in the whales, but of course, we treated them as royalty. I didn't feel good giving them muskets, but I suppose that as long as they are not using them on us, then perhaps we are helping to bring civility to this coast. The Maori are definitely not competing with us on any significant scale for the whale, so I do not consider them a nuisance overall. However, this gentleman may be on his way to wearing out his welcome.

Perhaps he will be a man of his word and bring the Harper back to me. It is a whim, I know, but I really do not like losing anything of value. We are very busy, and our resources are limited in our short time here. That boy needs to at least pay for his passage over here before I consider him dispensable. Besides, if what the Australians say is true about his being out in their skiff, he shall be severely punished.

Chapter 14

BLACK AND BLOODY

K umari and I were walking the sky that night. I was telling her about thunderstorms; and about how the air smelled when lightning came down out of the clouds before it rained. Her love made me feel like when I breathed that air before the storm, I was telling her.

We thought it was a whale at first. Bearing down on us, it blended in with the black bay, only the white caps on the bow breaking through the night to be seen on the beach. We were celebrating before it came. Before *he* came.

Ruaoneone had lifted the ban on fire for one night, and look what happened. It was my fault really. I know now for two reasons my presence could have shaped the fate of that night; but which one and why I knew not then. Nor perhaps might I have wanted to.

For had any of Te Rauparaha's intentions been known, they would surely have stripped my soul of any of its naïve preconceptions about having reached my romantic destiny sitting there with Kumari in my arms; or even fulfilling some preordained charmed existence with this peaceful and loving tribe. As the looming figure of Te Rauparaha's massive war vessel glided menacingly up to the shore, our music stopped and the mood froze.

II

"Dammit, I really didn't feel like working tonight." Ruaoneone said to his wife as he dropped his roasted pork leg in the sand. She echoed his displeasure with a grunt and a look of disdain toward the uninvited visitors. The Chief stood up and motioned for the usual welcoming committee to assemble and do their duty. They responded quickly, also sharing Ruaoneone's disgust, but not wanting to upset their leader further. The women gathered up the children and traipsed languidly back to the higher ground of the pa, knowing that any activity subsequent to the wero would be relegated to the realm of the men, given the late hour and rudeness of the visit. "I don't know what to expect from this joker, so make it a good one, men." Ruaoneone prompted his warriors.

About that time, Te Rauparaha stood upon the bow of his boat and began to wave a pair of large fern branches, one in each hand. This being the Maori symbol for a peaceful visit, all of Ruaoneone's men felt a sense of relief. There would be no bloodshed tonight, they thought. Te Rauparaha signaled his men to remain on the boat, and he approached Ruaoneone. The two chiefs clasped hands and touched noses. They talked in low tones as the village men milled around idly awaiting the outcome of this meeting.

One of the men on the beach that night was Black Jack. He had been enjoying a quiet evening, arm in arm with Kumari, when the towering shadow had sailed in. Now, as he watched his young lover file up the hill along with the other women, he felt a sense of apprehension creeping over the night. He watched the two chiefs talking, sizing up the famous chief about which he had heard so much. The man really didn't seem that impressive, Black Jack thought to himself. Without boasting to himself, Black Jack realized that he was at least a head taller than the man, and some forty years his junior. Without all those men and a nasty reputation behind him, thought Black Jack, the little general before him would be nothing to fear. Black Jack had heard that the same was true for Napoleon: A little man with a big army and a bad reputation. Black Jack thought from then on, he would call Te Rauparaha, 'The Maori Napoleon'.

Ruaoneone began to glance at Black Jack as he spoke with Te Rauparaha. He beckoned Black Jack over after a time; and the three engaged in talk. Ruaoneone said to Black Jack, "Black Jack, this is Te Rauparaha, the great chief from the North. He comes in peace tonight to ask our help."

Black Jack respectfully addressed Te Rauparaha, "Ah, yes, I have heard many good things about you. It is an honor to meet you." Te Rauparaha acknowledged his respectful greeting and the two engaged in hongi.

Ruaoneone spoke up again, "Black Jack, it seems that Te Rauparaha has some official business concerning your ship. Your Captain and the honorable Chief here have been negotiating some rites of passage issues. The issues are delicate and complex; and the Chief would graciously like to request your assistance." Ruaoneone spoke authoritatively to Black Jack, even though both of them knew that neither had the slightest knowledge of Te Rauparaha's true intentions.

Black Jack turned and spoke directly to Te Rauparaha, "The Captain would like me to return to the ship then?"

Te Rauparaha broke his arrogant stance briefly, and assured Black Jack with a smile, "No, no, son. Nothing of the sort. Your captain has given up hope of your returning from your newfound life here. He merely wishes to see your face and to know that you are getting along. He mentioned that you were about the area; and I told him that I had briefly seen a man of your description. We both agree that you would greatly facilitate talks between your good Captain and me. Don't you think so?"

Black Jack was actually impressed with Te Rauparaha's congenial nature and the smooth manner with which he made his request. He looked at Ruaoneone as for advice; however, his mentor seemed to be at a loss for words. Turning back to Te Rauparaha, he said, "And I am to sail with you? When will we go, and how far is it?"

Te Rauparaha hid his appreciation of Black Jack's boyish curiosity, and replied, "We will leave at dawn. It is just about an hour up the coast to Te Awaiti by water. My men and I are going to visit some other neighbors tonight where we will sleep. In the morning, we will swing by and pick you up here; and we will have you back by midday. How does that sound?"

Again, Black Jack fell victim to Te Rauparaha's polite charm, and with no opinion being offered by Ruaoneone, he accepted Te Rauparaha's terms and agreed to the favor. Te Rauparaha seemed pleased, and with parting pleasantries, he bid his hosts goodnight and set sail in his floating fortress.

As its immense form slowly disappeared around the rock cave corner of the bay, Black Jack and Ruaoneone shuddered as if awaking from some unknown spell.

Black Jack asked Ruaoneone as they were walking up the hill, "Do you believe him, Chief?"

Ruaoneone said, "He came waving the green branches of peace. As a Maori, he is bound by his word to spare us. Obviously, he needs you; so perhaps your help will help us all. Just be careful, my son. I will look forward to your return." With that, Ruaoneone returned to his whare.

As Black Jack found his way under the soft blanket of his own bed, he discovered the firm, supple, young skin of his eager bride waiting to quell his fears about the coming day.

III

Arthur adorned himself in full Maori war dress. He was proud of his new life with his new tribe; and he wanted to show it. If it were true what Te Rauparaha had said, then he had nothing to fear from his former captain. Perhaps, he thought, the riches of a successful season, along with the local scenery, were softening the old man. Regardless, he told himself, there was no way that Arthur could return to the ship now, given his present circumstances.

Te Rauparaha's canoe rounded the rocks just before the rising sun breached the hazy horizon. Black Jack stood at attention, a solitary figure: Brazen fireball bronzed warrior facing the glittering sea, solemn black silhouette back to the flat, wet beach. He threw a hailing hand into the air at the approaching boat. Te Rauparaha did not smile; nor did he look into Black Jack's eyes, as he despondently returned a half-hearted wave.

"Get in." said Te Rauparaha blankly.

Black Jack had not known what to expect from his new acquaintances, nor had he given it much thought in the overnight. However, now he became aware of the acute lack of communication from his host as he stood awkwardly in the middle of the boat. Any instructions from his new commandant would have been appreciated, no matter how blunt. Black Jack was ready to respond, whether as a civilian or a militant; however, no orders were forthcoming. The void of directions or decency heightened his dilemma and brought on a hint of resentment within Black Jack. Te Rauparaha certainly did not seem as gracious now as he had when asking a favor. It bothered Black Jack, but he held his tongue.

For close to an hour Black Jack stood, riding the waves from his vantage in the bow just behind Te Rauparaha. The Chief turned his head from side to side periodically, as a monarch surveying his kingdom. Black Jack began to get a sense of Te Rauparaha's arrogance; and it did not bode well in light of the man's reputation. Black Jack began to think that the trip held a clandestine significance which he was in no position to question; and he did not like the thought of being helpless in a bad situation. Helplessness was the predecessor of Death, he reckoned.

The day itself was beautiful. The weather was clear and dry, and a light, cool breeze stippled the china-blue water of Tory Channel. Along the way, they had seen the odd spout or two of wayward whales; however, now they were in the thick of a group of migrating whales which clogged the channel. The backs of the whales bobbed and dipped intermittently like pickles in a barrel, bumping the boat gently from all directions. The whales were inbound like the boat; and so as they approached the ships at Te Awaiti, Te Rauparaha and his gang heard the distant cry of the lookout and saw men scrambling on the beach.

Black Jack's captain and his crew were called on deck by the combined commotion, and they clamored about the ship, confused as to which party should gain precedence. The Captain leant his expertise to their priorities.

"All hands stand fast. Lower the ladder!" he boomed as Te Rauparaha's boat pulled alongside. "Let the shore crew do their job. You do yours!" he added, as he scanned the long vessel for his anticipated parcel. He recognized Arthur instantly, and his face dropped in disapproval. "Harper! What is that ridiculous outfit that you have on?" he demanded.

Te Rauparaha quickly stepped in front of Black Jack on the bow as he shouted up to the Captain in broken English. "Good Sir, do not be too harsh on the boy. We found him in this horrible state in the hands of a rogue tribe just down the coast." He turned to Black Jack and whispered reassurances in his ear, "The captain is upset. He was terribly troubled with your disappearance and he has been worried sick. Pay him no mind. I will handle this." Te Rauparaha smiled widely and hailed the Captain as he made for the rope ladder. He smiled and spoke loudly as he climbed. "Good Captain, I have brought you your man, and I assure you that he is in excellent condition. If we can conclude our bargain, then I will be on my way. I see that you are very busy." he said as he stopped near the top rung to cast a glance at a skiff in hot pursuit of a whale.

The Captain relaxed momentarily and looked in the direction of the hunted whale. He forced a smile and said, "Ah yes, Robulla. We are doing all right these days, thanks to you. Please, forgive my rudeness. Do come aboard."

On cue, Te Rauparaha smiled graciously and resumed his climb. Stepping to the Captain's side on deck, he exclaimed, "Do you not think it is a beautiful day, Captain!" The Captain quickly agreed with conciliatory nods and smiles. Te Rauparaha continued, "Captain, now that we are out of ear shot of your man, I feel that it is safe to tell you." He lowered his eyes and voice as he put a hand on the Captain's shoulder. He carried on with feigned concern, "Captain, your boy believes that he is a Maori now. It is going to take considerable effort on your part to reinstate a sense of discipline in him. I suggest that you take it slowly, for your sake."

The Captain looked worried and asked, "What do you mean?"

Te Rauparaha buried the hook and said, "He is wise in the ways of our warriors now. He could be a threat to your crew's safety if he is angered. He is like a wild beast now." Te Rauparaha waited for the full effect of his words to hit the Captain as he glanced over the side of the ship. He continued, "Now my advice is to let me counsel him on what your wishes are and the conditions he must meet for returning to proper service. He is aware of our proposed deal, so allow me to have the guns so that I may show him your sincerity. Once the muskets are safely in the ship, then I believe that he will feel that you are receiving him with a forgiving heart. Ooh, look, they've got him!" Te Rauparaha pointed excitedly to a flailing harpooned whale as he finished his suggestion.

The Captain considered his words in a newly distracted and excited state, and replied, "Yes, certainly. Show him that I mean business, I mean need business, I mean need him back . . ."

Te Rauparaha seized upon the opportunity and said, "Yes, yes, Captain, certainly I will help this matter. I see the crates stacked over there. If your men could just chuck them down to my men, then I will go down and prepare your boy."

The Captain, eyes still fixed on the frantic harpooned whale, issued the order for the guns to go down. "Yes, yes, away with the muskets, just as discussed at morning quarters. We've got more pressing business now!"

Te Rauparaha scrambled down the ladder as the narrow, long, wooden boxes were lowered down with ropes. He stood talking quietly to Black Jack while stealing glances up to the inattentive captain. As the last of the crates were lowered down, Te Rauparaha ushered Black Jack to the ladder and stood there alongside him looking up. He stopped Black Jack by the nape of the neck, as he shouted up to the Captain, "Right, then, nice visiting with you Captain. We'll be away now." Te Rauparaha flicked his fingers at his rowers and the great boat set off.

The Captain of The Elizabeth cast a glance down at the boat, then looked calmly back to the jumping whale. Suddenly, he turned and scanned his deck wildly for his cabin boy. Seeing nothing but the sniggering faces of his busy crew, he then looked down at the departing boat and the back of Black Jack being led aft by Te Rauparaha. The Captain yelled out in panic, "You there, scoundrel, whatever do you think you are doing?"

IV

The sound of nails being pried from resinous wood, the timberous slapping of pine boards being discarded onto a solid hardwood hull, and the continuous beat of five-hundred paddles all colluded and conducted themselves within the streamlined skimming symphony being comported down the coast.

Te Rauparaha looked one-eyed down the matte-silver barrel of a new musket. "The old man was glad to see you, son." he said, as he fired a dummy shot. "Nice." he said as he sequestered the nodding approval of the oarsmen nearby. "All right, who's got the powder?" he demanded, looking around the boat. As a man came rushing forward carrying a small animal-skin bag, Te Rauparaha smiled at Black Jack and then at the coast. He took the sac from the warrior and loaded a charge. He cocked the hammer back, raised the gun, and again looked straight down the barrel. He squeezed the trigger. A beautiful silver cloud and white sparks erupted over Te Rauparaha's head; and a resonant, full-bodied blast of sound echoed over the water toward land. Te Rauparaha lowered the musket, visibly pleased, and said to Black Jack, "They just get better every year."

Te Rauparaha instructed his men to throw the crate scraps overboard; and to go ahead and load a full shot with ball for each of the twenty-five muskets. He then engaged in friendly conversation with Black Jack. He said, "You see, all in a day's work. And back for lunch, just as I promised." Black Jack nodded apprehensively. Te Rauparaha continued, "I must admit, you are a unique fellow. I have never seen a man speak the White man's tongue and have such dark skin. How does this come to pass?" Black Jack cracked a smile, and explained his story as he had for Ruaoneone; and he rounded out with telling Te Rauparaha about his nickname, 'Black Jack White'. Te Rauparaha chuckled and said, "The first White man at Te Pukatea is black! How about that? That is the stuff legends are made of, I must say." Te Rauparaha continued to shake his head in amused wonder. Then he asked, "Well now, the Captain called out to you as 'Harper'. How do you explain that?" Arthur proceeded to tell him the painful story of how he had been duped and hired under false pretenses; how he had fallen from grace with the Captain; and how his English name had come to be bastardized through an act of spite. Te Rauparaha listened with an apparently sympathetic ear. He spoke up, "Well yes, subordination can be like that. Just thank your lucky stars that you are free now." Black Jack found this sincerity touching, and he admired Te Rauparaha's cultural savvy. The Chief added, "But you are quite large and strong to be regarded as a boy. I don't think that your captain appreciated your full potential as a warrior. My goodness,

you are as large as any Maori!" Black Jack was truly flat-
tered by Te Rauparaha's comments. He basked in the Chief's
words of praise as they blended with the rays of the blazing sun. The Chief went on, "You have been a great help
to me today. I consider you an asset, and I hope that I can
count on you again someday soon. You will make a great
warrior, and perhaps even a chief one day." These words
bathed Black Jack's ego; and his head began to swell along
with the beaming waters around him. Te Rauparaha concluded by saying, "Be my ally, Black Jack White. I will
make you into a great Maori chief like myself."

Black Jack pulled himself back from the brink of brag-
garts and grasped onto his humility. He said, "I don't
know."

As the two men fell silent over the proposition, Black
Jack noticed two objects approaching the boat from the
coast. They were two additional yet similar canoes to the
one he rode; however, they were about half the size and
carried the proportionally fewer number of men. The warriors onboard these vessels wore distinctively different
markings from those of Te Rauparaha's men; however, they
shared the same level of readiness for war in their dress. Te
Rauparaha signaled to the heads of each of these boats as
they pulled in along behind.

Black Jack asked, "Who are they?"

Te Rauparaha, hiding his initial flash of annoyance,
said, "They are warriors of another tribe. We all train together periodically to maintain good relations." He smiled
reassuringly at Black Jack.

Black Jack asked quickly, "Do you ever train jointly
with Ruaoneone and the Rangitane people?"

Te Rauparaha replied flatly, "No."

As the main war ship tarried southward back toward
Pukatea, one of the smaller ships broke toward shore just
north of the destination. Te Rauparaha signaled its leader

with a knowing nod. As the large ship rounded into Black Jack's home bay, the second of the smaller boats continued south.

"Training's finished." said Te Rauparaha gleefully. "Time to eat!"

V

Ruaoneone and his entire village ambled down the hill to greet their expected guests. The women had left lunch simmering in the ground, and now they laughed and chatted as they leisurely strolled toward the beach. The small children scurried here and there; naked, giggling, and carefree. The young men walked in loud boastful groups; and the elders rallied around the Chief. They all assembled on the beach; and Ruaoneone signaled for them all to be silent. As they hushed simultaneously, he smiled and put his hand in the air as a salutation to Te Rauparaha. He was so happy that the old dog had mended his evil ways, thought Ruaoneone.

Te Rauparaha also raised his hand high in salute; and there was a powerful moment of silence as the two chiefs locked eyes. As Te Rauparaha's smile eerily faded, his hand came down slowly. At the moment it dropped, every man in the gigantic boat stood in perfect mechanistic synchrony. Te Rauparaha picked up his musket; and twenty-four of the front warriors followed suit in harmony. The remaining four-hundred and seventy-five men removed their whalebone mere from their belts.

Black Jack did not recall any mention of a military display for the day's entertainment. He looked around nervously for Kumari. She peered at him from behind her mother, smiling. Oh Lord, they're gonna put on a show, he thought. Hope they don't go slappin' no one with those paddles, he worried.

In the next second, Black Jack's fears of a military parade were put to rest as Te Rauparaha fired the first shot. The musket ball tore through the neck of one of the elder men, as the sound of the blast followed on the heels of the fountain of blood. All Hell broke loose. The women screamed and fled in all directions, scooping up children as they ran. Te Rauparaha's men sent a volley of musket shot into their backs. Some fell, and others were spared by the misfires of the first round.

Ruaoneone and his stunned men were mostly unarmed; however, they managed to grab for their ever-present meres. Black Jack had absorbed the first two seconds of the scene from the bow of the boat; and he remained paralyzed in terror as Te Rauparaha reloaded in front of him. He remained an observer and witness of the horror, being unarmed, and strangely ignored by each side of the siege.

Te Rauparaha and his musketeers fired another round, taking out more women and children, and wounding some advancing men. The men with meres in the boat jumped and met Ruaoneone's men on the sand. Black Jack stood transfixed as he learned first-hand the true use of the mighty mere. For as the great flat round battle-axes were wielded with wild chops, rather than his previously proposed slaps, Black Jack saw men's skulls being precisely sliced open and freed of their caps and the top portions of their brains with one quick, clean swat. Men from both sides fell like zombies in mid-stride or half-chop; and bodies began to sink and tangle, sickeningly slumping like dung into mud.

Black Jack fretted frantically in a cold sweat, unable to join his comrades on the beach, or attack his enemies in the boat. He retched at the carnage, staring wildly at the scene while fearing for his life. Te Rauparaha and his gun-

men fired another round, taking down countless more innocents. The hand-to-hand combat on the front line had
strongly favored Te Rauparaha's numerous men; and now
only Ruaoneone and a handful of his young warriors remained in a circle of flailing arms and mere. Suddenly, Te
Rauparaha gave a signal, and his men stopped fighting.
The gunmen and the foot soldiers surrounded Ruaoneone
and his men, who seemed relieved by the momentary
standoff. Te Rauparaha yelled a command up the hill.
Black Jack recognized several men from the smaller boats
encountered earlier. They were forcing what women were
still alive, among them Ruaoneone's wife and Kumari, to
walk back down the hill. Black Jack felt ambiguous relief.
Several of the men kicked children along as well. One of
the men carried a round stone, a Patu Aruhe. Black Jack
recognized it as the fern pounder.

Te Rauparaha ordered all the surviving women, children, and men be lined up along the beach on their knees.
He ordered all of his men back into the boat as he climbed
in himself. He looked at Black Jack who huddled on the
bow dumbfounded. He called out to the warriors of the
mysterious new tribe; and they brought Ruaoneone to
front-and-center of the terrified line. As Te Rauparaha raised
his hand, his men launched the big boat into the water.
He held his hand up for a moment, as if taking in the
scene on the beach. The man with the stone held it high
above Ruaoneone's prostrate head. Ruaoneone's wife and
daughter began to sob, along with the other women in
the pa. Te Rauparaha dropped his hand. The executioner
brought the stone down swiftly, and he proudly exclaimed,
"Te Rauparaha!"

As the boat moved out into the bay, Black Jack managed to glance back long enough to see a man with his
mere methodically moving down the line as bodies fell
one by one.

Te Rauparaha calmly produced a bloody scalp from somewhere, and scooping out the remaining matter, licked his fingers and smacked his lips. "Sorry we had to eat and run. I promise a better supper." he said to Black Jack, staring straight into his quivering soul.

VI

"People often warn that hating someone is the fastest way to become exactly like them." Arpur said wisely to his Maori judge. "Of course, it is only looking back now that my consciousness is fully returning from that moment. For if it is true that an angry man sees red, and a coal which burns hotter than red is white, then I surely turned white that day with hatred for Te Rauparaha. However, in my white-hot flash of hatred, I did not realize that it was happening; but I lost my mind and became like him. I think it was my own defense against going completely insane with rage." Arpur said in deep reflection. The Maori judge and his family continued to eat their supper, transfixed, and nodding in wholehearted agreement.

For days the killing went on. Te Rauparaha and his men were as pirrhanas on land, murdering and feeding on flesh ravenously and ruthlessly, with method and yet without thought. Black Jack and Te Rauparaha worked as blood brothers in both rank and initiative; the Chief issuing no orders and his new prodigy needing none. It was mass killing by instinct and available means; and once it gained momentum, then it all came naturally to anyone involved. Black Jack became as an entire British regiment, threshing through body and limb with the simultaneous skills of several infantry soldiers.

The band swept south from Pukatea, following Te Rauparaha's pre-ordained and meticulously planned campaign. They would ambush unsuspecting pas at intervals just beyond the capability of any messengers, thereby preceding the spread of any word of their onslaught. They sailed day and night, killing entire tribes while they sat to eat; or slaughtering them in their sleep: Their timing was unselective.

To minimize injury to his army, Te Rauparaha always thinned the opposition with several rounds of musket shot, before proceeding with his ground attack. At one point he grew so bold in his ways that he waited for one hapu to complete its wero, yawning arrogantly as they danced, before blasting the third warrior as he lay the token down. The tribe did not even have time to respond before they were shredded.

The army gorged itself on human flesh as it went. Te Rauparaha would order the vanquished tribe's hangis cleared of their food, and the dead people chucked in. While the bodies cooked to his taste, Te Rauparaha would rape several of the surviving women. When he was finished with them, he would treat them to the ceremonial scalp slice with his mere and use their brains as garnish for his human meat. What pleased Te Rauparaha the most, however, was experiencing the flowering of his new understudy: He liked the way that the boy from Mississippi had become a promising young warrior virtually overnight. Looking at him now from a recumbent and satiated position, he offered his young friend a hand. Shaken, Black Jack refused. Despite all his slashing and raging and killing, Black Jack still had not tasted of human flesh.

He must, insisted Te Rauparaha, if he were to become a true Maori warrior. He must eat people and plenty of them. They were the enemy, and they deserved it; he reasoned with Black Jack.

Black Jack, still charged on blinding anger, began to become tired. He had raged for three consecutive days, never eating nor sleeping. He was exhausted and he didn't know it yet. His mind told him that he was enjoying himself, that he could go on killing forever without rest. He was intoxicated on blood.

Te Rauparaha continued with his persuasive argument. He told Black Jack that the killing was necessary, that it was a cleansing of the entire Maori soul; and that he had been chosen to carry out the work. He didn't really enjoy all the rampaging, he explained to Black Jack; it just had to be done for the good of all. Besides, he told Black Jack, he was very proud of him; and he was impressed with his performance. There was only one thing preventing Black Jack from totally joining the brotherhood, he told him; and that was the eating of the enemy's flesh. He further explained to the young man that it wasn't just the act of eating another person; it was a very deep and profound symbol of the warrior's respect for his fallen foe. It was a perfect circle, the killing and the eating, he explained. He rambled on about the significance of the ritual, and the actual honor that it bestowed upon the defeated tribe. It was a good thing, a purification, a necessary evil.

Te Rauparaha went on and on, as he gnawed on a young lady's neck bone and sucked his fingers. His talking mesmerized Black Jack as he fell from his elevated state of agitation. Arthur began to feel cold, tired, hungry, and bewildered all at once; and as Te Rauparaha continued to drone on about the merits of cannibalism, Black Jack reached out for a portion. There beneath the clear Kaikoura night sky, at the base of the majestic, craggy, green mountains by the magical sea, Black Jack sampled his first morsel of fellow man. Te Rauparaha continued as Black Jack chewed, never mentioning the part about the final insult and humiliation of the slain foe being the best flavor in the rainbow.

VIII

Weeks went by without Black Jack's awareness of time or season. He became a hardened man; not from concerted effort on his part, but from his inescapable focus of purpose in callous matters. The business of murder did not permit the luxury of thought; and the outward display of his skill and competence were merely the dubiously fortuitous manifestations of Black Jack's involuntary involvement in decorated genocide. Black Jack had not even had the opportunity to stop and wonder if he feared for his life; whether from the perils of the battlefield or the unspoken threat of his captors. Come to think of it, he pondered, he had not really sorted out whether or not they did hold him captive. Somehow he had assumed that his cohorts held control over him, either through intimidation or his own lack of resistance to their assault.

One night as Black Jack sat around a large bonfire on the beach, he experienced an odd sensation. He was sitting with a group of warriors and Te Rauparaha, laughing and talking. The fire was warm; and Black Jack was surprised to find himself enjoying the food and the company. It was all quite jovial. As he went to place an arm in the fire (a dead man's), he began to hallucinate that the arm was actually his. It did not burn; however, it alternated in his mind between being his arm and the dead man's arm. Suddenly Black Jack was besieged by shadowy figures which tapped at him like diving birds as they swooped. He was popped several times, randomly, and then in succession. He began to flail his arms, which were both on fire now, as the mysterious objects continued to pelt him.

Black Jack awoke on the endless, cold, dark beach. The coast along Kaikoura was starkly different from Cloudy Bay: It was straight and rocky for as far as the eye could see. And now in the still darkness, Black Jack struggled to shake off sleep and focus his eyes. There was no fire. What he saw were the carcasses of hundreds of people, partially decomposed and strewn randomly up and down the beach. His party was literally camping in among the remains, while the seagulls and wood hens roved and picked around them in the darkness. Black Jack had become accustomed to the stench. As he looked around, he was startled by another pair of eyes gleaming back at him nearby.

The figure stared at him, as its outline gradually became visible. It was Te Rauparaha, sitting up now from having been asleep. His agitation was beaming through the night. "You were having a bad dream. Go back to sleep. We have a busy day tomorrow."

Black Jack lay there, watching the stringy clouds stream past the moon; and listening to the waves wash the shore. He was numb and on edge at the same time. His nerves were raw, and yet his senses were fuzzy. His head felt dull and his memory was foggy; yet a blinding light shone into his tired eyes from somewhere in the back of his brain. He squinted to focus his mind. It was as if he were awakening from a night of too much grog. He knew where he was; but he felt no connection to the place. He knew the sequence of events leading up to his presence at that moment; yet it did not answer his question of why he was there. He was experiencing an educated amnesia; being given enough recall to preclude his innocence yet not enough to convict on motive. His reality was a nightmare; and with the narcotic effect of fury fading fast, he faced his most painful and difficult feat for some time: Rational thinking.

His thoughts reeled back up the coast, racing over rocky cliffs and battlefields still full of bodies; and the image of a face floated like a feather over the furlongs. Like a flag unfurled on the map of his memory, he flew toward her fleeting image, faster and faster along the coast; until at last he fell at the feet of his forgotten flame: Kumari.

Black Jack's gut wrenched and his eyes burned as he stifled his sobs among the warriors. How the pain of that second suddenly caught up to him: The instant of his separation from her, suppressed until now, slamming him like stone. Oh, how he felt as the torn bleeding arm of a fatally wounded body: Being the sole source of the mortal condition and begging reattachment. He agonized over whether she were alive. He obsessed on that one idea; and the vicious circle which the thought formed in his mind created a fragile protective shell that prevented him from destroying what was left of his own psyche.

Brothy ocean vapor saturated his heaving lungs and threatened to suffocate his mental valence. How would he take his leave from Te Rauparaha? he wondered. He thought back to the nights that he lay awake plotting his escape from the plantation Master. There was no comparing his past to the present situation. The two were vastly differ-ent, yet they shared one thing in common: The courage to be successful against all odds, he realized. Lying in the oppressive, stale heat of confining squalor, or lying among cold carrion and callous cannibals; it made no difference: He knew that he possessed the character to overcome. But how far and how difficult would it be this time? he asked himself.

Traveling through southern America in winter had been tough; however, this would be as tough in its own way. There had been others to help and guide him once he reached the hills. The trails through the mountains were full of Negroes, northward bound just as himself. There were horses and wagons, tents and camps: A veri-table secret society of freedom seekers who had helping one another refined to an art. It had almost been enjoy-able reaching New York, Black Jack remembered now.

Leaving Te Rauparaha's army would be different. It would require a more radical approach all together, Black Jack thought. He did not think that the direct method, such as a daring escape, would be a viable plan. No, he thought, the conditions called for a little bit of the fox that Arthur still proudly held secretly in reserve, releasing it slyly from its bottle when life demanded. And from that bottle, Black Jack assured himself, Te Rauparaha was going to drink a little of his own medicine: A bit of guile, steeped in ruse, to be washed down generously with revenge.

In his heightening sense of awareness, Black Jack hatched a plot there in the early dawn on the beach. He would not ask for what he wanted, Black Jack surmised; rather, he would tell Te Rauparaha what the Chief needed. In that way, he figured, Black Jack could avoid a direct battle of wits with the cunning chief. Without raising Te Rauparaha's suspicion of ulterior motive, without giving the chief a chance to consider Black Jack's change of heart; Black Jack would simply request that he be given command of his battalion. Yes, that was it, he thought: Why would the chief have gone out of his way to pay such particular attention to Black Jack if he were not grooming him for a greater role? He decided then that he would tell Te Rauparaha that he was ready to lead an arm of the Chief's army. However, he would not be so direct about it. Tact was necessary, he thought, if he were going to outsmart his adversary and achieve his true goal: To return to Te Pukatea and Kumari.

IX

"Today we stand down, my son." said Te Rauparaha to Black Jack at the morning meal. The warriors were wandering around the beach, most in partial dress, attending to various articles which had been neglected in the long heat of battle. Some repaired small items on the boats which had been accumulated through pillage, while others fished or just sat and smoked. The bill of fair had reverted to seafood, much to Black Jack's relief. Eating of the copious fish and other sea life, Black Jack felt as though he were feeding another version of himself. The simple creatures seemed to supply a section of his soul sitting just above simple plant consumption. Set just above that was animal meat eating; and then the unthinkable which he had actually performed, he thought. Each group now seemed for him to fit a state of mind: A hierarchy of peace correlating to a selection of diet, each level of food items being a symbol converging closer to its corresponding set of behaviors. That is to say, plant eaters may merely forage for and occasionally grow only what they need to maintain a harmonious balance with their surroundings; whereas animal eaters must either hunt or subjugate their prey; and cannibals must actually eat their own kind, which in the absence of, or even the presence of some absurd manifesto, is essentially devouring themselves directly without the luxury of any philosophical or spiritual spacer between the means of providence and the nutrition itself. So Black Jack thought as the warriors' smoke and Te Rauparaha's words wafted over the waves.

"But I thought that it was going to be a busy day today." Black Jack replied with a juvenile tone.

"No, I lied. I only wanted you to get your sleep. Besides, I didn't want you wandering off in the night." said Te Rauparaha.

"Well, what will we do today, then?" asked Black Jack, baiting his prey.

"We will rest. We deserve it. You have done quite well,

I must admit. You have been a great help and a boost to morale overall. I am quite pleased with our rapid progress." Te Rauparaha said with sincerity.

"Ah, so we are finished, then." Black Jack said, knowing the contrary.

"No, no, not quite my son. We will continue south tomorrow. Kaikoura is just my favorite rest stop. In fact, this is my best campaign in years. Perhaps we will stay two days." said Te Rauparaha, his mood bordering between mellow and serious.

"Then you think I am truly a good warrior then?" Black Jack asked with a leading tone.

"I told you I did. I meant it. For what little experience you have, you show exceptional natural ability. A real killer instinct!" Te Rauparaha said light-heartedly.

"Do you think that I have what it takes to be a chief?" Black Jack asked curtly.

"Wait a moment, now. Let's not get ahead of ourselves. In time my son, in time. Why do you ask?" Te Rauparaha responded with obvious surprise.

"Well, if not a chief, then your First Warrior, or some such position of authority." Black Jack said, accelerating the proposition.

Unfamiliar with the European concept of rank, Te Rauparaha replied, "There is no such thing. There is me, and I tell them what to do." He waved his hand over the beach at the hundreds of warriors. He continued, "A chief is not made, he makes himself through ruthlessness and aggression over other tribes."

"But you were once a warrior, were you not?" asked Black Jack argumentatively.

"Yes, but I became a chief by killing other chiefs and assimilating their tribes." said Te Rauparaha pensively confident.

"And so, that is how I am to become a chief? Whom

do I kill? A chief of another tribe, or my own chief?" Black
Jack asked with coy earnestness.

Te Rauparaha was taken aback by the question which
he somehow knew was inevitable, but which had come
too soon at the hands of this fine young cannibal. He gathered himself and said, hiding his concern, "My son, you
may kill whomever you choose; however, hear this: Of
course killing me would be foolish because of the awesome responsibility that you would immediately assume.
Besides, you and I make such a great team! Also, taking
command of any of the tribes we have recently vanquished
would not only make you vulnerable to them; but would
also put you at direct odds to me. Does that make sense?"
He tried to sound convincing to his young student.

Black Jack, quick with a defense, rallied, "Not necessarily: You may need someone in command here to hold
these northern posts while you carry on southward. Don't
you think that you are overextending yourself?"

Te Rauparaha, becoming visibly angry with his
subordinate's impudence, yelled, "Don't tell me how to
do my job! When you think that you know better than
me, then we will match our mere. Until then, I say who
lives or dies around here!" Black Jack sat unfazed by this
sudden outburst. He had expected this response. Te
Rauparaha, on the other hand, played into Black Jack's
hands perfectly with his alternative. He offered, "Now, if
you insist on playing a more important role in my operation, then I have a job for you." Black Jack watched the
words tumble from Te Rauparaha's mouth as a gambler
watches the cards fall from a dealer's hand. He anticipated
Te Rauparaha's gift. Te Rauparaha continued, "You may
return to Te Pukatea and hold the peace there. You will be
accepted back by your own people; and you are to tell
them that I have put you in charge. They will accept your
innocence in the matter and obey you in good faith."

Black Jack bit his lip in excitement. However, he flatly replied, "No! I cannot travel that far north. I am weak; and there is absolutely nothing there for me. Besides, it is so close to the White man and his treachery. I refuse."

Te Rauparaha's anger was quelled by his enjoyment of Black Jack's displeasure. He said, calmly smiling, "Precisely. I need you at the northern extent of the South Island, right between the threat of the White man and the village of my first conquest. You will be as a piece in that game the White man plays when he does not have the courage for real war: You will be a knight. Is that high enough a rank for you?" He began to laugh, as a father making concessions in his delegation of chores to a resentful child.

Black Jack played his scowling adolescent part to the hilt, while bursting at the seams with joy. He replied, "I don't know. I'll have to think about it."

Te Rauparaha changed stance to the offensive. He said, "No, no. It is not your choice. You will leave today. I will send a group of my best warriors with you in one of the smaller boats. They will help to enforce your express commission. Now get ready!"

Black Jack stood, persisting with his pitiful pout. Inside however, he was taking a flamboyant bow, as he had done so many times while performing at the old-timers' shack.

Te Rauparaha, of course, was only pleased with the convenient placement of his bargaining chip.

X

Black Jack's soul was free. To draw any analogy to his freedom would be to fall short of the very icon for which an archetypal comparison could be derived. Quite simply, he was as free as a thrice-escaped man; and moreover, he was as free as Black Jack White: An African-American man, born into slavery, and now influencing captains of empires and kings of great lands. He was as stoked as a furnace fire. That fire glowed a phosphorescent vermilion, in stark contrast to the hinterland pallor of the coastal valleys. New Zealand was painting one of its beautifully dismal days: A solid ceiling of clouds hanging low enough to impose upon vision and dampen wind noise, yet not impede distant visibility and ground-level sound. Like a toy sailor in a child's terrarium, Black Jack soaked in the sights such as sharply defined puffs of mist rising from blanketed blue hills and dales, and associated exotically colored South Pacific birds roosting in trees along the overcast shore.

His henchmen rowed efficiently. So well, in fact, that their powerful rhythm carried them all the way to Pukatea just as night was falling: An entire day without rest, food, or water; and they showed only determination and respect to their new leader. They had not even mentioned to him the throngs of seagulls perched on a myriad of bones along the way. Nor had he dug up the topic himself, remaining entirely silent the whole voyage.

As the boat approached the beach, Black Jack's anticipation dueled with his dread, his optimism of hoping that Kumari was alive winning by a slight margin. He could barely contain himself during the wero; and when the token was placed, he bounded for it and continued hurriedly past the procession in search of his bride. It was a new regime all around at Pukatea, he knew; however, he had no idea as to the extent of the human devastation. As he dashed from hut to hut, Te Rauparaha's diplomats explained the situation and Black Jack's new role. Finding none of Ruaoneone's people present in the pa, Black Jack breathlessly returned to the circle of Ngatirarua negotiators on the beach.

One of their warriors spoke up. "The one you seek is not here." he told Black Jack.

Black Jack replied indignantly, "And who are you to presume to know whom or what I seek?"

The warrior held his ground and said, "The princess Kumari. She has gone."

Black Jack was visibly stunned by the man's knowledge, and he was forced to concede his shock. He queried, "And is she dead?"

The warrior responded factually, "No. We have word that she escaped with her betrothed, Chief Pakauwera, to an inland pa."

Black Jack was aghast. He asked, "Her betrothed?" He could not comprehend the mention of her matrimony.

The warrior explained, "Yes, you see, Pakauwera was Ruaoneone's most senior advisor in the tribe. He was in line to succeed Ruaoneone as Chief. He had also declared his love for Kumari. That is, before you arrived."

Black Jack felt light-headed. He vaguely remembered Pakauwera now. "Go on." he said.

The Ngatirarua warrior continued, "When Ruaoneone granted her hand in marriage to you, Pakauwera felt extremely betrayed. He held his tongue, but he silently swore revenge. That is how word traveled to us, and then to Te Rauparaha, about the 'Fern Pounder' comment."

Black Jack's blood began to boil cold, feeling both fear and outrage at Te Rauparaha's spider web of influence. He said, "So now she is married and living with this man you say."

The warrior respectfully answered, "Yes. They and a handful of Rangitane are but a remaining few who escaped Te Rauparaha's wrath. Word is that they are in hiding until their numbers grow strong again."

Black Jack could only imagine how they were managing to increase their numbers. He felt sickened by his struggle between jealousy for Kumari and loyalty to the threatened tribe: His tribe. His plan had failed. He was now among strangers, having to assume the role of their faithful leader while suffering the ambiguous loss of his true love. He prayed for strength.

The warrior continued, "We have heard about your fierceness in battle, and your loyalty to Te Rauparaha. We have heard much more recently about the 'Black Giant' who fights with the rage of ten in his eyes. It will be an honor to serve you." The other warriors moved closer into the circle and hailed Black Jack with cheers of support. The other villagers, all transplants, also crowded around noisily.

There he was again, Black Jack thought: The reluctant hero. His heart ached for Kumari, yet he put on a brave face. He knew immediately that any plan of action must begin with biding his time here until the right moment. Besides, Fate had strangely tossed him an offertory bone, he discovered, as he looked around the crowd and saw her: The woman from the grog shop. She had apparently moved south with her tribe after the raid took place.

She came to him now; and with a look, he knew that she would suffice as his pill of solace during this painfully poignant waiting period.

Chapter 15

WITH EYES PEELED

Black Jack pushed his chair back from the long table and looked around nervously. He contemplated continuing with his story in front of the Judge's children. The Judge perceived his concerns and pointed sternly out of the room. The three children, two girls and a boy, obediently departed for bed.

"I wasn't sure if I should continue. I am becoming quite personal with my tale. It is probably boring you senseless. I shall go." said Black Jack sheepishly.

The Judge's wife entered the room with a pot of fresh, hot tea and began to pour her husband a cup. She looked around and asked, "I didn't miss anything, did I? Black Jack-cup of tea?"

The Judge broke in, tapping her outer thigh for her to sit down, and said, "No, no, Black Jack-I mean Arpur-was just about to continue. Please go on. I have the day off tomorrow, right dear?" His wife gave an agreeable nod, as the Maori Judge smiled and placed his chin eagerly upon his clasped hands. This moved his face into the light of the oil lamp, illuminating the sincerity in his eyes.

Black Jack collected his thoughts, and said, "Those years were not my own. I felt as if I were someone beside myself. My mate was a comfort to me; but that is about all. I pretended to love her, yet all the while, my heart yearned for Kumari. I thought about her constantly. My pain did not subside: It merely congealed, dried, and crusted over like a wound. A thin scab it was that formed on my soul; and I shielded it well, hiding it from anyone who might start my heart bleeding once again for all to stare at.

"However, I did run the tribe quite well. I immersed myself in the business of being Te Rauparaha's authority; and the villagers did respect me. It was an apparitional existence though: I was a ghost walking through life without actually touching or feeling anyone or anything. I told myself that it was a part of growing up. As long as I went through the motions of day-to-day living, then everything would be all right. That is how I survived.

"Ironically, my reputation was that of a vicious warrior; and everyone feared me. Inside, I was a broken man; having tried and convicted myself of crimes that I had been manipulated into committing. I was a ball of confusion and resentment, and I wanted revenge. It was my excruciating struggle with that concept, however, which eventually broke my will completely; and which set me on a course of action which would transcend my hatred for Te Rauparaha and set both captive and captor free of their spiritual bonds.

"In the meantime, though, I had come to be known by a name which I myself forbid anyone to use in my presence. It was a reprehensible misnomer, involuntarily earned, and aggravatingly injurious to a healing mind. I

heard them in distant circles of casual conversation call
me, 'Bloody Jack'. Meant as a Maori compliment, it dogged
me like a stain: One more cheetah's spot in my running
chronological collage. However, I decided to make the best
of my self-imposed sentence and capitalize on my ruthless
reputation. You see, as a reformed cannibal, I embarked
on a campaign to win these people's affections, not literally their hearts; but to turn them against Te Rauparaha.
It was a valiant and simple plan."

II

Black Jack began a campaign of reason. It was not a
popular one, but in the end it accomplished its goal. He
did not rely on his laurels to help him make friends with
his subjects. Rather, he trusted in his own wit, charm,
and confidence to slowly form a real, personal, and lasting
bond with the tribe members. Perhaps their fear of him
gave Black Jack an initial advantage in gaining their respectful attention; however, his genuine kindness could
not be disputed by them and he soon won everyone's hearts.

One night after a tribal wedding banquet, Black Jack
utilized the open forum and his command of the crowd to
make a bizarre speech. He posed the question to everyone,
"Did you enjoy our little celebratory meal?" There was a
unanimous and positive response. Black Jack smiled and
said louder, "Good! That was Te Rauparaha you were eating." The people gasped in unison and stared at him
blankly. He allowed the pause to continue for emphasis.
Then he said, "I am only joking. Ask yourselves this
though: What if I weren't?" The quizzical question served
its purpose; as people resumed talking, but in higher and
interrogative tones. Soon they settled back into the festive
mood of the evening and moved onto other topics; however, Black Jack knew that they were each and everyone

digesting his suggestion, even if they had not taken the time to completely chew its ramifications.

For days following, Black Jack fielded questions from all walks of the tribe. Some such as the elders would openly and frankly inquire as to his meaning; while others would wait until an opportunity arose to beg his pardon and ask if he minded explaining his intentions. Questions ranged in their coverage of aspect from whether he actually wanted to defeat and eat Te Rauparaha, to whether or not he were feeling well.

None of the guesses hit the target; and Black Jack had not expected them to. In fact, had any of the people of the tribe realized his point, then he would have been surprised that someone had not previously brought up the issue which he sought to presently illuminate. One day after many weeks had passed without mention of the incident, a young boy brought up the subject out of the blue. It seemed that in preparing for her wedding, the youngster's sister had jested with him about 'eating Te Rauparaha' at the ceremony; and this comment had left him subsequently very disturbed. Even at the age of seven, the boy was very familiar with the Chief's persona.

He innocently walked up to Black Jack during an elder's meeting and asked, "Are we going to eat Te Rauparaha?"

Black Jack tenderly asked the child, "And what makes you so concerned about this, young warrior?" By this time, the boy's mother had approached to retrieve him.

The child responded, "Because my sister is getting married and she says that we are going to eat Te Rauparaha." The shock of the boy's naïve audacity caused his mother to gasp in embarrassment, and this reaction drew the attention of many more onlookers. They focused on what their chief had to say.

Black Jack said in a serious tone, "No, my son, we are not going to eat Te Rauparaha." The crowd which had gathered now seemed to expel a sigh of relief. Then Black Jack's face lit up. He said smugly, "Well then, we shall eat your sister instead!" The crowd reacted in horror at his words and welcomed the fleeing boy into their arms. They stared in disbelief at Black Jack.

One man spoke up, "Why do you torment the little boy, my Chief?"

Black Jack responded confidently, "Drastic times call for drastic measures."

The man shot back, "Perhaps I might understand if I knew your point; but I don't understand why it must be made using a child's innocence."

Black Jack replied, "If the simplest arguments cannot be made with the simplest people, then they do not hold much water."

The man seemed to agree; and the crowd realized the good intentions of their leader. However, the man asked, "Then why all of this talk about eating people? Are you trying to tell us something?"

Black Jack said, "I am not trying to show you anything that is not already right before your face." The crowd now paid strict attention.

The man said, "Is it about our eating flesh? Do they not do that where you come from? Well, that is our tradition. It is a very sacred one, which has much spiritual meaning. We do not expect you to fully understand."

Black Jack said, "A spiritual tradition. That is fine. Then what will you eat when there are no more bodies; and where will the spirits live then?" The crowd had become highly interested, slightly surprised by the man's boldness.

The man said, "Why does it concern you so? It is not as though we are eating our own people, as you seem to suggest. We eat those slain in battle. It is an honorable thing."

Black Jack said, "Ah, but are not all tribes under one people, the Maori? If you were vast in number like the Pakeha, perhaps then you would have the luxury of eating all of your people that you desired. But look at you: You know that the Maori are dwindling. Believe me, I know this: The White men are great in number, and they will come here. Most importantly, they don't eat their own kind; nor will they eat you. However, you can rest assured that they may kill plenty of you, just as they killed the red-skinned people that occupied the land before them."

Now his tribe seemed really confused. The man was dazed, but he struggled to recover. He said, "That is well and fine; but like I say, it is our tradition. It is the way we have always done it. We don't expect you to understand it."

Black Jack said, "I understand that it is a reckless and dangerous tradition. I can think of nothing else that threatens the survival of your people more. Killing is one thing. But killing and eating? That seems to me to only further fuel your lust for blood. And you say that you are not eating your own tribe. Well with such small numbers of Maori left, if neighbors are eating neighbors, then why not eat yourselves? Go ahead and take the next step! All traditions have a beginning: Go ahead and start your own!"

The man became incensed; and the crowd seemed to reflect his sentiment. People looked at Black Jack with disgust, pity, confusion, and awe. Most thought that he had gone mad. The subject was not breached again for some time, although many would secretly discuss the issue among close friends. For some, the answer was as simple as the one for the question, 'Why does a bird fly?'; or 'Why does the sun rise?'; while for others the question seemed to be similar to asking, 'Why does a green branch symbolize a peaceful visit?' Regardless, the debate sparked controversy without completely undermining Black Jack's authority and trust; and he continued to enjoy a peaceful reign over the tribe. The people remained confused, however, as to how someone that they knew as 'Bloody Jack' could suddenly be taking issue with their cannibalism.

III

Months passed and a new year came. For Black Jack, January brought a snowless summer and a bittersweet anniversary. He reflected fondly on Lalani and the child which by now must be born; and he considered the consequences of his broken promise. He mourned the fact he might never know his child's birthday. His partner here had not conceived; nor had he wanted her to, he thought. He still longed for Kumari. In fact, it was his burning love for her that drove his thoughts and actions everyday, and that gave him the will to carry out his plan.

Life within the pa had settled into a peaceful routine, without the outside influence of either marauding Maori or wayward White whalers. Te Pukatea remained tranquil and serene, and everyone seemed happy. An underlying restlessness remained though, amid rumors that Te Rauparaha would return.

These were indeed true. In a land that was mostly free of natural threats and disasters, the fear of the roving butcher had substituted for the dread which was reserved for the likes of unexpected earthquakes or floods. Such was considered the magnitude of the destruction he brought; unlike the also absent perils of venomous snakes, poisonous spiders, crocodiles, wild cats, and the like which merely would have presented horrific encounters for unfortunate individuals. The specter of Te Rauparaha encompassed all known lethal things, like the cloak of death itself. In addition to his deadliness, his treachery graced the other edge of the sword; and it was that latter trait which Black Jack set about to exploit next.

At the tribe's mid-summer feast, much food was prepared. Also, many celebration rituals were performed. The occasion was larger than usual, and it brought with it the commensurate amount of festive activities. All the traditional native items were on the menu; excluding any of the neighbors.

Everything was high-spirited and light-hearted; and then as the tribe began to eat, someone joked to Black Jack about the fact that Te Rauparaha was not being served. Everyone laughed; however, Black Jack suddenly turned serious.

He said, "Ah, but what if he were to return and make a feast of you all?"

The banquet crowd fell silent. Everyone began to look at one another as if to say, 'Oh no, here we go again!' Under obvious pressure from his peers, the perpetrator begged forgiveness from Black Jack in an apparent attempt to forestall the inevitable; however, it was not to be granted, and Black Jack seized the convenient opportunity to begin a debate which lasted through dinner and was not done until well into the night. The sparring went somewhat along the lines of this: Black Jack asked just how loyal the tribe felt Te Rauparaha was to them. There was an uproar and objection at first, but giving the calming effect of the copious food, serious consideration of the question ensued as the temperament of the group settled. They eventually responded with a collective opinion that slightly resembled Black Jack's desired outcome of the discussion; and that was that no, they did not feel entirely safe and secure as subjects under Te Rauparaha's rule. But why ask, and what was the alternative? they demanded. Was he attempting to undermine the man who put him in charge, they asked Black Jack; and if so, was it out of some resentment or fear? Why this obsession with the man who had given him so much? they demanded.

The topic generated so much excitement and agitation, that Black Jack laid it to rest. However, he was pleased that he had accomplished what he had set out to do: That is to put yet another seed in the minds of his followers which would continue to grow and have the opposite effect of the pounds of pork, potatoes, and seafood which were now settling in their satisfied stomachs and seducing them to sleep. He knew that now they would begin to think about Te Rauparaha not as a protector, but as a possible problem. For as surely as the magnificent Black Whale migrated south to spawn in their beautiful waters, Te Rauparaha would someday return north along the coast to Kapiti. That is when, Black Jack assured himself, Te Rauparaha would receive his comeuppance.

Revenge was not necessarily the way that he wanted to go at this stage, Black Jack thought. Although he had once been angry enough to, and also possessed the desire to do in his adversary in a similar fashion that the murderous chief had done to so many, Black Jack restrained himself now in the pursuits of a higher goal. Besides, killing Te Rauparaha outright would only destroy any possibility of discovering where Kumari might be. Also, he definitely did not have any desire to eat the old chief. So a more subtle plan emerged in Black Jack's mind. Something of a nobler ideal than slaughtering the man out of hatred. More of an ambush, thought Black Jack. That would take some intricate planning, he thought; as it is one thing to kill a man in outright battle and another thing completely to surprise and capture him, especially when he is surrounded by his own army.

In addition, thought Black Jack, a surprise attack requires readiness; and more importantly it dictates that one know exactly when one's enemy is approaching. Black Jack currently had no idea as to when Te Rauparaha was coming; or whether or not Black Jack's own warriors would be willing to cooperate. He decided that one more convincing argument and a fine tuning of his plan should do the trick.

IV

Years passed with no mentionable incident; and as it turned out, this period of peace served not only as a time for Black Jack to educate his people, but also as a time for the teacher himself to further his philosophical enlightening. Strangely, the entire scenario of Black Jack's rule over the pa emulated that of a cloistered student at a great university. Not being required to work or occupy his day with menial tasks for mere survival, he was at liberty to sit and think all that he wanted to. All his meals were provided, and all his needs were generously attended to. He was exposed to a vast array of new information; and he was free to assimilate and learn whatever he chose. It was like a school without limits or rules; and he was in charge. Black Jack had discovered that he liked to think about everything and anything for long periods of time on the ship; however, he had always had to pay at least partial attention to his work.

Here at the pa it was different. Nothing interrupted his thoughts; and there was no threat of being accused of daydreaming by a superior. Black Jack was the supreme local being as far as anyone was concerned; and rather than

wield his authority as a Genghis Khan, he chose to become more like Buddha, spending his days in meditation
and contemplation. Slowly, he came to know exactly what
he would do about Te Rauparaha.

One day in 1833, however, the peace was disturbed
by news from the north that a White man's ship had been
driven ashore by a storm and wrecked. The word from the
messenger was that a less peaceful tribe than Black Jack's
was in the process of harassing the survivors and looting
the ship.

Black Jack thought back to his time at the whaling
station. He remembered how the Maori there had lived in
peace with the White man. He knew that that was not
always the case, however. He was not certain as to who
normally instigated the violence in times when there was
trouble between Maori and Pakeha; but in this instance,
he decided that he wanted to find out first-hand.

Black Jack gathered a group of his warriors and set out
for points north in his canoe. He had a general idea of
where the ship wreck had occurred; and he knew that he
could perform a reconnaissance trip in one day. Traveling
up the coast, his party soon encountered the delicately
fingered outline of the shore which curved in and out in-
tricately to form a maze of sounds along the top of the
South Island. The cistern pattern of the bays made for
slow going, as it significantly increased the actual length
of coastline which they must canvas. Eventually, though,
they came upon the barque.

Black Jack ordered that his canoe be beached out of
sight of the stranded sailors, in the event that the hostile
activities were already in progress. He and his men could
see a group of White people on the shore; and the broken
hull of the ship remained nearby in shallow water. Black
Jack led his men along the edge of the bush to a vantage
closer to the marooned group. As they drew nearer, Black

Jack saw that much cargo had been dragged from the ship and strewn along the beach. The group of Whites now huddled among the broken crates around a fire of burning scrap wood. All looked despondent and fearful, except one: A large, burly, black-haired man who paced boldly back and forth as if keeping watch for attackers. Nearest to him were a woman and two small children.

Black Jack recognized him as the man from the whaling station. The gruff but friendly man who had first inspected a young and fearful nubian named Harper: The man they called Jackie. Black Jack's heart leapt as he fought the urge to hail the man he knew; but he hesitated upon realizing that the man may not only fail to remember him, but also may seize upon him in his full Maori garb. It was an odd spot. He wanted to help his old acquaintance; however, he did not want to create a conflict. With his small number of supporters, Black Jack was in no position to launch an offensive upon anyone, or properly defend himself either.

Suddenly, a rustling in the bushes behind his group startled them all. As they looked, several Maori warriors from another tribe appeared and made their way toward the beach. Before they got far, however, Black Jack called out to them.

"You there, what are you doing?" Black Jack demanded. They were all out of earshot of the Whites.

Looking stunned, the other warriors whipped around. Their apparent leader said, "Who are you and what business is it of yours?"

Black Jack replied, "We are from Te Pukatea. I am the Chief there, and these are my warriors. We have come to help the White men who are in distress."

The warrior responded, "Well go home. This is our territory, and what these Pakeha have is ours. We have come to kill them and take what is left."

Black Jack said, "You will do no such thing. Let these people go in peace. They have done nothing to you. If you harm them, believe me, you will have more trouble than you can imagine."

The warrior said, "Ha! From you? We will kill you and eat you for supper. Now go, before you anger me further."

Black Jack said, "My son, I am a chief, and I could kill you so fast with my greenstone, that I could then eat you while you watched. Now do not anger me. I have told you what I want. Go and tell your chief that these people are not to be harmed. Is that understood?"

The warrior glared at Black Jack in defiance; however, he reluctantly signaled his men, and they retreated. Black Jack and his men looked once more upon the pitiful mob on the beach and then rowed for home. It would be a long time before he learned their fate.

V

Around this time, Black Jack began to think seriously about his fate. Seeing the vulnerability of the Whites on the beach that day had caused him to consider his bizarre situation in this remote and exotic land. At the age of twenty-two, he felt that he had matured enough to handle such an extraneous life; but oh, how quickly, he thought. He wondered if anyone else had had such an incredible growing-up experience. In his wildest dreams, he never could have imagined that he would ever be in such a sce-nario, and with so much responsibility. Along with his own, however, he could not ignore the overshadowing fate of Te Rauparaha; and how their two destinies had become intertwined.

The incident with the shipwreck also served to heighten Black Jack's wariness of Te Rauparaha's imminent return; and it also increased his sense of urgency for devising a plan of action against the murderous chief. Black Jack had often thought of posting lookouts from his tribe to give early warning from down the coast; however, this had never actually seemed practical. Black Jack knew from first-hand experience that the Chief moved faster than any word of mouth or running messenger. If Te Rauparaha were coming, he would speed swiftly up the coast and strike without warning, he thought. Either that, or he would cruise right on by back to Kapiti, not to be seen again for years. Black Jack could not afford to have that happen, he thought, for the sake of finding Kumari's whereabouts. Black Jack knew that Te Rauparaha had not already returned north for one simple reason; and that fact became the last key idea that Black Jack required to turn his people against Te Rauparaha once and for all.

On the way home on that fateful day, Black Jack and his men had passed another canoe that was heading north. It was a large canoe; not quite as large as Te Rauparaha's, but big enough for about one hundred warriors and some odd number of passengers. Black Jack recognized some of the men as Te Rauparaha's warriors, and he waved in recognition of them. They acknowledged him briefly and dutifully, and continued rowing. Onboard the canoe were various other Maori men, women, and children in clothing with markings which Black Jack did not recognize. He asked his warriors what this was about; and they replied that the people were slaves, captured in battle and bound for Kapiti. Black Jack's blood ran cold. Even in light of the horrible atrocities that he had witnessed, he could not believe that the practice of human slavery was being carried out in this beautiful land: And not by the White man. Maori enslaving Maori: Because of his personal experience, it struck an even deeper nerve than the cannibalism. The killing, the eating, and the enslavement: It must all come to an end, he thought. The best way to convince his people, he reckoned, was to tell them about the evils of slavery that he had learned by personal experience.

Armed with his final argument, and the evidence that Te Rauparaha was still active down South, Black Jack needed only to devise the solution to the Te Rauparaha problem, he thought. The solution was a dilemma, however. If solving the problem meant killing Te Rauparaha, Black Jack thought, then that would constitute murderous revenge; and that would completely nullify all of Black Jack's beautiful arguments. He would then be a tyrannical hypocrite in the eyes of his people, he thought. No, he realized, it was justice he was after, not revenge; and perhaps he could even convince Te Rauparaha as to the evil of his ways. But even with the backing of his people, how would Black Jack go about making a captive audience of his rival? he wondered.

Back home at Pukatea, Black Jack began to go on long walks to think about his plan. He also wanted to scout out a possible ambush site south of Pukatea. As it happened, the lay of the coast could not have provided a better place to stage a surprise assault on a northbound vessel.

What hindered the early warning ability of a lookout would also work to the advantage of an ambush party. That is, the coastline directly south of Pukatea created a blind in both directions, making it impossible for anyone to see or be seen in and around the small coves until directly upon them.

Black Jack began to play military strategist in his mind. He wanted to pull off the perfect ambush, preferably with no combat or injury on either side. He believed that he knew how:

About three miles south of the gently arcing bay of

Pukatea was a long straight beach of flat, smooth sand. One could see along the beach on a clear day for about ten miles to a large outcropping of land that formed a cape. At the north end of the beach, closest to Pukatea, the mountains abruptly shot into the sea forming a rocky face toward the long beach. The rocky cliff came to a point at about the low-tide line, so that when the tide was out, one could scamper through shallow surf around the point to the other side. What lay there was a very interesting sight to behold.

The cove rose slightly onto a small beach which was like a hollow column rimmed by a high rock wall all the way around. One needed to strain his neck to peer up the wall face to the bushy ridge above. On the north side of this inlet was another high, sharp point which also just barely touched the water. Black Jack was able to walk, therefore, from the long beach, to the cove, and to what lay next; and all were occluded from view of the others. Strangely, what lay next was virtually an identical replica of the first cove. Black Jack was having trouble believing his good fortune of finding such an ideal hiding place for his army; and then he really made a fascinating discovery.

Running between the two coves, near each of their rears, was a small cave. The cave was almost perfectly formed, just large enough for Black Jack to walk through slightly stooped over. It simply amazed Black Jack that the entire place could be so fortuitously created and positioned where it was. His plan of attack practically devised itself as Black Jack strolled around, beaming and admiring this wondrous geographical creation. It was all clear to him, he thought. He would go ahead and station a group of warriors in each cove, with a scout on the ridge overlooking the long, flat beach. The scout would always have time to alert the army in the first cove, no matter how bad the visibility or what time of day.

Once warned, the first group would wait for Te Rauparaha's boat to pass the point and then begin a vigorous challenge dance in an attempt to enrage the Chief and lure him in. As he approached and landed, thought Black Jack, the second army would storm from around the other rocky point and surround Te Rauparaha's men. Then, Black Jack and his men would confiscate Te Rauparaha's muskets and force him to negotiate. It all made perfect sense to Black Jack as he sat there daydreaming in the isolated cove. Convincing his people, he thought, would be another story, however.

VI

The girl stood in a great Maori house, flanked by a line of royal warriors. She knelt obediently before a large dark figure, bowing her head of long, black hair. With a sudden rushing sound and a sweeping motion of the specter's arm, her head became separated from her body cleanly at the neck and rolled across the floor. The neck attached to the head oozed green melon as the face contorted in anguish.

Black Jack awoke with a sharp pain in his chest. He was breathing heavily. It took him many seconds to realize where he was. He got up and took a walk around the pa before the sun rose.

"Where is Kumari?" Black Jack asked his senior warriors at breakfast.

"We do not know, as we have told you many times." one said plainly.

"Is she a slave at Kapiti?" Black Jack asked.

"Perhaps. It is possible, but we do not know. All we know is that she was taken from here under orders from Te Rauparaha."

"That is all I need to know. Whether she is at Kapiti

or somewhere else, I know that it is a place that is not her choosing; and that is slavery to me." Black Jack said.

"And what do you know of slavery?" another warrior boldly asked.

Black Jack paused in apparent anger; however, he was actually glad that the man had breached the subject. For it was Black Jack's final argument against Te Rauparaha's rule; and Black Jack had planned on bringing it to light that day. Now was as good as time as any; for he knew that word of his secret would spread quickly around the pa. That, he figured, would give the idea even more validity than publicly announcing it. He replied, "My son, I was born a slave to the White man. I know first-hand what it is to live as a slave; and what it means to gain freedom. So do not question my authority on the issue. I will forgive your ignorance, however." The warriors were stunned; and they sat in quiet reverence of their chief. He continued, "I want it all to end: The human suffering. There is no need for it in a place that is so beautiful; and yet this man, Te Rauparaha, actively seeks to continually spread terror throughout the lives of all Maori. Certainly, he has allied with your tribe, but at what cost? And what guarantee do you have that someday you or someone you love will not end up on his dinner table, or working in slavery? Is that what you want?" The warriors looked at one another in serious contemplation; and shook their heads in response to Black Jack one by one. "No. I did not think so. Killing and terrorizing are not strength. Love and peace are the will of the soul. Te Rauparaha has forgotten that. I do not think that he is evil. He has just become power hungry and overzealous for what you yourself have told me is Maori 'tradition'. Well, I say that it is time for a change. Do you agree?" Black Jack asked. The warriors nodded in agreement, their faces lightening with the lifting of some unspoken burden. "Good then. I have a plan. Te Rauparaha will be returning soon. I know this because I had a dream last night; and I am very intuitive and wise." Black Jack said, beginning to grin with a sly confidence. The warriors began to smile with their chief. "I have it all worked out; and if all goes well, Te Rauparaha's mind will be changed just like this:" Black Jack said, launching into his detailed and elaborate plan.

VII

Cold effervescent mist hovered in the dim air. It bubbled in Black Jack's nose and tickled his throat. The vapor emanated from the foamy turbulence which was the shallow washing of the tide into the cave. This was so different from the cavernous home of his humble beginnings at Te Pukatea, thought Black Jack. He celebrated the dissimilarities, however. For one, the moisture; but it was the overall feeling of the place that stimulated Black Jack's thoughts. The cave had a mystical quality, a spiritual power which Black Jack sensed as he lay peacefully inside near the south entrance. He was able to lie there comfortably, owing to the fact that the cave floor sloped downward to the tidal pool gradually as it ran north. Therein; its walls were moist and the air was humid, but the atmosphere of the cave was not clammy. Strangely, thought Black Jack, the tepid, moist conditions seemed to give the place energy. The water within the cave seemed to exert a pressure, a vital push outward, he thought. He liked it.

The small pool near the north entrance of the cave formed via a diminutive rivulet that ran between the rock face and the sandy beach in the north cove. Unlike the rest of the beach, it was affected by the rising and falling of the tide, so that at any given time the pool may have been anywhere from a few feet deep to merely a wet sand floor. The tidal pool also undulated with the waves, so that the sound of the surf was ever present throughout the cave. Instead of muffling the surge, however, the cave acted to channel and sharpen the sound so that near one end, as where Black Jack lay, it gave the illusion that the shifting water was always nearby. The truth was that the cave was roughly one-hundred feet long. More interestingly still, the cave had a sharp bend where the tidal pool formed near the north end. This gave the effect of allowing an eerie light to glow upon the pool without one being able to see directly through the cave at any one point except from the center of the pool. This catch could act as an advantage or a dilemma, thought Black Jack. He lay there, meditating on his plan and enjoying his unusual surroundings, until someone summoned him to the midday meal.

As Black Jack enjoyed his food, he perused the small canyon in which he sat. From the center of the beach facing the sea, he looked up over his right shoulder. There high above him in a clump of dense bush he could just make out the form of the appointed Lookout atop the rocky ledge. This man was the only pair of eyes that could presently see beyond the cliff and down the beach, while hundreds of other eyes remained locked within the blinders that were the walls of the small cove.

Black Jack looked left and saw the small cave in the large high wall that was the north side of the south cove. On the far side lay the mirror image of his present camp with hundreds more of his finest also enjoying their meal. A small miracle, marveled Black Jack, was this fortuitous arrangement of the twin coves. He had become as a playful child, running back and forth between the two beaches through the cave. He had issued the order that he be the only one allowed into the cave; not as a selfish whim, but out of practicality for his plan to be the second messenger, relaying the word of Te Rauparaha's approach once Black

Jack had heard. That's how it would be; and then the second herd would storm around the front of the face to Te Rauparaha's landed flank. Black Jack continued to run through it, amusing himself with the fluid interaction of the various parts and sequential actions of the scheme. As he sat there basking in the high noon sun, grazing and gazing, a shadow fell across his food.

The Lookout's dark form partially eclipsed the sun and his voice filled the cove. He yelled, "The big canoe! Coming fast!" Instantly, hundreds of men jumped to their feet with amazing synchrony. They looked to Black Jack and he gave them an affirmative nod of reassurance. He bolted into the cool cave and ran through to the other side. The other group of warriors could sense his urgency immediately, and they began to prepare their surprise. On his way back, Black Jack noticed that his feet splashed through only a few inches of water in the pool. Low tide, he thought: *Excellent.*

Back in the south cove, Black Jack positioned himself hurriedly behind his lines of warriors and watched the Lookout for the signal that Te Rauparaha's bow was about to cross the cliff face and show in the cove. The tension became as lightning in the air, and everyone remained silent and frozen. Suddenly, the tip of a boat appeared around the south rocks; and the haka began. The warriors displayed ferociously, with the same passion and precision that had straightened the hair on Black Jack's spine that day in Pukatea long ago. They yelled their chant vociferously and moved with methodical muscularity slowly down the beach to the water's edge.

They managed to gain Te Rauparaha's attention almost immediately; and he seemed genuinely surprised to see a full regiment in a cove which he knew as only a small empty oddity on his mental map. Standing on the bow like Napoleon, he pointed for his men to land. He knew that it would be his choice to fight; and it appeared as though he were giving the option deep consideration.

His time for making the decision did not last long, however, for as his boat made a hard landing, the dance ended immediately and the men charged. They were simultaneously joined by the second army coming through the surf from the north; and the two forces converged on Te Rauparaha and his surprised entourage. They never had time to react. It was such an unexpected breach of protocol by a supposedly subordinated tribe, that Te Rauparaha was overwhelmed by the entire experience. All the muskets in his boat were quickly confiscated as he stood watching; and his warriors sat bewildered as their ship was plundered.

Black Jack came running up with the wave of men and seized Te Rauparaha with an arm around his neck. He so overpowered the small chief that he was able to easily drag him up the beach and into the cave. He shouted at Te Rauparaha as they went, "You're not so big without your guns, eh Chief? Answer me!" Te Rauparaha could only manage muffled gurgles as he struggled to remain on his feet. Black Jack dragged him into the cave and down to the pool. As he grabbed the chief's mere, he flung him from his grip.

The old chief fell to his knees, breathless, and looked mournfully up at Black Jack. He said, gasping, "My son, you are going to kill your Chief after all?"

Black Jack said, "Perhaps." He was attempting to secure the chief's undivided attention. His physical prowess over his former mentor was acutely obvious by this time; and it would have been no problem for him to finish the old chief with a chop of the Patu Pounamu.

Te Rauparaha was obviously overwhelmed with the situation. As a chief, he knew that it was his honor and duty to submit to his conqueror, no matter how long he had reigned or how great his own conquests. However, the suddenness and surprise of the ambush had left him seriously without the will to die so soon. It had been a good run, he thought. The reality of its ending was sinking in only slowly. Te Rauparaha said finally, "Then let it be. You are a worthy successor. Be merciful and kill me swiftly with my own dear Papu-tahi." He was speaking of his personal, sacred, greenstone battle axe.

His words only served to further incense Black Jack, who replied, "I do not want to kill you, old man. Nor do I want any part of your ill-gotten kingdom. I will not answer evil with evil, although you have forced me to answer force with force merely to capture your attention. For that offense, you will now pay."

Te Rauparaha's eyes widened as he looked up at Black Jack's angry face. The old chief was kneeling in the center of the tidal pool which by now had filled to the level of his waist and was surging with the incoming waves.

Black Jack continued to wield the Chief's mere with a raised hand as he stared down into his eyes. He said, "No, death would be too good for you. You know that living in shame and dishonor would be far worse, don't you? What would they say? Ha! 'The mighty old chief, bested by his little Black boy apprentice. A White man's slave!' I know you. You would sooner kill yourself than sit and listen to that. A lifetime of glory and your remaining days spent in anguish, as if none of the former had taken place or even mattered. But no, you will live. And if you give me what I want, I will even spare you the misery and pain of losing your reputation. You will walk from this cave with your head held high; and you will still be able to tell your men that you and I are allies, and that we still rule this great land together. Years will pass, however, and they will be amazed at how gentle their great chief has become. How kind, how tolerant; and how he eats the flesh of his fellow man no more, nor kills innocent men, women, and children. Doesn't that sound wonderful, Chief? Can you imagine that, old man: Glory without bloodshed?" Black Jack raised his voice louder and louder as he became increasingly sarcastic with his tirade.

Te Rauparaha's eyes had begun to show a different kind of fear. Now, he thought Black Jack to be going mad; and he did not know what to truly expect from his captor. Also, the water was now up to his chest, and he had begun to fear the rising tide as much as Black Jack's sharp words. He asked, "What is it? If there is something that I can serve you with and retain my dignity; then by all means, let me help us both."

Black Jack angrily said, "In good time, Chief. I want to first make sure that you fully understand my mission. Hear me now: No more killing and eating! Not only for the sake of sanity, but for the sake of your people! Look at you: You used the decimation of your people by the White man's sickness to take advantage of them. How cowardly was that? Your people dying, and what was your answer? Kill more, and rule and enslave the remaining few. Ha! Do I need to tell you how foolish that makes you look? The White man writes things down. Your people, on the other hand, talk about their past. What do you think the White man's books will say about you when there are no more of your people to tell the story. 'A great Maori Chief whose services to eradicate his own people were procured for a few muskets and some tobacco'. Is that how you want to be remembered for all time? If it is, tell me now, and I will swiftly make your exit from this cave all the more swift." Black Jack raised the mere as if to strike.

Te Rauparaha's eyes widened with terror and the realization of his own stupidity simultaneously. He stammered, "No, no! Spare me. I understand what it is you say. But look at me, son! Who is it that you think you are dealing with?" The water was brimming over his shoulders as he looked up at Black Jack. He continued, "I am the child of highest Maori royalty. My parents ruled this land long before Captain Cook ever set his blue eyes upon it. I was raised to be a great chief from the time I was in my mother's arms. I do not do the things I do out of malice toward my people. It is my duty as a good Maori, my destiny as a chief; and it is tradition: My people expect it, because that is the way it has always been done."

Black Jack's brow rose at the sound of his last words. He said, "Ah, there it is: 'Tradition'. The way things have always been done somehow makes them right. Well, I only have to say, that if doing things as they have always been done leaves you with no people to do them, then that makes the things you do rather pointless, don't you agree?" Te Rauparaha nodded, mouth gaping and eyes bulging. Black Jack added, "Besides, 'always' is a long time. For your people, 'always' has only been the last few-hundred years. Who do you think the first person was that suggested eating other people? Do you think he was very popular?" Te Rauparaha shook his head with a negative response, and the same dumbfounded expression. Black Jack said sharply, "No! I didn't think so. So how did it become so popular, you ask? Because stupid people went along with it until it was 'tradition', that's how! So don't tell me that rubbish, or you'll only make me madder!" Black Jack was livid at this point. His saliva sprayed in Te Rauparaha's face as he yelled. He still held the raised mere, waving it wildly.

Te Rauparaha asked meekly, "What do you want?"

Black Jack cut him off, shouting, "I'm getting to that! Now, just be quiet. I want you to understand me perfectly, that's what I want. I want you to know that I am doing this for your own good, for the good of all Maori. I want you to understand that when you leave this cave, that you are the man who is going to change this country. Not me, you! You got that?"

Te Rauparaha, resigned to Black Jack's raving lecture, said quietly, "Yes." The water was starting up his neck.

Black Jack started again, quietly. "All right, from the beginning: You are going to resume your rule of the Maori in your domain as a peaceful and kind chief. You are going to stop fighting other Maori not under your control, and work toward peace and unity with them. Now, this is all because you not only need to preserve and strengthen the remaining Maori; you also need to prepare yourselves for the coming White men."

Te Rauparaha looked surprised. He asked, "What do you mean?"

Black Jack said wisely, "There are many, many more White men than there are Maori. Believe me, I know. They will come and try to take everything you have. Trust me, I have seen them do it to my people and other people many times. More importantly, the Pakeha do not fight with one another as the Maori do. They do not kill for the sake of killing; and they do not eat one another. They are a unified force coming to this land. You will need all your strength and numbers to stand up to them. Do you understand?"

Te Rauparaha showed a cognizant expression, as well as a look of concern about the threatening water level. He asked eagerly, trying no to sound desperate, "I truly do. You have enlightened me, young man. My heart is opened. What is it you still want?"

Black Jack saw sincerity in Te Rauparaha's eyes and truth in his voice. He said, "There is a Maori woman. She was my soul mate before you came and destroyed what we had. I want to find her. Tell me where she is." He spoke as if he thought Te Rauparaha knew.

Te Rauparaha said, "Tell me who it is you speak of, Black Jack. There have been so many that I have sent away." He spoke with true concern.

Black Jack, flaring, said, "Kumari!"

Te Rauparaha looked suddenly perplexed. He asked, "The daughter of Ruaoneone? Does she know you?"

Black Jack grew angry once again and shouted, "Know me? We were married, you fool! We were in love as much as the sky loves the sea. You destroyed that. Where is she?"

Te Rauparaha, swallowing hard, said, "She is alive, my son, take heart. I hear she is inland, just south of here at a small Rangitane pa. You can reach her in a day or two. I will tell you where. But . . ." The old chief paused. The water had reached his chin.

Black Jack asked warily with anger still in his voice, "But what?" He was beginning to realize the prospect of seeing Kumari.

Te Rauparaha said cautiously, "But that tribe was marked for death by me. The order has been issued, and the surrounding unfriendly tribes will not know of my sudden turn around. I cannot reverse everything that I have set in motion over the last few years with a wave of my hand. You yourself will be in danger if you go and show yourself to be friendly to the few remaining Rangitane."

Black Jack said quickly, "Leave it to me. I will not make you or me look as though we have gone soft overnight. Even I realize that weakness is no advocate of peace. Come on, you may go now." Black Jack reached out to help his captive up from the water; however, as he touched his head, he quickly plunged it below the surface.

Te Rauparaha resurfaced with a look of confusion. He said, sputtering and bursting with suppressed anxiety, "Oh, thank you. I will not forget what you have told me. From now on, I owe my life to you. You have taught me well, my son. Please, carry my Papu-tahi in good faith and may it keep you always."

Black Jack held the gifted mere proudly in his right hand, and he embraced the old chief with his left arm. They walked from the cave shoulder to shoulder, now laughing as men who have bonded out of mutual respect. They hailed the awaiting warriors.

Black Jack gave the signal, and Te Rauparaha his; and the warriors abandoned their standoff. For the rest of the afternoon the two troops played the Maori version of rugby with much camaraderie; and the two chiefs ate heartily while they worked out a plan for lasting peace.

Chapter 16

A CRACK AT HAPPINESS

Virgin valleys opened up before Black Jack as vast, verdant, velvet vistas, spreading out over rolling hills and peaks as they beckoned him to venture on. The sun sailed over a completely clear and cloudless sky, its heat having eloped with the humidity. Freshly perfumed, the cool air sauntered among the trees, awaiting its chance to steal a ride on a passing warm steed called the breeze which rustled the leaves as it ran. The wind sang Kumari.

Inland was a new experience for Black Jack. For the first time in New Zealand, he saw no sea, and no sign of man for as far as he could see. Te Rauparaha's directions had been simple. Black Jack needed only to travel down the great straight coast toward the cape. At the mouth of the great river, he was to turn toward the interior and follow the water until he began to reach the mountains. At a certain point, Te Rauparaha had said, a very distinctive lonely peak would appear on his left. If he headed straight for the lone mountain away from the river, he would meet directly with his old tribe near its base. It was a beautifully sensible place to relocate, thought Black Jack now, as he looked around the nearby mountain ranges.

Standing by the clear river, he took a drink of the sparkling water and admired the sculpture of the surrounding earth. For the first time, he saw the ranges to the north: A succession of ridges, each large in themselves, increasing in height at even intervals and their respective distances. It was like a stairway to heaven, thought Black Jack. Perhaps that was the reason for the local Maori naming it 'footsteps to the rainbow of the gods', he speculated. Regardless, he considered it one of the most beautiful works of creation that he had ever seen. Its unique set of textures and shapes made him want to reach out and explore it with his hands. The valley floor was broad and flat, spreading for miles in places where its fingers reached into the craggy hills. It was like an African savanna interspersed with large green and brown pyramids. Black Jack found it hard to believe that he was only a few miles from the ocean. What excellent farm land the area would make, he thought.

The group carried on, bolstered by hope and Black Jack's enthusiasm for his long-awaited goal. He had selected several of his best warriors to accompany him on the trip, and they formed a lively entourage as they tramped along in high spirits. Their mood was a combination of the carry-over from their glorious day with Te Rauparaha, and the promise of the joyous reunion which lay ahead. What a day it had been, thought Black Jack, to see the faces of the men on the beach as he triumphantly brought Te Rauparaha, humbled and repentant, from the cave. The warriors had seemed confused at first; however, when they had discovered the benefits afforded by the two chiefs' truce, they had responded with resounding support. It

was a win-win situation for everyone involved; and now
Black Jack, feeling as though he were the worthy engineer
of events, was heading off to claim his prize.

How would Kumari respond to him after seven years?
he wondered. His love had never wavered; but what about
hers? he worried. He knew how he felt, and that was all
that mattered, he thought. He knew that he truly loved
Kumari, and that what they had shared at Te Pukatea was
not a childhood infatuation. At least not for him, he
thought. She had been his first true love. He had thought
that he had loved before; however, that false love had only
given him grounds for comparing what he had felt with
Kumari; and what he still felt now. But what of her feelings? he asked himself again. He knew that she had been
betrothed to Pakauwera; but had she loved him? he wondered. Had it lasted? he pondered. And if so, would she
consider having two husbands? Black Jack loved her that
much, that he would share her with another man, if need
be. But he wondered if her custom, or if she herself, would
allow such an arrangement?

Black Jack was willing to make that small sacrifice for
the overwhelming joy of having her back by his side, even
if only for part of the time. The thought of just seeing her,
face to face; or of smelling her hair and feeling her skin: It
all made the years of absence seem like minutes. The time
spent with her seemed perfectly preserved in his mind, as
if encased in crystal, never to age or be touched by time. It
were as though Black Jack could envision eternity with
her right here on Earth, he thought, in the paradise in
which he now walked. His mother had spoken of the Garden of Eden, and of the perfection within which the world's
first man and woman lived. Black Jack wondered if he had
actually been given the chance by God to live out a ver-

sion of that existence. It certainly felt like it, he thought. His steps quickened.

Late afternoon yellow gave way to early evening rose as the troop neared the area of expected occupation. They had seen the mysterious single peak and headed for it; however, they had seen no sign of Maori. As the valley floor narrowed, they came upon a small stream. Stopping to refresh themselves, they noticed various things floating upon the water. Glittering like silver flakes were the loose scales of fish; and floating feathers followed those. The final clue came in the form of fern leaves and potato skins flowing in the swirl; and the warriors knew that people could not be far. Everyone began to hurry on the heels of Black Jack, who rushed ahead swiftly to confirm the findings of their aquatic archaeology.

Bush began to open onto cultivated land. The tribe had begun to plant crops, Black Jack thought. Trees had been cleared, leaving only the odd one standing here and there around fields of high grass, corn, and potatoes. Black Jack marveled at the width and breadth of the pa. Mud huts began to appear as the path became more distinct, finally opening up onto the main area of the marae. The men ran as a pack now; and people began to emerge from various places and dwellings to see them. Black Jack became breathless in his excitement as he ran back and forth along the main corridor of the village toward the center, and the great community house. Most people he did not recognize; however, a few from his former tribe pointed and waved as he hurried by. He acknowledged them in his mind only, as he took no time for formalities in his search for his one objective. His men flanked him, intent only on following his lead; for it was only he who would be welcome here, if at all.

Suddenly, warriors from the tribe began to flow from the Great House in haste, preparing to meet their challengers. Behind them came Pakauwera with a stern look on his face. Seeing Black Jack, his demeanor immediately changed, and he ordered the warriors to stand down. Black Jack's party had arrived right before supper time, and many women and children were milling about the back of the house preparing the meal. Black Jack approached Pakauwera at the front door, and the two clasped hands and touched noses and foreheads. They patted one another on the back, and exchanged pleasant greetings along with sentiments of surprise.

Not wanting to be rude, Black Jack humbly apologized and asked forgiveness for his unexpected visit. He added, however, that he was on urgent business. He said, "If it pleases the Chief, and if time has healed the wound between us, then I would like very much to see Kumari."

The Chief answered immediately and without malice, "Of course, my brother. It is an honor that you have come. I know what you and Kumari shared; and you are completely welcome to see my wife now."

Black Jack hid his anxious desire, and asked, "Ah thank you, Chief. I desire only a brief talk with her for old time's sake; and then my men and I will impart to you our message from Te Rauparaha."

The Chief replied, "Nonsense. Spend as much time with the beautiful princess as you like. We will all enjoy a great meal together; and you can explain your mission after supper. Kumari is just around back there. Go and see her." The Chief pointed casually around the house while remaining in the doorway. "I will wait inside." he concluded.

Black Jack's heart leapt. He gave a quick anxious glance at his warriors as a child entering a candy shop; and proceeded to lead them around the house. The question as to

why she was around back with the common women briefly
crossed his mind; however, he quickly dismissed it in his
delirious rush to bring her long-lost form into his vision.
Rounding the corner, he scanned for her among the smattering of women, toiling to and fro at various tasks. Some
were sitting, peeling vegetables and tending pots; while
others walked around carrying various animals and children.

Then he saw her. Near the back of the yard was the
recognizable outline of her slender back. He melted. Gathering his nerve and his calm, he slowed as he walked toward her. His men remained at the back corner of the
house. Crossing the yard, passing through paths of busy
women, he remained intently focused on the back of her
head. From afar, he could tell that she still had her full
head of long, shiny, raven-black hair. In slow-motion, he
envisioned her turning, smiling, flashing her white teeth
and green eyes, her smooth, brown skin glowing radiantly
in the setting sunlight.

As he reached her, he noticed that she was sitting on a
tree stump. From behind, he could tell that she was preparing something: She seemed to be chopping fish with a
whale bone. He drew a final breath; prayed; and reached
out and lightly touched the back of her shoulder. She
turned slowly without expression. Suddenly, there she was,
in all her beauty, looking up at him. He felt the Earth
drop a few feet beneath him and the sky sway. His head
grew light and his insides felt as though he were plum-
meting from a great height. His scalp tingled and his groin
swelled with hot and cold fluids. His Adam's apple
struggled to set itself free from his constricting throat. He
felt his spirit rise above his body and then come back down.
She smiled, and his heart went into labor. He wanted to
devour her, be inside her, and satisfy the longings of her
soul all at the same time. He wanted to make love to her

there on the spot in front of all of the people of the village while she screamed his name in ecstasy. They were re-united, at last!

As he prepared to speak, he noticed a small, pink, chunk of fish on her forehead near her hair. He smiled as he reached to brush it away: A wayward piece of the Pisces the poor girl was wailing on, he thought. The flesh-col-ored bleb remained unmoved. Black Jack cautiously placed his fingers along her hair at the bump and pushed her locks aside.

The pink furrow stretched from the top left corner of her forehead across her temple diagonally to a loose flap of skin which folded into a dark chasm within her skull. There, on the side of her head, normally hidden by hair, was a shadowy section of a spidery map of pulsating blue rivers of blood coursing in and among a sickly gray and shiny pudding. Black Jack pulled back his hand and let her hair drop to conceal the unmerciful work of an unsuc-cessful mere. His ears began to ring and buzz, and the air became thick. He searched her eyes for a spark of life.

Remarkably, she sprang to her feet, still smiling, and began to speak. What came out of her mouth, however, accompanied by the drool and partially-chewed food from days gone by, was closer to the crowing moans of a child in the midst of a nightmare than to any words that Black Jack had ever heard. He was able to make out some of what she said as Kumari yelled, "Bwak man! Bwak man! I know you!"

Black Jack stumbled backward, searching her face for signs of her remaining intelligence in light of her awkward claim. He said, "Yes?"

She continued, "You're da bwak man!" These last words came from a place that Black Jack knew was devoid of mind or memory of him and his love for her; and he turned away from her in horror. She ranted on as he walked away, "Da bwak man is here, everybody. See da bwak man? See him?" Black Jack's steps quickened as he reached the back of the house and his warriors. His face was a green black; and small beads of sweat covered his face. He vomited as he reached the corner. He hurried past his men who fell in behind and flanked him on both sides, not sure what he would do.

Kumari pursued the group, all the time saying, "Wook! Wook at the bwak man! He is bwak!"

Black Jack could take no more. He wheeled around on his heels and lunged at Kumari. His men caught him and struggled to restrain his vigorous charge. He leapt, clawed, and screamed at his former lover as his men used all of their strength to hold his thrusting and writhing body. He began yelling as loudly as any man could yell, "Kill her! I'm gonna kill her! Please, dear God, let me kill her!" His face swelled grotesquely as his eyes bulged and turned red; and sweat and saliva flowed effluently as he flailed. His veins stood upon his skin.

Kumari stood watching him, unscathed by his attempted assault, and pointing, she said, "Wook. The bwak man is not happy. Why are you sad, bwak man?"

Black Jack made one more tremendous heave with all of his strength; and then his eyelids fluttered as his eyeballs rolled back in their sockets. His body went limp, with one arm outstretched and fingers gnarled. In a fading, raspy, voice, he said, "Kill her."

II

Light, mellow smoke sharpened in the crisp dawn air as it stung Black Jack's nostrils, awakening him to the accompanying sporadic crackling of many small fires nearby.

His head felt as a torn muscle cramping; his throat seared; and his bones scraped one another along with parts of his innards as he struggled to stir. He thought at first that perhaps he had fallen from a great height. He wondered where he was; and then he remembered. He ceased his efforts to rise, and closed his eyes with a long, groaning sigh. He continued to live and breathe despite his utter lack of will or desire to do so. Through the physical pain and mental quagmire, he reached down into his soul to collect his thoughts for the inevitable day.

Black Jack sat up and peered from the hut. There among the women preparing the morning meal was Kumari, seated on her stump, walloping fish as though she had not moved from the previous night. The clarity of the early morning leant strength to his thoughts, and he stole the opportunity to look upon her and reflect without her knowledge. With her back to him, he could view her fondly from a distance, her living image now serving as a symbol of her former self, simulating her semblance as a succor to his sorrow. He stared. She stood. He noticed now for the first time that she was with child. Black Jack was far beyond being capable of reacting or having a reaction; he merely contemplated deeper. He was detached from his feelings for her now, he realized. He was only an observer of an object, forming opinions about someone—or something—who for so long had formed the core of his life. He reflected now on what it was that he had wanted with Kumari: He believed that it was Heaven on Earth. Black Jack's mother had often told him about Heaven, and the promise of a perfect life after death for those who were saved; and Black Jack had thought that he had found that paradise in his lifetime. His and Kumari's love had been perfect, he thought. Black Jack could not envision a more fulfilling and happy life than spending the rest of his days with her in this veritable Garden of Eden.

Yet, she was not dead. Black Jack questioned his own authority to judge the value of her life now, to herself or anyone. Who was he to wish for or ponder her death, either as a merciful release from the shackles of her seemingly empty shell, or as a possible passage to a restoration to her former glorious self? he wondered. Black Jack simply did not know which fate he would choose for her, given the right; and yet she remained there-alive-to torment, mock, and continually remind him that no matter what his choice or spiritual knowledge, he must pull himself together and go on living without her. Black Jack wept. There in the shadows with his grief, he quietly mourned the loss of her from his life, separately from and unbeknownst to her body standing not forty feet from him. His farewell to Kumari respectfully bid, Black Jack rose to meet with Pakauwera.

III

With a look of guilty apprehension, the Chief met Black Jack at the door of the Great House. The Chief said, "Please come in. We will catch up on old times and celebrate your return."

Black Jack replied with a tone of general disapproval, "No, thank you. We will be on our way this morning." He paused, selecting his next subject carefully.

Rushing to ease the tension, the Chief said, "I did not know how to tell you. It has been very hard on all of us. As you can see, I still love her very much. She has borne to me three children and we are doing quite well."

Black Jack relented in his look of disdain, and said, "Well, yes, I am happy for the tribe. I still consider the

Rangitane to be my people. That is also what I need to discuss with you."

The Chief raised a genuinely curious brow, and said, "Oh? Does it have to do with Te Rauparaha?"

Black Jack said, "Yes. You know that I went to war with him, right?"

The Chief said evasively, "Well, I had heard rumors."

Black Jack continued abruptly, "It's not important now. What matters, shall we say, is that Te Rauparaha has had a change of heart. He has not promised the world overnight, but he has given me his word that the threat to this tribe has been lifted.

The Chief's eyes lit up, and then attempting to downplay his excitement, commented casually, "Really."

Black Jack said, "On one condition:"

The Chief looked concerned again, and asked, "And what is that?"

Black Jack continued, "In an effort not to appear weak to some of his outlying enemies, he has requested that a massacre be staged. He wants you to use some of your old bones and tell any messengers that my visit left many dead and dying."

The Chief's ears perked up. He looked as though he were going to laugh. He at last said, "I think that we can arrange that . . . Bloody Jack!" He began to chuckle nervously as a child who has revealed a forbidden secret.

Black Jack's eyes flared at the Chief, and he snapped, "Stop it!"

The Chief erupted into uproarious laughter. Black Jack stormed out of the village with his warriors, as the Chief continued to bellow with laughter behind him. Black Jack reaffirmed a decision to himself which had been in the making for some time: He was through with living with the Maori for a while.

Chapter 17

FROM KAPITI TO KAKAPO

So with hardened heart, Black Jack headed for home. Part of him had died in his endeavors to find lost love; and yet a new aspect of his person was coming to life. Not as beautiful as the hope of eternal love, this side of him had perhaps lain dormant or obscured by more innocent or naïve folds of his soul; however, now in his burgeoning state of callous resolve, the thing inside him reared its ugly head to offer solace in the absence of warmer and softer comforts: It was the lust for wealth.

Black Jack began to think back to the words so long before which had not made a large impression at the time, but which were coming back now clearly to entice him. They were the statements of Happy and Groggy Jack concerning the profitability of whaling. After having lost his desire for all the ways of the White man and his money, ironically, now Black Jack was returning full circle to seek out a possible position at one of the reeking bastions of raw greed for blubber.

II

"I decided that I truly had become a free man; so I could do what I wanted. Even if it did mean going back to live with the White Man. I decided first that I wanted to see the place called Kapiti. That's where Te Rauparaha ran his operations from; and I figured that it would be a good place to start my soul searching. Besides, I wanted to tell him how bad he had messed up my life, even though I had already forgiven him." Black Jack said as he sipped his second cup of tea. He asked his hosts, "Now this is a whole 'nother story. If'n you don't want to hear it, I'll understand."

The Maori Judge swallowed hard, eyes wide, and said, "It is all one story. It is your story. Please continue. Biscuit?"

Black Jack sheepishly accepted the cookie and cleared his throat. With the first bite and a hot sip, he continued, "I went alone to Kapiti Island in my own canoe, leaving behind the people I had come to know at Te Pukatea. They said that I would be back; although I tried to explain that I was returning to the ways of the White Man. That was another reason for going to Kapiti: I knew from experience that it was a crossroads for the whaling ships.

"When I arrived, Kapiti Island was teeming with Maori and Whites alike. It was like a frontier town where everything is in demand and easy to get. It was not difficult to find Te Rauparaha, and from him I learned that most of the Maori were slaves that he had suddenly freed. This had created a new problem, however, in that most of them had no way of making their way home, or anywhere else for that matter. They had become as nomads in their own land, marooned in a place that was too small to support them all by honest means. Most had resorted to chicanery or outright begging to get what they needed from the whalers. One of the ship's doctors had told Te Rauparaha that he had a 'social crisis' on his hands. Te Rauparaha had asked him if that was another of the Pakeha's evil spirits.

"I told Te Rauparaha about the fate of Kumari and the other Rangitane. I told him how part of me wished that I had not forgiven him so soon; and had slain him in the cave that day. He said that he understood and that he was sorry, he had reformed, he said. Not only because of his realization about his wrongs against Maori, but also because he had learned that what I warned him about the Pakeha was true. I asked him what he meant, and he said that he had had a run in with some whalers that had turned bloody. Many Maori were killed, he said. He said that he was partly to blame, but he thought that the Whites had overreacted. It was something to do with a tribe taking some White children and their mother.

"I told Te Rauparaha that I was returning to the White Man's world for a time. I told him that I had a wife and child back home; and now with the loss of Kumari, I wanted to try and make some money and return to them. He said that he understood. He said that he had recently taken a new wife, and that his feelings had changed about everything.

"He also said that he had good news about the Pakeha. In his mediation of the incident with the kidnapped family, he had actually negotiated a purchase with the White whaler for some land back down South near Te Pukatea. The man was on his way back from Sydney with supplies to set up a shore-whaling station he said.

"I asked if it was a big burly man with black hair, and he said yes. My heart jumped. I asked if the wife and children were all right, and he said yes. I was overjoyed. I told him that I had actually helped to kill a whale before we met.

"Te Rauparaha said the whalers looked for Maori who would help them set up camp. He said that I should offer my services as a Maori and not as a former black White man, and see how I get on. It did seem like a good idea. He told me to go on down there and tell the Maori that he had sent me, and that I had first shot at helping the new whalers. He said it was at Kakapo Bay. Just follow the coast up from Te Pukatea, he said.

"So we said our farewells, and he gave me his assurances of peace in the region, with Whites and Maori. I told him again that the White people would not go out of their way to kill any Maori if he helped them and did not pester them. He said he agreed, but he still was not gonna go all soft. We laughed and did the hongi, and I set off with a little better feeling in my heart.

"When I got to Kakapo, I really liked it. It was a little bit like Pukatea. A nice, small bay with hills and trees running down to it, and a good, flat beach. I thought that Jackie had picked a good spot to buy for a few guns, blankets, and a keg of tobacco. I wouldn't have minded purchasing some land; but first I had to earn some money. I stayed with the Maori there. They had heard of me, and they respected Te Rauparaha's wishes. They were waiting for the whalers with all the wood and things that they would need to get started. Some of the men had even been out on a few whale hunts down at Te Awaiti before the owner's shipwreck. One woman wished she was a whaler's wife as well.

"When the ship pulled in, I greeted them in full warrior dress. I wondered if Jackie and his wife would recognize me. At first, it seemed like they did. Jackie's eyes seemed to light up; and he said I was the blackest Maori that he had ever seen; but beyond that, our veiled familiarity seemed only to stem the initial tide of trust without revealing our former brief acquaintance. I was happy to leave it at that. They seemed happy to have someone young, big, and strong to make their life easier at their new home. It was all good. They got off to a flying start, Jackie being eager to pick up his business at the pace of his former station.

"From 1836 to 1843, it did go surprisingly well: Like a dream, in fact. That period of my life was as exciting and interesting, in its own way, as my time with the Maori; and until a similar and untimely end to it, I can honestly say that I had again begun to glimpse happiness.

"The whalers at the bay were amazed at my ability. They had never seen such raw savagery from a seeming novice; and they often asked me to be their headsman. There were many times that I was first to the whale, and many more that I would leap upon its back and finish the beast fearlessly and single-handedly. Without boasting, I can say that I became a legend of the seas during that time; only because my keenness for killing, which sprang from a former life, had now become one of my few satisfying pleasures. When once I had blindly slaughtered my fellow man, I now boldly butchered the Black Whale with the same senselessness. I will now recount only the more significant events from that era of my life as a Tonguer."

Chapter 18

THE WATCH

A large wobbling droplet falls from a low gable through a worm's-eye view in slow motion to the ground. Another drop falls backlit by the cool gray sky, then another. The rains come again and the sound is like hushed sandpaper rushing in around the lone house as the winds from the shore brush its drab sides and stir the low bushes growing down to the sea.

On the beach a large kettle, a try-pot, smolders over its guarded coals. The rain spatters and hisses on the hot iron; tiny bombardments vainly stipple the skirting ashes surrounding the glowing embers; and meteoric craters form in the boiling surface of the sludgy, smoking oil brimming in the one-tun pot. It rhythmically belches a timely puff of greasy, steamy smoke as the rancid vapors take flight from this irreverent cauldron of the end of the whale's remains. The muffled bubbling harmonizes with the constant sizzle of repelled rain, in concert with the steady

downpour. The kettle sits alone, hovering confidently despite the barrage, above the smooth black sea pebbles which
generously crowd the beach and allow to mingle among
them the scant, gray sand which washes in and out with
the punctilious tide.

The sheets of rain stacking and sailing sideways in the
torrent sweep the beach until they slap into the royal blue
water of the virgin bay, now penciled charcoal murky in
the premature dusk imposed by the storm. But look, now
a long line of white curves rises from this lonely sandy
stage; a row of whale ribs bleached by the absentee sun,
almost glowing in their alabaster radiance and in mockingly stark contrast to the cast and pall of the day. A holy
cathedral of sorts, a collection of flying buttresses suited
for the Notre Dame itself, undermined by their cruelly
ironic resemblance to carefully arranged headstones.

Now see how they frame the simple outline of the
grog shop up the hill, with the din of its seafaring occu-
pants quelled by the strong beating of the wet tympani
outside. Across the bay, the homogenous fluid chorus
pauses momentarily, as the rain ceases, and a woman
emerges from the house onto the mist-soaked deck and
releases a bellowous cry, "Suns breaking! Whale Watch,
post!"

The white door of the one-room grog shop slams open
as the clamor of many pairs of greasy, muddy boots on its
wooden deck almost drowns the crashing of the shattered
pane situated within the path of the poorly placed portal's
knob.

"I've told you about that door, mate, about a thousand goddamn times!" yells the shopkeep. The whalers
take no notice of him in their ruckus as they flee from
their dim, dank den and carry on loudly in song and boastful talk en masse toward the beach. One man remains on
the deck, however, as he has drawn the day's honorary

position of 'Watch', considered a fortuitous role by many because of its amenities and benefits the least of which being free grog and tobacco, for the duration of duty; but not without its onerous responsibility and the expectations of his mates that no whale within a hawk's eyesight be not only spotted but vociferously and promptly announced.

The job carried prestige owing to its direct obligation to produce: A position which in its cost-effectively allocated slot of one, carried as much weight as a boatful of its harpooned hunting colleagues; and with this honor came the pride of being skillful in such a potentially complex role, and the pleasure of relaxing into the job when an experienced Watch's confidence and competence so permitted.

Besides, there were many horror stories about the proverbial neglectful and unproductive Watch, who when at the end of the day, had spotted nary a whale, was sharply castigated and ostracized by his 'mates' for days on end; so that by the completion of the roster rotation, his senses had been keenly honed and sharpened by his sympathetic cohorts and he was once again deemed 'fit for duty' with the condition that a second fruitless watch would result in a verdict of his total failure as a Watch, whether there had actually been any whales about or not.

Such was the pressure placed on this focal member of the whaling team; and the average leviathan chaser had no problem with it after one or two weeks following his arrival at the bay, so that most of the men enjoyed the trust and faith of their fellow flenchers, save for the odd bugger or two. But by-and-large, everyone kept an eye out for the Black Whales that roamed the bay.

Chapter 19

ONE SUMMER MORNING

Black Jack awoke before dawn. From his hut, he could still hear the revelry of the shore-whaling party down the beach. The conversation was unintelligible from his distance; however, the pattern of sounds was a continual repetition of the same things: Low muffled bantering with occasional highs of grumbling, followed by a peal of laughter and various hoots and hollers for a period of time; and then more low grumbling. It was like listening to a rainstorm blow in and out of the harbor; however, this particular morning was clear, calm, and warm. It was summer.

Other than the sailors, there was no particular noise throughout the pa. The dawn was close to breaking; and so the light blue-gray hue was beginning to backwash the stars; and the landscape was becoming visible to those who cared to look around. The gang's bonfire was dying down; and the party was showing its usual signs of disbanding for the night. It was the off season; and an unwary pass-

14601-GARD

erby might have become guilty of being too kind and generously overestimating the amount of work that the whalers now attended to on a day-to-day basis. That is to say: Absolutely none, except for the barest minimum of effort required to survive. Gathering food, shifting goods, and perhaps occasionally doing odd jobs around the hut for the missuses: Other than that, summer was a time of leisure and recreation between arduous and dangerous hunting seasons; and everyone treated it as such with no exception.

As the party broke up, Black Jack could hear the bay returning to virtual silence. As there was no wind, the only vague sounds he could make out were the small breakers scrubbing the tide line, and the occasional brushing of men's shoulders on low bushes as they made their way through the winding foot paths leading to their respective huts. The bay cove was like a large amphitheater facing the ocean. Huts were arranged randomly along the paths at varying heights and distances from one another as they scattered down the inside of the bowl to the beach. The hillside was covered with the low native scrub brush that grew from the high tree line down to the sea, interrupted only by the small footpaths and clearing for each hut. All in all, it made for a very peaceful setting for this small whaling village.

The quiet following the retiring of the men lasted for approximately one-half hour; when suddenly, the silence was pierced by the exquisite singing of several Bellbirds, with their melodious wild music that emulated small silver bells. This was followed by the crowing of the Kaka birds, which added an element of baritone to the arrangement. Then, the Kakapo chimed in with its intermittent mid-range notes; and this symphony was completed by the staccato interjections of the Takahe as they strutted around the yards of the villagers. It was a variegated, multi-textured, melee of natural sound; and Black Jack lay there enjoying it in the gauzy pre-dawn light.

This concert went on for a few unspoiled moments, when Black Jack became aware of a different sound mingling with the others. It was a bird he could not readily identify. Among the bell sounds, between the low crows and the middle warbles, came a soft murmuring sound in starts and stops. Eventually it began to come in regular intervals; and actually became quite rhythmic: Like breathing, though Black Jack. The sound became more like a moan from a large beast; and yet it did not sound like the distressed groans of an injured animal. It more resembled the pleasant pulsation of the creatures around him. Suddenly, there was another set of shorter, higher sounds, further up on the hill; and the two sets of sounds faded in and out, intertwining with one another in differing tempos but with similar timber. Then, a third such sound, this one deeper in quality, began emanating from a spot a few yards below Black Jack's hut. He sat up, straining his ears to listen between the singing of the birds and the playing of the mysterious bellows. And with his ear perched at the window, he heard a new and different sound altogether, echoing throughout the cove in the clear dawn air.

Coming in waves, it seemed to increase in volume in direct relation to its rapidity: That is, as it became faster, it got louder. Black Jack listened to its various directions and sources; and he determined that the new sounds were coming from the same origins as the hidden bagpipes. The sounds were like bird beaks softly striking the trunks of trees; or like children's feet gently hitting floor stones as they ran. Slap, slap, slap; (then louder) whap, whap, whap; (then softly again) slap, slap, slap. All intermingled with the moans; all ranging up and down the hillside in various tones.

Then, Black Jack realized a certain characteristic of the sounds: A voice-like quality; and he recognized one of the voices behind the low throaty sounds. It was the missus of one of his fellow shore-whalers! And then it all came to him as the dawn broke and orange virgin sunlight spilled onto the bushy green hillside: The moans of all the wives. And the moans, one by one, gave way to a cacophony of shrieks and cries as the birds took flight in a confused synchrony; and the valley became silent once again.

And then Black Jack heard giggling outside the door of his hut. He got off his mat and walked to the doorway; and outside he saw a row of women sitting along the hillside next to his dwelling. They looked at him and laughed quietly as the first one stood up and moved toward him. He recognized them as all of the unmarried Maori girls from around the pa, numbering about twelve in ages ranging from sixteen to early twenties. The first one motioned that she would like to come in; and Black Jack, bewildered, allowed her to pass him in the doorway. Once in, she hastily disrobed and made her way under his wool blanket, smiling and beckoning him to join her. Black Jack hesitated; and peered out the doorway, only to see the long line of ladies waving him on and coyly cackling. He looked around the hill, and upon seeing no other eyes, set about to completing the task at hand. He reckoned that it would be rude to refuse the collective offer of the coquettes' honor; and he realized that time was of the essence if he were going to finish the job before the rising sun exposed his unplanned scheme.

II

Hurriedly pressing on, Black Jack pushed to complete his duties with the unloved women of the pa. It was always an uncelebrated affair, of which he made no fanfare

nor any complex attempts at elaborate posturing. He
merely pleasured each one in turn discretely in the most
direct manner, while the others sat along the walls of his
hut. The women would chat and laugh, seemingly uninterested at times with the primary activity in progress.
They would gibber on excitedly about the ordinary, using
animated hands, frequently breaking into long trills of
heightening tones; as a piano keyboard being suddenly
run in scales from bass to treble. Other times they would
sound like birds, chirping in a cacophony of conversation
between groups of twos and threes criss-cross around the
room; and then cutting sharply into catty banter apparently pertaining to topics of harmlessly negative connota-
tion. All the while as Black Jack kept a methodical and
modest pace atop the current occupant under his blanket.
There was never any time for luxury. With the burden of
his work continually threatening to outrun his enjoyment
of the task at hand, he scarcely managed to restrain himself throughout runs that frequently extended to a dozen
customers. He had become extremely shrewd and adept
at detecting even the more reserved partner's displays of
satisfaction; and he would prudently require their resignation and withdrawal from the race after only one rack of
shudders. It going without saying, come the last contes-
tant, he often pounced and finished her with a confident
sprint, both hound and hare deriving pleasure from the
proverb of the 'lucky last.'

"What is sovereignty?" a deep male voice asked earnestly, sending Black Jack bolting upright beneath his
blanket and silencing the gallery. Te Rauparaha stood at
the door peering in. He seemed unconcerned with the
internal affairs of the hut. Black Jack scrambled to throw
his clothes on; and then he stepped outside with Te
Rauparaha. The old chief cracked a smile as he looked

back over his shoulder and asked, "How are things going my friend? Well, I hope?"

Black Jack walked on, guiding the old chief away with a hand to his back. He replied sheepishly, "Yes. Well, I've been a bit tired lately."

Te Rauparaha chuckled and said, "Ah, that is fine, my son; however, summer is supposed to be a time of rest for you whalers." He continued to grin.

Black Jack pursed his lips in embarrassment. He stopped, turned, and faced Te Rauparaha twenty-odd paces from his hut. They did the hongi. He asked, "Now, my friend, what is it that I can help you with?"

Te Rauparaha casually resumed with his prior questioning. He asked, "What is sovereignty?" The last word he pronounced in English.

Black Jack looked at him, slightly puzzled, and replied, "That is an English word. Why on Earth are you asking me about that?"

Te Rauparaha responded, once again in Maori, "The White man is here in great numbers out on the bay today. Myself, Te Rangiarata, and other chiefs of Cloudy Bay are meeting with them to discuss an agreement between the Pakeha and Maori; and possibly to sign it into treaty."

Black Jack looked concerned, and said, "A treaty? What is all this about? It is the first I have heard of it."

Te Rauparaha's brows lifted, and he remarked, "Well, that is what you get for living with the Pakeha. You expect them to tell you anything?" He began to laugh.

Embarrassed, Black Jack laughed with him. He replied, "No, my friend, but this sounds serious. What does this word you mention have to do with it?"

Te Rauparaha fixed a serious expression upon his face again, and said, "All right. Here it is: All the captains of the ships are on this one ship, and they've got us all gath-

ered around this barrel, pointing to this big piece of paper. It's got all kinds of Pakeha writing on it; and at the
bottom, it's got a little picture of some kind of flower and
what looks like a chief's headdress. Only, instead of feathers, it's got stones and metal on it. Does that sound familiar?"

Black Jack thought for a moment, and then said, "It
sounds like they want you to sign some sort of contract.
Like the one that made me a slave to the ship. What are
they saying it means, again?"

Te Rauparaha seemed slightly annoyed. "I'm telling
you, they are talking about, 'Sovereignty of the Crown'
over Maori land. I don't know what they mean."

Black Jack's eyes began to light up slowly in realization. He said, "Well, if I remember correctly, it means the
same as you sittin' on a hill and overseeing your land. Yes,
that's it: Being master of all you survey, without no one
tellin' you what to do. That's what that means!" Black
Jack was impressed with his own interpretation. "Or wait,
maybe it means being master of your own destiny. I can't
remember which." he said, looking perplexed.

Te Rauparaha looked confused again. He said, "Master of all I survey? What, they want to take all the land, do
they?"

Black Jack considered the idea quickly, and then shook
his head. He responded, "No, no. I'm sure they wouldn't
be foolish enough to try that on you. Remember what I
said about the White man coming? I told you there's a
whole heap of them. They're probably just makin' sure
that it's all right that they start comin' down here. You
know, so there's no trouble with the Maori and all."

Te Rauparaha replied in a reflective tone, "Well, there
won't be any trouble if they don't try to take what isn't
theirs. Besides, we don't really own the land. We belong

to the land. The White man doesn't seem to understand that: It's why I'm so confused about them wanting to officially declare this 'sovereignty' thing on paper. How much land do they think they need? They act as if they are going to fill every available inch!" He laughed at his own idea.

Black Jack said, "Yes, well, I know what you mean. It is not enough for the White man, it seems, merely to use the land sparingly for what he needs. He seems to have a burning need to subjugate the land, as he does animals and people. That may be a good thing, however."

Te Rauparaha stiffened. He asked, "How could that ever be a good thing?"

Black Jack, slightly surprised at his own wisdom, replied, "Well, it is also true that the White man prefers to subjugate, rather than kill. He seems to kill only that which he cannot farm, enslave, or domesticate: Such as the whales for example. Perhaps in signing this treaty, you may lead the Pakeha to believe that he has successfully subjugated the Maori and his land. Maybe that will ensure peace for all. Let the White man think that he has ownership and control."

Te Rauparaha became indignant. He said, "That is ridiculous. Whatever gave you such a revolting idea? If the White man thinks that he is Master, then he is. How do you rationalize that?"

Black Jack fired back, "Not necessarily. Now think about it: I said the White man will kill what he cannot control. That means he will try to control you, but can he really? Can he control your soul, my friend? No, and we both know that no one can control the soul of the land."

Te Rauparaha seemed to see the sense of Black Jack's words. He nodded as he contemplated his options. He said, "Yes. I see. They can kill the body, but they cannot kill the soul. Very wise, my son. Perhaps you should come and sign this contract, this 'Treaty of Waitangi'."

Black Jack smiled at the compliment and said, "No, I leave that for the Maori to decide. You must remember, old man, I am merely a black White man myself. Besides, the White men you are dealing with now are not the people of my land. I believe that if these Pakeha do you wrong in this deal, then perhaps they will have the man from my land to deal with someday."

Te Rauparaha returned his smile, and turning to walk away, said, "Ah, but you are, and always will be, so much more to me. Thank you, my son. Now perhaps you should return to your business." He pointed toward the hut as he departed.

Black Jack, turning away, said, "It is finished."

Chapter 20

THE DISGRUNTLED

"Five seasons full on, and what do I have to show for it?" he asked with a snarl, speaking more to the pot than to the men around him.

"Ah, well, you've got quite a nice stroke there, mate!" one man belted out; and the others laughed mockingly.

Cook continued to stir the large try-pot, the one at the back, while he chucked chunks of blubber into the two closer pots with his free hand. "Thanks, mate, but I mean seriously: What have I got after five years of whaling?" Cook asked again, partly humbled, but mostly annoyed by the taunts of his cohorts. Richard ('Dick' as his mates called him) Cook, his face eerily lit by the glowing coals of the furnace under the pots, sat on the vertebrae of a whale while he stirred the hot oil with a steady sway. He was an American shore-whaler, a 'Yank' as his colleagues unaffectionately termed him; and he had been a regular among the throngs of nubile and seasoned harpooners alike who had come and gone over the years in and around Kakapo. Jackie's Bay was what he and this tight circle of compatriots called it now; for anyone who had worked the channel for long came to know Jackie: And knowing Jackie meant respecting the large, burly man who had started the shore-whaling trade in this corner of the world; as well as realizing that he was still in control of life and law as far as the inhabitants of this stretch of beach were concerned.

"What are you on about, mate?" one of the men inquired as the laughter died down. He was one of the older, more experienced whalers; and he felt entitled to question the validity of Cook's concern. Besides, he had no fear of Cook, and certainly little respect for the Yank, who was not to be confused with the great Captain Cook. Now there was a man, he thought: A fellow subject of the Queen who had risked all to discover this great land and claim it for the Crown. Not like this crybaby Yank, who had had the backing of more ships than could fit into Tory Channel; and who had still managed to fritter all his earnings away.

"You know what I'm talking about. They work us like dogs when the whales are running, happily take our money for grog and lodging; and then expect us to bugger off somewhere else as soon as the last whale does!" he said, as he raised his voice higher and higher.

"Pipe down, Cook, you don't know what you are talking about." said another man, this time an Australian. "If you got along with any of those captains . . ." he said as he waved his hand over the line of ships moored quietly out in the calm moonlit bay. "You'd be out of here to follow the whales with the rest of the lot. Now whose problem is that?" he asked with a rise of his brow and a challenging stare.

"No, no, you know that's not right . . ." Cook quickly replied, his frustration masked by his own sincere belief

that he was correct. "I've given outstanding service on every ship that I've served on." he said in a defensively asser-
tive voice.

" 'Service on every ship that I've served on.' That makes
sense!" one of the group chimed in, with an almost antici-
patory timing. "Sam, Charlie, have you given 'Outstanding service on the ships you've served on'?" he called out to
the others lounging among the fireside troop.

One shot back theatrically, "Why yes. Yes I have 'served
with outstandingly servile servitude' on the ships I've served
on!"

The other said immediately, "Serves you right!" Everyone but Cook laughed uproariously.

Cook's face had gone pale as he silently stared at the
boiling oil, withdrawn from the revelry being played at
his expense. "Yeah, right." he said despondently. "You
know what I mean."

"All I know," said the older man with a suddenly serious tone, "Is that none of those ships wants you. They'd
sooner see you go over the loggerhead tangled in the line
than have you hanging about the boat like an albatross.
And that's no one's fault but your own." The others grew
silent at the accusation.

Cook bristled. "What do you mean?" he asked skeptically.

"Ah, c'mon mate," said the old whaler. "You're always
on the piss, even when the rest of us have called it quits.
That's where all of your money goes. And then you're too
drunk to stand a proper watch, if you can stand at all. And
as far as your reputation . . ." he was cut short in mid-
sentence.

"Now don't get on about that!" Cook shouted in defense.

"You know it's true!" the veteran shot back. The others stared at the coals, nervously exchanging sideways glances as the argument between these two men heated.

"Now that's not fair." Cook sputtered back as his voice broke.

"Fair, blah! You are the worst watch out here. Hell, what has it been now, three watches in a row you've let a fish get right out from under your nose? Ask Patrick! He knows! You saw that one while you were on the pots the other day, right Norton?" One of the men nodded slowly in silent agreement, looking down so as not to fan the flames of the spat. "You complain about not having anything, mate. You're lucky you're still here at the rate you're losing mates and allies!" roared the old man.

"I know, I know." Cook quietly conceded. "But listen: You guys know I'm not a bad bloke. I don't know what it is. I've just had the worst luck lately."

"Luck! Get off it mate, it's you!" said the old man, disgusted.

"No, listen really, I've got it all figured out." Cook uttered desperately. He continued with his soliloquy while the others half-listened, resigned to letting him vent rather than waste their breath. They listened as he began quietly, with how it all began: His descent into destitution. They listened to how he had been a fairly successful farmhand; until his employer had accused him of stealing, and his reputation had suffered among the townspeople. They heard about his hearing about whaling in the South Seas; how lucrative he had heard it was; how a man could make his fortune in only a few years. He explained how it had been a new start for him. They listened as he told about not adapting well to sea-faring life, and the code by which sailors live by, being just a simple farmer and all. He went on and on about how suddenly no one liked him or helped him with unfamiliar tasks, and how the entire crew had

ceased to speak to him. He spoke of the months of isolation, though he was surrounded by men, and how one
day he found that "he could do nothing right"; and that
he thought he was going insane.

And that is when the corporal punishment began. His
superiors began to present mysterious charges against him
to the First Mate. Small violations at first, such as unsatisfactory tidiness in his quarters; even though, he swore, the
state of affairs of his fellow sailors was "ten times worse."
The First Mate had seemed helpful at first, offering his
counsel and advice on the little matters; and always finishing their closed-door talks with a fatherly, "I hope that
I've helped you, and that you can do better in the future."

However, Cook asserted, that with the increasing frequency and seriousness of charges against him (he did not
eat the Captain's chicken!) the understanding nature of
the First Mate had started to fade; and he even began to
treat him with the same impersonal disdain that the rest
of the crew had long since perfected.

It had become his professional duty, the First Mate
informed him one day, to report him to the Captain as a
serious threat to the operation of the ship. This had surprised Cook, he said, that his trusted friend had turned
on him so swiftly and coldly; and that standing before the
Captain, he had found not even a trace of sympathy or
warmth that had once been exhibited to him by the First
Mate, and even the rest of the crew at one time as he
recalled.

The Captain had quickly dismissed him, as he would
a parcel being delivered to shore; and the First Mate had
explained matter-of-factly once outside the Captain's cabin
that Cook was to be reassigned to a sister ship in the
company's fleet which was short-staffed. The Mate had
said further that the 'offer' only came with a disciplinary
mark in his service record: Or else he would be dismissed

from service altogether; and he would have to find and finance his own passage to wherever. Without much of a life to return to in the States, Cook said, he had quickly taken the former; although he had misgivings about starting out on a new ship with a black mark against him.

Things had actually gone well on the next ship, he was surprised to say; even getting camaraderie and support upon freely admitting that "no one liked him" on his previous ship. "We like you just fine!" always came the chorus in the ship's galley; as he became a hail-fellow-well-met, and a bit of a celebrity as well, being the only Yank on an Australian ship. He had even discovered that he was quite a skilled seaman, rather than the incompetent buffoon that the others had made him believe; and he had excelled on this Aussie ship, even advancing a rank with the increased pay and rations to boot.

But then had come the night that he fell asleep on watch, and had been reprimanded by his superior; and it seemed that within a few weeks the entire cycle was repeating itself. That happened on three more ships, until he could be transferred no more; and he was relegated to the permanent status of shore-whaler.

"See, it's all you." the old man said after a pause.

Cook sank from his oratorical posture into despair. "You don't understand." he said, having expected at least a modicum of empathy from his audience.

"I understand you're a self-pitying lag, Cook!" the old whaler exclaimed; and the men erupted into satisfied laughter once again, relieved after their long dutiful silence.

"Hear, hear!" they all shouted in unison. "Now go to bed, Cook. You've got first watch tomorrow; and no excuses this time."

Dick puckered in confused, pent anger. As he continued to stir the scrag he thought, what did they mean by that? "You know what I'm all about, right Jack?" He spoke to one dark figure who had been sitting among the now disbanding mob, not laughing, not speaking. He had remained seated, staring at the coals under the cool indigo sky.

"No, mate, I'm afraid I don't." said the Black man with a low, husky voice.

"C'mon, you've had your share of hard times. Everyone knows your story: How you were mistreated by your kind and all. You did what you had to do and now you're all right. So you know what I'm talking about when I say I've been tread on, right?" implored Cook. He had unwittingly touched on more of Black Jack's past than his fireside partner cared to acknowledge; however it produced no more sympathy for this man within Black Jack's heart.

"Ain't no one treading on you, Dick. You's mucked up inside: You need to sort that out." Black Jack said with candor.

Cook perked up and stirred more vigorously, happy to have entreated someone into further discussion, if even half-heartedly, about his problems. "No, really Jack, look at us! Hell, you were a slave; and now look at us! I'm sitting here doing the same thing, over and over, day in and day out. Look!" he said sprightly as he exaggerated the motions of stirring the hot pot. "Boil double, toil and trouble!" he said mockingly as he began to laugh at his own joke. "This is slavery, Jack! The same thing over and over. We should be free!" he said as he became more agitated. "See what I mean?" he queried, searching for agreement in Black Jack's eyes.

"No." said Black Jack bluntly, hedging his annoyance. He took a deep thoughtful breath, and said, "Mate, I've got my freedom. Not bragging on myself, but I've paid my dues and now I am what I consider to be a reasonably successful free man. My freedom came the minute I was thrown off that whale and swam to shore. I was a success the second I walked up out of the waves at that little bay down the way here." said Black Jack as he casually pointed south. "Even though it didn't seem all that great then, it sure does now. I'm gonna be famous for that bay one day, you watch and see!" Black Jack said in modest boasting. "Now, if it's work you're afraid of, mate, then there might be your problem. Of course, shore-whaling ain't glamorous; and you won't hear the other men go out of their way to say that. But it's what you get in the end that's important. No one really likes to work, mate. Is that what you wanted to hear?" Jack asked in a sincere yet slightly patronizing tone.

"No, no, you're getting me all wrong." Cook said as he became flustered. "I'm not afraid of work, but look!" he said, as he threw out his arms; and Jack looked around also, not quite sure what he was getting at.

"Yesss?" Black Jack asked, with a cautiously curious tone. He took over the idle stirrer as a polite gesture to his storyteller to continue.

"Look at what this guy has!" Cook exclaimed.

"You mean Jackie, or Wynen?" Black Jack asked, not meaning to be coy.

"Both! Either! Jackie's got his little outpost here with all the modern comforts, all set up for him and his family. And Wynen, the shopkeeper: He's got us all by the purse strings. Ah, the first store on the South Island. How difficult is that?" Cook asked indignantly with a sarcastic tone.

"Well, what's wrong with that? They're both trying to make an honest living, just like the rest of us." Black Jack said as he assumed the role of the Devil's advocate.

"On our backs, Jack, on our backs!" he yelled as the veins bulged beneath his red neck. "And honest? Huh!"

"What are you implying, Dick? You don't think they charge a fair price?" Black Jack asked more sincerely, surprised at his converse's sudden lucidity.

"How would we know, eh Jack? Think about it: How would we know?" Cook asserted more than he asked as he became more confident.

"Well . . ." Jack replied, actually beginning to listen to Cook for the first time. "Why would they cheat us?" he asked innocently.

"Wake up, Jack! Do you think they really give a damn about us?" Cook demanded as he sensed his audience's increasing interest.

"Meaning?" asked Jack, finding Cook's allegations toward his fellow White man ever more intriguing.

"Meaning, just look! Do they have any women around here for us?" Cook asked.

"Oh, so that is what this is about!" Jack said triumphantly.

"No, no, don't steer the subject, mate." Cook said as he became arrogant and seized control of the argument. "Look at Jackie! He's got his little Missus from way back. You think he cares about us?" he grumbled.

"It's not his job to provide us with women folk, Dick. Besides, I did my best to set us all up when I first got here. And you ruined that chance!" said Black Jack quickly.

"I know, I know," said Cook, stinging from the verbal blow. "But she's still around here somewhere, saying she's my wife; and besides, how many of these blokes are still truly hitched to the horse they rode in on? Look at the other one up the hill!" retorted Cook.

"Wynen?" asked Black Jack.

"Exactly!" Dick exclaimed congratulatively. "Look at what he calls his wife."

"Darling, I suppose." said Jack smugly, and chuckled.

"No, Jack. His little Maori princess. The one up on the hill running the store." Cook said, as if he had uncovered a great secret.

"So." said Jack dryly.

"So! So he's got another Missus up in town; with other children running around by her. This one here is just his little holiday mistress." said Cook pointedly.

"Really?" Black Jack mused, allowing his surprise to show before saying, "Well, what business is that of yours?"

"What business? It's everyone's business mate! It's not fair, him holding himself up as a pillar of the community and all; expecting us to pay top dollar for everything and then expecting us to show respect and gratitude on top." Cook ranted. "And what about you? Wouldn't you appreciate a little female company now and then?"

Cook, with his unexpected turn in conversation, had unwittingly struck Black Jack with a sensitive subject; and he let it be known. "Now don't you worry about me, mate." he said in a suddenly serious and gruff manner. "I've had my share of White ladies and Maori princesses alike." he flatly told his mate; and in a further retaliatory tone, "I don't have a problem in that department, like some people."

"Well you can avoid the issue all you want Jack." Cook said in an attempt to save face. "I've seen how it works around here, and I don't like it." he said with a nod of his chin.

"Well, why don't you just leave then, if it's all that bad." said Black Jack in a disgusted, slightly sad voice as he got up to go.

"I might just, Jack, I might just! Anyplace is better than here!" yelled Cook as the haunting words dogged Black Jack's fading form.

II

Cook stewed awhile longer as he resumed stirring his steaming cauldron of blubber. No one understood the problem, he thought: They all chose to close their eyes. He knew, though. He knew exactly what was wrong; and as he searched his pockets with an alternating free hand, he began to get quite angry about all that had transgressed that evening.

Blast! Not even a shilling for a tin of tobacco. His anger began to mount with his frustration. Why was he always out of tobacco, and money for that matter? he asked himself. And the store! What absurd hours for the only damned store for miles around. Here, of all places, where the sun did not set until nine o'clock, the shop closed its doors promptly at six o'clock! It always infuriated him when, after a long day of stirring or flenching without so much as an offer of a relief from one of his mates, he would run bounding up the hill to the shop; only to see the doors being closed and the sign turned. It was a constant hassle. There he would go, humble as a Booby bird, dipping and bowing, asking his pardon; could he please purchase a tin, it had been a long day; and always the same reply: Sorry, mate, we really can't, and 'why didn't you get some today', and all the patronizing stock anecdotes reserved for the smallest of children.

His blood began to boil as he took large, cumbersome steps up the steep, grassy slope toward the shop. He noticed as he walked that the grass was becoming increasingly slippery. Was that dew? he thought. The sun hadn't set but an hour ago! And as he looked around, he noticed his path becoming darker; and a glance upward revealed that clouds were swiftly sliding in to obscure the silver moon. Rain, he thought. Wonderful, just what he needed!

A soggy smoke before a restless, wet night under a skiff. That is, if he even got his tobacco.

He could see the strong light of a single oil lamp through the shop door's windows as he stepped up onto the deck. A chance, he thought. Perhaps they would be understanding this time. He saw her through the glass working over the day's books at the bench. He tried the door, and easily slithered in. She turned with a start, saw it was him, and quickly told him the shop was closed.

"I know ma'am, but it really is urgent." he said as he mustered his most polite personality. "You see, me and the men, we've been working late these days, finishing the season . . ." he had been saying when she cut him short.

She had even looked as though she were listening; and then she said as emotionlessly as before, "We're closed for business. Please come back tomorrow. We open at seven."

He sensed her familiarity with him and his prior en- counters with her husband; her slight disdain at having had to say so many words to a useless customer; and her knowledge that the shore-whalers were all at work by six: He perceived all of these things in her one bland mono- logue. He also sensed something else behind all of the others: Fear. "Ma'am, if I could just get a tin of tobacco, I will promptly pay for it tomorrow." he said, as his voice carried up at the end of his sentence. He slid closer to her.

She seemed to struggle for an instant between sympa- thy and assertion; and she said, "My husband, Mr. Wynen the shop owner, is away for the evening on business. It really is not up to me to let things out of the shop." she said. "Please come back tomorrow; and he will take care of you."

Something in her voice crawled under his skin; and as he stepped up to her stool, he said, "What is it?"

The Maori woman stared back at his face, dark and

twisted with anguish in the flickering light. She clung to her courage and without blinking an eye, said, "What is what?"

He could not believe that he had to stand there being humiliated by such a beautiful woman in her evening sarong. She seemed to mock him with her resolute gaze and her flower-print gown. "What is it, Squeaker, that you people have against me?" he asked in a breaking voice, tears beginning to well in his eyes.

Her heart leapt at the sound of her nickname; and as her head began to swim with thoughts of her sleeping children in the next room, she said sharply, "I'm sorry, you are going to have to leave now!"

His weepy frown suddenly puffed into a blustery crimson grimace as he grabbed her hair. "Why don't you like me?" he screamed.

No one but her waking children heard her screams; and no one their screams; nor the blood splattering the ceiling inside as the rain swept in from the sea and washed the wooden outside walls of the shop.

Later, as he enjoyed a calming smoke under the emerging moon, he watched the shimmering rainbow streams of oil slip from the sands into the soothing waves of tranquil Jackie's Bay; whence they came.

Chapter 21

A JUST DELIVERANCE

"Black Jack, is that you?" asked Cook in a sleepy voice, rubbing his bleary eyes with sandy hands. He struggled to peer up at the silhouette of the large looming figure backlit by the blazing moon. The form stood on an earthen rise, accentuated by the accompanying shadows of crooked trees which strained to share the rays of the celestial spotlight in which the feathered phantom stood.

The darkness spoke. "I think I can help you. Come with me." said Black Jack in a low, forceful voice.

Cook gathered his shabby self from the sand, and staggered behind the specter. He asked, "Why are you dressed like a Maori? Where are we going? What time is it?" Black Jack silently motioned for him to follow; and he led the disoriented whaler to the dark and shimmering shore.

Black Jack said, "The clock in the shop just counted

the Apostles. It is at this moment as late and as early as can possibly be."

Cook shook his head at the comment, and with a puzzled look, asked, "What are we going to do at this hour?"

Black Jack stepped into the canoe. He said in a reassuring tone, "Just come with me, Dick. I want to show you something that will help you out of this mess." The two lighted in the boat and Black Jack shoved off. There was only his one paddle. Cook sat in the bow, back to the water. Black Jack propelled and steered the small vessel.

The 'mess' he referred to was Dick Cook's life. Since the death of Kueka, things had gone from bad to worse for him. He was a prime suspect. Having been the last one to see him that fateful night, Black Jack was not necessarily in a rush to condemn his colleague to the crime; however, he had had to give account of the evening simply to clear his own name. Of course, all the stories of the other sailors present that night concurred; and the authorities had begun to point fingers. In such a small and remote community, the heat had quickly piled onto Cook, and his unsavory behavior had worsened under the pressure. It was a fitting response in the eyes of the accusing villagers, they concluded, for a man who comported himself in such an irresponsible and slovenly manner. His drinking had increased, his fitness for work had become not even worthy of consideration, and his presence was tolerated only in the least desirable places in the pa. He had become a pariah, stranded in a limbo between precluded guilt and his skillful self-destruction.

Cook said, "I'm not helping here much, Black Jack. I wish that I had a paddle." The cool night air blew softly off of the smooth sea and served to sharpen his sleeping senses.

Black Jack said, "You are all right. Just relax and enjoy

the journey. I will see that we get there." The words soothed Cook, and he settled in the bow, still uncertain as to the purpose of the outing. Black Jack said, "I know it's been hard for you lately. I thought that we could just get away for a little while and talk about it." Black Jack spoke in a soft, low tone as he rowed slowly.

Cook said, "A talk with the Tonguer! Now there's a fitting therapy." He smiled at his own attempt at humor. It was the first time that his spirits had lifted in a long time. His act had caused serious problems for everyone around him, as well as compounding the troubles of his own life. Maori and Pakeha relations, having settled into a smooth symbiosis since Black Jack's settlement with Te Rauparaha, were now flaring again because of the murder of one of their own. Kueka had been a Maori princess, and her marriage to a prominent Pakeha businessman had helped to weld a foundation of trust and weave a framework for furthering the bond between Brown and White on the South Island of New Zealand.

Black Jack had even felt the heat from his Maori counterparts, owing to the fact that it had happened on his watch, so to speak. That is not to say his lookout for the night, but more importantly, his word to Te Rauparaha that he would watch over the White Man and his progress; and report periodically on the state of affairs. This was their bargain, the two 'Chiefs' having agreed that the success of peace between the two peoples required constant monitoring. Kueka's murder, however, had been completely unexpected.

To make matters worse, a Maori had recently killed a White person on the North Island. In keeping with the conditions of the Treaty of Waitangi, and in a show of good faith, the Maori of New Zealand had allowed the man to be tried, convicted, and executed in accordance with English law. In the case of Kueka, Cook had been tried; and although an overwhelming preponderance had pointed to him as the killer, he was let go on claims of circumstantial evidence. The Maori were outraged, and trouble had begun to brew.

"Everyone thinks I'm guilty, Black Jack. It's driving me crazy. They got that Maori fellow, though, didn't they!" Cook said with the exuberance of an adolescent.

Black Jack said, flatly, "Yes, they did. It's a shame they haven't found who killed Kueka."

Cook looked sideways at Black Jack, and said, "Yes, it is. The trial was hell; but they couldn't prove a thing! Yes, they got the wrong man." He stopped, and the silence fell between them in the darkness. Black Jack continued to row slowly and rhythmically. Cook asked, "Where are we going? And why are you dressed like that?"

Black Jack replied, "I know some people who can help ease your pain. They are some Maori friends of mine; and it will make it easier if I appear like this."

Cook shifted on his seat. He seemed uneasy as he said, "Maori friends? Why do we need to see them? What makes you think that they can do anything for me?"

Black Jack responded, "Well, believe it or not, I used to live as a Maori. Right down the coast here in Te Pukatea. I know that getting away from the White Man for awhile can simplify your life; maybe clear your head up a little. I'm gonna take you to the tribe I lived with and they will take care of you. You'll get better, you'll see."

Cook became more restless, and said, "Get better? Black Jack, what are you talking about? I don't need to get better. I just need to make some money and get out of this place." He looked around and padded his pockets. He said, "Ah, damn. I left my tobacco back on the beach. You didn't bring any, did you?"

Black Jack said calmly, "I don't smoke." The silence swirled and thickened in the darkness between them.

Cook laughed nervously, and asked, "Damn, then I reckon you didn't bring anything to drink then, either?"

Black Jack said flatly, "No."

Cook lifted his chin and craned his neck, and said jokingly, "I knew you wasn't good for nothin', man!"

Black Jack let the comment fall into the water. Another minute of silence passed between them. Black Jack spoke up and said, "They will feed you well. You won't have to work, so you can catch up on your rest. There may be smoke, but probably no drink. However, you will quickly find that you do not need it. You'll soon find yourself feeling happier, I promise."

Cook digested Black Jack's words, and replied, "Geez, Black Jack, you've got this all planned out. I wish you had told me. I don't know about living with the Maori: It may have been all right for a fella like you, but I'm White! How do you think they're gonna take to me?"

Black Jack feigned ignorance and answered his question with a question, "How they would take to anyone, I suppose. Why should you be any different?"

Cook hesitated, surprised by Black Jack's response, and said, "Well, I don't know. You know how I am with people, right?"

Black Jack suppressed a knowing and satisfied smirk, and said, "Well, yes. Sort of. What do you think your problem is, Dick?"

Cook instantly perked up, delighted at the prospect of discussing his problems. The cool air, the isolation, and the sole company had suddenly become good things to him; and he felt free to open up. Almost as pleasurable as a drink and a smoke, in fact. He started, "I don't know. Well, look at me: I don't have a woman for starters. Everyone else does, but I don't."

Black Jack interrupted, "Do you have problems with

women, Dick? I told you that everyone at the station has a fair shot at a wife."

Cook said, "Yes, but that's a Maori wife. You know how I feel about that."

Black Jack said, "No, I did not. How do you feel? Do you have something against the Maori?"

Cook broke into a relaxed laughter and said, "Hell, Black Jack, I've got something against everyone!"

Black Jack asked genuinely, "What do you mean?"

Cook said, "I hate people."

Black Jack, slightly surprised by his honesty, said, "You what?"

Cook reemphasized, "I hate people. Every one of them. I mean everyone acts like a goddamn saint. But they're not. Everyone's got the same problems as me, but they all act so 'holier than thou'. Everyone's always saying, 'We're just trying to help you', but no one gives a damn about me. I'm all alone in this world. And with women: Hell, try to find a woman who's a soul mate, Jack. I never have! They're all so demanding. I don't trust them as far as I can throw them, either!"

Black Jack contemplated his passenger's words and then asked, "So you don't form bonds with people, is that what you are saying?"

Cook rambled on, "Hell, I don't know. I guess so. Yeah, that's part of it. I try to be friends with everyone, but they all shit on me. I never try to take advantage of anyone, but look at them have a go at me! It's not fair. Everyone has always treated me like a child. I have never been respected by anyone. No one has ever told me that they liked me. You know that, Black Jack?"

Black Jack grunted in the dark. He choked out an, "I guess so."

Cook asked childishly, "What's wrong? Do I talk too

much?" He looked around anxiously and rubbed his arms and said, "Brrr. It's getting chilly. Are we there yet?"

Black Jack strained to remain civil, and said, "Mmhm."

Cook stopped his antics, and in an apologetic tone, said, "Well, I don't expect a fellow like you to understand. I know you've had a simple life and all; and you haven't done half the things I've done. But I appreciate you trying to listen to me anyway."

The remainder of the trip was spent in complete silence, save for the methodical strokes of Black Jack's paddle.

II

Under the full moon the two in the canoe pulled into Te Pukatea around two.

Black Jack said, "Wake up, Dick."

Cook stirred, and in a disoriented voice, asked, "Where are we? What time is it?"

Black Jack said, "We are home. Here is where you'll stay for the next little while."

Cook glanced around, confused, and said, "But no one will be up. What are we going to do?"

Black Jack said, "No, no. Don't worry. We are going to do something first, before everyone gets up. I want to show you something."

Cook said, "I don't know, Black Jack. I'm so tired."

Black Jack said, "That is exactly why I am going to show you this. It will revitalize you."

Black Jack paddled over to the southern corner of the bay. It was the rock corner with the cave arch that looked out over the sea. Beside the arch was a large, flat, rock terrace which jutted into the sea. At the far side of the terrace, a section of rock continued out into the sea, around, and back to form the rim of a deep tidal pool. It was oval, about twenty-feet across at its widest, and roughly fifteen-feet deep. On the ocean side small channels, slightly wider than a man's head, opened onto the ocean allowing the water to rush in and out with the waves. At high tide, the water would surge just over the rim, rushing into and through the pool violently; and finally wash up onto the rock terrace. The rock walls of the pool were covered with large mussels from top to bottom. It was high tide when they arrived.

Black Jack told Cook, "I want you to get in and pull some mussels for us. Because it is high tide, you need to actually be in the water, so you can pull the mussels when the waves go out."

Cook watched the waves churn into and out of the pool, forming a deep swirling froth. He said anxiously, "But Black Jack, those waves are only four or five seconds apart. I don't know if I can do anything in that time. Besides, it's cold! What do we need the mussels for, anyway?"

Black Jack said, "The mussels are very good; and they're good for you. They are very satisfying, with healing properties as well. They will help you to give up your vices. Also, they were my first meal here. They hold a very special meaning for me. Get in." Cook hesitated, and then stepped out of the canoe, and onto the rock rim. Black Jack got out of the canoe and dragged it up onto the rock terrace. He turned to look at Cook. Black Jack said again, "Get in, Dick."

Cook stuck one foot into the water; and then slowly lowered himself down to sit on the ledge. He said, "I'm gonna have to leave my clothes on, else I'll be cut to shreds!"

Black Jack said calmly, "You'll be fine. Now get us some of those mussels. I'm hungry."

Cook obliged the man who had done all of the work along the way. He gently slid into the water, carefully avoiding the edges. He began to tread water in the center of the tidal pool, as he came to terms with the surging waves. He shouted up to Black Jack, "Good God, man, this is work just staying off the rocks. I don't know about picking any mussels."

Black Jack said firmly, "Try."

Cook struggled to swim closer to the ledge under Black Jack's feet. He waited and watched as the waves washed up and down the wall within a span of five to six feet. He saw the mussels become exposed briefly; and then be swallowed up again by the surging sea. Finally, he made a desperate attempt to get close to the wall. He allowed himself to drift, and then timing his descent with the water, bobbed down and grabbed at shells. The waves surrounded him; and he popped up to the ledge, waving sliced and bloody hands. He said, sputtering, "I don't know, Black Jack. This doesn't seem like the right way to do this."

Black Jack asked, "What's wrong, Dick?"

Cook pushed back from the rocks in earnest, trying desperately to stay afloat. He stammered, "Black Jack, this doesn't feel right. I'm getting tired really fast. Look at my hands!"

Black Jack asked nonchalantly, "What about them?" He slowly drew his mere from his belt. Its green stone shimmered menacingly in the moonlight.

Cook looked up at him and said, "Well hell, if you're gonna use that, I might as well get out. I'm bleeding like a madman here!" Cook paddled over to the ledge and placed his hands near Black Jack's feet. He prepared to climb out with the help of the next surge. Black Jack squatted and slapped the broad side of the pounamu down on Cook's hands. Cook yelled, "Ouch, damn!" as he released the ledge and floated back to the center of the pool. He shouted, "What'd you do that for? The mussels are down there!" He pointed a bloody finger below Black Jack.

Black Jack said, "I'm sorry, did that hurt, Dick?"

Cook replied, "Well, yes! This is getting a little scary. I'm getting out." He lunged once again for the ledge.

Black Jack met his fingers again with a slap of the mere. He asked, "Do you think Kueka felt anything before she died, Dick? Or do you think she was too scared to feel? Which do you think would be worse, Dick?"

Cook flailed his arms desperately now in the water, and screamed, "Hell, I don't know. What are you askin' me for? You're scaring the Devil out of me. I thought you were my friend!"

Black Jack said, "I am, my friend, I am."

Cook suddenly bolted for the ledge again, seeing that the wall was exposed by a lull. As he reached out for the ledge, however, he instead placed his hands onto a ridge of mussels just below the lip of the rim. These mussels, having been only partially submerged by the high tide, remained open. There they sat, like hard-shelled Venus flytraps, awaiting some non-existent prey. As Cook reached, his fingers mistakenly slipped into the open mollusks, their shells snapping shut like so many small steel jaws. He tried in vain to rip his hands free before the onslaught of the next wave, but his attempts were futile. The swell came over him and he disappeared from view. When the water receded, his limp body waved loosely behind his outstretched arms.

"Rest, my friend, rest." said Black Jack peacefully.

III

Rowing back to Kakapo, Black Jack contemplated the ramifications of his actions. He had not intended to pass judgment on his peer. He had truly wanted to help the troubled man in the best way possible. The healing time he had planned for Cook at Te Pukatea was real enough in his mind, he recalled; but as he drew nearer to the place, and closer to what he believed to be the truth, he had felt compelled by some outside force to follow his chosen course of action.

Black Jack's mother had always said, "Judge not lest ye be judged", and "Thou shalt not kill"; and he had always tried his best to adhere to those guidelines. In this case, however, Black Jack had agonized over the murder of Kueka and his responsibility to it. Who was he to judge what killing was, he wondered, with his history? With time and thought, though, a difference had been discerned in his mind between the mutual slaughter of people in armed battle, and the mindless murder of a defenseless woman and her children. The entire affair had dredged up the painful memories of Kumari, along with the ordeal of his early days with Te Rauparaha. In the end, Black Jack had been faced with a decision consisting of the same components of consideration as that when he was forced to deal with his Maori nemesis: To choose between revenge and justice. Black Jack's final resolution came about from his realization that although both required a certain involvement of the sin of judgment, the difference between justice and revenge lay in the addition of an emotion called anger.

As he rowed steadily over the still waters toward the whaling station, Black Jack was alone with the troubling reality that his act of justice had not been accomplished without a certain amount of his anger. It was akin to the same feeling he had felt when he had faced the fate of Kumari; and it had all flared up inside him while standing at Kueka's funeral. "Vengeance is mine, saith the Lord," had gone the words of the Pastor, there amidst the amber waves of tall grass blowing in the wind atop the hill overlooking the bay. "Do not seek ye then to take an eye for an eye, nor a tooth for a tooth." Black Jack had only listened with one ear to the eulogy as tears of rage welled in his eyes and scenes of the crime raced through his mind. Partially blinded, muted, and deafened by emotion, he could not immediately foresee the implications of the murder of this beautiful, young, princess relative of Te Rauparaha. Neither was he as fully affected as he may have been by the response of the good Reverend when he humbly requested to receive a copy of the Bible. The Preacher had seemed bothered and said, "My son, it will do you no good if you cannot read what is inside it."

Chapter 22

THE MASSACRE OF TRUST

B e it from a breakdown in the lines of communication, or an outright resistance to the flow of information, word of Cook's death not only failed to appease the stalwart appellate of the Cloudy Bay chiefs, but it also did nothing to put the people of Port Underwood on a course for peace. So, at the end of a long, misguided path of embroilment, confusion, and mistrust, the following scene has unfolded:

Cloudy rays fall on the tattooed face of an old man as his eyes yearn skyward. With outstretched and uplifted arms, he cries, "Farewell, oh Sun, farewell thou world of light, come, oh night, come on, oh Death!" He is standing on a flat plain near a stream. Beside him is the sprawled body of a dead constable in uniform, still clutching the handcuffs and leg irons which he had brought to capture the Chief.

Several feet away, a Black man in whaling clothes holds

aloft a Bible and a staff, as he proclaims, "Have faith, Te Rauparaha, have strength. Not a hair on your head will be harmed, by the grace of God. Believe that, and you will be saved!"

The old chief continues to tremble and chant heavenward, a revolver in one hand. Around the perimeter of the clearing lie strewn the bodies of four Maori and twenty-two Pakeha. Countless others, weaponless or wounded, cower in the bushes along the small river. The magnitude of the scenario at Wairau is done more justice, however, by backing up a few paces, and tracing the steps which have led to the site of the massacre.

II

January, 1843:

News of Kueka's murder does not fall well upon the ears of Te Rauparaha at Kapiti. In good faith and out of respect for Black Jack's wishes, he awaits the outcome of the British trial. He is naturally outraged at the acquittal of Dick Cook, a White man, on lack of evidence. This coming shortly after a Maori man's being hung for the murder of a White woman. Immediately, there is talk of utu, or vengeance, for Kueka among the Maori.

April 1843:

Te Rauparaha steps off his canoe at Te Pukatea following rumors that the White man has been extremely active in the area. Pakeha ships have been pulling into a port at the top of the South Island, and White men have been seen carrying on strange activities all down through the Waitohi valley to Tua Marina, just inland of Te Pukatea.

The Chief is met by Reverend Ironside, who has been a missionary to the Maori since the signing of the Treaty of Waitangi. He has learned the native tongue well, and he is a deft interpreter between the Pakeha and Maori. He tells the Chief, "Do not be alarmed, but there are two gentlemen here under contract from the Crown to survey and name all desirable tracts of land."

Te Rauparaha, taken aback and slightly indignant, replied, "But they already have names. Does that not matter to them?"

The Reverend responded, "I mean that the places are receiving English names. For example, they have named Te Pukatea, 'White's Bay'."

Te Rauparaha sardonically replied, "Well, now, isn't that creative! They're not short on modesty, I'll give the White men that much."

The Reverend, with an air of amused sympathy replied, "No, no, Chief. They have named it after Black Jack White, the American Negro. Do you remember him? The Maori here have told me much about him."

Te Rauparaha arrogantly replied, "Ha! The boy from Mississippi? Remember him? He is like a son to me!"

The Reverend seemed humbled by the Chief's response. He said in a serious tone, "Perhaps I should warn you before you travel inland."

The Chief looked at him with genuine concern.

Moving over the hills from the shore, Te Rauparaha and his warriors reached the flat floor of the wide Waitohi valley. What they encountered, they could scarcely believe: Spread out in all directions for as far as the eye could see, were white stakes standing in the ground at regular intervals, knee-high, like so many small grave markers. It was as though the entire basin had been turned into a massive cemetery. The fact that it had all been done without Te Rauparaha's consent did not quickly escape him, regardless of his delayed response; for he was soon hopping mad and ordering his men to pull up each and every baton blanche. Satisfied that he had stopped the current encroachment upon his sovereignty, the Chief encamped at the namesake of his student-turned-teacher, in case there were further trespasses.

Within days, of course, a team of indignant, self-important investigators stood upon his doorstep at White's Bay, demanding an explanation of his vandalism. He simply replied that no permission had been sought to survey the land; and certainly nothing had been paid to the Maori of Cloudy Bay for the acquisition of any new lands. The men were adamant that he had signed a deal which encompassed the Waitohi valley; and the chief was equally vociferous in expressing that he had not. The argument heated and spread to many more parties, coming and going, over the next few days; until finally the order was issued that a constable with armed assistance be sent to arrest and shackle the great and illustrious Te Rauparaha for contempt of the Crown's orders.

What ensued was the mess at Wairau. Some say that it was merely an incident, causing the death of only a few people. Other accounts claim that it was a massacre involving hundreds. The truth is that it happened; and it served to shatter what trust had existed between Maori and Pakeha, as it also threatened to fracture the fragile trust which existed between Black Jack White and Te Rauparaha. Perhaps only the tall Titoki tree, which stands there still today by the stream for which the site is named, knows the full story.

III

Something happened to both of them at Wairau. It was a transcendental transformation for both Black Jack and Te Rauparaha. Exactly why or what is hard to explain; but beyond the sheer magnitude of the event around them and its obvious outward ramifications, something big happened within each of these men that changed them forever. One man rebounded at the sight of the shackles, and the other saw Jesus.

For Black Jack, the shackles held obvious and ominous significance. Seeing them along with the horrible tragedy ripped open wounds and laid bare parts of his soul which caused him to rethink his returning to America for many reasons. Of course the possibility of being sold back into slavery entered his mind; however, much deeper issues concerned his immediate thoughts. He now considered the heinous cuffs and leg-irons as evidence of what the British were planning for New Zealand, and how evil their intentions may be after all. The entire ordeal aroused in him a sense of higher purpose and duty toward this new land that he loved; and his ideals of loyalty and commitment were strongly evoked. He suddenly felt as though his place were here, and that he was morally obligated to stay and fulfill his destiny in this country. That destiny, he concluded, included standing by the now disadvantaged and vulnerable Maori: Standing for truth and justice in the face of the now White threat; and standing up for the land itself.

In the case of Te Rauparaha, he was actually and ironically saved by the White man's savior. From the short time that he had spent with Reverend Ironside and the converted Maori at White's Bay, Te Rauparaha had learned enough about Jesus Christ to believe that he knew who had kept him from coming to harm at Wairau. Of course, it didn't hurt that Black Jack had recently begun to reexamine the good Word that his mother had so often imparted on him, her having been fortunate enough to hear the sermons of many a traveling parson in her role as house

maid; and it also didn't do any harm having him jumping
around unarmed in the thick of the shooting with a Bible
in his hand, swearing that Te Rauparaha would be un-
harmed.

Miracle or no, the whole experience was powerful
enough to convince Te Rauparaha to accept the Lord as
his personal savior. This spiritual awakening in the midst
of a life-threatening crisis helped the two to form a brotherhood that dispelled any mistrust that may have arisen
between them stemming from Black Jack's previous inac-
curate predictions as to the pilgrim's projected progress.
That is to say, Te Rauparaha was not inclined to accuse
Black Jack of giving bad advice on the signing of the Treaty
of Waitangi, or of being in cahoots in any way with the
White man with which he had lived long enough to somehow influence them to name a bay after him. All of that
palled in comparison to Te Rauparaha's new soul.

Even greater than their first summit for peace, the
two embarked on a renaissance of good will. All mistrust
between them was laid aside in light of their mutual belief, and they exchanged proposals for the protection of
New Zealand and New Zealanders. They agreed that given
the thorough and convincing thrashing which they had
received, the White settlers were no doubt adopting a less
aggressive stance for the future and retreating to the more
conservative and most likely original interpretation of the
Treaty of Waitangi. Therefore, suggested Black Jack, a peace
offering of disarmament would not be a bad idea. In return, he thought, the Whites would probably offer a token 'purchase,' or exchange of goods, for the relinquished
guns. Te Rauparaha was not thrilled by the idea, but he
relented to the wisdom of the prospect.

Furthermore, Black Jack suggested that he move away
from the White whaling settlement of Kakapo, owing to
his involvement at Wairau and the problems that that may

pose for him. He said to Te Rauparaha as they strolled White's Bay a few days after the massacre, "Chief, I have a plan. First, we're gonna go back to Kakapo, just you and me. Now you know and I know that those are good folks, and they've always treated me and your people reasonably well. They didn't have anything to do with this latest land grab; and they've certainly been there long enough to belong. Let them be the first to whom you make an offering of peace. Take that rusty old revolver that you shot that constable with and offer it to them for some blankets or tobacco. See how that strikes them! Surely, word of that will make it around. That's bound to have an effect."

The old chief looked as though he thought the idea were odd, and then smiling, said, "All right. You have been right about most things so far. Let us go and do this thing. What do we have to lose?"

June 22nd, 1843:

They seemed scared, thought Te Rauparaha. Two British ships and a slew of sailors in the bay, and still they were standoffish. He set the six-barreled pistol upon the table at which he sat. Several of his women counted shillings, saying that the shore whalers should sell them something. Their money was as good as anyone else's thought Te Rauparaha; and besides, it seemed as though this family would be slightly grateful for his actions surrounding their shipwreck so many years before. Also for selling them this damn land, he thought, holding his anger. Why were they so nervous? he wondered. He had not instigated the problems at Wairau, he thought; and now he was even showing a real effort to make total peace. What more could he do than give them his gun? he asked himself. What good was money if it did not seal a bargain with trust? he wondered. The entire experience left a bad taste in his mouth, and he departed the whaler's house disgusted. The only man who seemed to have any respect for Te Rauparaha, he thought, was the man who had married Kueka. This Pakeha was now busy running back and forth between the house and the ships in the bay. Te Rauparaha asked him if he was scared, or if there was another reason that he could not stop to talk. Everyone he encountered gave him the answer that they were simply too busy giving account to the authorities on who was responsible for the events at Wairau.

Later that day in a discussion with Black Jack at White's Bay, Te Rauparaha said, "I just don't trust them. They all seem to be bothered by something, and totally uninterested in resolving the differences between Pakeha and Maori. They were all running around like they each had a bug up their ass. It was driving me crazy, so I left."

Black Jack seemed slightly skeptical, and asked anxiously, "Well, did you discuss disarmament with them? You know, reestablishing a truce and affirming the original goals of the Treaty of Waitangi?"

Te Rauparaha acted disappointed, and said, "I gave them my gun and tried to talk with them. I even tried to use some of their kind of money to buy some goods; you know, to show that I could deal on their terms."

Black Jack enthusiastically asked, "And?"

Te Rauparaha gruffly responded, "And nothing. They milled about the house tensely as if I was a dog they wanted to let out. It was humiliating. I've never been made to feel less important, even by you!" The Chief made the slightly humorous remark with a serious look. There was a moment of pregnant silence.

Black Jack, trying to maintain his positive bias, said, "Oh well, at least you made the effort. They will remember that."

Te Rauparaha snapped, "Bollocks! They were sweeping the dust out on my heels. I don't know how you have lived with those people for so long. And you consider yourself one of them now, don't you!"

Black Jack looked down, lowering his tone, and said, "No, not really."

Te Rauparaha took the offensive, and said loudly, "But what of the great whaler? You've been doing so well for years. Has all that changed?"

Black Jack defended himself, "Look, Chief, since Kueka's murder, I've become disillusioned myself. Just like when I finally found Kumari. It hasn't been easy for me losing my faith in two peoples. I've had to become my own person completely, with a little faith. You've learned that yourself." The Chief relented with a nod of agreement. Black Jack continued, "So believe me when I tell you that my trust in the White man isn't exactly that great right now either. I've seen a lot of bad things that I don't like in my many years of whaling. One of them being, the slaughter of whales. At first, they were just dumb beasts to me; but now it seems that they are just as beautiful as any of God's other creations. And the White man is destroying them in huge numbers. In just a few years, I have seen their numbers dwindle; and I cannot face staying and watching them become none, as I once feared that the Maori would."

Te Rauparaha seemed to digest Black Jack's words, with more earnestness than skepticism; and he said, "I hear you, but what about the money? I thought that you were going to become the great wealthy whaler and return to your homeland in triumph over the White Man. What has happened to that dream?"

Black Jack responded as if he had anticipated the question. He said, "Chief, I feel that I now have a higher calling here. Besides, I have not become wealthy. Whaling in

Winter and lazing in Summer does not make a man rich. That type of wealth does not interest me anymore anyway. It is spiritual wealth that I seek now. This is my home, and I want to defend it. I do not feel the yearning to return to America that I once did. I want to shape the destiny of this new land along with my own. I too do not trust the White Man's intentions and system of trade; however, I do believe that he can be guided to do the right thing with this land and its native people. Seeing those shackles alarmed and motivated me. They were a warning that the evil of man against man can spring up anywhere; but that evil can be thwarted by good men such as you and me. I am leaving the White Man for awhile, as I left the Maori; and I am going to live as a monk in complete solitude and silence."

Chapter 23

THE SCOUT

Solid black night and deafening silence. No bells tolled the hour, as no watch kept the time. A set of hands carefully sifted through soft ashes like hot snow in the dark; and two lips came together and pursed as a pair of cheeks poised to puff. He blew gently over the smoldering stone, and orange light oozed briskly from the core of the coal. Beating to each breath, the ember pulsated from red to yellow radiance, like a diamond heart on fire, pumping bright life into the face of its reviver and his room. Heat flowed on the cold heels of fleeting shadows; or rather, the vast area where light was lacking fell backward when the wavering warmth waned with his lung wind. At last satisfied with its steady strength, he removed the burning rock from its pale with blacksmith's tongs and placed it in the ready stove where it promptly ignited the waiting tinder. Peering in upon his new home's first flames, Black

14601-GARD

Jack cheerfully said aloud, "Merry Christmas to me, in 1843."

The whalers had helped him move. They all thought he was mad to leave such a lucrative profession at its peak. Black Jack assured them that he was making the right decision by virtue of the fact that he had prayed a long time about it. Besides, he had noticed that the last couple of seasons had seen significantly fewer whales come into the bay; and the supposed 'shore' whalers had had to search further out to sea for the great creatures: Something that they seemed slow to admit. A 'trend' they all said: Nothing to become alarmed or concerned about in the long run for whaling as a whole. Two slow seasons did not a bust of the business make; and besides, there were just too many whales for their small operation to have affected the overall number of the leviathan. That's what they all had said; but Black Jack knew better. His common sense told him that killing the calf along with the cow would eventually mean no more cattle: A simple principle which was as true in whaling as it was in farming. Trying to tell the whalers that the world was a farm and that they were more like cattle rustlers than good farmers was for Black Jack like telling a drunkard that the brewer was going belly-up. They would hear none of it. They all joked him about something called 'Amistad'; as it seemed to them that his sudden upheaval from the Pakeha village was a sign of his rebellion. In the end, however, all farewells had been handled in good spirits with no hard feelings between Black Jack and the crew from Kakapo. In fact, to show their good will and appreciation, they had helped him shift in toto from the seaside village to his newly selected site.

"Are you going to be a hermit now, Black Jack?" one of the men had asked jokingly.

"Something like that." Black Jack had replied, smugly

concealing a plethora of motives and ambitions for his new life that his smirk only alluded to.

They had banded together to help build him a 'proper' home, with sawed timber beams and plank walls. It also had a wood shingle roof instead of the manuka branches that served as the watershed for so many Maori huts in the pa. The wood had come from sheers that were either splintered or showed the first signs of not being shipshape; and once they were shored within the small building, they served their purpose well. Supplies were brought as well to give Black Jack a sterling start to his strive for independence. He was stocked with the following: A sturdy double-bladed five-pound long-handle axe; a one-pound hammer; an assortment of nails; a cast-iron pot, one frying pan; one plate, cup, and set of utensils; and a hoe. All had been carried on a small cart pulled by a mule, along with a potbelly stove and a large copper water cistern. It reminded Black Jack of home, he thought, being complete with the iron chalice for containing the hopefully eternal fire.

Saying his goodbyes during the holidays, the sailors had insisted on his staying for one last sendoff; and he had obliged them a sentimental soiree of celebration and singing at the grog shop. Almost as festive as his fateful night following his first flenching, Black Jack ended the fun and fanfare early; and fetching a pale of flame, he fended a phalanx of spear grass and fern as he fled for his new castle and fortress of freedom. Having desired to provide himself with all of the creature comforts, Black Jack had ironically once again been faced with debating whether the perpetual furnace would become his servant or his master. As the first droplets fell from the threatening clouds and a cool wind followed, he felt that he had done the right thing for Christmas Eve. There was one more thing that the gang had managed to get specially from Sydney to help Black Jack pass the long nights alone: A brand-new mouth harp.

In the meantime since the Wairau massacre, much had transpired with Te Rauparaha as well. He had actually stood trial at the hands of British authorities for his alleged crimes, and had been acquitted. The governor at the time was sympathetic to the Maori as a whole owing to the fact that the Treaty of Waitangi afforded them protection as any other subjects of the Crown. The unauthorized grab for land at the hands of anxious settlers, therefore, was deemed a violation of local Maori rights; and the case was dropped. This had an understandably calming effect upon the chiefs of Cloudy Bay, including Te Rauparaha, who saw that the treaty actually had meaning in relation to their control of the land.

Not being truly local to Cloudy Bay and the South Island, and not feeling as though there were any need to remain, Te Rauparaha began to consider moving north again as to home. This decision was aided by a handful of factors. First, he saw a map of all of New Zealand made by the White Man. In it he saw the North Island next to the South Island, and all the territory that he controlled either directly or indirectly. It was large, but nowhere as big as he had thought. It surprised him to see the other coast of the islands so close to where he was. Then he laid eyes on the map of the entire world with New Zealand in its proper perspective. This really had a profound effect upon the Chief. For the first time, he realized that he did not rule the majority of the world, as he had always thought. He also had the chance to see how much of the world was controlled by the Pakeha; and if he were drunk on power before, that really sobered him up. Being a prudent man at heart despite his propensity for zealousness, Te Rauparaha remembered the words of Black Jack about yielding to the Pakeha. Even in the calm following the trial proceedings, he was left with an uneasy feeling about the future role of the Europeans in New Zealand.

This tempered concern led to Te Rauparaha's agreement with Black Jack as to the resigned warrior-whaler's role in the new order of Maori-Pakeha politics. The two proposed a strikingly similar purpose for his post at Para. That was the Maori name for the area in which Black Jack had settled. Directly inland over the ridges from White's Bay, and just north of the massacre site near the Tua Marina stream, Para was an area of flat, flax-covered land which lay at the absolute heart of the Waitohi Valley that extended south from the waterside pa of the same name. To the west were steeper mountains still, so that this stretch of ground provided an ideal path for anyone traveling from points north to the mouth of the broad Wairau River where it met the sea down south. In other words, both men knew that no parties would pass no matter what their intentions, without the knowledge and scrutiny of Black Jack White. He was to become, in fact, the unofficial gatekeeper for the newly surveyed valley.

Speaking of which, the survey map had no small effect upon the old chief either. Seeing the valley cut up into hundreds of crossecting lines, all perfectly straight and mostly at right angles in total opposition to the natural lay of the land further convinced him as to the confusion of the Pakeha. Why did they persist in slicing the land into little confined spaces which beckoned filling in? he wondered. Why not enjoy the varied features of the land as they existed? A lake here, a river there, a mountain and a volcano in the distance: That's how the land was put together, not with straight lines and points on a map. The lines on the land were like shackles on men, he thought. The land would tell the men where best to live, and not the other way around; and in keeping with that principle, Te Rauparaha looked at the White Man's map and saw that one of his favorite places in the world, Lake Taupo, was actually the largest lake in New Zealand and dead-center in the North Island. How appropriate, he thought; and perhaps why he had always felt that it was a special place. Regardless, it was going to be his retreat for the next few years, he decided.

Black Jack, on the other hand, had the peace and quiet of the big valley to look forward to. His orders were quite simple: He was to report the intentions of the White men he encountered to the Maori. Te Rauparaha was amazed at the difference in the White Man's attitude toward a brown-skinned Maori and his friend, Black Jack White. To any Pakeha first meeting him, he appeared as a simple Negro posing no threat of intelligence or interference. To the Maori, familiar or not with his conquests, he repre-sented a formidable black giant with incredible strength. To the whalers, he posed an enigma: Since first returning to the stations as a Maori interpreter, none of them had been quite certain as to his exact origin. For the sake of the mission, however, the choice of identity was clear. Black Jack White would be the humble ex-slave from America with a helpful attitude toward the gullible and unsus-pecting settler. It was a beautiful plan, agreed the two. Over their farewell feast, they laughed about it until their sides split.

II

So once again, not since being in the crow's nest on the high seas, Black Jack settled into the role of being the sole lookout. He found that he truly enjoyed his silent solitude. Unlike his surviving three short days of it at White's Bay, here he was faced with an indeterminable number of years, beginning with 1844.

He started simply again. All he needed was food, wa-ter, and shelter for one man. He soon found that the task of procuring three meals a day was enough to keep him busy from dawn to dusk. December would have been still plenty of Spring left for planting a vegetable garden; however, without even the beginnings of a plot cleared, he had to rely on the local fauna and flora for the first few months. It was back to duck and fern. He did not have a gun. He relied on his spear. He broke up the soft, dry dirt around his hut with the hoe during the hot, sunny days. He huddled around the stove at night, letting its low light crack the darkness only when he chucked in an odd faggot or two of wood. However, he found that he preferred the darkness. With open doors and windows, his cabin was as one with the outside air; and he found that his eyes would eventually adjust to any level of the ambient light. Besides, he took delight in the images which played in his mind, those being brighter by far than any candle or lamp. He had brought only one book, his Bible; but he couldn't read it. So what else was there to do, he thought, than to reflect fondly upon the illustrious events of his wonderful life until he became sleepy?

One of his early projects was to build a real bed. He had always wanted one; however, time and fashion had not permitted it at the whaling station. Now he had the saw, the wood, and heaps of leisure within which to construct his dream bed. A simple frame of planks, posts, and slats came about; and for comfort he started with a standard flax-leaf mat. In later days, though, he would accumulate enough feathers and flax fluff to fashion a proper mattress.

Most days were arid and clear. Even summertime, though, rarely saw him sweat. The heat could sharpen and come upon him suddenly if he weren't cautious; but it was always mild in comparison with the humid swelter of the Mississippi Delta. Black Jack reveled in it. At the age of thirty-two, he felt like a kid again. He had seen the

Master's children playing games such as frontier soldiers
and Indians, and he had lamented his inability to join in
and enjoy such sport. Now that he was self-appointed sentry, scout, and scoundrel, he was free to play with himself
all day long if he wished to do so. However, he was ever
conscious of the seriousness of his command post, never
allowing his amusements to distract him from his duties.
And that job, quite simply, was to be right where he was,
day after day.

There was a Maori trail that ran alongside the entire
length of the Tua Marina stream through the valley. A
creek running perpendicular to the stream branched off
toward Black Jack's hut a few hundred yards away. That is
where he spent his time, from the moment the sun came
up to the moment it set: Somewhere between his hut and
the main stream. It was plain logic: Anyone traveling for
the purpose of business would come only during daylight,
and they would take the major trail, the path of least resistance. So Black Jack was a guard, in essence, marching
back and forth to the little river periodically throughout
his long days. Besides, he had a clear line of sight to the
creek bank, reducing the urgency with which he must
monitor the passageway. A month went by before he actually saw anyone, and they were a Maori fishing party. As
far as keeping tabs on the White Man, he thought, his life
was going to be easy.

However, the long days and nights of solitude began
to take their toll. As summer stretched on, the incessant
song of the cicada was sometimes the only salvation of his
sanity. He had purposely relinquished all vices, leaving
behind all alcohol and tobacco at the pa. At night, with
hands idle however, he found that he could only play his
mouth harp so long before the torment of boredom lighted
on his shoulder. The activities of day and night remained

separated. In the mornings, chopping wood could entertain him for hours, the same being true for picking flax in the afternoons. But neither of these had any place in the night; and that is when his mind would awaken fully.

Staring at the stars became a passion. Dazzled by their brilliance on the clearest of nights, he could entertain himself with their beauty until the sun came up. He had learned a few constellations from the sailors, but more than the static stellar features; it was the blazing trails of meteors and the unidentifiable flickering objects that captured his attention most. On gloomy nights, though, he was unable to remain unaffected by the weather, and he would succumb to bouts of melancholy.

With plenty of time to think at night, his thoughts turned to the child whom he knew now that he would probably never know. A child who now was the same age as he had been when he made his escape. A child who was still a slave. Black Jack would sometimes sob at this thought; and then he would take heart in considering that his child might also one day break the bonds of slavery. He had told everyone where he was going, thought Black Jack, unlike his father; and it was totally conceivable that his son might find his way down to what now was a world-famous whaling destination. Black Jack became fascinated with this thought; and it bolstered his spirits more often than its rival. Also, he hoped that Lalani had remarried and found happiness.

In his time during the day, his thoughts were more inclined toward work; and if time allowed, Black Jack would be quite inventive. His first creation was a windmill. He sawed two boards of equal length, whittled them with his knife, and warped them with steam. Then he nailed them together at the center; and fixing them to a crude wooden axle, nailed the assembly to a post set in the ground. The simple machine delighted him, although it performed no work beyond its entertainment. He knew that some Europeans harnessed the wind in their native countries; but he wasn't exactly certain as to how. His next discovery involved the Sun. He found that if he left the cistern in the sun all day, then by evening he would have enough hot water for a bath without having to heat individual pots and porting them from the stove. One day, he had the bright idea to build a platform on his roof and allow the cistern to sit there, collecting rainwater and sun alternately. Therein, he turned the sudden shifts in the weather to his advantage. This gave him hope, that he was no longer so much at the mercy of the climatic mood, and he began to feel that he was a deserving master of his beautiful surroundings; furthermore, that they were rewarding his strong kindness.

Then the rains came; and with them came a sense of terrible loneliness.

III

Sometimes it rains so long I think it's never gonna stop. It rained in Mississippi, but not like this. Never like this. It rains until I think it won't stop and then it does for a little while and I think I've got lots to do but then I remember I don't. I don't ever remember being this lonely though. Sometimes I think about going out in the rain and getting things done but then I realize its not worth it. Not with all the time I've got. I forget that I don't work for no one no more. Just myself. As good as that sounds, sometimes that's harder than working all day for the Master.

But I find ways to stay busy. You better believe that. Ain't no way I'm ever goin' back. I'll find plenty to do here. Plenty to eat, plenty of sleep, and I might even teach myself to read that Bible that keeps starin' at me over there. If I learn to read, then maybe I can write. That way maybe someday somebody will remember me. As a person, a free man, someone who shaped his own destiny with daring acts of bravery. Yes sir, a real legend.

Right now, though, I've got the sadness something terrible. This place gets fiercely muddy outside all around, and I can't stand to go out and even rustle up something to eat. I laid in some firewood for days like this, but it's almost gone. I boarded up the windows to keep the rain out, but the damp just seeps right through and into my bones. Sometimes, the only way I can get warm is to stay in bed under my wool blanket. If I run out of wood, though, I'll have to start sawing pieces from my bed, and then soon I'll be back to sleeping on the floor. If I run out of tinder, I might have to use some pages from the Bible; and I really don't want to do that.

Soon, it's gonna be gettin' colder than this. Away from the sea, I know it frosts pretty bad some mornings. I ain't lookin' forward to that. I don't think the stream will freeze up, but you never know. I have seen some mighty snows fall on these mountains 'round here. That's why the Maori stay down by the water mostly. It's all right, though, I'll make it just fine by myself. I pray it stops raining one of these days. Or at least if it's gonna rain so much, it could thunder and lightning as well. It's just this steady, soggy, blowing rain that makes my head feel so musty. If it wasn't for the threat of the water comin' into the floor of my hut to keep me on edge, I guess I'd just curl up into a ball and die. I didn't bring no coffee either; and I thought I was sick of blubber stew, but oh how a hot bowl of that would warm my soul right now. I'm like a moody child, with no parents to discipline me. I don't even sleep regular when it's like this. I find myself wakin' at odd times, and even my soul feels tired. I think I might need a companion, and then I think it's not worth it. Most times now, I don't even feel the urge to be with no one, not even women folk. Thinkin' about the way it used to be with Kumari, and then thinkin' about the way she is now makes me sick. At least I don't have to worry about the way things could've been between us. Or else these drops I hear on my roof would be my tears. Next sunny day, I'm gonna gather as much flax as I can so on days like these I can start spinning yarn like Mama used to. Me, the great warrior chief, in exile doing housework! Maybe I'll just make enough yarn to fashion a rope and hang myself. Ha, ha, I jest, perhaps a bit too much. And how many years was my agreement with Te Rauparaha?

IV

To a Maori guide in the fall of 1845: "Relay this message to Te Rauparaha in Taupo. From Black Jack White, your ally in the South. I have experienced the incident of meeting the queerest of two Pakeha gentlemen. It seems that they were sent on official business from the Crown. I intercepted them at the Tua Marina stream, and they became quite excited when they learned that I was a Negro and former whaler with a knowledge of the area and the ability to speak Maori. Their excitement grew when they learned that they were only a couple of miles from the site of the Wairau massacre; and that the stream they were following intersected directly with the Wairau River. They went on and on about the fact that Waitohi would be such a better place for the settlers to land, rather than Nelson, which is so far north and over steep mountain ranges. Hell, we could have told them that! Well, let them all suffer in their stubborn ignorance if they refuse to take advice from the locals. They probably wouldn't like the advice I gave them anyway.

"I took them down the road to the Wairau (they let me ride a spare mule); and we paid the Maori to take us across. The Englishmen, a Mr. Fox and a Mr. Stephens, seemed scared. They complained about the boat being 'scarcely more than a plank' and about the fact that the

horses had to swim alongside. They said they had heard of
even Maori drowning in such canoes. Back home, they
said, the horses and men all rode across on one big flat
boat, not one that was only four-inches wide. I told them
that they were free to swim with the horses. They didn't
like that idea much.

"At first, they did seem to have a genuine appreciation
for the land and the people. We spent several days together; and I accommodated them at my humble abode. I
was happy to have the company. They were strange men
though. They both slept in my bed together, whilst I bed-
ded down on the floor. During the day, we traveled
throughout the whole valley and even ventured into the
mountains. I liked riding an animal; it was easy on my
legs. The two men spoke to each other about what they
saw in the most flowery and sensual manner that I have
ever heard two men talk to one another. One man spoke
freely while the other uttered agreements and faithfully
scribed it all down. They talked about simple things in
the most fantastic phrases. For example, we came upon an
area of hidden lakes which seemed to be previously undis-
covered; and I thought that they were nice and all, but
they went on, 'We will call this land of lakes Tarndale, for
the smattering of tarns which lie about; where the blue
whistling duck delights in rocky mountain streams, with
the Paradise Goose, and an occasional teal or widgeon,
whilst the unsophisticated wood hen is often amused by
us, pecking and prying with quaint attitude and curious
eye around our encampment. Lake Tennyson lies in an
amphitheater of lofty peaks bold in outline, dark in color,
except where brightened by sunlight and relieved by
patches of snow scattered in clefts of the rock. On its banks
clumps of birch trees, here and there, hang over the water,
or stand grouped over a smooth down, towards a wood,
on the side; whilst in front, the river, leaving the lake by a

pebbly way, flows away down the level grass plain.' I tell you, Te Rauparaha, they went on and on like that the whole time. They literally seemed to be in love with the entire land.

"Then they did the strangest thing. I am still so stunned by the bizarre nature of their actions, that I have yet to come to terms with it through my anger. Perhaps you can help me to understand. As we finished up our sightseeing and headed for the valley floor, they began to set fire to everything behind us. At first I sat bewildered, not knowing the extent of their intent. Then as it became clear that they were burning indiscriminately, I became irate. I demanded to know what they were doing, and they simply laughed and sniggered in a farcical manner, as if they found my concerns to be funny. I was forced to flee the flames on the half ass' back until we reached the valley floor, at which point I told them that I would keep the mule as payment. That seemed to sober them slightly, but they still continued to frolic with one another. I told them that they better not ever show their faces again, or it would not be me who would extract payment from them. That was the last I saw of Fox and Stephens."

The news, understandably, did not settle well with Te Rauparaha; and he began to reconsider his peaceful stance on the Pakeha. In the summer of 1846, Te Rauparaha witnessed first-hand the shock horror of vast tracts being burned to wasteland by settlers, careless as to whether the fires spread to land which had not been purchased. It was a greater insult to Te Rauparaha's pride and intelligence than the shackles had been; and the old chief felt compelled once again to take up arms against the White Man.

Of course, the once complacent attitude of the newly arrived settlers soon turned sour toward this man of whom they were already suspicious; and heightening tensions quickly found the government forces capturing and incar-

cerating Te Rauparaha on July 22nd, 1846. This only served
to further incense the Maori Nation; and what ensued as
their retaliation was known as the Maori Wars. It was essentially an all-out onslaught against the White Man in
an effort to show him who controlled New Zealand. However, one irony caused a catch in the entire fabric of the
plan.

Tamihana, the son begat by a former wife of Te
Rauparaha, had been raised as a Christian by missionaries. He was part of the first generation of Maori Christians
growing large across the land; and he was leader of the
first church at Kaikoura. He preached a message of peace,
in loving opposition to the methods of his father; and the
Maori heart was divided. Therefore Te Rauparaha, now
nearly an octogenarian, remained imprisoned in a makeshift cell upon a British ship moored just off the coast.
There he simmered for two years while the war raged over
land. For a man of his importance approaching eighty to
have suffered that long, locked away on a bobbing boat,
they might as well have sent him away to Hell.

V

October Sixteenth, 1848:

*Lord, an endless storm without lightning and thunder is
like a long, watery torture. I'd rather shrivel up in a bath and
melt away than live here and endure this mush. One of the
settlers finally got it all together and found his way down to
Waitohi. He moved on down the valley a little; and sometimes
I think I can hear his cows if I listen real hard. But it's after
midnight now, and I know they're just standing there, huddled
and still, in the cold pouring rain. People say they're the dumb-
est animal, but I think they're pretty keen. They know what's
going on: Who's cruel, and who's kind; and stuff like that. I*

seen a bull gettin' it one day. Surprised the hell out of me. It must have been at least seventeen inches long, and slimy. Not like a horse's, but more like a dog's; with the inside part showing and no skin around it. When he mounted, it found its way up inside the cow just like a snake, twisting and turning for home like it had eyes or something. The cow's eyes bugged out, and she let out an awful sound as she tried to run away. But I could see that he was quick; and something shot up in there.

Now I think I hear the rain stopping. Sweet Jesus, it is! Three days on and it's gonna quit just like that, I can feel it. I don't care what time it is, I'm gettin' up and lookin' around outside. My goodness, I can see the moon breaking through. I'm puttin' my shoes on and goin' out. I've been sleepin' all day anyway. Ever since that Maori brought me news about Te Rauparaha. Poor old bugger. Close to two years now out on that ship with no relief in sight. I don't know what to do for him. The whole thing kind of messes up the plan we had. The wars don't seem to be doin' any good either. The settlers just keep comin'; and now they have a reason to dress up in their soldier suits and act all important. They ask me if I'll join up. They say I have the perfect spot to be one of their scouts. I act all naïve and say yes; and I am very happy to take their free rations. Poor dumb bastards. Sometimes when the Maori come for my report, we crack open a government tin and eat and laugh. It is a great time then; even though our hearts are with Te Rauparaha. The Maori have issued a strong warning to the Pakeha concerning his release. Even the land seems to want utu for his captivity.

For crying out loud, I can barely see now out my door. The fog has come up so bad following the rain, the sky and the ground have become invisible again. It is a dense, warm, fog. Very fine though, it is, like smoke. With the rebounding rise of vapor from different herbs and soils, it almost has a flavor: Like thick tea. A nice deep breath of it seems to cleanse my lungs and revive me. To heck with it, I know the land well enough after all these years. I'm going for a stroll. I still can't believe there's no snakes in New Zealand. Not one. No possums, raccoons; no rabbits, neither. Come to think of it, when the birds go in, I don't think I've ever seen a critter after dark. Sometimes the skeeters don't even seem interested in biting; and the flies are so lazy you can swat 'em right out of the air. Yes sir, I think that it's got to be the gentlest land in God's creation. There's no wolves, deer, antelope, crocodiles, alligators . . . I really can't think of anything that's wild here 'cept the fishes and the birds. Well, me, of course!

All right, here I go into the soup with no lamp or nothin'. There ain't another soul around for miles. This is fantastic. My senses are on edge. Just one foot in front of the other, that's it. Like explorin' another world. Remember where the creek is: Ah, yes, I hear a little trickle now. All right, I'm on the path. There's the edge of the water, I can walk on down the trail now. I'm travelin' in fine style now. What a strange smell the air has, though.

Here it is October, and it's already gettin' warm. At least it was when I first set out. Now it seems to be gettin' a little chilly. The fog seems a little crisper, a little thinner. I can just make out a dim blue glow in it. This has got to be the very definition of eerie. I'm slightly frightened, but it's more than that: It's a feeling coming not from fear of the unknown; but of the possibility of this being all there is to know. Like that man in the Bible Mama used to tell me about. The one that was damned to wander the Earth for eternity without rest. This must've been what it was like for him. Wandering through the dark fog, acutely aware, never seeing anyone, and nowhere to go.

Well, I know where I'm goin'. There's the Tua Marina stream, right where I 'spected it. It's got a nice strong sound that'll keep me company. I'm gonna head north up the big wide path, just for the Hell of it. Maybe I'll make it all the way up to the dairy before I get tired and want to turn around.

I guess I've been walkin' for close to an hour now. Haven't seen a thing! There's just somethin' in the air, though. Can't quite put my finger on it. It's got me all charged up, though. Must be around two in the morning, and I'm not even tired. I wonder how old Te Rauparaha is doin', out on that ship. I wonder if he's wide awake right now. I've heard about two people talkin' to one another in their minds, under just the right conditions. If ever there was two people who could communicate without talkin', it would be us! At this distance, I don't know. I think I'll just think about him anyway, to make myself feel better about the whole situation.

Hold on, what's this? That's not a light up ahead, I know it. That ding-dang dairy ain't this close. Besides, they wouldn't have a light on this early. Well, maybe. I hear tell these milkers get up pretty early. Not this early though. It can't be much past two, I reckon. Now, wait a minute, I'm not walkin' that fast. That thing is movin' toward me. Is someone comin' down the river? This is gettin' stranger by the minute. This bloke or chap or whatever this is must be daft. Now I know this ain't some whaler lost his way all this far inland at this hour. Besides, he'd be on the piss somethin' fierce and couldn't stand on no stream. Hold on, here it comes. Wait, it's still far away. Hell, I can't tell what it's doin'. I keep walkin' toward it; and it just seems to be floatin' all around. Here it is. No. Don't tell me. There ain't no building out here. Where the Hell am I? All right, there's the stream. That is the Tua Marina, right? Then what's this? I'm slapping the first wooden step with my boot. It's ringing out solid and true like any good solid plank should. She's here, all right! Well, I'll be. I must be lost, or maybe I need to get out more often. Seems like I would've heard them building something this close. It's like the grog shop over from the station just up and floated its way here.

Now, are those Pakeha voices I hear? I'm walking across a wooden stoop through the fog. I'm opening the door, and the stagnant, foul, warm air of the place is hitting me in the face as I step out of the mist. Everything seems real. The smoke, the stench of stale beer, the clinking of glasses. The sailors at the bar? I know I definitely did not smell the ocean outside. Where did I turn? No one seems to notice me. Hell, I've got enough, I'll have myself a beer. Hmm. Tastes real enough. Imagine that, an actual house of entertainment, out here in the middle of nowhere. And how did these blokes get here? They're not whalers, they're sailors. What are they going on about?

"And I hear tell the son-of-a-bitch would sooner eat you as look at you. They say that he didn't get goin' strong 'til he was in his sixties. Then he showed everyone a thing or two." said one crusty old sailor.

"Yeah, well mate, you talk him up like he's a war hero or something. He's nothing more than a low-down, bloody savage. The whole lot of them are. I say a musket ball for every one. That'll show 'em." chimed in another younger but equally patriotic seaman.

The third man at the bar added thoughtfully yet loyally, "Well, mates, they've got him down in the hole now. He's almost eighty, and he's sure to rot away there. His kind are jumpin' up and down and chanting their voodoo rubbish, swearin' that the spirit of the land will take its revenge on us all. Hell, sometimes they sound scarier than the Catholic Church!" The three burst into raucous laughter and hoisted their mugs.

After a moment of revelry, the first man o' war, having taken notice of Black Jack, turned from the bar and said, "Well let's ask this gentleman. Good sir, what do you think we should do with the renegade Maori chief?"

Black Jack hesitated, having become aware of his actual presence in the pub only through the present patrons' eyes. He gathered himself, and self-consciously said, "I personally believe that you will be sorry if you do not release the Chief. If I remember correctly, the original

Governor's report cited the New Zealand Company as the aggressor in all land disputes. Also, the charges against Te Rauparaha such as arson and murder were either fabricated or exaggerated. That's what I think." He finished, holding his mug and looking at the men.

The sailors stared at him in stunned silence for a brief moment; and then all at once they charged Black Jack in a torrent of vituperation with yells of "traitor", and "overboard!" They swept him backward off his feet and in one rush pushed him through the shop door, over the porch, and into the creek with a splash. Still holding the shattered handle of his pint jug, Black Jack struggled to stand unsteadily as the shop door slammed. Whether he had drifted a ways downstream, or whether he had staggered unaware, the steamy silhouette of the ship seemed to be moving away in the misty darkness. Once again the light from the fogged windows became blurred and fuzzy, as if at a good distance; and then again not yet so far. Regardless, he climbed out of the water and started moving further down the slippery path toward home. He was even more disoriented and baffled than before; and he allowed his quest for the comfort of his cabin to outrun his curiosity about the queer apparition he had encountered. Not having fully accepted the experience as real, he took a quick, last glance over his shoulder after the fleeting form.

Oh, God, I gotta funny feeling about that place. I didn't like that one bit. I'm feelin' awfully strange now. How long was I there?

As he turned his head to look behind him, his foot struck a large rock on the path in front of him. The next moment seemed to freeze for Black Jack, as he spun back just in time to see the large stone spring into the air.

Oh my God, I've kicked that rock up in the air. Now the ground is dropping. Am I dizzy? I can't stand. My face is on the ground. My mouth is full of mud. The Earth is knockin' me in the head like a hammer over and over. It's loud. I'm up on my knees. My stomach is swingin' underneath me. I'm gonna be sick. My arms are burnin'. I can't hold onto the ground, it's shakin' so bad. I'm terrified the whole world's gonna drop out from underneath me, but there's nowhere for me to go. God, how long can this go on? I'm startin' to choke on dust. Rocks are hoppin' toward me. All right. Did it stop? My head is buzzing. That beer is coming up. Ah yes, that's better. I'm scared. I don't think any of this is happening. I'm going home now. I'll just follow the . . . wait a minute, there's two streams now. Where did all those boulders come from? These cracks look real. I'm so tired. Lord, have mercy on me.

Black Jack found his way home through the foggy dark and promptly went to sleep. The weather went forgiving, and the next day saw the sun come out. Black Jack spent the day pouring over the land around his hut. He noticed that the ground had shifted more than a foot-either up, down, or sideways-in many places across the valley floor. He made a day trip following the Tua Marina stream north again. Very far north he found a farmer fuming over his ruined dairy and some shaken cows; however, there was no sign of a wooden structure anywhere else along the trek.

VI

Whether the great earthquake of 1848 actually had anything to do with the subsequent acquittal and release of Te Rauparaha later that year can now only be a matter of conjecture and superstition. However, the magnitude of such a coincidence, whether real or imagined, was overshadowed by an even greater event the following year. On the twenty-seventh of November, 1849, just a few days short of his eighty-second birthday, Te Rauparaha died a peaceful death. And whether he was in fact the Devil himself as some had claimed, or the Savior in disguise as others had said; he was nonetheless laid out in a traditional White Man's coffin, as opposed to a Maori canoe, with each of his bare feet proudly displaying their six respective toes. In contrast to his earlier career, but none less important to note, was the fact that during his final year, he made no exhibition of resentment; neither upon his release from the brig, nor nearer his death. He lived quietly and unostentatiously, accepting with as good grace as he might the new order of things; and he even sought to assist his people in reaching a higher plain of civilization. Some have said that his perpetual anger had given way to continual prayer; and he adopted the doctrine of 'peace on earth, good will toward men' over his former heathen 'blood for blood' philosophy.

It was rumored that he had become stricken with an internal complaint, the precise nature of which was never ascertained; and it necessitated his taking much rest. It was during that time in which he delighted others, Maori and willing White alike, with the stories of his glorious war campaigns.

To the staunch Pakeha, his death served to end his 'mischievous scheming and insatiable cupidity', as they so kindly put it. Having never truly taken faith in Te Rauparaha's newfound religious fervor, the Pakeha perhaps got their deserts with the Chief's successor, his heathen nephew who loved tobacco and rum but loathed the White Man. Te Rangihaeta had been present at the signing of the Treaty of Waitangi; however, his sentiments lay strongly on the side of his people. He was a stubborn rebel and a Maori patriot; and his opinion of Pakeha aggression could best be summarized by his statement to the Governor, "We are driven into a corner, and yet you covet that also." He evoked the hatred of the whalers, so much so in fact that they often tried to poison him with a salutation of

rum laced with arsenic. In the end, though, their measles
got him. Regardless, the Pakeha-Maori political climate
mellowed on the South Island, as the crux of the wars
moved north. This left Black Jack suddenly relieved of his
military duties on both sides, and bereft of a close and
brotherly compatriot.

Chapter 24

THE POSTMAN

"Hell, no, I won't go!" came Black Jack's confidently indignant reply to the boys in uniform at his door.

His defiance spattered on their shocked faces. One in the front, holding a piece of paper, said, "But you'll lose your orders, Jack. You'll be discharged without pay; and there'll be no more rations." The junior officer sounded almost as if he were pleading.

"Honestly, I could care less. I am not leaving my homestead to fight some damn crazy Maori up north. No sah. Now you boys carry on. Good day." said Black Jack, as he closed the door emphatically. He had tried to sound convincing and authoritative to the members of the new regiment; in order to avoid being called up to Nelson on charges. He hoped now more than ever that the once impromptu colonial army command honored its original clause of being a strictly 'voluntary' service. Only time and the god-awfully slow mail in these parts would tell, he thought.

Besides, after such a tumultuous and unusually harrowing life, he thought, Black Jack desired to, and felt entitled to, begin enjoying the pleasures of an altogether simple and ordinary life. One that was not in service to anyone. Despite the occasional skirmish and squabble over land here and there, it seemed to him that the Maori-Pakeha relationship had settled into a balanced, if not tolerable, level of tension. Fighting and expansion now seemed to be the norm after the ten years since Waitangi; and as one man who could have remained neutral to the conflict the entire time, Black Jack felt that he had actually helped each side tremendously and should deservedly and perhaps selfishly serve his own needs for awhile. He cynically joked to himself that he had in his short life been all things to all people, and now he was completely alone.

The wars didn't seem to matter in the larger scheme of things, anyway, he thought. In just the last year since Te Rauparaha died, houses had sprung up all over the valley. Men came streaming down, building huts out of manuka branches; and within months had constructed large English houses with verandahs and big, comfortable rooms. At the mouth of the Wairau, there was now even a new hotel where bottled beer and other creature comforts could be had.

Black Jack now found his silent and tranquil valley full of the sound of pounding hammers and ripping saws all day; and the night was presently pestered with the desperate bleating of thousands of misplaced and unconsciously homesick sheep. All across the plains he saw them, wherever he scanned: An endless decoupage of uniform gray and white speckles on an infinite newly-laid green lawn. If that was not enough to shatter his once unpierced transcendental shield, then a final addition to the landscape, and a certain insult, was woven in among the wool to completely destroy his calm: The shepherds' new dogs barked all day and bayed all night.

As if some dark force of misfortune had followed Black Jack full circle from his fateful flight so long ago and found him finally half-way 'round the world, the sign of the canine flagged an omen which caused his teeth to clench and the hair on his back to permanently bristle. His hatred for dogs grew to an obsession. Although he would not have any direct conflict with the new fanged residents of the valley for some time, he nonetheless aided this separation through his exercise of other avoidance techniques and practices. Namely, he steered people away from his land. He had no shame in doing it, either.

If a White settler were stupid enough to ask him, he reckoned, then he would tell him flat out that the land all around him for two miles was all claimed. If he were feeling particularly ornery due to the frequency of interruptions to his otherwise peaceful day, then as a parting gift and a proverbial kick in the ass, he would point the persons in the direction of the farthest available piece of swamp land on the survey map. What really topped his tulips, however, was when settlers, trudging back from the lowlands to Waitohi for supplies, would stop and sincerely and vigorously thank him for his expert guidance. Amazingly still, he marveled, was that he managed to begin charging some people a fee for telling them where to go, and even received plenty of return business and referrals by word of mouth.

II

The time told. The soldiers returned with papers. Anything official with writing on it scared the Hell out of

Black Jack; and he showed his fear out of respect as he stood at attention in the doorway of his hut.

"Yes?" he asked stiffly.

The same young officer, now looking seasoned from time in the field, held the paper and read, "I, Governor of Nelson, do hereby command by proxy, that one Arthur Alesworth, commenced to fulfill his reserve duties; and to be sworn hereto, this ninth day of November, in the year of our Lord, eighteen-hundred and fifty-two. The duties shall be as follows: To serve as mail carrier for the postmaster at the new Wairau branch post office. The fulfillment of these duties will endure until such time as I see fit for the cause of the war. Failure to commit to this charge will result in arrest and imprisonment. That is all. Signed, Governor Eyre." The soldier dropped his town-crier tone, and said, "You need to sign here, sir."

Black Jack, feeling a certain amount of relief, put on a staunch stance and said, "Goddamn, I am never volunteering myself for nothin', or signin' anything ever— EVER—again. I got a job! You know that? I've been running odds and ends down the stream for people goin' on two years now. How'm I 'sposed to do both now? What does this pay?"

The young officer remained reserved and respectful in the wake of Black Jack's tirade, and replied, "Sir, we'll bring you your tin of flour every month." He seemed proud to declare this.

Black Jack, bridling his disgust, said, "Flour? Flour! I don't bake boy. What'm I gonna do, cook some biscuits? Did you bring me an apron as well? Hell, give me that pen. I'm sick and tired of this whole business." And with a stroke of the pen, Black Jack became the first postman for the Waitohi valley; a job that he had to balance between runs of supplies to a small settlement downstream which was becoming popularly known as 'The Beaver'. It

was a place which was situated at a polar opposite to the
town at the top of the valley; and it would soon become
its rival. One prominent figure from Waitohi township
wasted no time in setting the undeclared feud in motion
when he sardonically remarked, "The beaver town is beautifully situated in a hollow, or swamp, nicely adapted as a
natural basin to receive the overflow of the Wairau river as
it frequently does." It was a place which Black Jack would
one day find to be an interesting destination.

III

In reporting to his station of work, Black Jack was
promptly informed that in addition to his humdrum duties of delivering civilian mail to various places throughout the valley, he was also going to periodically carry out
runs to different regiments in full military capacity. That
might include war hot spots on the North Island and the
accompanying extended time away from home. Wonderful, he thought.

Taking his medicine like a man, Black Jack pulled up
his bootstraps and got on with the daily routine of working two jobs that had somehow worked their way into his
busy schedule of semi-retirement. He adopted the demeanor of a truculent yet cynical middle-aged man who
has too much to do and who would rather be gone fishing. Becoming a bit of a celebrity because of his suddenly
visible position in the community, Black Jack would smile
cheerily in hailing patrons and sigh wearily as he rode off
into the dust between stops. It seemed to him that he was
always on the go, with no time to catch his breath until he
went to bed at night; although he knew somehow that he
was probably not working any harder than he ever had. It
was the expectation of having wanted to slow down that
added to his burden, he wisely presumed. He chastised

himself for having to enjoy his work to make it easy, although he did not have a ready remedy for his own perceived immaturity. At least he still worked alone, he thought, mostly unsupervised. That had always been one of his strong points, he recalled: To get on top of a job from the start, so others would leave him the hell alone.

So out he rode, day after day, on a mule he called Independence. If he were going to be tasked with carrying the White Man's written words, then he would do it with pride. Besides, folks in these parts actually seemed friendly and genuinely happy to make his acquaintance, he thought. It almost made him feel guilty for secretly hating their guts. As time went on, however, it seemed that Black Jack ended up doing just about everything but deliver the mail.

"You're that fellow that can grow just about everything under the sun around here, aren't you?" asked one gentleman at his gate. "Tell me now about the difference in this Maori potato and . . ." he went on, and Black Jack spent the better part of the afternoon with the man in his garden.

"You know how to cut and cure this confounded Totara wood, don't you fella!" exclaimed another hardy settler, anxious to dry in his new house with a solid roofline. Black Jack spent half a morning there talking about native wood grain.

"Partner, I hear tell that you tamed this wild flax all the way into a pillow. Is that true?" asked a curious older woman. Black Jack patiently demonstrated his techniques with her and her husband. She wanted yarn. He wanted rope. Black Jack knew it all.

Within a month he was the handyman and Jack-of-all-trades for the entire trotting area. His knowledge and expertise were in constant demand, and he was held in high esteem throughout the community; although not entirely undue to the retention of his humility and good sense of humor. He sardonically thought to himself that if not for the all-out thrill of it, he at least liked the reward that came with working. He enjoyed being appreciated, and not being taken for granted. A sense of importance began to take root in him; and as he lay in bed thinking one night, he realized that he was actually seducing himself into aiding the enemy. He needed to regain perspective, he thought. He needed to reach down inside himself, he realized, and bring out that ruthless edge that had emerged in his youth. He lay there scheming, wondering how to resist the slippery grip of collusion; when in a sudden flash of brilliance, the answer revealed itself to him: The mail!

Once again, he rejoiced, the White Man had tossed the keys to the inmates. Black Jack could neither read nor write; and yet he realized that a large part of the solution to the Pakeha problem was carried under his nose every single day. He also knew the man who could best utilize all of that information which was flowing into the land in neat little packets by the boat full: Tamihana.

Tamihana, having been raised a Christian and taught the language of the Pakeha by missionaries, would be the perfect candidate for deciphering intercepted civilian and military mail. The only problem, thought Black Jack, would be to convert him to the cause.

IV

To a Maori guide in the Spring of 1853: "Relay this message to Tamihana, son of Te Rauparaha, in Kaikoura. From Black Jack White, an ally of your late father. I realize that your Christian faith and gentleman ways have prevented you from taking up arms against the Pakeha in the land wars. However, I am sure that you would agree that

these wars have nonetheless escalated in the North; and
that they threaten peace for us all. Something must be
done. I am therefore calling on you, in addition to preach-
ing your message, to take action in a manner that I will
impart to you. Can you please make arrangements to visit
me, as I cannot leave my post? Thank you."

Of course Tamihana knew the entire story of Black
Jack White; and he was more than happy and honored to
travel to White's Bay. There in Black Jack's hut on a hot,
sunny afternoon, the two chiefs had a meeting of the minds.
Tamihana came with a reverent and open mind. The two
exchanged pleasantries, laughing about good memories,
and mourning the bad. Then Black Jack literally dropped
his plan into Tamihana's lap. Dumping out the contents
of his mailbag, Black Jack let fall a multitude of letters and
packages as his companion watched them tumble into a
pile on the floor.

"I know it's not the Christian thing to do; and I know
it's an invasion of privacy: But I think it's the answer to
stopping the war." said Black Jack sincerely, standing
proudly with the empty, open bag in his hand.

Tamihana looked at him blankly for a moment, and
then brushing letters aside as he stood, said, "No." He
calmly made for the door.

Black Jack stepped in front of him and hurriedly said,
"Now wait a minute Chief. Let's think about this . . ."

"No." said Tamihana flatly, cutting him off.

"Just how better to see into the mind of the White
Man. Think about what it will mean in the long run . . ."
said Black Jack.

"No." said Tamihana again, walking against Black Jack's
hand.

"To your children, to everyone's children if you can

honestly say that you helped to stop the bloodshed." Black Jack continued.

"No." said Tamihana, a little more firmly, as he pushed through the door past Black Jack.

"Chief! What are words on paper in comparison to piles of bodies? Maori bodies!" Black Jack screamed at the departing man's back. Tamihana kept walking. Black Jack, in desperation, blurted, "No one likes you, you know! I hear them saying that you're too soft, that all your words about peace and love are for the birds; that they do nothing for the Maori."

Tamihana, having been walking slowly and calmly, jerked to a halt; lifted his head; turned on his heels; and charged back toward the door. He grabbed Black Jack by the throat and said angrily, "You are an evil, evil man. Do not anger me with your mischief . . ." The Chief's voice faded as he looked at Black Jack and his size. He released him and dropped his own head. He said in despair, "Oh, you are right, I suppose. All the prayers and hallelujahs grow tiresome when only half the people are in church." He lifted his head and said, "And only half of them are listening." The two men chuckled with relief. Tamihana stepped back inside as Black Jack moved aside. "Tell me about your plan my friend." said Tamihana wistfully, as the two sat down again to talk.

V

Hours later found them laughing until they choked and tears welled in their eyes.

"So then I said, 'Oh yes sah, you'll find plenty of water down there on that piece of land . . . '" said Black Jack, as the two grabbed their sides and stomped their feet in uncontrollable fits of laughter.

Tamihana, whooping with delight, fell back into his

best impression of a naïve settler, and stammered, "Well, thank you, kind fellow. I surely appreciate your help." He struggled not to laugh.

Black Jack said, straight-faced in an imitation of himself, "Well don't mention it sah . . . to anyone!" His eyebrows went up, and the pair ripped loose with wild laughter again.

Catching his breath, Tamihana wiped a tear, and said, "All right, time to get serious. Now you say you'll be carrying some actual military orders on the North Island?"

Black Jack responded, "That's what they say. And you know what else?" He smiled.

Tamihana asked curiously, "What?"

"They actually think that I'm gonna go coast to coast, Wellington to Wanganui, inland by mule!" Black Jack flashed a pensive grin to drive home the full effect of his words.

Replying with the initial percolations of laughter, Tamihana asked, "Not by the coast in a canoe?"

Black Jack, holding his laughter, said, "No. And can you hear me now when they ask how the jungle was? 'Ah, you know, tough as nails, sah, but I managed sah.'; or when they ask about crossing the rivers: 'Oh, you know me, sah. I swam . . . and I helped the mule swim across too." The two slammed the table in unison as they laughed hard in each other's face.

The pair hammered out a simple plan. Tamihana would send some of his brighter young Christian Maori who were literate in English. They would live with the tribe at White's Bay, and coach others there in the finer points of the scheme. Whenever Black Jack received orders, he would recruit readers who were also adept at doctoring the mail so as to avoid detection; and then the mail would be distributed by canoe all the way up the coast of the North

Island to its appointed post. By that time, most of the information would have been acted upon and countered, making its message meaningless and its mission moot. The best advantage of this system, of course, was to help avoid bloody conflict altogether. The best part of it for Black Jack, was that most times he didn't even have to go along. He stayed at White's Bay and made a working holiday of the entire operation, until word of its success returned to him and his swollen belly.

Occasionally, he would make a cameo appearance, borrowing a mule on the other side of the strait and popping up at some checkpoint near Wellington. A few soldiers knew of him just through general appearance and mention of name; however, most of them would have been hard-pressed to formally report any specific times or places of his actual presence. An icon to the Maori, recognized instantly by strangers from description alone, he was a convenient nobody to the White Man, remaining effectively anonymous to the majority of his superiors for the duration of his postal career. A true civil servant. Plus, he looked absolutely killing in a uniform. On more than one occasion, it no doubt helped him to knock off the odd piece of lonely, homesick settler's wife whose husband was too busy mending fences or shifting livestock between paddocks. And amazingly, between the days for espionage and his long stops for morning and afternoon 'tea', Black Jack received a commendation for 'timely and efficient performance' of his duties.

VI

One day down by the river, Black Jack ran into one of his old whaling station captains. He was working on three small boats, all newly built. They were painted yellow, with red trim, and a red placard on the back with letters which Black Jack supposed were their names.

Recognizing Black Jack, the Captain called out, "G'day mate. Gosh it's been years. How ya goin'?"

Black Jack took a moment to place the face, and then recognizing the whaler, said, "Oh, fine. My legs could be better; but I'm gettin' along all right."

"All right? I hear you've been running the mail around here. And when you're not doing that, you're running supplies in my competitor's boats." said the Captain good-naturedly.

Black Jack said humbly, "Oh, well, I do what I can to get by. How 'bout yourself?"

The Captain, slightly embarrassed by the question, replied, "Me? Well, see for yourself. I've started a new business now that the whales are gone. Just built myself these three new beauties. I'm just about to christen them. Yes, sir, ferry transport: It's gonna be the next big boom 'round here. Join up with me now, Black Jack, and you can get in on the bottom rung. Whad'ya say?"

Black Jack said, "I don't know."

The Captain, having held his breath for a response, said, "Bah! Sure you do. This is where it's at. Good pay. Plus commission, your own boat, and you get to spend some nights down in Beaver Town. I'll even put you up at the hotel. C'mon."

Black Jack said, "I don't know. I don't think my other employer would like that too much."

The Captain, closing in for the kill, said, "Bah! Jim? I'll take care of him. You just leave it to me. C'mon Black Jack. He's small time compared to what we're gonna be. Help me christen these babies. We'll have a beer!" Black Jack relented, and the two maneuvered onto the small pier with their bottles. The Captain cleared his throat and puffed

out his chest. He said, "All right, ready? Nothin' fancy
now. I, Captain Samuel Bowler, do hereby commission to
service the following boats, this first day of January, eighteen-hundred and fifty-five: The Mary, the Gypsy, and
the Necromancer." The captain gave a nod, and Black Jack
smashed his beer bottle over the bow of the Gypsy, the
bottle spewing the remainder of its contents onto the other
boats.

Black Jack liked his new job. He liked the little boats,
and the way that Sam had designed and tailored them for
the swift, shallow, and narrow streams which intercon-
nected the townships of the valley. They weren't like the
clumsy and unruly boats of his previous boss. That man
had just hurriedly adapted some old whaling skiffs when
he abandoned his station. No, these digs were smooth,
thought Black Jack, as he cruised in style on the clear wa-
terways lined with emerald grasses. So much better than
fighting the riptide on coastal runs to Nelson, he thought.

He had gotten a good feel for the job, and had made a
handful of local runs. Then came the day that Sam gave
him his first big assignment. He was sent down the big
river to the Beaver Town with a full load of bottled liquor.
It was bound for one of the new hotels on the main street;
and delivery and off-loading came with a complimentary
meal and a night's lodging.

The Captain told him, "Now this is one run I'd usually keep for myself, but I'm busy with some other things;
and I can't take the whole day and night to go down to the
Beaver. I want you to be real careful with this one. You're
full to the gills with cases of gin, and I can't afford for
these to even get wet, let alone dumped in the drink. You
should be fine, just take your time gettin' down there,
this being your first time and all. It's real simple: The
Beaver has grown a lot in the last couple of years, but she's
quite easy to get around. The river comes around a bend

right at the end of her main street. You'll see the three
hotels there in a row, along with some other shops; and a
garden park at the far end. That's all there is to it. Just
dock the boat, and the boys will be waitin' there for you.
Got it?"

Black Jack accepted his assignment with a modest level
of excited anticipation, and said, "Yes, Captain."

The Captain said, "Good. Now I've loaded up the
Necromancer. Make sure the guys are from the right hotel. They'll say they're from the 'Gin Palace' when asked.
That's how you'll know. Good luck." With that, Black
Jack put pole to river bed and shoved off for Beaver Town.
The 'Necromancer' Black Jack repeated to himself: He
had asked the Captain what the name meant; but he had
only gotten more confused. Something about a man who
had power over death, he thought.

Black Jack made his way to Beaver Town with a slow,
steady stroke of his staff. The river became broad and the
current less swift as the inviting waters spread out before
him. Summer was upon the valley; and all living things
seemed to thank the giving sun. Butterflies flitted among
the flowers and grass; and songbirds darted low in the
meadows. The stream's sparkling spattered scattering rays
into the staring eyes of the clear blue sky. Sheep frolicked.
Cows grazed. Horses whinnied and chased one another.
The warm air tried on new fragrances as Black Jack floated
by. Fish glimmered among the undulating weeds beneath
the crystal surface. The mountains casually showcased their
majestic beauty. A building broke the horizon.

As he rounded the bend, Black Jack saw that a lawn
extended to the banks of the river, forming a promenade
up a gentle slope to the main street of the town. On the
grassy way near the base of the rise into town was a large
shade tree under which sat a bench. A wooden staircase
had been erected near the bench up to the street. Up the

stream further and on the opposite side, Black Jack could
see nothing but wild bush. A small dock extended into
the water across the green strip from the stairs.

The men were waiting for him, and they greeted Black
Jack well, being happy to receive their vital cargo. With
first case in arms, he was shown the hotel just over the
hill; it happening to be as red as the box he walked with.
For good reason, as it turned out that a thirsty and ready
town without a sawmiller would sooner build with anything available than wait. So the 'Gin Palace' as it came to
be called was put together using the red wood of the containers that arrived waiting for a home: Perhaps a standing
tribute to the constructive influence of the spirits upon a
wanting mob; and possibly a plausible answer to the mys-
tery of the manpower behind the Great Pyramids. There
never were better brewers, in fact, than the mighty Egyp-
tians with their vast plains of grain along the lengthy Nile.
Why is it that water, wheat, and a little yeast should cause
Man to rise to such heights? Is it for the inevitable fall?

Black Jack was done by dinner; and after a twilight
meal and a gin and tonic, specialty of the house, he took a
stroll about the town. He headed west up the main street
toward the town center. Along the way, every open door
seemed to be another hotel pub or grog shop, each with
its ample array of differing patrons; all engaged in varying
stages and positions of grumbling, laughing, talking, and
drinking, their poses being frozen for an instant as his eyes
passed the entry way. Amidst the aimless and uniform
babble, he believed that certain audible phrases quickly
and sharply rose above the drone and darted his ears: Words
such as, 'There's a queer fellow'; and 'you can tell by the
way he walks'; or 'there's that man'; and 'always alone';
and so on down the street. The clock struck seven as he
reached the square. Of three alternative routes, he chose
left and carried on with his grand tour of the Beaver. The

first building he encountered was another hotel chock full
of loyal customers; and then next came the street which
ran along the back of his hotel at the far end. He noticed
that at this hour, no one else seemed to be walking along
the town streets. They were all either in the pubs or on
horses or horse-drawn carriages. People even glared at him
as if he were odd; and he wondered if it had anything to
do with his solo walking.

In fact, it seemed to him that for such a small town, it
had a very large number of horses and carriages. The entire village's populace, he thought, must be riding around
the handful of streets. He watched; and it did not seem
that anyone was performing any particular business: Not
even the perfunctory social visit with passersby in most
cases. They just appeared to be riding, riding, riding to no
end, thought Black Jack. It all began to annoy him: The
constant stares at him from people who were going nowhere in circles.

During the day, the town had been quite peaceful.
He had seen people walking from shop to shop in normal
fashion, performing the ordinary business of the day. No
one, save for the odd bugger, frequented any of the hotel
pubs; and hardly anyone carried on in a more than sublime manner. Now, it seemed, everyone was attempting to
make as much noise as possible. In particular, Black Jack
noticed, with a certain device that everyone had placed
conspicuously upon the reigns of their steeds. It was all a
bizarre spectacle to him: From the single dusty old filly
being ridden by a boy in rags to the richest of covered
coaches occupied by squires and ladies, everyone had placed
a large cow bell just behind the ear of their horses. Completely baffling to Black Jack was the fact that of the hundreds of bells that he saw, they were all identical, as if one
merchant alone had been fortunate enough to import the
item in vogue. As base and common as it struck him as

being, every single rider, poor or wealthy, made it a point
to drive their animal as hard as possible with the crop or
whip on a frantic charge down each stretch of street. This
would cause the bell to clang terribly, seemingly for no
other reason than for the sake of the sound; as the responsible person acted oblivious to—and the horse wholly dismayed by—the racket.

The entire strange scene began to annoy Black Jack
and make him weary; so he turned left again in an effort to
head for his hotel. Along that street, which was effectively
parallel to his destination across town, he passed the constable station. He wondered if there were any laws concerning the disturbing of the peace, or illegal use of equip-
ment on animals used for transport. Black Jack could see
the officers of the law sitting motionless behind the glass
of their building, seemingly settled in for another quiet
night in the Beaver. So much for correcting the issue of
the bells, he thought as he plodded on. Perhaps it was
him, he attempted to concede to himself. However, as he
closed his eyes to obtain a more objective opinion on the
matter, the constant cacophony and tumultuous din of
the frivolous devices actually began to make him angry.
He opened his eyes and walked on in disgust that such a
beautiful town at sunset should be marred with the barrage of a myriad of noise makers.

Turning left at the next corner, he was on the avenue
along the river winding its way quietly out of town. Black
Jack could see the shade tree. As he approached the corner
which would point him home for the night, he thought
that he saw a familiar face within the shop which occupied the first spot on the block closest to the stream; however, he did not stop to investigate in his agitated state.
Once upstairs in his room, he promptly closed the large
window overlooking the street. He was in room thirteen,

the last one down the hallway to the left: The closest to the river.

After a time with his head beneath a pillow, Black Jack realized that it had grown dark. He moved a chair to the large window and began to watch the people of the town once again. Noticing that the steady stream had dwindled to a select few of roving groups, he opened the window. A period of silence and cool breeze remained unbroken for several seconds. Oil lamps glittered in the street, and charming buildings smiled in their glow. Shades of blue twilight matted silver flecks and softly frosted swashes over dusk-tinted distant mountains. Black Jack inhaled it all and held it in contented appreciation. Then around the corner they came.

Barreling down the boulevard, bells clanging, the parties in the coaches seemed to Black Jack to be oblivious to the natural beauty around them. They seemed unaware, he also thought, of just about everything in fact. Around and around the town they went, in clusters, pairs, and alone. Sometimes they would follow one another in trains, other times spreading out to canvas the area. Groups would stop then and again along certain parts of the street to congregate and engage in casual conversations. These associations often fell along apparent lines of monetary status, owing to the decor and condition of the carriages that huddled together. Other times, young and old, commoner and citizen of class alike would share a parking lot. All of the people merely seemed content, in Black Jack's eye, to commingle and pass the evening in a singular meaningless manner: In the trivial pursuit of commotion. It was a race to gain victory over utter and complete boredom at the urban hub of the middle of nowhere; and everyone was the odds-on favorite to show. That is not to say, however, that it did not make for at least an interesting spectacle.

As Black Jack sat watching from his window above the

hotel entrance, a regal carriage with very well-to-do passengers called a halt to its endless chariot race and stopped
out front. In the coach was a party of finely dressed men
and women. Two couples: One young man stepped down
and helped his lady companion out with much chivalry,
as the other pair remained seated. Then, their mischievous antics began to tell their age. Their patting and paw-
ing, slapping and teasing, along with their constant giggling, let Black Jack know that they were probably well
less than twenty. The other couple in the carriage became
fully consumed with one another, as the standing pair
waited for the driver to unload the lady's bags. Two Maori
men, attendants of the hotel whom Black Jack had seen
earlier, stepped graciously up to assist with the handling
of the young aristocrats' arrival. Black Jack strained an ear
to gather what was going on.

"No, Love, you know what Mum and Dad would say.
Besides, you'll be fine here. It's only for one night; and
you won't be sleeping that long. We've still got the rest of
the evening!" said the young man with a reassuring peck
on her lips.

She held his hands clasped to her bosom, and with a
worried look, said, "I know, Charles, but it's so hard when
we're not together. It will be even more difficult now that
we're right in the same town. I can't wait 'til we're married!"

He lowered his voice and spoke as if to a child, "I
know, Love. Soon we'll be together every night. Now
c'mon. Run along and drop these bags in the room. We've
got celebrating to do!"

She turned briskly, happily reassured about their future, and followed her luggage in the hands of the house
boys. Black Jack watched as the young man, top hat in
hand, waited anxiously in the street for his fiancée to return. Then he heard the sounds in the hall as the bustling

entourage stormed to the door of the room next to his. He heard the two men conversing about the room and fumbling with the lock. The jingle of the skeleton key sounded success, and the door was booted open. He heard the clumsy, large window slide open, the bags hit the floor, and the men march back down the hall. Black Jack saw the young man wave and smile as the young lady yelled something in a high excited voice from the open window next to his. Then he heard the door slam, the key turn, and feet softly and swiftly move down the hallway. A moment later she appeared by her future husband's side; and they were off.

Black Jack did not see them for some time. Being more than summer lovers, he expected them to slip away to some secluded spot and sit beneath a tree; or perhaps find a dim corner of one of the nice eateries in town. However, soon enough, around the corner they came. Rambling along, with other horses and riders alongside, they hooted and hollered as they held up bottled libations and imbibed unashamedly. He saw them go around two or three times in rapid succession; and then they disappeared from the lineup of hopeless contestants. Perhaps an hour or more later, they reappeared, louder and visibly less sober than before. They truly did seem to be having a grand time, thought Black Jack, if even in such petite style. Who was he to judge? he wondered, as he noticed that they at least had one another.

At one point late in the evening, the street cleared altogether; and Black Jack was free once again to enjoy the silent beauty of the Beaver Town. He counted to thirty, and amazingly no sound interrupted his serenity. Then suddenly, from across the street, an entirely frightening and unfamiliar sound erupted atop one of the opposing buildings. It emanated from one spot; and as he scanned the darkness for the source of the ruckus, Black Jack's eyes settled upon a stream of white steam and black smoke being pumped from a gray box with wheels and pulleys attached. Black Jack had heard of the new machines called coal-steam engines which were capable of doing the work of many windmills; however, he had no idea what the function of this particular one was, or why it should be in operation after eleven o'clock at night. He only knew that it was one more horrific disturbance of the peace in a place where he thought that there should be absolutely none. The horses belonged on a racetrack; and the engine belonged in the building's cellar, he thought.

The horse-and-carriages began to dwindle in number and intensity of activity, and tranquility began to return to the town in longer lengths shortly after the center clock struck midnight. It was around then as well that he saw them coming down the street. Pulling up in front, the foursome seemed finished. Visibly inebriated, the young man from before struggled to stagger out of the carriage and remain standing. His lovely partner, also affected by the night's alcohol, tumbled into his arms and planted her unsteady feet. The two embraced one another for dear life as the sober driver stepped into the lobby to retrieve some assistance. The Maori gentlemen from before gingerly approached the couple as the driver remounted his perch and took the reigns in eager anticipation of reaching home. Black Jack heard the Maori men and the young man talking.

"Where is the house maid? My fiancée here needs attending to." said the man, slurring his words.

"Oh, she's gone to bed for the evening, sir. It's late. The young lady will be shown to her room tonight and attended to in the morning." said one of the Maori men as the other eagerly nodded in agreement.

The young man, swaying as he held his incoherent

lady friend, said, "Shee that see ish! I have to go now, but we will be back in the mornink. Be sir that see ish up!"

The two men gesticulated humbly, smiling egregiously and rubbing their hands. "Very good, Sir. Yes, Sir. She will be shown to her room straight away, Sir." said each man in alternating repetition of the other.

The young man pushed her into their arms and stumbled back into his seat. Black Jack watched as the carriage drove away and the two men each took an arm of the lady and braced her on their shoulders. The men were not what he would call young and handsome: They impressed Black Jack as being the product of one of the first generation of Maori men to grow up completely within the lifestyle of the Pakeha. Now, in middle age and having had drunk too much, eaten unhealthily, and smoked the same, they showed the effects of being weathered by vice. Their guts protruded heavily over their English belts; and their black hair, although still thick, was receding and peppered with gray. Their features had begun to droop prematurely from the ravages of long nights of libation; and several teeth had since headed south. They were crusty and salty, but not without a certain authentic masculine charm: Much like old yard dogs.

Although walking partly under her own volition, the young lady did not seem to Black Jack to be entirely present of mind as the trio passed beneath the lighted marquee of the hotel and out of sight. He heard them come quietly down the hall after a time, and then begin to whisper outside her door. He decided to crack his door open for a peek at the parental progress.

As he peered, he saw her bury her face in the chest of one of the men while the other struggled with the door. Upon his success, he turned and exchanged glances with his mate, and the two scanned around in all directions. The girl began to babble and look around, seeming to comprehend her arrival at her proper destination. With a concerted rush and a slam of the door behind them, the threesome disappeared into the room. Black Jack, tired from the night watch, lay down upon his bed and listened for the pair's departure.

Inside her dim room, she could barely follow their dark forms as the light of the street streamed in past the musty yellow and brown floral drapes, mixing with the glow of the room's oil lamp upon the peeling green foil fleur-de-lys wallpaper. As she felt herself sit heavily upon the bed against the wall next to one of the men, she heard the other man mumble something about "checking on things" from the toilet. Crossing the room, he extinguished the low lamp, filling her eyes with strobing rings of murky colored light rippling over pools of darkness. She strained to focus as she heard the cumbersome wooden window being closed and the curtains drawn, cutting off the flow of the cool night air. Small, smooth, round and wet stones rolled and clacked within her cranium, as she became aware of the smells around her. The pungent warm scent of stale red wine and cigarettes snuffed in beer closed in around her along with the sharp, oniony body funk of a presence breathing in her ear. Her neck swanned and jerked, falling forward to meet the dusty wool coat and musky aroma of the man now standing in front of her. She struggled to breathe, see, and stop spinning as she felt the coat brush aside her long, fine hair. Why couldn't the house maid attend to her, as was proper? she wondered. Why were these men taking such care to see her to bed? Thinking that she had heard the room key jingle in the standing man's pocket, she raised a wavy hand of protest and query, only to find the large, naked belly of the imposing Maori. She instinctively recoiled, though clumsily, her hand re-tracing its sloppy trail back down the slope. She felt the weight and breadth of the man's protruding gut. In her altered state, it reminded her of a heavy wool blanket, fresh from the wash, which her mother and she would have lovingly wrung before it was hung. The first pang of fear passed through her navel, starting from her heart and flowing cold down within her inner folds. Then her hand discovered a happy and anxious child, swaddling beneath the man's bulky spread: The organ grinder's cheeky assistant, springing to touch the rims of her supple sipping portal. Sporting a plum hat and dashing vest, it slipped over the moat, through her pearly gates, and clamored over the castle's royal taster, planting a serviceman's homecoming kiss at the rear of her reception chamber and receiving a reflexive hug in return. Utter shock and terror flashed across the top of her head; and then something strange occurred: As the festooned creature playfully probed and burrowed curiously within her face, like a macaque in the caves on the Rock of Gibraltar, she felt the fear take flight; and warmth melted over her. Had her hand betrayed her, she wondered, failing to shun this uninvited visitor at the door? Her fingers held out the last bit of resistance at the threshold, where upon further investigation she found the bold guest's luggage. She felt her bottom becoming as hot butter. The other man, whose hands had been upon her bosom, now gently grasped her ankles. The two men consorted, and they laid her back upon the bed. She realized that she had never seen a man's face so close to her down there, nor had she felt a man drink from the fountain from whence her bubbly debut vintage now flowed. She wondered if it meant that she would still be a virgin in the morning.

Black Jack drifted through the gentle warm waves of waning consciousness, imagining that he heard frantic scraping, thumping, and rapping upon his wall between the two rooms. He also heard a sound that challenged his memory. Desperately searching in semi-sleep through his mental archive of sensory experiences, he stumbled across a time, when as a young boy out hunting, he had first heard the stifled, squeaky mews of excited bunnies busy within their den. He was privy to that sound now over and over again, almost waking to it several times throughout the long night.

VII

The next morning Black Jack awoke bright and early, having left his curtains and window open. Another fine, sunny day greeted him as he stood and scanned the still street just after sunrise. Making his way downstairs, he carefully stepped over empty and tipped bottles, fag butts, and piles of assorted discarded gastric goods in various stages along the digestive path. Once clear of the last step on the front of the hotel, he did not look back. Black Jack walked briskly toward the river and his boat that would carry him home. Down the stairs and to the dock he scampered, a sole enterpriser, risen with the birds; and aside from them, he was alone in his endeavors: Or so he thought.

As Black Jack finished checking his draft and prepared to cast off the lines, a lone, dark figure could be seen sitting slightly slouched on the seat beneath the big shade tree. Startled, Black Jack reflexively cried out, "Hello there. How ya goin'?" Black Jack could see in the gray light of the early morning that the stranger held what looked to be a letter in his hand. The large man was darkly-complected with a head of thick, black hair and a bushy but neatly trimmed red beard. He wore a long seaman's oilcloth coat, and high black boots with pointed tips. Black Jack could not tell from a distance whether the man was Maori or Pakeha.

The solemn figure replied strongly, "Good, mate, but you might not be."

Taken aback further by this comment than by the stranger's ominous appearance, Black Jack replied, "What do you mean by that? Do I know you sir?"

The man shouted across to the dock, shaking the letter sternly, "No, you don't know who I am; but I've heard plenty about you. Come closer and I'll tell you."

Black Jack, still wary of the stranger, would only step out of the boat and walk to the head of the pier. He asked, "What business is it that you have with me, sir? I am busy, and I must go." Black Jack could see that the man had piercing blue eyes.

The man said, "I think that you will stay when you hear what I have to tell you."

Black Jack, attempting to feign bravado, said, "Well, out with it then, sir. I have not the time for games and such."

The man said, "So, you like to read other people's mail, do you? And what satisfaction does that give you?"

Black Jack felt cold chills; and his bowels twinged with the threat of desertion. He demanded, "Who are you? What do you want?"

The man sat up from his slinky position and said, "I want to know why you feel compelled to invade other people's privacy. Is it for some higher purpose? Do you think that you are helping history in some way?"

Black Jack said, "Well, I'm not admitting anything until you tell me who you are."

The man said, "In good time Black Jack. Suffice to say that I have it on good word what crimes you've committed. I could have you put away for a very long time. Now, let's say that you are innocent. Let's take a walk and let me show you some things that may influence your thinking on the matter."

Black Jack, still maintaining his ignorance of the evidence, said, "I'm not going anywhere with you, 'cause I haven't done anything wrong."

The man said, "Black Jack, let's not beat around the bush. I've spoken with Tamihana as well, and he's confessed everything. Now, you can either cooperate, and I can help you; or you can refuse, in which case I will make things very difficult for you. It's your choice, Black Jack."

Black Jack hesitated in the breech. He said after a moment, "All right. But where's this walk you're talkin' about? I don't have all day."

The man said with a smile, now standing, "Follow me."

The two walked in silence as the mysterious gentleman led Black Jack along a trail through the dense brush. After the better portion of an hour, the bushes began to spread out; and the trail became sandy. Sea grasses began to appear; and the breeze picked up. Black Jack saw gulls and smelled the ocean. The men exited the scrub and walked onto a broad, sloping terrace as the water appeared in the distance at its edge. Black Jack could not see a shore line. It seemed as though the grass of the meadow extended right up to the water's edge. He followed the man, until suddenly, an abrupt edge appeared before them. It was the end of the sand and grass, and the beginning of a vertical cliff which stood towering one-hundred feet above the beach. Black Jack caught his breath as he stopped, his head swimming from the height. He stepped back a couple of paces. The man remained standing at the edge, peering down, the wind from below buffeting his hair. He turned and looked Black Jack in the eye.

"Please, have a seat. I have much to tell you." said the man with an extended hand. Black Jack sat, head perked up, ready to listen. The man continued, "Your plan was not without its merits. Your good intentions should probably be rewarded by some higher authority; and in some

respect, your intentions will probably reap their own reward with the minimal influence of events that they effect. But Black Jack, reading so much mail on such a large
scale? Did you really think that that was the right thing to
do?" The man began to pace; and as he did, he wandered
in his steps to a point behind Black Jack. From his new
vantage, he went on. "Did you really think that you would
get away with it? I mean you know, and I know, that this
amounts to treason. You could hang for this, Black Jack!
And what about the safety of those you wish to help and
protect? How do you think the Pakeha would react if they
knew? Wouldn't you feel terrible if they retaliated against
the Maori in some horrible way? Think about it, Black
Jack." The man went on and on about the morality and
ethics of the activities in which Black Jack was engaged;
and slowly, Black Jack began to ignore him. He began to
daydream as he gazed out over the ocean, the man's voice
droning in the background.

Suddenly, Black Jack was stricken with the oddest sensation of sinking, and as his mind raced into focus, he
realized that the sand in front of him and beneath him
was pouring over the cliff like the flow through an hour-
glass. Black Jack became horrified; but as he struggled to
fight the stream of sand, he found himself coming un-
avoidably closer to the edge of the cliff. It was actually a
new edge, as the old dropped away, grain by grain, to the
beach below. Before Black Jack could do anything, he found
himself coming to rest on the sheer face of the cliff, buttocks perched on a small, shifting ledge, and shoulders
below the lip of the meadow rim. He was instantly terrified. Looking down, his head was protruding from the
cliff, face further out than his feet, giving him a view straight
down. He was completely vertical, he realized. Looking
around, his eyes were dead level with the grass and sand of
the terrace of land behind him. There was no sign of the

stranger. Dust blew into his eyes, forcing him to turn back
and face his falling fate. Although there appeared to be no
ledges save for the one on which he seemingly sat, he instinctively spread his arms and tried to dig in with his
elbows. He clawed with his heels to gain a hold, but to no
avail. He felt as though his seat were slipping. Suddenly,
birds appeared around him. Not a flock, nor a multitude,
but a handful of large, white sea foul flew here and there
around the cliff and lighted on various small ledges. Black
Jack in his state could still tell that they were not gulls,
nor were they albatrosses. They were something in between.

His sides and lungs tightened in panic. He was afflicted with the overwhelming sensation of being in continual freefall. He felt as though a large timber had been
braced from below and wedged beneath his ribs; or perhaps more to the point, that he was already speared upon
the rocks so far below. He was in the vice-like grip of perpetual death, though cursed with the remaining life to
suffer it infinitely. Finally falling would have been a relief
from the hell that he hung over.

The odd-looking birds began to engage in a strange
activity. As Black Jack watched, they would fall head first
from their perches and dive straight down. Tucking their
feet behind them and their wings back, they would achieve
full speed before snapping their wings open. Their wings
would unfurl like sail sheets, with a sharp crack and a
flapping sound; and the birds would then arc up and
around steeply to reclaim their original ledge. It was an
agonizing spectacle for Black Jack to witness, their mas-
tery of the fall seeming to mock his perilous predicament.

Suddenly, two strong hands grasped his arms and
pulled him up onto the meadow. "How did that feel?" the
man asked. "Like slowly suffocating, or something else?
How would you like to face that for an entire day?"

Black Jack, too shaken to react with anger, stammered, "How did you . . . why have you..?"

The man interrupted, "No, no. Don't worry. All will be revealed. Walk with me. I have more to explain." Black Jack, still perturbed by his ordeal, cautiously walked beside the man. The stranger continued, "Do you recognize that bird?"

Black Jack, still distracted, said with annoyance, "No. It looks like a sea bird, but I don't know its name."

The man said in the tone of a patient teacher, "That is the Booby. Its name betrays its flying ability, wouldn't you say?"

Black Jack, now giving his full attention, said, "Yes, I would say so. I've never seen any other bird that large able to do such things."

The man said, "Ah, yes. Very astute of you. And do you know how it came to be known by such a derogatory name?"

Black Jack said cautiously, "No."

The man said, "Because, when the first English sailors set foot on land here, the bird sat upon its nest and eggs as it watched the men walk straight up and bash its brains in. Therefore, the sailors thought that the bird was the stupidest creature that they had ever encountered."

Black Jack, curious but not committed, said, "Really."

The man said, "Yes, really. But do you know why the bird was so trusting?"

Black Jack said, "No."

The man erupted, "Because it had no goddamn predators on this entire island! It had no reason to be scared-of anything!"

Black Jack asked politely, "I'm sorry, predators?"

The man said, "Nothing ate the Booby. It was master

of everything it saw as it sat and nested. It was free to frolic and fly as it wished, without fear."

Black Jack, digesting what he heard, said, "Oh."

The man said, "Yes, and do you know which bird is even more free?"

Black Jack said, "No."

The man said, "The Kiwi."

Black Jack said, "The Kiwi? But it doesn't have any wings. It can't fly. How can you say it is free?"

The man said, "Because it doesn't *need* any wings. That is because it does not need to fly away from any predators. Well, at least that was true before man came along. But regardless, the truth is that it is a bird; and at one time it had wings. The first one to be born without wings, once this land separated from Australia, survived. It went on to make more wingless baby birds, none of which were eaten either. They made more, and so on; until there was an entirely new variety of bird."

Black Jack said, "That is very interesting, but you still haven't told me how that makes the Kiwi free."

The man, surprised but patient, said, "Because, Black Jack, flying is hard work. Have you ever tried it? Birds came along because they could fly away from their enemies; but it was still hard work. The Kiwi doesn't have to work to survive anymore. Therefore, it is free. Does that make sense?"

Black Jack said, "I don't know. I guess so."

The man shook his head with a smile. Their walking had brought them back to the dock and the tree. The man said, "All right. I've confused you. Here, sit with me while I try to explain further." The two sat upon the bench in the shade. Black Jack was uncertain whether the sun had partially blinded him or whether his eyes were playing tricks; however, the tint of the slightly overcast sky and the grass seemed to reverse; and many colors went to gray. The man continued, "Look, Black Jack, perhaps this will convince you."

Suddenly, the ghostly forms of Maori children, sitting in rows between the bench and the river, began to materialize. Black Jack could make out the hazy outlines of writing slates and chalk in their hands; and a man and woman walking among them as teachers. The entire scene was an apparition in motion, a slice of the past being reenacted and projected before Black Jack's eyes.

The man beside him said, "You see, Black Jack, these children were being taught to read and write in English by Christian missionaries, much like Tamihana was."

Black Jack, mystified by the moving images, said, "But when . . . who are they?"

The man said, "Ah, Black Jack. I think you know. You see, on a day when so many had turned out to mourn the loss of someone you know so well, a man who fought and died so bravely, who was given a proper hero's burial by the White men . . ."

Black Jack, beginning to realize something, stood and said in a crowing whisper, "No!" Coming down the river, he saw a canoe filled with what seemed to be several Maori warriors.

The man continued, "The same White men who could not forgive their losses at the fallen hero's hands so long before . . ."

Black Jack, trembling, said, "No, please."

The man said, "Oh, yes. And with so many Maori in attendance at his funeral, it made such perfect sense to the Pakeha to take what they wanted from the few who remained . . ."

Black Jack, feeling sick, moaned, "Oh, God."

The man said, "The few innocents from a tribe living

inland, who were slowly making their way back to the coast. It was such a beautiful spot to stop and camp for awhile; on their way back to a seaside home so long ago forsaken . . ."

Black Jack, now in panic, ran from the bench toward the phantom group as the warriors leapt onto the shore. He said, to no one in particular, "Stop it! Please, stop it."

The man said, "You see, Black Jack, you thought all along that you were helping to change history for the better. Well, you couldn't have helped this day . . . not while you were stuffing your face at Te Rauparaha's grave!" The warriors began wading into the crowd, chopping wildly as they went. Small heads, hair, and limbs began to fly. Black Jack ran back and forth among the figures, passing through them in futile attempts to rescue them. The man went on, "But this was prime property Black Jack! Sakes alive, flat farm land along a river so close to the ocean: Why, it was to die for!" The man said the last with wild sarcasm. Black Jack began to scream and yell with tears of rage and despair, now recognizing members of the tribe. The man said, "What better day and more appropriate way to extract revenge and avoid revenue than to ambush a bunch of innocent people, eh Black Jack? There they were, learning the good Word of the righteous Pakeha, on their little tablets carried straight down from the Mount, when lo and behold, along came a pack of out-of-work whalers, desperate to help the Crown in any way they could. They were more than happy to dress up, play savage, and kill some luckless Maori for a price. Hell, they'd been doing that for years!"

The man kept up his smiling soliloquy spiked with cynicism, until Black Jack fell to his knees and cried, "Havoc!" at the top of his lungs. The slates, tumbling to the ground, resembled tiny, scattered headstones. As the bloody fallen figures faded and the whalers went to wisps, Black Jack turned toward the man on the bench.

There on the bench beside the man was Kumari. The man was holding the letter from before. His skin seemed darker than ever: A gray going toward a dusky purple. His eyes shone brightly blue from the shadows. He said, "What do you think of intervening in people's lives now, Black Jack? Still like the idea?" The man smiled a toothy grin; and stroking Kumari along the back and shoulders with his left hand, he set down the letter and unbuttoned his long oilcloth coat with the right. Standing from the man's left side at a distance, Black Jack could only make out shadows and patches beneath the coat; however, he could see that the man wore only his leathery skin. Holding up the left flap of the coat, the man gently placed his right hand upon Kumari's head. She had begun to drool, and her eyes were crossed. Her face descended and disappeared behind the flap of the stranger's coat. Black Jack watched in horror as he saw what looked like a tail slither and whip once before it dipped out of sight behind the raised coat flap again. It had not been a tail, Black Jack suddenly realized; as it looked slimy and skinless, like the sign of the excited bull. Kumari made a muffled sound, like the surprise of a delighted child; and her head began to move slowly up and down.

The man, picking up the letter, looked Black Jack in the eye and said, "You want to know the future? I can show you that. Right Kumari?" She again made a giggling noise, vocalizing her full agreement with a humming, hidden smile.

The man waved his hand, and all the tints of the landscape shifted to reds, yellows, and golds. "Take a look, Black Jack!" the man said. Suddenly, there were fantastic carriages, made of metal and glass, racing up and down the main street of the town, now grown to a small city.

The machines belched gases and loud noises as they moved. Women walked about in tight men's trousers and blouses that seemed to form a second skin, exposing the sleek lines over their calves, buttocks, and breasts. The protrusion of these outlines into the air was accentuated by long, narrow pegs placed beneath the heel of their shoes; which gave them all the appearance when they walked, thought Black Jack, of the half-human hoofed beasts he had seen in pictures of Greek mythology. A great tower stood overlooking the center of town, crowned with a huge engine that roared and whined at regular intervals. The man continued, "This will be a great center one day, Black Jack. Livestock will be sold by the thousands, farms uprooted and overturned by the mile, and vines planted by the millions; all to make way for the mighty grape! This entire valley will flow with wine, and every year a great festival will be held in tribute to the god of the grapes. There will be much consumption and many drunken souls will take to the town in blind revelry. Men, women, and children, all stumbling and staggering about the streets; and I'll be there, in all my glory, to oversee the celebrations. People will come from all over the world every year to partake of pleasure in this peaceful place; and every year a soul will be sacrificed for the sake of the harvest. Don't you want to be there? Sign up now!" Black Jack looked around the city in bewilderment, amazed and terrified at the glimpse of the future the man had provided. The man continued, "I found out I didn't need my wings, Black Jack. Now I'm free. Let me show you." Black Jack, beginning to realize that he was in mortal danger, started to back away toward the boat. The man said, "That's it. Run have a look see at that shop on the corner. The first place of business in the Beaver. Whose is that do you reckon? The illustrious husband of the late Kueka, you suppose? That's right. That's what a man does when drowning his own sorrows will not kill the pain. He seeks to drown others! I can give you everything, Black Jack. All you need to do is sign this letter. Come here, I want to give you something. Right, Kumari?" Again came her verbal nod. Black Jack, realizing that the boat would be too slow, began to run past the man toward the stairs. The man said, "Don't go, Black Jack, I want to give you something. Please, you'll like it!" Black Jack glanced over his shoulder as he ran. He saw Kumari lift her head; and as she did, he noticed that her tongue protruded, having become one with the specter's shiny, wet scepter. It sawed back and forth over her lips, as she looked Black Jack square in the eyes. He turned his head and ran for his life. Up the steps and into the main street he scurried, hearing the man's fleeting words as he fled. The man finished with "All your valiant talk to Te Rauparaha about the soul being free. Ha! I can kill your soul, Black Jack. What do you think of that? I can kill your soul! Where would you be then? Someone's going to own you again, Black Jack. Trust me, I know. If not me, then someone! Someone's coming, Black Jack. There'll be plagues, floods, and earthquakes. He's gonna own you!"

The ground began to shake as he ran. It trembled as violently as it had years before; and he was knocked to the ground, falling unconscious as bells clanged chaotically.

Chapter 25

A DIG FROM THE PAST

Spreading out in all directions, the big head floated toward him with a solemn look of determination.

In a flash, the figure flipped upside down and melted into a warped and wavy form staring him in the eyes. Wobbling and shimmering, the man hovered just in front of him, beginning to disappear into fog.

Black Jack turned the spoon over again and stroked the surface with a fine cloth until the brilliant gleam returned his reflection to its former glory. Ebony on silver complemented the crystal well, he thought, as he stood setting the table in the large dining room. He admired his mirror image some more, straightening his black tie whose knot was tied securely around his muscular neck. He was the picture of a man who had accomplished so much; and yet this was the first time that he had stopped to visibly reflect. Indulging in a taste of vanity as he polished, he allowed himself the luxury of looking at his own time-worn face; and also to ponder why after so many events in his life, he had not paused to actually peer upon himself before. Looking at his own distinguished features, he told himself that at the age of sixty, he deserved to admire his own good looks and to reflect on everything that had occurred over the years. His mind wandered back through time as he put the final touches on the place settings for the evening's honored guests. A small folded card on one plate read, "Thank you for attending our special dinner party, Rev. Ironside. With best wishes from Kennington and the Baillie family. Sunday, March Ninth, Eighteen-Hundred and Seventy-Three."

II

After having failed in his role as the Maori Moses, Black Jack became in a sense a Noah figure for the plains which twice were flooded in concordance with a thankfully past and greatly unpleasant prophecy. Having come to grips with his present fate as a farmhand, butler, and flaxmiller, he could now look back on certain events less bitterly. Like the day that they came:

Dashing in the distance, to and fro, through the valley over tracts of land still undeveloped, the couple rode red-breasted on horseback. With hunting caps on, horns blowing, and hounds in tow, they cantered regally, relentlessly pursuing their elusive quarry and maintaining a purposeful appearance. Still refusing to show any sign of doubt or deterrence, they strode confidently up to Black Jack's shack. He was home in the cool and shade, counting his tins of flour that he kept to mark his time in service. The man and wife, remaining mounted as they jockeyed assumptively upon their unsteady steeds, called out from the yard. Black Jack, happy to offer his help to the hapless horsemen, humbly stepped outside.

"Yes?" said Black Jack, standing in the late afternoon sun.

"Good fellow, have you happened to see any hares?" asked the gentleman hunter.

"No." said Black Jack flatly. He had never seen one; however, that fact was in keeping with his knowledge of the entire missing menagerie whose list he had amassed in his head. "I've never seen anything worth huntin' 'round here." he added, looking down and around contemptuously at the panting dogs in his yard.

"Well, I say, that is odd. Something should surely be done about such a sorry state of sport." said the gentleman, exchanging glances with his wife.

"I do say, Charles, it sounds like a good opportunity to demonstrate your expertise in stocking. " she said with an insidious grin. The two looked at one another knowingly for some time. Black Jack became annoyed with their secretive smiles.

"Righto, we're off then." said the man finally, and the pair bolted as the dogs leapt to attention and followed. Black Jack thought them completely rude, and he went back to watching his eighty-one containers of now wormy wheat powder.

Some time later, the couple returned. Carrying covered cages, they carefully dismounted and looked around. The dogs had been left behind. The two were smiling arrogantly again as they surveyed their surroundings. They gave Black Jack the creeps, in their pretentious hunting jackets and riding pants.

"Sir, we bring good tidings from Picton." said the gentleman.

"Picton, where is that?" asked Black Jack.

"Why, haven't you heard, good man? They changed the name just over a fortnight ago." said the gentleman.

"No, I hadn't heard that. I don't get much news out here." said Black Jack, not revealing his disappointment.

"Well here, take a look at this." The gentleman handed Black Jack an official piece of paper.

"Sir, I cannot read. I'm sorry." said Black Jack without shame.

With a look of skepticism, the gentleman retracted the sheet and said, "Very well, I will read it aloud to you then: 'The Governor doth hereby, in further pursuance of his plans, constitute the town of Picton, heretofore called Waitohi, to be capital of the said province of Marlborough, this first day of November, eighteen-hundred and fifty-nine.' Now, how does that sound?"

Black Jack said, "That's the ugliest name I've ever heard. Is that English? What was wrong with Waitohi?"

The gentleman eyed Black Jack suspiciously and said, "Yes, it's English. The other name was Maori, as I'm sure you know. Besides, good man, how did you file for your property without knowing how to read or write? Did you employ a solicitor?"

Black Jack did not appreciate the gentleman's tone, nor his audacious questioning. "File, sir? However do you mean?" asked Black Jack.

"For this tract of land which you occupy. Surely you have the paperwork to prove ownership." said the gentleman.

Black Jack said, "Sir, I have filed no such paperwork, nor is any in my possession."

The gentleman, stunned, said, "Well how is it that you claim rights to this land? I notice that your accent is not British. I was under the distinct impression that this land had been purchased and cordoned off for subjects of the Crown."

Black Jack, swiftly switching the subject, said, "Sir, I have more rights to claim this land than you will ever know. I have been here for sixteen years on this same spot; and if this land is not mine by squatters' rights alone, then I don't know why not."

The gentleman, gaining a gleam in his eye, said reassuringly, "Well, it is not a matter for me to debate. I was simply curious. My wife and I had seen this big empty tract for some time, and thought what lovely hunting grounds it would make. Didn't we, Pooch?"

"Quite right, Hunter." said the woman.

"Right. Now, we have some business to attend to. We were hoping that it would be all right if we started a little project out here in the middle of the valley, my good man." The gentleman uncovered the cages, revealing their contents of four rabbits: Two mating pairs of different varieties. "Would it be all right if we released these rabbits on your land for the purpose of stocking the Wairau area? It will be a momentous occasion, and a monumental achievement if successful."

Black Jack seemed amused, and he replied, "Well, I don't know. I don't see why not. I'd be curious to see if we can't get something else to eat around here besides birds and fish. I'll be surprised, though, if they stick around these parts."

The gentleman, anxious to do his deed, and ignoring Black Jack's last comment, began to open the cages. He shooed the rabbits, and they ran swiftly in all directions. When each was a few yards away, the four stopped suddenly and sniffed the air. They then began to converge on one cardinal point; and soon they were all headed off in more or less the same general direction. All three people stood in silence for some time, watching the rabbits' forms dissolve into obscurity.

Finally the man said, "Right. Well perhaps we will see them again some day. For now, it's farewell to you good man. Thank you for all your help."

"No worries." said Black Jack.

III

Dressed in their Sunday best, they arrived in a caravan of uncovered carts. A young yet mature-looking gentleman dismounted and stepped to the door of the shack. He stroked his muttonchops beard, fiddled with his military sword, and looked back at his beautiful bride, smiling in reassurance. Finding no one about, he rejoined his family troop and sat purveying the vast plot with them. According to the deed, it ran from the Tua Marina stream at its eastern boundary for five hundred yards, to the base of the foothills on the western end for the same north-south width. Having failed to conquer the bush and swamp on his initial property near Nelson, appropriately and ironically named, 'Erina', he had decided to give a go in kinder country. The piece of land he sat looking at was surrounded by farms. He was told that it was a 'real gem', overlooked by clerical error for years on end, until it had recently been brought to the attention of the magistrate by a couple who, oddly enough, were on holiday at the time and had no interest in claiming the land.

Captain Baillie, on whom fortune had smiled throughout his thirty years, found it no great surprise to suddenly acquire five thousand acres at the stroke of a pen. He considered it his birthright and just reward for his military service. Now a squire, he wished only to live a quiet and comfortable life; shunning the shearing he had received when sheep had dropped suddenly below a shilling the previous season. A big house with a nice view was all he wanted now. He would call it all 'Kennington'.

First was the matter of this odd man, however, of whom he had heard so much. An American Negro, or possibly a mongrel Maori or unknown mix, who had given a go at whaling, and now lived by himself: Who was this Black Jack White? Still full of life, and already a legend, the Captain had heard. The man had a geographical landmark named in his honor; was still working full-time in the service of Her Majesty; and had managed to learn and teach others everything there was to know about living in New Zealand. What an amazing person, thought Captain Baillie. He felt honored to be receiving the parcel of land that this Yank Black man had cared for so well. He couldn't wait to shake his hand. In the meantime, they pitched their tents and unloaded provisions in preparation for building.

Arriving on the scene near sunset, Black Jack tempered his exhaustion and put on his friendliest face. He said, "Stopping to rest for the night? How far down the valley ya goin'?" He scanned his mental map for the scarce areas that remained, to his knowledge, unclaimed.

The Captain said, "Ah, you must be the famous Black Jack White. I have heard so much about you. I'm Captain Baillie, and this is my family and our servants."

The word 'servants' pierced Black Jack's side like a cold blade. He stifled his reaction, and replied, "Likewise, Captain Baillie. Yes, Sir, I've been here for years and years. I used to be a whaler. Now I deliver the mail for the army. Plus I help people settle in here around the valley. I could help you all, if you like."

The Captain said, "No, no. You take your time. We've got plenty of help of our own. You just let me know if we can be of any help to you."

Black Jack did a double take, and said, "Help *me*? How do you mean, Sir?"

The Captain said with a smile, "Well, you know, when the army has found you new quarters to relocate to. Let us know how we can make your move all the less difficult."

Black Jack went cold and his hair crawled. He said,

"Relocate? Sir, I'm not going anywhere. Now you can stay here for the night, but I think it'll be best for everyone if you be off in the morning."

The Captain said, beginning to understand Black Jack's misunderstanding, "Perhaps I haven't made myself clear. My apologies if I have angered you. This is our home now. We were awarded all of this land; and we will be here making improvements from this time forth."

Black Jack felt ill. He began to smell defeat. He said, "Awarded this land? I didn't realize there was a contest going on. As far as I know, this land belongs to me."

The Captain, easing in for closure, said, "Now sir, I can understand your displeasure. I know that it is an unfortunate event that you are not a subject of the Crown. Believe me, I am prepared to make things comfortable for a fellow serviceman, however, if you would be willing to stay and work with us."

Black Jack, tears of anger and disgust welling, shouted, "Goddamn, ain't there nothin' in this world that the White Man won't take? Hell, I was here before you was born! Don't that count for anything? I got to think about this one. I'll be back." He stormed off into his darkening hut, leaving the Captain holding his hat and looking at the ground in contemplation. As he stood there in the purple dusk, tins of flour began to land around him, discharging clouds of white dust loudly as the lids popped like so many falling canister bombs.

IV

Although semi-retired, Baillie's experience at clearing difficult land was not lost on Para. With his guidance, his workmen had soon converted it to arable soil, with the trees being sold to the sawmiller. With money literally rolling in and little work to do, the Captain's interests turned toward local politics. Despite his earlier failures, he was courted and recruited on the grounds of his exceptional land management skills; and he won convincingly the seat of Superintendent of Waitohi in 1861. Baillie was a scrupulous and generous leader. He poured funds into public works and local projects, mainly roads and bridges. The area from Picton to Tua Marina benefited greatly from his managerial foresight, becoming a shining example of British ingenuity and engineering in New Zealand. Baillie could not foresee one thing, however, despite his overwhelming popularity; and that was the great flood of 1862. By great, it can be said that water overran or washed away every newly-built road and bridge, covering the land and the first story of every building from the bay at Picton down to the river at Beaver Town. It was as if the entire valley was merely a vestigial inland inlet for the ocean to reclaim as it saw fit. It also claimed the political career of Captain Baillie. How he could come to be blamed for an act of God is enlightening testament to the nature of the early colonial political climate.

Sparks of another kind flew in the valley, however, when the first telegraph lines were installed in 1863. It effectively put a welcome end to Black Jack's mail-carrying days; and ironically, was the same year as the Emancipation Proclamation in the United States of America. That fact would not be discovered by Black Jack, however, until he heard it from some Yank goldminers the following year.

Disheartened by the loss of his 'sovereignty' over Para, and now fully retired, Black Jack was willing foughter for the fire that swept the area in 1864: Gold Fever. Having already become seasoned veterans, the '49ers from America led the way in making and working claims once gold had been discovered. Miners came from all over the world, determined not to miss out on the next big rush, as many of them had done in the States.

The strikes in New Zealand were rich. Men could become wealthy in a matter of months even from small claims; or they could, as in most cases, lose everything that they had left behind to unsuccessfully chase the elusive nugget. Men frequently fought and died in drunken brawls in conditions very similar to the old whaling stations. Once the abundant alluvial gold-the loose stuff lying in the river that was the most visible and romanticized-was depleted, then the glamorous job of gold prospecting became a treacherous and dreary daily routine of drudgery and dredging. Men stood in cold, muddy water waist-deep shoveling gravel and dirt into sluices which washed the rocks and precipitated the dust, yielding only a few dollars a day. People could make more money in wages while shoveling manure back home; and yet the allure and the mystique of the metal invariably dragged out the insufferable idiot and perpetual loser from the best of men. Within weeks, Black Jack had been wise enough to wistfully watch his worthless pan being whisked by whitewater downstream as he waded away toward home. Returning to Para, now grown up with workers' cottages all around his old shack, he humbly asked the Captain for a job and the hut.

A plague of sorts ended the gold rush in wool for a time. The dreaded 'scab' disease virtually eliminated sheep from New Zealand in 1865, the same year that the thirteenth amendment was ratified in the U.S.A. From that point on, it was illegal to own human beings in that country.

In 1867, the actual felling of the sold trees began. They quickly went, as 300,000 acres of their kind disappeared from the surrounding land. What had once been dense forest and scrub brush was now smooth and barren, save for the patches of grass the White Man planted. Houses were the most popular crop, and Captain Baillie kept up with the times. He had a fourteen-room house built, eight of which were bedrooms. Milled on the grounds, Kennington, affectionately known as the 'Big House', was the New Zealand equivalent of an English squire's manor house.

Patience paid off in 1868; as the pains of past precipitation provided pleasure, Baillie having placed the porch of his palace above the previous flood plain. Another great flood had come, and a shimmering lake spread out before the mansion, the house serving as a veritable ark for the cottagers whose shacks now showed only shingles. One rare guest, the hare, was readily added to the refugee menu, however, as the rabbits had reproduced rampantly in recent years. They overran the ramparts by the thousands when the river rose. Black Jack thought that perhaps the sly red fox could provide the remedy for the silver-gray bunnies, once the water had receded. Had he thought to return to the United States that year, he may have been granted citizenship in his mother country, regardless of his color.

Flaxmilling began on a large scale in 1869, with several plants springing into operation throughout the valley. Black Jack leant his expertise to all of them, having had become intimate with the wild filamentous fiber that thrived in the local bogs. The Industrial Revolution had brought machines and automation to the mills, and with them came the monotony of the humdrum factory job. The many years that Black Jack spent spinning flax in his later life were not without interesting incident, however. As it happened, one of the most popular products of the mills was rope.

One day, it seems, Black Jack overheard many men talking while on their morning meal break. He heard things such as "Not me, not for all the money in the world."; and "Well who are they gonna get to do it?"; and "Why us?

Just because we make the rope doesn't mean we tie the noose!" His supervisor had finally approached him and told him that there was a pressing errand in Picton, and to please ride over there pronto.

Black Jack, upon arriving at the center of town with the best rope available, was whisked behind a stage, given a hood and a pair of gardening gloves, and told what to do. Once on the platform with the bound and blindfolded murderer, he had simply said, "Do not be afraid, my friend. You are going to a better place." before tightening the knot and pulling the lever.

V

Greenstone ground to powder with a whetstone, placed into white flour and wet to a paste: That was Black Jack's secret silver polish. Ironically, he had discovered it quite by accident when he had attempted to sharpen the old chief's pounamu. Fine green glass flecks had gone everywhere, irritating his eyes and skin. Upon touching the tins, he found that a gleam arose where once there was merely a dusting of rust and a thin, dull tarnish. Gleaning a vicarious glow from the results of his laborious buffing, he had become obsessive about the shine of the silver. He would stand and polish the entire set for hours on end some days, staring into the smooth, scratchless surfaces. Such was his fascination that he had started suggesting such things to the Captain as, "Sir, you could make your silver into coins and start your own country."; and "Sir, you could make a money for the Maori and Pakeha alike and unify the land."; only to be laughed at in that loud, fatherly, condescending tone that the Captain seemed to reserve for Black Jack and his comments.

Captain Baillie would say things like, "Black Jack,

where do you come up with some of your ideas?" while the family would snigger and scoff.

"You handsome devil." said Black Jack as he took a final look into the last spoon to be set. He looked forward to the Reverend's arrival. Having to work on Sundays, he had been unable to attend the valley's newly constructed church. Therefore, he had many unanswered questions about his spirituality which he hoped the good Reverend could help him with. Black Jack went and changed out of his house attire and into his field clothes; and he waited for the man of the cloth. He would not be attending, nor serving, the evening's meal.

Riding upon a donkey, the Reverend arrived at roughly three ticks of the clock past half-past three; just in time for hors d'ouevres. He was heralded by a bell tied behind the animal's ear. Lone, low muggy clouds clung to the threatening sky. Black Jack greeted the Pastor with a blanket and promptly ushered the covered burro to a stable stall. Returning to the house, he saw the Minister speaking with the Captain, a glass of champagne in one hand and a deviled egg in the other.

Black Jack went to his shack to retrieve his Bible. There were so many things that he didn't understand. He wanted to ask the Preacher. His reading lessons with Baillie's daughter had uncovered so much within the scriptures, and yet the truth had confused him. He took up the Good Book and went to the yard, waiting patiently near the porch. He paced as he practiced his questions in his mind. He could barely hear what the Captain and the clergyman were conversing on.

"What in the world is he doing? I've never seen him act up like this." said the Captain in a hushed tone, giving a sideways glance toward Black Jack.

The Reverend followed suit in an equally reserved voice. He asked, "Good Lord, is that the Bible that I gave to him all those years ago? Has he even learned to read yet?"

The Captain replied, "Well, my daughter has been teaching him a few things. I don't know, he may have mastered the language by now." He paused as the two held their pose of simulated conversation on the porch, ever watchful of the Black man striding back and forth on the lawn. The Captain called out to Black Jack, "I do say, is everything all right, Black Jack?"

Black Jack stopped and turned. He said, "Yes, Sir. I just need to speak with the Reverend about some things."

The two men on the porch exchanged quizzical glances. The Captain turned and asked, "What sort of things, Black Jack? The Reverend and I are rather busy."

Black Jack said urgently, "Just some things, Sir. Important things."

The two on the verandah held their sideways glances for a moment. Then the Reverend said, "I'll be with you in a moment, Black Jack."

The Captain said to the Reverend, "I'm so sorry, I don't know what this is all about . . ."

The Reverend smiled and raised a hand. He said, "It's quite all right. I'll take care of it. Just don't sit down to dinner without me." With that, he walked down into the yard and began to walk away with Black Jack. He said, "What is it, my son?"

As they walked toward Black Jack's shack, Black Jack said, "I don't know. Lately I've been having trouble with my faith, Father."

The Reverend said, "Your Bible contains all the answers that you will ever need, my son."

Black Jack said, "But I can't read all that well, Father."

The Reverend said, "Then you should come to church, my son. All will be revealed in readings and sermons there."

Black Jack said, "But I can't make it to church, Father. My work won't allow it."

The Reverend said, "Then you can always pray, my son. The Lord will answer your prayers."

Black Jack said, "Well, that is just it, Father. Lately, I don't feel that he has."

The Reverend asked, "How do you mean, my son?"

Black Jack said, "Well, take my life for example. I just don't feel as though I've been rewarded with the things I deserve."

The Reverend asked, "How do you mean?"

Black Jack said, "Well, look at me. I've worked hard all my life. I've been in this land since before most of the White people. The handful of White folk who were here when I arrived are dead now. And I'm not even considered to be a citizen, or worthy of owning land. I wanted to be someone too. I escaped slavery in my country, and now all I am is someone's house servant."

The Reverend said, "Well, that is something, isn't it? If you are comparing yourself to Captain Baillie and the way in which he has been blessed, then you are looking at apples and oranges."

Black Jack perked up and asked, "What do you mean?"

The Reverend said, "Well, the Captain is a righteous man. He gives a proper tithe to the Church, the one that he donated funds to in order for it to be built. He's a pillar of the community and the salt of the Earth. That's why he's living large and reaping what he has sown in his mansion on the hill there. It's all a reflection of what God thinks of him." He beamed a doting glance up the hill at the Big House.

Black Jack said, "Living large? So you're telling me that I'm living in a tiny shack with hardly any money because God hasn't smiled on me?"

The Reverend made a sour look and said, "No, no.

That's not what I meant. I'm saying that perhaps it is a spiritual problem on your part. Perhaps there is some sin that you are still guilty of that you haven't confessed to God. Perhaps you don't pray enough. You've really got to get off somewhere all by yourself, away from all these people, and really spend some time and effort at it. Have you ever tried that? Maybe that is something you can work on in your spare time. Perhaps you are working too much. That can be a sin as well. I don't know what's going on with you and this young lady, but I know it's improper for a man and a woman to spend time alone together where people can talk about it and bear false witness. And lastly, it may just be yourself, Black Jack."

Black Jack, now totally bewildered and becoming perturbed, asked, "What do you mean?"

The Reverend said pedantically, "Well, Black Jack, the Captain is quite a refined gentleman of good breeding and manners. He's a real people person with a great personality. God likes that."

Black Jack asked, "So without a personality, my spirituality is going to suffer, you say?"

The Reverend said, "Well, aside from salvation, the Lord gives us liberty. After that he gives us talents. For some it's music, for others it's writing, and perhaps for a few it is the arts. However, for a select group, the talent may be the ability to win friends and influence people. God rewards those people; perhaps a bit more than ordinary folks."

Black Jack asked, "So after all this time as a good person, I may still never be fulfilled spiritually because I don't have a dynamic personality?"

The Reverend said, "That may be part of it. I really don't have all the answers, Black Jack. It is between you and the Lord. If he has seen fit to make the Captain your master, then it is up to you to be obedient. Besides, the

Captain, despite his wealth and prosperity, is just as accountable to the Lord as you and I. Your riches lie in Heaven."

Black Jack said, "That is all well and fine, but what if I don't go to Heaven?"

The Reverend, becoming tired, said, "That is between you and the Lord's grace, Black Jack. It all goes back to what I was saying about sin. Only you know what is in your heart. I've heard some things about you, Black Jack. I'll be honest; the Maori have spoken of things, which if true, would cast serious doubt on your chances. At least in my mind. And then there's the Captain's daughter. I don't know what's going on there. I know that if a man lies in sin with a woman that he may never wed her. I might just count my blessings, if I were you, and be grateful for what little you do have. You see, Black Jack, I think that I know your true personality; and now you may be getting just what . . ."

Black Jack could take no more. As they reached the shack, he grabbed the Reverend by the collar and jerked him around the side of the hut. With his other hand, he brought the heavy Bible swiftly and squarely down onto the preacher's nose, smashing it and causing it to bleed profusely. Dropping the book, he clasped both hands firmly around the Reverend's neck and began to shake him violently. The clergyman began to turn purple. Black Jack yelled, "You have absolutely no idea what the Hell you are talking about! Do you hear me? You're not a man of God! You're a farce! Do you have any idea who I am and what I've done in my lifetime?" The struggle went on for several seconds.

Suddenly, the Captain and some of his workers appeared; and they managed to pull Black Jack off of the Minister. The police were summoned. The Reverend pressed charges. Black Jack was arrested for assault and

Captain Baillie subsequently posted bond. Upon hearing the testimony of each man, the Judge bound both parties over the sum of twenty-five pounds to keep the peace for six months.

Chapter 26

A PRIVATE LESSON

She always dressed formally when she came to call. According to the custom of the day, that included a full blouse with bodice and hoop skirt, full-length black, laced dress boots, and a bonnet with its assortment of fastening pins. Being one of Captain Baillie's daughters, nothing less would be expected owing to her position in life and her status in the community; even if she were just tutoring cottagers on her rounds most Sundays.

Lessons always came after church; and depending on how many people had signed on for the day, could last from mid-morning to late afternoon, with the compulsory break for lunch. The Captain's daughter would start at the Big House with a round of chit-chat and the obligatory 'catching-up' with her mother, father, and siblings; and they would discuss her travels and doings over the previous week. Conversation would invariably turn to the arrangement of cottages scattered down the hill and throughout the valley, with mention of each occupant's progress in the arts of reading and writing. Everyone received the highest praise from their gracious tutor's mouth, although she never admitted that certain persons' attitudes and aptitudes rose above the others; or that certain students shone in her eyes brighter than others.

No, she was fair and impartial to the last, and no one was the wiser as to how well the others were doing, or how poorly as the case might have been; and she managed to instill a sense of confidence and accomplishment in all of her pupils as a result of her cheerful and generous nature, aside from her personal sensibilities.

In the course of conversation, however, it was understood that special mention be made of a certain favorite topic, that being one 'Black Jack' whose progress in the disciplines piqued a greater curiosity due to his unique character and personal standing with the family. Black Jack had never learned to read and write, in all of his sixty-two years; even though his service in the local regiment as a mail carrier had required that he at least be able to scrawl his name. But he had always wanted to read and write. Since his escape so many years before, he had yearned to keep a journal of all the incredible things that he had suddenly become privy to as a free man; and with freedom should come education he had always thought.

And so, in these later years when he had "done most of his living", he welcomed the opportunity to receive the personal attention of the good Captain's daughter on his days of rest. Sunday afternoons off were a luxury bestowed upon him by the family in these later years, in return for the many years of fine service that he had provided them; and also in recognition of his military service which had been quite heroic in the eyes of his countrymen. Now that he was in the golden years of his life, he thought, he wanted to take the time to reflect on the magnificent occurrences within his life; and to possibly write them down. Besides, he had always wanted to send a letter back home, and try to figure out what had become of his kinfolk.

Separation and time had long since quelled the fear that his former captain and owner, or some authority vested therein, may someday return and enslave him once again. He knew now that his old captain must be at least retired, if not dead; and his fear had given way to a mellowed bitterness which gently compelled him to wonder about his former life and the possibility of a reunion with his fellow Americans.

But Black Jack was happy; and he did not let remorse enter into any of his reminiscing. He had lived a full and exciting life; and this was home now. Unless something drastic occurred to change his life here, he thought, Kennington would be where he was laid to rest. It was more a contented realization for him than a committed resignation to the twilight years of his life; and he had begun to savor every moment there in the hot, sunny valley that had become his sanctuary.

She knocked softly, with her usual rehearsed hesitancy, and waited in equally premeditated nervousness just outside the open doorway as an eager reporter might wait for a celebrity. She tugged at the hem of her wool vest, and tipped her hat as she assured herself that the pins were not showing through her tightly bound hair buns. With a final ruffle of her hoops and petticoat, she put her arms to her side, clutching her attaché stuffed with lessons; and waited for him, eyes straight ahead. She really didn't know the source of her girlish anticipation: She had just always liked Black Jack. Perhaps it was the way that everyone always talked about him, or the fact that he was such a unique fellow with such a decorated past; or perhaps it was just the opportunity to help such a nice old man to learn an important skill he had never possessed despite all of his accomplishments. Yes that was it, it occurred to her: The chance to teach something so important to the man whom she had grown up around, who was nearly three times her age, and who still stood so high in the community. It, he rather, made her feel important. Perhaps that was the reason she always visited Black Jack last, in the late afternoon, and stayed with him the longest.

The hot sun sprayed down upon her; and her eyes strained to see into the dark doorway. It seemed to be filled with a grayish-blue mist; and she knew it must be cooler inside the workingman's hut than it was standing in the full rays of the three o'clock sun. And slowly, a darker area of the interior became framed by the dim portal; and it moved toward her, filling in the blue with black until suddenly there he was: All six-feet-four of imposing yet lean stature.

"G'day Miss Baillie, how ya goin'?" he said with a huge yet respectful grin. "Would you like to come in?"

At once her formal posture broke and she pushed past him with the good-natured impatience of a long-time mate. "Would I ever, Black Jack! You know better than to keep a lady waiting. And in this heat!" she huffed half-jokingly as she turned to cast her eyes upon him, as if castigating the family dog.

"Sorry, Miss Baillie, I was busy and didn't hear you knocking." he offered in sheepish apology.

"Having a bit of a lie-down, were you? And you know when I call, don't you!" she impressed further.

"No, ma'am, always working. You know me." he said with a light sarcasm that showed the cheekiness and spark that she had come to adore in this big man.

"Well, alright then. Won't you offer me a seat?" she said, retreating from her stance, and offering a conciliatory laugh to break the uncertain tension. They both laughed hardily; and broke into random shuffling about the room, like a disjointed and careful dance in the search for their respective places.

"Here, Miss Baillie. Take this one." said Jack, as he swiftly moved a chair into the middle of his one-room hut. "I'll take this one." as he shifted another, identical chair, facing opposite the other at arm's length.

"Oh, Jack, when are you going to get a proper desk?" she jibed him again, semi-seriously.

"Now Miss Baillie, you know I can't afford any desk. Besides, where would I put it?" he said, as they both looked around the cramped cabin and then returned gazes.

"I will see what I can do." she said curtly as they both sat. She ruffled her petticoat; settled her skirt; and placed the lessons upon the large lap created by her hoops. "Now let us begin." she said sternly.

The lesson went well, as had always been the case; and Black Jack showed what he had learned in his home-work, while adding to his knowledge during the current lesson. Miss Baillie had 'developed' a method for teaching whereby, at least in Black Jack's particular instance, she would have him recount episodes of his life, one or two per lesson, and write sentences which highlighted the topics of mutual interest. The technique worked quickly for Black Jack; for over a cup of tea, he would mention several subjects that thrilled Miss Baillie while she jotted down what she considered to be pertinent and useful words. These were the 'big' words, as Black Jack called them: The names of places, the action words from his adventures, and the various birds, fish, and other animals that he had come across in his travels.

Miss Baillie believed in her method, because although the words she chose were generally more complex and less obvious to acquire than the more common articles and pronouns of simple sentences, she thought that Black Jack's emotional connection to these words and the imagery which they evoked would provide a greater motivation for him to learn. Besides, it seemed much more interesting, not to mention dignified, for a grown man than starting at the 'beginning' with the alphabet and trying to teach Black Jack the sounds of the letters; assembling the sounds into words, and then stringing the words into meaningless and childish sentences. She thought that might bore them both to tears; and Black Jack's interest in spending time with her in lessons might quickly wane.

Her theory proved correct, as the two of them embarked into many hours of lively conversation; none of which seemed to either of them to be contrived or designed solely for the lessons at hand. She would wait for the end of a story, or perhaps for an appropriate interval when they might be laughing uproariously at one of Black Jack's anecdotal hyperboles, or even staring intently into one another's eyes as Black Jack sauntered deeper into one of his, "There I was, surrounded . . ." tales. At that point, she could toss out a couple of words at Black Jack; and sit back to relax and enjoy her tea while he struggled to piece together familiar letters and sounds to form the words.

He had long since become aware of all of the building blocks of English, working backward from the words she had selected in conversation; and he would merely put together his best rendition of these words on paper while she looked on. Inadvertently, he had even learned some Maori language along the way, with its peculiar sounds and syntax; and he had even joked to several around the valley that, through the help of Miss Baillie, he was becoming bilingual. This of course did not speak to the fact that he had learned much of spoken Maori from his earliest days in New Zealand. He didn't think of that much these days, though.

"I wuz at wyroo." he uttered, asking if it were correct.

"Good, Black Jack!" She was always sure to praise him

before correcting him. "Now, let's start with the easiest. How do you spell, 'was'?"

He thought hard, knowing that he could have spelled it correctly the first time; but he always opted for the phonetic spelling to impress her with his speed at writing complete sentences. "W-A-S." he said. A lot of spelling made absolutely no sense to him; and he let her know quite often.

"Good. Now let's start getting these right the first time, all right Black Jack? This is very important." she said firmly. She also placed a hand on Black Jack's writing hand as she leaned forward in her chair. He knew that she meant only to show caring emphasis for her words; and that she implied nothing more by it. His respect for her was immense; and they had formed a professional bond in their serious endeavors together. Each of them sensed their mutual admiration.

After Black Jack had completed a full page of sentences, complete with corrections, Miss Baillie graded his paper with her usual 'excellent' and relaxed into a less formal mood. "Ah, Black Jack," she said, "You really are progressing quite well. I'm proud of you."

He was unsure how to take the compliment; and so he carefully hid any embarrassment so as to spare her the same. "No worries, Miss Baillie. You are certainly the best teacher that I have ever had." They both laughed loudly.

Miss Baillie pulled herself together; and still half-laughing, said, "Ah me, Black Jack, you are a true card. Who says you can't teach an old dog new tricks?" They both ripped with laughter again.

Black Jack delighted in her ribbing; and he shot back, "Watch who you're calling 'old', Miss Baillie, or I'll go up there and tell your father about your apparent lack of respect for your elders!"

She suddenly stopped laughing; and in her flushed state said impetuously, "As if he'd listen to anything you have to say about his honorable daughter, you old goat!" And she let loose with even more guffaws. Both of them knew what she was hinting at. Everyone knew that although Black Jack was still a laborer for the family, he had attained an almost cult-figure status with the entire family; enjoying almost all of the amenities of a close friend, save for the invitations to estate dinners and functions. This was understood to be in keeping with the social expectations of some lesser refined local associates and community pillars; and also in general consideration of the fellow cottagers and their working families who might feel a bit put out by Black Jack's special treatment. However, none of that prevented these two from becoming close friends, within the boundaries of discretion; and they enjoyed their time together without belaboring the fact.

The last remark dug slightly into Black Jack's skin; and without showing that he had been stung, replied, "Old goat! Why lady, if I didn't owe your father so much gratitude, I'd take you out and show you a thing or two on this farm." There was a pregnant pause between them as they each realized that there were two possible retorts to that statement: One of which had to do with the place no longer being a farm, and the other remained unspeakable even between them.

"Well, with that young man, I had better take my leave; as I believe a certain someone has learned all that they are capable of today." she snapped coyly; and stood to leave. However, as she stood, the hem of her dress caught the leg of her chair, sending her and the seat rolling backward in a flail of arms and a flurry of white flaxen petticoat and gray wool. Her hat flew into the corner; and there was a cacophony of pins scattering across the hard floor as her long hair came tumbling down and streamed past her shoulders. She instinctively threw her arms back, landing on her palms and rump simultaneously with a thump and a whoosh of air blowing across the small room in all directions. Jack had reflexively reached out to catch her; but in rising up and forward, had only managed to flail along with her as he witnessed her descent in slow-motion. With a thud she stopped, head turning up immediately to look into his eyes staring down in the subsequently awkward silence. Then suddenly, tears began to form in her eyes.

"Oh, Black Jack, what am I going to do?" she importuned in a high-pitched, singsong voice that made Black Jack feel badly as well. He helped Miss Baillie to her feet; and they surveyed the damage, with her spinning head over shoulder, and him walking around her in the opposite direction.

When all had been seen, she cried shrilly, "Black Jack! What am I going to do? I can't leave here in this condition. What will they say?" Her dress was covered in the beige-colored dust that now clung to the wool; her dress was turned so that not only part of her petticoat showed around the top and bottom; but also a portion of her corset had become visible in the area between her blouse and skirt. Worst of all, it seemed that all of the hoops had slipped their rigging; and were turned outward and pointing in all directions.

"Now, Miss Baillie, just calm down. It doesn't look like anything got torn. We'll have you fixed up in a flash." he assured her; even though he himself had become unsettled by her near shrieking. The last thing he needed was for her to bolt out of his hut in her present condition and run yelling up to the Big House. She was twenty-three, and mature enough to handle herself in most situations since returning from the university; but still, Black Jack thought, he knew how women could fly off the handle.

"Besides, I'm an old whaler from way back, Miss Baillie. These are whale bones, and you know I know my way 'round them, right Miss Baillie?" he said in an even calmer, deeper, and slower voice.

"Oh, Black Jack." she whined once more.

"Oh, nothin', you 'jes hold on, you." he said almost gruffly now, as he placed a hand firmly between her shoulders and guided her to the back of his chair. She relented in silence, yielding to his touch; and relaxing her tense stance. Jack pushed her gently forward; and she knew to put her arms out straight and grasp the top of the chair back. He began the task of briskly brushing the dust from her dress with one open palm, steadying himself as he leaned down with the other gentle hand on her back. He stood up, carefully slipped fingertips under the waist of her skirt; and with a swift tug, pulled it right again.

"Black Jack, I don't know." she said softly; even though she was reassured by his quick progress with the state of her dishevelment.

"Shhh, Miss Baillie. Jes' hold on. Now this next part may be a little tricky; but you just trust your trusty Black Jack." he said smugly; and managed to get another chuckle between them. She relaxed a little more; and he thought that to be good for what he was about to attempt next. For although he was familiar with the concept of whale-bone hoop skirts, it had never occurred to him to actually study one to learn all of its little secret ins and outs. He proceeded with caution.

He knelt down behind her and very carefully began unbuttoning the long line running from the floor to her back straight up the middle. It was a potentially odd moment; however, they both knew that several more layers of petticoat would prevent him from becoming privy to anything remotely improper. And besides, this was the only way for a handyman to access the more delicate inner work-

ings of what was more of a contraption than a lady's ac-
couterment. He quickly folded back the flaps of the outer
dress and began to manually inspect the folds within for
the covered outlines of the elusive underpinnings. Up high,
above the hip, he discovered the origins of the first row of
'ribs': A small, more slender set of bones which sat just off
the hip in bilateral, semicircular halves. These were easy
to manipulate into position, needling them with fingertips through the thick cloth until they came around and
dropped with curves parallel to the hips.

"One down, Miss Baillie. Just a little bit more." he
said with the assurance of a tailor at the local haberdash-
ery.

"That's fine." she almost droned with a sigh, having
resigned herself to the situation several moments before;
and since having begun to daydream and drift into thought.
She trusted Black Jack; and this seemed like nothing more
than a private consult between a lady and her attendant,
although she had never thought of Black Jack as being
beneath her in any way.

He continued with one of the larger rows of bones,
down around her knees; so as to have a lower as well as
upper reference for all the bones in between to line up
against. Black Jack wrestled with rustling frill and lace
bodice; and remained keenly intent on the bone which he
could not see directly, but which he must picture in his
mind as he gently moved it. It was as a surgeon working
blind; as he had seen Captain Baillie do on several occa-
sions when he operated on actual peoples' bodies, hands
hidden in blood.

Black Jack felt the large bone roll into place, carried
by its own weight around its axis, and come to revive the
largest curve of the outermost circle of the dress. Black
Jack leaned back on one knee to take a gander at the outline of the skirt. He felt proud of the way it was coming

together, and he leaned in to finish the job. "I'm gonna get these ones in between, Miss Baillie. I'm almost done." he said, almost praising himself more than reassuring his subject.

"Whatever, Mr. Alesworth." she said with a coyly feigned annoyance. "Just hurry, please. I cannot be late for supper. And have you noticed how hot it has become in here?" She grew louder on the latter part of the question, as if a slight delirium had besieged her.

"No, ma'am, but I'll take your word for it." he said, as he fumbled for a medium-size bone. He had been careful not to breech the private confines of her protective petticoat. He had grown increasingly confident with the success of his earlier attempts; so that now he fluttered freely through the folds of her undergarment without fear of encountering any part of the outline which made up the lesser known areas of her person. He might as well be working on the large drapes in the great dining hall, he thought, as much chance as he had of encountering the secret boundaries of Miss Baillie's womanhood. He made a sweep to the outer left and easily found the bone there in its twisted sleeve; and he followed with a swift check to the right to confirm the complementary arc there. All he need do now was to trace their respective paths to the middle and line them up. Then he would be one step closer to having Miss Baillie on her way.

As he began to cross over, he brushed superfluous fluff this way; and frilly folds that way, all the time working blind with his hand buried in the stuff. He brought his other hand down to the small of her back to better steady himself as he anticipated feeling both ends of the bone halves meeting at the center. As he walked his fingers slowly along the right bone, he leaned his head in and cocked one ear so as to aid his search by listening to the muffled rustling of his progress. His forefinger reached the end of

the bone first; and he planted it there for reference as he
stretched his thumb out into the breech to feel for the
blunt end of the opposing bone. His thumb began to
stretch beyond the point where he had envisioned the end
of the other bone; and after a few conservative swipes of
his thumb into open air, he made one last desperate, broad
stroke, all the while resting his remaining fingers on the
found bone.

His thumb struck something wet. Instantaneously, she
lurched forward and gasped, precluding the need for him
to withdraw his thumb. She spoke in a tone that let him
know that she had been far away. "Arthur?" she said,
sounding as though she did not really want, or perhaps
feared, his reply. There followed a profound silence; as she
seemed not to dare to turn around or change her stance.
She remained, grasping the chair back. Black Jack continued to work, now hurriedly, to fix her clothing.

After a few quick flicks of her undergarments to create
a futile distraction in the fleeting seconds following the
incident, Black Jack leaned back again to inspect her petticoat from a distance. They both knew what had happened, though. But how? each of them thought. He scanned
for any sign of an opening: A tear perhaps, or a flap, or a
fold sewn overlapping. Nothing, though, revealed itself;
and he was left to reinspecting her folds. Black Jack suddenly noticed in the silence that it was growing rather
warm in the hut. He was bothered by something else as
well. He began to realize what it was: Her silence! It baffled
and somewhat annoyed him at the same time. Kneeling
there, staring at her backside, up her back and over her
golden locks of hair and resolutely turned head. It bothered him! She had made no attempt to leave or make empty
comments to abate any humiliation she might be suffering. Nothing! She just stood there, legs gone rigid and

straight. And she had called him 'Arthur'! No one had ever used that name with him, except . . . his mother!

He began to ruffle her pleats more rapidly, in a frustrated attempt to locate the other bone faster. It had been right there! Where was it? he asked himself; as he rifled through the folds, his face becoming flush. Why did she just stand there? All of it brought up the past and threw it into Black Jack's face. He remembered feelings that he had forgotten when she had left for school. He began to remember a time when, regardless of her class standing, her age would have made his futile thoughts of her forbidden. It had always been her clothes, he thought: How he would watch her in the cool, foggy mornings making her way down to the road for school. Her freshly washed face and neatly braided hair in a long ponytail down her slender back. Her sheer, white blouse modestly boasting of newly flowered buds; and her crisp green-and-black plaid, short, wool skirt, all dangling delicately over smooth, tan thighs and knee-high socks. A very smart uniform, indeed, he would comment to himself as he dressed for work. His fascination would sometimes turn to surprised anger as he often fell for the flour-in-his-boots trick which one or all of the Captain's daughters frequently played on him. Was it her? he wondered. The one who smelled of early morning dew when he would help her upon her horse? There had been a time when she had sat upon his lap for some reason or other. They were alone in his hut, he remembered not why now; but he had felt the pangs of something powerful rising within him for this girl who was quickly becoming more than a child. He had wanted to feel guilty, but he had assured himself that it was something more.

Then she had gone away to the university. It was hard for him; however, he had tried to forget her. It was just fatherly concern, he had told himself. Nothing a little work wouldn't help him forget.

Reports from school had not been favorable, though. Over the years, there were her unscheduled visits home which he did not think were holidays. He heard rumors of her difficulties: Problems with discipline, threats of expulsion for disorderly and 'unladylike' conduct, and something else about a trip to a boy's school.

On one of her small sabbaticals, she had visited him, looking all of a woman. It surprised him. She spoke as an adult; and they conversed freely about life and growing up. She went on about a recent charge by the staff concerning a certain theft of school property. She had maintained her innocence, although the Headmaster's baton had been found during a search of her hall. She had sworn to Black Jack that she never used it on anyone. He had told her that he understood.

Suddenly, it showed itself, the mysterious cleft in her underpinning that had apparently been torn there by a misplaced bone tip. The opening mocked him, as she continued to stand fast, seemingly unaware of his discovery.

She said suddenly, "Arthur, do you remember when I used to sit in your lap after school?"

Black Jack, surprised by the question, said, "Yes."

She said, "I never came straight here like you thought."

Black Jack, hesitantly, said, "All right. And what is the point of telling me this now?"

She said, "Me and the girls used to talk about you. I used to duck home first and ditch everything from under my school skirt before I'd come down here. They said you wouldn't notice, but I said you would."

Black Jack asked, "Why are you telling me this? What is your point, young lady?" He was becoming dismayed at her apparent disrespect.

She said, "But you never noticed, you old goat. I used

to sit and listen to your babbling for hours, waiting for you to scold me; and you were never the wiser. You old fool!"

He could take her teasing no longer; and with a disgusted grunt he jumped to his feet and moved in close behind her.

She made no movement, as if she had resolved her opinion on the matter long before; and it seemed to him that Black Jack's latest actions did not surprise her in the least. She finally broke her silence, "I don't know, Arthur . . ." she said as she trailed off in a slightly disarming tone. But she knew, as well as he; and as a ball of fire suddenly combusted deep inside of her, she came to know that Black Jack had assumed the role of tutor for the remainder of the afternoon.

"The girls and I, young lady." he said.

II

She came several more times after that. And more frequently than her normal Sunday visits. Baillie's daughter became inflamed with an insatiable lust for the kind, old, able black man who worked for her father; and her affection began to manifest itself in detailed attention to his particular needs. Her dress and accoutrements, and in particular her personal grooming, became lavish in the extreme, with her outfitting herself some Sundays in what some cottagers began to say was "beyond appropriate" for casual schooling. It had also not been missed by several eyes that her clothing remained in the utmost condition until the moment that she was seen leaving a certain man's cabin. Wet tongues began to wag.

On one occasion, she brought Black Jack the desk that she had promised. She also brought a very fine pocket watch. "Now we can keep proper time of our lessons." she said.

"I've always had a good eye on the time, Miss Baillie. I've lived here nearly all my life. I can tell you what day of what season it is just by looking at the Sun." said Black Jack, bragging slightly.

"Oh, Arthur, the Great One! I know how magnificent you are. I just want to be sure. You know, just to be safe."

"Yes, I know, Miss Baillie. We wouldn't want you to tarnish your sterling reputation by being late." said Black Jack sarcastically.

She blushed. "This desk will help us study properly, too. No more fooling around." she said, attempting to sound stern.

"Oh, no, we wouldn't want that to happen." he said, grinning widely.

She blushed again and pawed at him. "Now, stop, Arthur." she whined. "Try to be serious. Now I've brought you some very interesting books that should make our lessons easier. These books will help you to learn to read better, because I think that you will be able to identify with them. They've all been published recently around the world, so they're all on current topics." She began to pull books from her large canvas shoulder bag and read their titles and descriptions aloud. "Now here's a book by a gentleman by the name of 'Melville'. He wrote about chasing a white whale called 'Moby Dick' around the world with an insane captain."

"Sounds vaguely familiar." said Black Jack reservedly. "He's just now gettin' 'round to writin' about that?"

"Here's one about a Black man in the United States who escaped to the North and lived to write about it. 'The Heroic Slave' by Frederick Douglass." she said.

"All right. Well where's the second part? He just stayed in America after he escaped? What's so great about that?" he implored.

She flashed him a perplexed, sideways glance. "Here's one by a man named Whitman who wrote about the American president who set the slaves free. It's called, 'O Captain! My Captain!' How about that one?"

"I might check that one out. Is he Black?" asked Black Jack.

"I don't know." she said. "Here's a couple of books by a man who decided to drop out of society for awhile and write in a cabin he built by a pond. One's called, 'Walden'. The other's called, 'Civil Disobedience'. Either of those sound interesting?"

"Hell, I could sit around here and write about plenty of disobedience." said Black Jack wryly.

"Then perhaps you should read this one." she said, condescendingly. "It's by a gentleman by the name of Dostoevsky. 'Crime and Punishment.'" She looked at him smugly.

"Sittin' out here alone for years on end has been punishment enough for two men's crimes, darling." he shot back coyly.

She laughed. "Oh, here's some you'll like: 'The Innocents Abroad' by Mark Twain. Or, his 'Roughing It'. Those might suit you."

"Is he a Southern man?" asked Black Jack reflectively.

"Yes. A humorist. Now here is someone a bit more morose. Friedrich Nietzche. Not a man I would want to spend a lot of time alone with." she said. "Wrote 'The Birth of Tragedy'."

"Ooh." said Black Jack. "Keep that one away from me."

"The list goes on." she said. "Jules Verne: 'Around the

World in Eighty Days'. That one came out just last year, 1873. Then there's Longfellow, Poe, Wordsworth, Tennyson, Dickens, Tolstoy; oh, and one for the ladies: 'Little Women' by Louisa May Alcott."

"I don't know." said Black Jack sheepishly. "I'm not a Poe, Dickens, or Longfellow. All of those men sound so up themselves."

"Well, now, Arthur, keep in mind: Most of these are just popular works of fiction. Perhaps you would prefer some of the more traditional classics?" she asked earnestly.

Black Jack, becoming slightly overwhelmed and frustrated with the flood of new information, tossed one of the books back at her. "Here, I'll write my own book." As she tried to catch it, however, the book bounced off her hands and onto the desk. It sent the watch flying to the hard earthen floor. She reflexively sprang from her seat and onto her hands and knees to retrieve the timepiece.

"Oh, Arthur!" she shrieked frantically. "How could you?" She found the watch, which was now missing its crystal face. "The glass, Arthur. You've lost the glass!" she yelled.

"Now calm down, Miss Baillie." said Black Jack. He remained seated so as not to step on the elusive lens. "Just hold on; you'll find it." He leaned forward and reassuringly placed a hand on her darting head.

She snapped her head up, meeting him with a desperate stare. "It's gone, Arthur! That's my uncle's watch! He'll kill me." she moaned, setting the watch upon the desk.

"Now, now, Miss Baillie. Just slow down. It's there somewhere." he said. He ran his big, dusky, black hand through her thick, long hair in an attempt to relax her. He then began to talk about the books to lessen her panic. "I guess the thing about those people that I don't particularly like is that they just seem to make up words. You know?"

She slowed in her search, occasionally casting a glance upward as she spoke, "Well, that's all right. You can make up words if you wish, too." she said.

"How?" he demanded.

"Well, let's see." she said, looking around the floor with eyes and hands. "The easiest way is to cross words. Say your name, for example."

"Why my name? What's wrong with my name?" he asked.

"Well, you told me that 'Arthur' was something only your mother called you. You still seem uncomfortable when I use it. Then there's 'Harper'. You've told me how that name makes you flinch. So why not combine the two, say, into something like 'Arpur'. How does that sound?"

"That sounds all fancy. I like that." He smiled and wriggled his shoulders as if mocking the name playfully as he repeated the word aloud. "Arpur!" he said, placing the major emphasis on the last syllable. "That sounds like a prince or something."

"My prince." she said, smiling slyly up at him.

"Do another one!" he said like an excited child at Christmas.

"Well, you can do these yourself." she said in her school-matron voice. "But I'll do one more just to get you started." She lifted one hand and began to stroke his knee as she raised the other hand to reveal the dusty crystal. She smiled triumphantly, placing the glass on the desk beside the watch. She quickly glanced at the watch hands before returning her face to rest upon her hands atop his knees. She ran fingers smoothly down his thigh as she smirked. "Let's see: 'Large' plus 'happy' gives you 'lappy'." she said, as her hand reached its semantic example.

Or 'harpy', he thought smugly as she latched.

III

Tooth marks spun in all directions, each bite overlapping the next in a circular cascade of rough swirls. Furry splinters leaned in odd patterns like tiny trees blown by some forgotten frozen breeze. Black Jack stared up at the ceiling timbers of his recent addition, and inhaled their sharp, sweet, freshly-sawn scent: A gift from the Captain. Now the cabin had two rooms, and it almost seemed like a proper house to Black Jack.

Lying down upon his big, billowy bed, his gaze and thoughts came to rest upon the coffin nestled among the new beams. Built within the last year, she had been in a position to notice it during one of her visits.

"Arpur, what is that?" she had asked like a little girl.

"It's my canoe." he had said in a fatherly tone.

"It looks like a . . . well, you know, a coffin." she had said.

"Same thing." he had said.

"What do you mean? Are you going somewhere? Are you dying?" she had asked ingenuously.

"No. I'm not dying. Yet." he had said.

"Well, what are you thinking about coffins for, then?" she had asked, with frightened concern.

"I've been thinking about a lot of things lately." he had said.

"Like what? Death?" she had asked.

"Not just that. Listen, I just built the thing because I realized that maybe I won't be able to soon. I just want a proper burial, that's all. Besides, it's a glorious thing to some, not something to be scared of or dreaded." he had said.

"Oh. Well, don't be thinking of dying anytime soon."

she had said, kissing him on the cheek as she rolled beneath the linens.

"Well, a glorious death may be all I get at the end of this life. I haven't got much else." he had said.

"How can you say that? You've got me! What more could you want?" she had asked.

"Well, look at your father." he had said.

"What about him?" she had asked.

"He's half my age; he hasn't done nearly half the things I've done in my life; and look at all he's got!" he had said, growing indignant.

"Well, what do you want all that stuff for, Arpur?" she had asked.

"I just feel that I deserve it." he had said. "After all I have accomplished."

"But he's a White gentleman, Arpur. You're a black farmhand. What do you expect?"

"Well, for starters, it would be nice to own some land. Maybe I'd like to build a big house and have a large family. Maybe even run for office."

"Oh, Arpur, you're so cute!"

"I'm being serious. Why shouldn't I have what every other man has, as hard as I have worked to achieve it?" he had said, growing angry.

"Oh, Arpur, now you are just being negative. Look how far you've come! You said yourself that you started life as a slave. Isn't it enough that you have your freedom now? You've had a full life. Now you've got a roof over your head, plenty to eat, and friends. I don't understand why you've got to be so hard on yourself." she had said sincerely. "I guess it's a man thing."

"You know, you've got an amazing talent for stating the obvious." he had said in resigned disgust, staring up

at the coffin in the ceiling beams while she had annoy-
ingly stroked his chest.

Looking up, lying in the same spot now, however, he
longed for her presence. She would be along soon, he
thought. He could suffer the tortuous agony of her misunderstanding his plight, he reckoned, if it meant having
her undying affection. It was a fair, yet frustrating, trade
he thought. No worse than the condition of his life in
general, though. She at least understood in some ways
more of what he was going through than most people could,
or had even attempted to, comprehend of his situation.
She offered empathy and sympathy: The latter he could
do without; but she was the only one who had ever offered
either. So he took the poisoned pair with a grain of salt. In
the midst of intimacy, however, he was alone to grapple
with his own personal struggle. That paradox compounded
his pain. If she could only truly understand. Ah, the short-
comings of love: So close and yet so far. With all of her
modern schooling and seemingly self-realized social awareness, she still could not see the forest for the trees. It actually made him feel better to pity *her*. *And* to crave her.

Wondering if it were possible to know someone right
down to the very core of their soul, he lay there as long,
thick bands of winter clouds swept by on the darkening
horizon. She was late, he thought. He got up and looked
at the watch. Six p.m. He wondered. She had never been
late. He pensively flipped the watch in his fingers, reading
the inscription on the back: "J.O. Western." Quite an ex-
pensive timepiece, he thought. Surely its owner must be
missing it.

A knock came suddenly at the door. Opening it, Black
Jack was met by a sweaty, breathless man. "It's Miss
Baillie!" he said. Black Jack's heart sank. "There's been an
accident."

"What is it?" he asked, remaining calm.

"I'm not sure. They say she's resting up at the Big House. The doctor's been summoned from Picton."

"Yes. And what am I to do about it?" Black Jack asked, still attempting to conceal everything which might be known.

"She's delirious. She's asking for you!" said the man. "The Captain wants you up there straightaway."

"Tell them I will arrive shortly." said Black Jack, shutting the door. He put his head down, hand still on the knob, and gathered his scattering thoughts. How much had she uttered? he wondered. What would the family think? Was she all right? He pulled himself together, and headed for the lights on the hill.

IV

She was all right. He could tell at the door to her room as the maid removed the wash cloth from her forehead. He entered and went to her.

"Oh, Arpur. I'm so glad you could make it. Thank you." she said. She looked around him to the maid at the door. "That will be all, Dora. Thank you." The maid genuflected and closed the door on her way out. "Oh, Arpur, it was horrible!"

"What happened?" he asked, still reserved as though he were being watched.

"Coming from Tua Marina, I decided to take a shortcut through a neighbor's field. Everything was fine, but I guess he thought I was a stranger or something. I don't know, but the next thing, his dogs are chasing my horse and we go galloping for the fence. I was so scared, Arpur. We were flying! I tried screaming at the dogs, but they wouldn't mind me. They just kept barking and gnashing their teeth alongside; and nipping at my horse's heels. It was terrible! We were going at full flank when we reached the fence. I was thrown so hard, Arpur. I thought I would break into a thousand pieces of glass." she said, as she began to cry and laugh at the same time. She daubed her tears with a cloth and said, "I'm so sorry, Arpur. I'm such a fool."

"No, no. You're not. Everything will be fine. It's not your fault. I'm here now." he said with a soft smile, kissing her hand.

She said, "No, you don't understand. I'm really sorry . . . about the baby. The doctor says that I lost the baby!"

Splinters jabbed and burned in various points throughout his body, and his temples throbbed. He held back tears of rage as he choked on his words and forced a smile. "Everything's gonna be just fine. You rest now, love. Just rest." He waited for her to close her eyes as her exhaustion finally arrived and unpacked its bags, evicting the previous tenant, her shock. As the tears streamed down his face there by her bedside, he silently and calmly devised his cold, callous resolve. No best friend of man could resist a tasty treat, he thought. This recipe, though, would be his final solution to the problem of the dogs.

Over the next few months, many canines were found scattered throughout the valley, lying peacefully with no sign of trauma whatsoever to explain their mysterious death. It were as though they had just lain down and died. Some dogs had been seen to grow progressively slower over a period of a few days; however, nothing they did or ate indicated anything unusual that might contribute to their demise. Even the Captain's dogs had not been spared: A fact which dismayed him and which he brought up in conversation outside one day.

"Black Jack, what do you make of all these dogs up an dying all of a sudden? Heart worms, you reckon?" he asked.

"I don't know, Sir. You've got me. I love these dogs."

said Black Jack, petting the new puppy which the Captain had just picked up. "Could be anything, I reckon."

"Well, I don't know about anything, either." said the Captain, eyeing Black Jack skeptically. "I just thought maybe you had run across something like this before."

"Naw, Sir. I ain't never seen nothin' like it before. But I got something that might help." he said.

"Well, let's have at it, then." the Captain said, somewhere between impatience and desperation.

"All right, Sir." said Black Jack. He went into his cabin and opened a tin of freshly-cooked biscuits. They were a special batch, baked from his private stash of government flour and laced with a secret ingredient: The glass grounds of the old chief's sacred greenstone. Black Jack emerged from the shack with a couple and fed one to the small, eager dog.

"Mercy, he's really going at that. What's in those, Black Jack? The little fellow is literally polishing that thing off!" said the Captain enthusiastically.

"Yes, Sir, he is." said Black Jack smugly.

V

"You've changed all the dates around." said the Judge, in a tone of sudden realization.

"Beg your pardon?" said Arpur.

"The dates . . . the events . . . and the places . . . you lied in my courtroom. Why?" he asked in a mystified voice.

"I didn't necessarily lie . . . I just withheld a little of the truth." said Black Jack, dodging the bullet.

"No, wait . . ." said the Judge. His voice trailed off as if he were interested not in confrontation, merely clarification. "You didn't want anyone to know. You were scared! Why?"

"Well, wouldn't you be?" challenged Arpur. "I mean, think about it. Would you admit that you took part in some of the bloodiest massacres in history? Would you admit that you were a spy and possibly a traitor? Thank God, my wisdom outruns my vanity."

"Perhaps. I don't appreciate your mockery of my court, though." said the Judge sternly. "But I can certainly see your point, given the scope of your situation. I will be understanding this time and say that your story grants you a certain license with the truth, in light of how others might unjustly perceive you."

"Thank you, your Honor." said Black Jack respectfully. "I appreciate your patience and interest in listening to the full story. I believe that you are the only one to have heard the entire account."

"It was well worth it, my friend. I do not believe that many people will ever live nor hear such a story as great as the legend of Black Jack White." said the Judge. "Before I retire, I want to take this opportunity to thank you for being such an inspiration."

"The pleasure was all mine." said Black Jack.

Chapter 27

A BAKER'S DOZEN

Brilliant burnt umber and sublime avocado green. Dusty olives licked by hues of orange, on a palate of saffron and chili reds: The Captain's wife had a masterful yet sensitive stroke.

"Stick the fork in it, Arpur!" commanded the Captain through the dark. Arpur fumbled with the utensil as he aligned the tines with the mouth of the hot funnel. Carefully nudging the tin cone into place, he brought the painting into focus as the light streamed from the lamp, through the lens, and projected the picture onto the plaster-of-Paris wall. "Perfect!" barked the Captain. The big house loomed, blazed; and with a flash it was gone, leaving only a white void.

"Now this one might require a bit of explaining." said the Captain's wife. Arpur had placed the slide of her work of art into the frame; and the beam projected its image across the room. A hot, still, silent sadness hung in the air

momentarily along with the dust settling through the
piercing ray of light that carried the shadows of the present
company's heads and pressed them against the apparition
of the absent family's portrait. "I painted this one at Christmas when everything had settled down and no one was
bothering me anymore. Can you see who that is, Black
Jack?" asked the Captain's wife, as if speaking to a child.

"Yes, Mrs. Baillie. I can see them just fine. Now just
'cuz you can't see me in the dark so well, doesn't mean I
can't see you." said Arpur. The Captain and his wife
laughed. "I mean, I am only eighty-one years old." he
joked to hide his pain. Sitting there with the elderly couple
of the estate-the Captain and his wife approaching sixty-
he felt like more of a caretaker for the fellow aging, and an
old and trusted friend; rather than a staff member who
was hanging on due to the kindness of his employers. The
mutual bond which had formed between the three helped
to buffer the blow struck by seeing the figures upon the
wall. He gazed at their faces as he remembered the people
and events of the past twenty years: The young girl, the
woman; and the man who had come for his watch.

II

September of 1875, the winter chill had not yet
yielded to the Southern Hemisphere spring; and a couple
lay cuddling beneath flax and wool near a crackling potbelly stove. They talked about a lost child and the way
things might have been. They talked about the way things
might be if only they could get married.

"You know that I love you, Arpur." she had said.

"I'm not so sure." he had said.

"How can you say that?" she had importuned.

"Why won't you marry me?" he had asked.

"Oh, Arpur, it's so complicated." she had said.

"No, it's very simple. You say you love me. I love you. What is stopping us? Surely it isn't . . ." He had dared not say the words.

"No, no. It's nothing like that." she had been quick to say. "I just want to be happy right now here with you. Can we not be so serious?"

He had relented and let it go. She had gone. Later, the man had come on horseback, knocking upon Arpur's cabin door.

"Where is she?" he had demanded, a young man dressed in fine clothes.

"Where is who?" Arpur had asked, feigning ignorance in the face of trouble.

"You know who I am talking about, nigger." he had said, pushing his way into the shack. "Don't make it worse than it already is."

"Sir, I . . ." he had tried to say to belay the inevitable.

"And what is this, then?" the man had demanded, spying the desk. "How did this get here?"

"I don't know." Arpur had stammered.

"I see. Perhaps a fairy carried it here." the man had said cruelly. "And in the drawer, what have we here?" he had asked, having discovered the watch. "J-O-Western. Do you know who that is, boy?" he had asked menacingly. "John Octavius-that's me! This is my watch. What are you doing with it?"

"I don't know." Arpur had said again.

"Right! It's her, isn't it! You listen here. I don't know what's going on between you two, but there ain't no way that my sweet Gillian is going to waste anymore time teaching a goddamn nigger to read! You hear me?" the man had stated.

"Loud and clear, Octavius." Arpur had said, mocking the man's name.

"Don't anger me, boy. I've got a right mind to have

you arrested for theft. In fact . . . right!" the man had yelled. He had stormed out with his final words.

Arpur was arrested shortly thereafter, Mr. Western having had wanted to preserve the honor and untarnished name of his fiancée, the daughter of the good Captain Baillie. Arpur never saw Miss Baillie again within a private setting; and sightings of her were rare as she only came around once or twice a year on holidays. She eventually became Mrs. J.O. Western, had a daughter a few years later, and got on with the business of being a proper gentleman's wife. Arpur toiled poignantly on into his latter years, as he tended to his garden and his heart, which had over the years so many times bended but never broken. As he mended the fences and the odd amenities of Kennington, he often appeased himself with thoughts of her while he chewed on nails and pounded the posts.

III

"They're coming with the honorariums for Bastille Day. We've got so much to do William. Are we ready do you think, Black Jack?" asked the Captain's wife aimlessly to everyone in the room and no one at all.

"Yes ma'am, we'll be ready." said Arpur after a pause.

"You understand then why we couldn't do much for your eighty-second birthday, then?" she asked.

"Yes ma'am." he said through the darkness.

"And you've eaten all your cake, then?" she asked.

"Yes, ma'am. I'm eating the last piece right now." he said sheepishly.

"That's all right." she said, looking forward at the picture illuminated on the wall. "You know the little one there was so funny about it."

"How's that ma'am?" asked Arpur, mouth full of cake.

"Well, it was her first try at baking; so I couldn't let

her waste my good flour. You were out and about somewhere or I would have asked first; but I sent her down
there to get some of that old Government Issue stuff from
your place. I figured it wouldn't matter much once it was
cooked up properly." she said, beginning to smile through
her words.

"Yes, ma'am." he said, trying not to sound objection-
able.

"Well Gillian was here, and we girls were all in the
kitchen doing other things while we tried to make time
for your cake and . . ." she was saying.

Arpur cut her off. "Miss Baillie—I mean Mrs. Western—was here?" he asked, sounding surprised.

"Yes, Black Jack. She stopped by to help with your
cake. She wanted to make biscuits, but I didn't think that
was appropriate. Now don't interrupt me." said Mrs.
Baillie.

"Yes, ma'am. Sorry ma'am." said Arpur.

"So things got very hectic and we kept misplacing various items while we were running here and there; and it
didn't look as though we were going to get around to finishing your gateau. No sooner had we put it in the oven
though, then the little one holds up the can to her mother
and asks if you are Polish!" she said.

"Come again, ma'am." said Arpur.

"That's what I said. Gillian picked up the can, and
she seemed puzzled. She said that in all her long talks
with you about your adventures that you had never mentioned one time about being in Poland. We figured it must
be one of your jokes, eh Black Jack?" There was a pause.
"Black Jack?" she asked again. No answer. There was a
flutter of motion in the dark as the elderly pair scrambled
from the couch and hurriedly lit all the lamps in the room.

Sitting there in the middle of the room, beside the
desk upon which sat the homemade projector, was Arpur,

head to one side and hands clutching at his gut. On the desk beside the apparatus were a saucer and a fork that held a bite of a half-eaten piece of chocolate cake. The projector utilized a lens from a watch which had been bought at the expense of six pounds, three shillings, six pence, and a day in court; and it sat atop a desk which had been thrown in with the bargain and brought back to Kennington as a show of no hard feelings.

IV

Awaking in the hospital, Arpur looked out over the cold, gray plains as they were pelted with winter rain. The day seemed as night; and even the nurses' cheery smiles could not lift his spirits as he lay upon the white sheets stamped in red letters: 'Picton Infirmary'. He listened intently from his bed as the doctor in the hallway told the Captain and his wife that all that could be done was to "make him comfortable." They came and stood by his side, expressing their sympathy and apologies for what had happened. They iterated their wish that they could do something for him. They left with best regards and gratitude for his long service to the family.

Shortly thereafter, she came. The daughter he rarely saw stood with her, the mother's hands upon her shoulders. They gazed forlornly at him.

"I'm sorry, Mister Arpur. I didn't mean to make you sick." she said sincerely, her little brown eyes twinkling and her nose twitching.

"Shh." said her mother, shaking her shoulders gently.

"I'm sorry. I should have known you never sailed to Poland." said Mrs. Western. He grimaced as he let out a half laugh. She smiled as a tear ran down her face.

"I guess this is one way to cleanse the soul." he said, laughing and grabbing his side. She sobbed and laughed simultaneously. "Thank you for coming." he said, grasping her hand.

"It is my pleasure." she said. They exchanged a pained glance for a moment. Then she said that it was best that they go. As they were leaving, the little girl broke from the door and ran back to Arpur's bed.

"Mama says she still loves you sometimes." she said. She ran back to her mother who flashed an embarrassed look at Arpur. She grabbed the little girl's hand and they disappeared from the doorway.

Arpur thought he slept for a time. He awoke to find Reverend Ironside standing beside his bed.

"How are you, you old dog?" asked the Reverend. "I've been sent in to give your last blessings."

Arpur watched as the man whom he thought had died years ago began to make the gestures of the Cross and to chant in Latin. Arpur turned and looked out the window. It was still raining hard as the sky grew dark under a hidden sunset. The priest finished his ceremony.

"They say there's a flood coming, Black Jack. What do you make of that?" asked the clergyman.

"I'm not ready for this." Arpur said suddenly, as he bolted upright in his bed. "I've got things to do." He sprang from his hospital bed in his gown and bare feet, and he headed for the door. As he was leaving the room, he caught a glimpse of what appeared to be a parrot lighting upon the preacher's shoulder.

"No, Dick, no!" squawked the bird.

Arpur ran down the long, dark hallway toward the main doors of the infirmary. Over his shoulder, he heard a large door open; and many big dogs began to howl frantically. He heard their claws tapping on the tiles, as they seemed to get closer behind him. Bursting through the doors, he ran out into the rain and headed for Para in the remaining daylight. The dogs pursued him as the water began to rise around him.

Splashing through deep puddles, he raced for home along the muddy road to Kennington. All his efforts were concerted for a single purpose: To reach his cabin and retrieve his coffin before it was too late. He wanted a proper burial. He remembered that some of the whalers who had married Maori women had been honored with a Maori burial. That included the placement of a huge canoe, standing upright and halfway in the ground as a grave marker. Arpur had decided that he would have what his great friend and comrade had chosen: A casket.

Reaching his shack, Arpur now stood knee-deep in water. The dogs, it seemed, had abandoned their pursuit. He quickly retrieved his burial box from the ceiling beams and climbed in, leaving the lid behind. Coffin or canoe, the point became moot; and he floated calmly on the mounting waters. They would find him, he thought, when the flood receded. They could bury him on the spot he was discovered on, for all he cared. He knew that he would be remembered at least.

The coffin began to drift around the basin as the roof to his hut disappeared. The flood was worse than he had expected. Suddenly, the rain stopped. The clouds parted, and the sun shone focused rays down around him. The water became as smooth as glass. He sat and looked around the beautiful still silence. Then he noticed that a strange unknown force seemed to be pushing his vessel gently toward the west. He was surprised by a splash; and a small Black boy popped his head out of the water a few feet from the coffin.

"Daddy, Daddy. Look! Grandmamma taught me how to swim. I can swim forever now." the boy said. He swam on ahead of the coffin and disappeared.

Where the boy had first appeared, Arpur's mother

sprang from the surface. Treading water, she said, "Oh, Arthur. He was such a joy to all of us. You would have been so proud, son! Don't worry, though. I took good care of him. His mama took ill in the head after he was born, though. The Master had to put her down. We gonna all be together now, though. You'll see. C'mon, it's just up ahead." The older Black lady swam strongly ahead and also disappeared into the sun-stained waters.

Arpur lay back; a sense of peace coming over him, as various other figures from his past swam by his casket. The box floated into the wavering streams of glimmering light, toward the blazing sun. A rainbow appeared in the distance. As he approached the setting sun, the bright yellow shine color blinded him, causing him to see green; and his canoe fused with the huge, luminescent, emerald crystalline orb as it sintered and solidified. Turning to a ring of greenstone, the jade pendant in the sky slipped into the darkness of its background as the air around it gave up its ethereal light and faded into the flesh which was his black chest, lying there on the white covers of the hospital bed.

The nurses gathered around; and with a "1-2-3," and a "heave-ho," they lifted him free from his bed and shrouded him with the sheets.

Epilogue

rthur Harper Alesworth died on July third, 1894, just two days before his eighty-second birthday. His funeral was well attended. His obituary in the local paper said that he was a trustworthy old man; and although he made no show of religion, dearly loved his Bible. The paper went on to say that those in the valley who knew him well had nothing but kind words for him and said that he would be missed there.

Black Jack White was buried at Picton cemetery in the dead of winter. He lies peacefully in a grave which to this day remains unmarked.

Printed in the United States
933600001B

9 781401 049706